The Fifth Law of Hawkins

Books by Charles Durden

The Fifth Law of Hawkins
No Bugles, No Drums

The Fifth Law of
HAWKINS

Charles Durden

St. Martin's Press

New York

Song lyrics from "One Toke Over the Line"
used by permission of Michael Brewer/Talking Beaver Music (BMI).

Design by Richard Oriolo

ISBN 0-312-93089-5

First Edition: September 1990
1   3   5   7   9   10   8   6   4   2

For Gabriella and Don,
Susan and Michael,
The Mother Superior,
and
Mr. Shapiro.
For T. Doherty and the
Seidperson, who placed
their bets and hoped
for the best.
For Ms. Jaffe and the
days of future past.
And most especially for
Joshua, whose sense of
humor, abundant love,
and abiding faith
kept me in the game
when the only chips I
had left were a
bad attitude and my
belief in the
Grand Scheme of Things.

— — — —

The moment I saw Jesus Christ standing in the bowels of the Baltimore train yard it occurred to me that I might well be headed for serious trouble. *He* had returned, just like all those Bible-thumping turkeys had said He would, and there I was, four fingers deep into a large jar of orange juice and tequila and about four hours into a flight on the magic-mushroom express. I definitely was not ready to meet my Maker.

Jesus was wearing crisscrossed bandoliers crammed with what looked to me to be gleaming rounds of .30-caliber ammo, and He was waving an M-16. He didn't look happy. In fact, He didn't look anything at all like those Sunday school images of Jesus-the-Lord-Savior I'd been force-fed by my Christian keepers in what passed for my youth. He did have the flowing robe and the sandals, the beard and the long hair, but the hair was matted, the beard needed to be trimmed, and his robe was made out of Mexican flour sacks. I knew the material. I had a pullover shirt made of the same material in my bag. *Chinga tu madre*, I muttered as I sat back and closed my eyes.

The train, on which I was entombed in something called a parlor car, collided with a force field. We had arrived at Whiplash City, one of Amtrak's many unscheduled stops on the run from Miami to Manhattan. My eyes popped open and I looked out the window as though I actually expected to find an explanation for the engine's sudden inability to move forward. And there stood J.C., laughing.

As abruptly as it had stopped, the train lurched forward and immediately smashed into a second, equally invisible barrier.

Fuck me, who's driving this piece of pig iron? I wondered. I looked outside again and there was Jesus, loping along, holding the rifle high over His shaggy head and shouting. Being locked behind soundproof, shatterproof, hermetically sealed windows, I couldn't hear Him, but His mouth was moving like a born-again Baptist missionary preaching to a Niger River revival meeting. He came abreast of my window, turned, and pointed the rifle directly at me. I grinned and responded with a couple of unmistakable Italian gestures I had learned from a friend in the backwoods of 'Nam.

J.C.'s knowledge of Italian semaphore was adequate. He lowered the weapon with a look of disappointment. I moved my head from side to side, my expression much like that of the disappointed parent who has secured a permanent seat on the High Horse of Superiority. God Almighty Himself would've had trouble jamming that .30-caliber ammo into the bore of an M-16, I thought, and I tried sending Him the thought telepathically. He may even have gotten it. He shrugged, as though to say, "What the fuck . . . it's just a game."

The train struggled forward, inching its way toward the station. Jesus was left behind, one more dumb shit lost in a time warp.

"The inmates are running the asylum."

The source of the unsolicited wisdom was seated opposite me, a middle-aged Republican in a wrinkled three-piece polyester suit, a clip-on tie, and black wing-tip shoes. A flag-shaped pin on his lapel read: REAGAN IN '80. I wondered for an instant if that was the last time his suit had been sent out for cleaning. I looked up from the flag to the face. He had close-set brown eyes that would have looked better on a newt. Satisfied that he had attracted my attention, he tacked a humorless, thin-lipped smile onto his observation and left it hanging there like a dangling participle.

"Lucky for us," I said in a tone I hoped he would interpret as an invitation to disappear into the ether.

Lord, I prayed, please don't let this asshole think that conversation with me would be any better than the misery of his own thoughts. Please? My brain is fried. Too much cactus juice and much too much psilocybin. I need a nice quiet Cosmic DMZ to stumble around in for the next couple of hours, and then I'll go back to being Mr. Nice Guy.

"*Ball*-ti-more!" The fat conductor lurched up the aisle, bellowing at something close to a hundred db. "Ball-ti-*more Station!*"

Right. I ask for a quiet Cosmic garden spot and You give me fuckin' Baltimore. And You wonder why I don't stay in touch? I closed my eyes with a sigh and pictured myself suspended beneath a hang glider, soaring above a forest that stretched down to the shoreline of an ocean . . . climbing higher and higher . . .

The tequila took over and then the magic mushrooms kicked in like the afterburner on an F-18. I went straight into the stratosphere, strapped to my psilocybin rocket chair, singing under my breath:

> One toke over the line, sweet Jesus
> One toke over the line . . .
> Sittin' downtown in a railway station
> One toke over the line.

The train shuddered and staggered to a rail-grinding halt as I came back to Earth in Baltimore station. My Republican observer cleared his throat and I turned to find him staring at me. A furrow had formed between his eyes and his thin lips were set in a line as unyielding as his view of right and wrong. He had the look of a Christian about to do his duty. My paranoia surfaced with a drug-fueled rush that threatened to lift me right out of my seat. I was raised in a house full of faces like that, all of them belonging to my mother. And since I escaped that joyless place I've seen enough of them elsewhere to know that there's never any real refuge from their determination to rid the world of conscious wrongdoers. The last time I had seen one of those faces up close it belonged to a pistol-happy sonofabitch working for the Mexican Federal Police. He and five of his dimwitted cohorts had just busted me for possession of the evil weed, and he had a .38 in my face. His eyes had glowed with self-righteous glee and

I knew he was primed to gun down another drug-crazed gringo. Fortunately, I wasn't even stoned.

"You don't look well," the Republican said in a slightly accusing voice. "Are you ill?"

"Virus," I lied. My voice was hoarse and to me it sounded about as sincere as my last words to my wife: "I'll be back in a couple of days." That was a couple of years or a couple of lives ago. It's tough to keep track when you're on the run. I unscrewed the top of the juice jar I was clutching and gulped down an ounce or two. "Vitamin C," I said as I capped the jar.

He leaned forward, as though closing the distance would enable him to see through the dark lenses of my sunglasses. "Are you on medication?"

"Midol," I answered matter-of-factly and casually turned my attention to the string of passengers wandering through the aisle. I searched in vain for a pretty female face.

"Midol!?" The word exploded from his mouth as it dawned on him that my answer quite probably wasn't an altogether sincere response to his question. It never occurred to him that none of it was any of his business.

"For my goddamn shrapnel wounds, you fuckin' half-wit!" The hot flash of anger shattered the fragile armor of his arrogance and he recoiled into his seat. The verbal blast also triggered a coughing fit which brought up a residue of tar from two months of smoking cheap Mexican cigarettes. Flecks of brown phlegm flew from my mouth. He pushed himself deeper into the chair, repulsed and close to panic. "I've also got terminal malaria, in remission, and herpes complex seven. All to save a bunch of pig-fucking slopes from the evils of Godless Communism." I tore at the buttons of my shirt. "You want to see the goddamn scars?"

"No!" Panic took control and his eyes were wide with dread, his voice little more than a whimper. "No, really . . . it isn't necessary. I didn't realize . . ."

"Didn't realize *what?*" I snarled as I pulled the sunglasses off my face. I knew the combination of emotion and tequila had given me the look of a wild-eyed lunatic, and the psilocybin made it all seem like an exercise in method acting. What a weird-ass combination, I thought. This shit should be illegal.

"I was against the war," Mr. Republican babbled.

"So what? I'm still a goddamn cripple. Is this the first time you've come face-to-face with the tattered remains of what you so cheerfully shipped off to fight the heathens? Well, I'm it! I'm what's left."

"Honest to God," he whispered as tears spilled from his eyes, "I was against the war."

I stared at him for a long moment, then replaced the glasses and settled back. "So was I."

■ ▬ ▬ ▬

Somehow, in the midst of all that, the debarking passengers had gotten off and the embarking passengers had boarded. The train was rolling smoothly out of the yard, headed north. Slowly I relaxed, grateful that no one had felt compelled to summon the conductor, or worse, a cop. Of all the people I choose to avoid, cops and copy editors always rank in the top three. I turned slightly to watch the slums slip by, hoping that Mr. Republican had had enough excitement to keep him busy with his own vapid thoughts. He had, whatever his reason, wandered into an emotional mine field and survived with nothing worse than a couple of small dents in his self-image. I took another swig from the juice jar and exhaled the last of the tension. Relaxed, I began humming under my breath again:

> One toke over the line, sweet Jesus
> One toke over the line . . .
> Sittin' downtown in a railway station,
> One toke over the line.

I was humming along when it suddenly hit me: Midol!? A chuckle slipped out. Hawkins, you fuckin' drug-addled retard, if you had five functioning brain cells you'd be dangerous. Midol, my ass. And shrapnel wounds . . . what the fuck would you have done if he had wanted to see them?

I turned to look out the window and saw my reflection. I smiled, but it didn't smile back. That sorry-looking sonofabitch didn't have any real sense of humor. He probably wishes we *had* been wounded. He's the same dipshit that married me to my WASP Princess wife and made all those promises she expected *me* to keep. Christ on a bike. I couldn't believe all the saccharine shit he spoon-fed her. How the hell could he have believed that I would go along with all that moonlight-and-magnolia madness?

The day of our wedding she said to him, "Jamie, this is the most important day of our lives . . ." He reached out to touch her cheek and I cracked up laughing. She didn't know what the hell was happening. It scared her and she pulled away, trembling. "Jamie . . . ?" Her voice was pitiful. He got all emotional and put his arms around her, crying softly. That made her feel better. "Jamie," she asked softly, "why were you laughing?"

Why, indeed. I was laughing because I was dying, choking to death on her innocence, desperately wanting to be able to swallow all of it in the hope that it would heal the real wounds, the ones she couldn't see, or couldn't bear to see. Fat fuckin' chance of that. I was so busy chewing on my own truth I couldn't have swallowed a raw oyster. All my illusions had been shattered long before I met her and the shards were embedded like splintered bone fragments in my psyche. I wasn't laughing. What she heard was the wind blowing through the ragged holes that were left when all that remained of my idealistic beliefs exploded in a storm of something called *friendly fire*. Try explaining that to the First Runner-up of Miss Chatham County, 1977.

"Can I buy you a drink?" The question came from what seemed an enormous distance. It took a few seconds for me to disengage from one reality and engage another. The Republican had his hand on my shoulder, and when he was satisfied he had my attention he squeezed it. "I'm gonna grab a toot before I take on the wife. Want something? A beer? Bourbon? Scotch?"

I hoisted the jar and managed a half-assed smile. "I'll probably do better if I stick with the o.j. But thanks."

"Okay. Something to eat? A sandwich, or some chips?"

I declined with a shake of my head and he responded with a joyless smile as he turned away. Jesus H. Christ, I thought, is he out to lunch or has "Reach Out and Touch Someone" become the national anthem in my absence? I watched his lonely retreat to the bar and felt a fleeting urge to comfort him. Why not? Have a couple of drinks, listen to his bullshit and maybe ease his pain for the moment. Jamie Hawkins, friend of man. Tequila madness. I opted to pass the problem on to someone else.

Sweet Mother of Christ, I prayed, hear me in my time of need: Find that poor miserable sonofabitch someone suitable to share his shit. I'm too fucked up to make small talk with a Christian Republican. Amen.

I sent the prayer winging its way into the ozone, took another slug of the tequila and o.j., and resumed staring out the window. The engineer whistled a crossing in a small farm town and as we thundered by the candy-striped poles and flashing lights I was seized by a yearning for the Norman Rockwell existence visible from my seat. Pickup trucks, fresh-faced clear-eyed girls in faded jeans, a volunteer fire department, a general store, a job in the local sawmill driving a forklift . . .

Forklift!? Something jerked me out of my reverie. Absurdity overload, probably. Jamie Hawkins, forklift operator? Shit! I leaned toward the window and pressed my forehead to the cool glass. Get a grip on yourself, boy. Life's too long to get trapped in that kind of fantasy. And simplicity fashioned from the whole cloth of wishful thinking isn't much of a shield against the realities of this world.

I pulled my portable typewriter from an overhead rack, rolled in some paper, and stared at the vast expanse of whiteness with my usual mix of emotions. As a source of anxiety it's difficult for me to find an object more frightening than a ream of clean white paper. I live with the dread that I've written my last sentence, that I'll go to the well one more time and the best I'll get is a burp. But on the other end of the string is unlimited possibility. Inspiration can come anytime and anything is possible. Not probable, but certainly possible.

For a few seconds I sat motionless. The ebb and flow of the psilocybin was in its ebb stage. I was coming down, slowly. Not a good time to look into the abyss and contemplate the unanswerable question: What in the name of Christ am I doing headed for Philadelphia? I started typing:

Philadelphia, Pa, Oct. 13 — James F. Hawkins, widely re-
garded by his peers as God's misbegotten gift to America's second-rate newspapers, arrived here today. Mr.
Hawkins, master of the wise mouth, expects to join the
staff of the Philadelphia Call within the week, and has
ben bean been (Goddamn stupid typewriter never could
spell) AND HAS BEEN designated as a feature writer on the
paper's dayside staff.
    Mr. Hawkins joins the Call staff after spending two
months in a Mexican federal prison where he was incarcer-
ated for possession of too much evil weed. He declined to
comment on the circumstances of his bust, nor would he
answer questions about his release and deportation.
    Prior to his incarceration, Mr. Hawkins was employed
by the Lynchfield, Va. Independent Union-Democrat where
he wrote a thrice-weekly column titled MISFIT.
    "The journalistic equivalent of type-casting," ob-
served Mr. Hawkins.
    Twice during his stint at the Independent Union-
Democrat his column was nominated for the Overset Alibi
Award, journalism's highest accolade for articles editors were too chickenshit to print. (Ed. note: Overset is
the term used to designate copy set in type but never
printed due to "space limitations.")
    Prior to his employment with the Virginia daily, Mr.
Hawkins worked as a feature writer and general assignment reporter for daily papers in Georgia, Tennessee,
Texas, and California. All were papers of less than 50-
thousand circulation, and none of them worth a flying
fuck.

(MORE MORE MORE MORE MORE)

Right. The question was, and is, and probably always will be: More of what? I wasn't sure how much more of the same old shit I could endure. Or was willing to endure. Playing the role of Jamie Hawkins, world-weary newspaper reporter, was a precarious way to make a living. Even worse was Jamie Hawkins, novelist. *Pane e chipolla*, the Italians say. A life of eating bread and onions. It's a boring diet even if it's supplemented by glowing reviews. Try paying your rent with a clip from the *Sunday Review of Books* extolling your work as a genuine

American voice shouting from the wilderness . . . whatever the hell that ever meant.

The truth is, I would have bet my last hundred against a shiny wax apple that I'd driven the final nail into the coffin of my checkered career when I was fired from the *Independent Union-Democrat* . . . better known as the Lynchfield *IUD*. It was aptly named, a rag owned by a bunch of pussies who used the paper to shield the town from any and all forms of contemporary enlightenment. The town was owned and operated by reactionary Bible-thumping throwbacks to Herbert Hoover and Elmer Gantry. The *IUD* was the third paper from which I had been tossed on my ass. Summarily, as they say. The charge was "insubordination" and I sure as hell couldn't argue the point. Even I'll admit that one shouldn't tell an editor to take his assignment, fold it five ways, and pack it up his fat ass.

What bothered me was that the deed was done, as I was told, for my own good. I have never had, nor have I ever heard of anyone else having something truly wonderful handed to them with the same comment. "Here's a check for ten thousand dollars and a first-class ticket to Greece. It's for your own good." Or, "We're giving you two weeks of bonus vacation. Let that be a lesson to you." The implicit message seemed to be that I would learn from the experience of being fired. The only thing I ever learned was that it didn't make a helluva lot of difference to me. Bad attitude.

Fired three times, and twice I walked out. Those two jobs had been little more than pit stops on a coast-to-coast run. Six weeks in Small Mountain, Tennessee. Six hours in Rio Blanco, Texas. You had to be there. The town lived and died with the rise and fall of oil prices and the editor proudly printed an editorial in which he declared that the best method for dealing with "those Arab ragheads who have seriously undermined the American consumer's right to plentiful oil and V-8 engines is with renewed commitment to nuclear power. About 25 megatons dropped in the middle of Khomeini's heathen capital should serve to remind All-America's Arab 'friends' that it was Americans who invented nuclear weapons, Americans who used them, and Americans who keep watch on the right of all Christian nations to live without fear of being forced to kneel before the pagan lords of OPEC."

Immediately after lunch on my first day as the *Rio Blanco Tribune's* police and court reporter/feature writer/business editor I had been ushered into the office of the editor and publisher, Tyrone L. "Lucky" McBride, by the managing editor. The m.e. introduced us and left the room.

Lucky was lucky to be alive. He bordered on obese, and it was anyone's guess as to which side of that border he called home. I counted three chins, visible, and I wouldn't have bet against the possibility of a fourth hidden in the folds of flesh that rolled over his collar. He wore a white shirt and a bright yellow polyester tie that was held in place with a tie clip fashioned to look like the skull of a steer, and he had a crew cut. He was dug in behind a huge old beat-up desk in an office that gave me new insight into the concept of chaos. Anchored to the wall behind him was a laminated blow-up of the aforementioned editorial.

He leaned back in his squeaky chair, swung his boots up to the top of his desk, and squinted through a veil of cigar smoke. He didn't speak, and he didn't seem to be waiting for me to speak. He just stared. An old wall clock in a walnut case ticked and tocked as the pendulum swung from side to side. About ten seconds into the waiting game I began silently counting the ticks and tocks. At Number Twenty-seven Lucky spoke. "I don' think you gon' fit in here, boy. You got that big city smart-ass look about you and people 'round here who wears sunglasses indoors is usually thought to be drug dealers."

I counted another thirty ticks and tocks before I spoke. "You may be right. I already got a ticket for parking in a slot reserved for deputies, heartburn from eating at Fu Lu's Chinese Chili Palace, and the runs from drinking the water in the city room cooler."

"Collect anything we owe you," he said, talking around the cigar, "then find the first on-ramp to the Inner-state and don't look back. You probably'd do real well in California. Lotta smart-asses and weirdos out there."

As it turned out, he was half right. I found a lot of stone-strange weirdos. But I didn't do real well there, either.

(MORE MORE MORE MORE MORE)

How much more, I wondered as I looked up to find my seatmate settling back into his chair. I quickly rolled in another sheet of paper and began typing.

Add 1: Hawkins
Mr. Hawkins, a native of Peach Orchard, GA, is a Vietnam veteran, winner of two Silver Stars, a Purple Heart, and was seriously considered for a General Court-Martial just before his discharge.

"Lotta bullshit," Mr. Hawkins commented when asked about the court-martial. He repeated the comment when asked about the medals.

After his separation from the army, and several months of aimless travel, during which he wrote a novel, Mr. Hawkins was hired as a general assignment reporter for the Mandell, GA, Daily Observer. It was from the city room of the Daily Observer that he launched his dubious descent into the world of small-town journalism. "It's been pretty much downhill since then," he observed.

Mr. Hawkins is presently separated (or quite possibly divorced--who knows?) from his wife, the former Marybeth Summers of Savannah, GA.

"She seemed to think I couldn't possibly have anything better or more interesting to do than spend my life

in Mandell, making babies and writing about poor-ass
peanut farmers," Mr. Hawkins noted. "She lives in constant danger of having her brain turned into a small jar
of Skippy's."

(MORE MORE MORE MORE MORE)

Fuck more.

"I'd like to ask you something," the Republican said as he rattled the ice
in what looked like a Scotch on the rocks.

I looked up from the paper. "Why?"

The question completely confused him. "What?" would have been okay,
and "Okay" would have been acceptable, but "Why?" wasn't on the list of
anticipated responses. He rattled the ice again. "I think you're on drugs and I'm
a Delaware County Pennsylvania auxiliary policeman." He squinted and tried
to turn his face into a Clint Eastwood mask, a trick he hadn't quite mastered.

I cracked up laughing. I couldn't stop myself. And the laughing set off the
coughing again. Finally I managed to say, "A Delaware County what?"

"Police officer," he snapped.

"*Auxiliary* police officer, I believe you said. Sort of like candy stripers,
right? In a state of emergency you'd be assigned to the field kitchen to make
coffee."

His face, already pink from however many drinks he had consumed at the
bar, turned even rosier. "I'm licensed," he growled.

That set off another fit of coughing laughter. "Licensed to do what?" I asked
when I got the coughing under control. "Shoot the shit?" I wiped the tears from
my eyes. "Listen, Sheriff, I *am* on drugs. I'm an outpatient of the Veterans
Hospital in Valley Forge. Two weeks ago they asked me if I'd volunteer for a
new drug they're testing. I agreed. They warned me not to drink, but I had a
couple and I'm wired." I smiled with a certain amount of rueful regret. "I
probably should've stayed close to the hospital but my sister just had a baby and
I went down to Virginia to visit her and my new nephew. Her husband's on a
destroyer in the Gulf . . ."

A look of genuine remorse displaced the anger on his face and he held out
his hand. "I'd like to apologize." I shook hands with him, determined not to
laugh. "William Payne, Senior."

"Jamie Hawkins, the one and only," I said with a grin.

"Actually, I guess I'm the one and only, too. My boy, Billy Junior, was
killed in Vietnam. His patrol was ambushed." He took a quick drink from the
glass. "One of his buddies came by a few months later, to see me and Billy's
mom. He said the patrol leader was smoking marijuana. They were supposed
to track down some VC sappers . . . do you know what they are?"

"Demolition specialists."

"Right, right." He nodded his head a few times, as though I had answered the key question on one of life's most important exams. (And now, for fifty bonus points, tell us: What type of explosive was most commonly used by Viet Cong sappers?) "I never was sure if he knew what he was talking about . . ." All those years of unrelieved sadness settled in his face. I looked away, out the window, not wanting to hear another story about another kid who died in fuckin' Vietnam.

"I warned my boy about drugs, right from the beginning. I told 'im, 'Billy, a bottle of Scotch is a lot better than a pound of marijuana.' I said, 'If you need a lift you let your dad know and we'll tie one on.' "

The train roared over the Susquehanna River, whistling a mournful call. The sun was low on the horizon. I uncapped the juice bottle and drained two or three ounces down my throat. Payne, aptly named, went on and on.

"Lots of times me and Billy would sit out under the trees at night, drinking and talking . . . He was always good with his hands and he planned on studying cabinetmaking. In his senior year, for his shop project, he built an altar for the church. He did a beautiful job. It was a very simple design, clean lines. He made it out of walnut. Bought the wood himself with money he made working construction during the summer."

Near the north shore of the river I saw an old rowboat bobbing at anchor. The captain and his crew, probably his wife, were fishing. The train hooted and the woman waved. Ah, there we are, I thought. Some of the colorful natives, industrious and hardworking, waving gaily as the visitors pass. Then, with nets full and nothing left in the grog bottle, the drunken sots weigh anchor and head for home.

"Killed by a drug user." Tears streamed from Payne's eyes.

"Mr. Payne, a lot of guys smoked dope in 'Nam. And a lot of guys didn't. Drugs weren't the problem. Booze wasn't the problem. Because in the end the dope smokers, the boozers, the bullshitters, and the hard-nosed professionals all had a common cross to carry."

He wiped his eyes with his free hand and struggled to find a lid for his emotions. I waited. Finally he heaved a sigh, gulped most of what remained of the watered-down drink, and looked at me with bloodshot eyes. "What was that?"

"Mindless arrogance. Denial of the obvious. Unmitigated stupidity."

"I don't understand . . ."

"Mr. Payne, we beat the Germans with industrial capacity. We beat the Japanese with two atom bombs. We haven't won a war since, and I don't think we ever will."

"That's Commie treason!"

"That's common sense. We tried to terrorize the Vietnamese with technology and firepower. It didn't work. It won't work, not in Southeast Asia, not in Africa, not in the Middle East. And it isn't just us. Look at the Russians in Afghanistan."

"What about Grenada?" he asked in a tone of triumph.

"That wasn't a war, that was live-fire combat maneuvers. I could have taken that island with a troop of fifty female mud wrestlers. Shit, I could probably have *bought* it for five or ten million dollars. They spent that much just planning it."

He sat quietly, occasionally rattling the few remaining slivers of ice in his glass, and stared in my direction. I think his thoughts were elsewhere. I looked out the window for awhile, wondering if William Payne, Sr., and William Payne, Jr., ever had any meaningful alternatives to the roads they chose. Was there another route that led to a happy ending? Probably not. A *different* ending, perhaps, but William Payne, Sr., didn't look like he had ever known a happy ending to anything. He had regret written all over him. Maybe, I thought, when you're an all-American suburbanite pushing fifty-five with ten years left on your mortgage and your waist measures three inches more than your chest, maybe at that point regret is all that's left.

I rolled the third sheet of paper into my typewriter and typed:

Add 2: Hawkins

Add what? I asked myself. Anything at all, or nothing at all. I rested my fingers on the keyboard and looked down into the well, as though some understanding was hidden beneath the cover. Nothing happened, no inspirational flash, no insight, *nada*. I pulled off the cover and looked into a six-month accumulation of Mexican dust.

"Something wrong?" I glanced up and Payne shrugged. "I'm pretty good with repairs on things like typewriters. Maybe I could help out."

"Actually I was looking for the key to a puzzle, and there's forty-four of 'em in there."

"*Wilmington!*" the fat conductor bellowed from behind me. I jumped half out of my seat. "*Will*-ming-ton Station."

"Well, that's me," Payne announced. He held out his hand, which I took. "Sorry I butted into your life like I did."

"Forget it."

"I don't usually let my emotions get out of hand but today was"—he shrugged—"difficult." He stood, rocking a little from side to side with the movement of the train, holding the back of the seat with his left hand. With his right he reached into his jacket pocket and withdrew a piece of folded onionskin paper. The train slowed to a stop, lurched forward a few feet, then stopped again. He held out the paper. I took it. "So long." He picked up an overnight bag and walked away.

As the train rolled out of the station I caught a glimpse of him walking along the platform, alone. His body sagged, his head was down. And then he disappeared from sight. I looked from him to the piece of paper he had handed me, and the realization of what it was came with brutal swiftness. He had apologized and offered his hand, but all the while he meant to have the last word. Or the last few words. I opened the paper and there they were: WILLIAM J. PAYNE, JR., rubbed from that goddamn slab of polished black granite, our monument to our monumental fuck-up.

Fuck you, William J. Payne, Sr. I've got my own pain. I've seen the pictures, listened to the ridiculous debates, read the reports, and watched families and friends kneeling at its base as though it were the Wailing Wall. I have not been and I doubt that I'll ever go. I saw them die. I don't want or need to be reminded that they're dead.

I rolled the paper into a thin tube and lit the end with my lighter. The onionskin burned quickly, and after a few seconds I dropped the remains into the armrest ashtray, uncapped the jar, and offered a toast to a comrade unknown: "Rest in peace, Billy boy . . ." I drank, and then I drank some more.

— — — —

Eighteen hours later I awoke in the viselike grip of tequila coma. My eyes opened, my bladder howled, and my body refused to move. All those little neural transmitters that ordinarily provide the spark for basic motor functions were misfiring. I blinked a couple of times. My eyes closed and opened without difficulty. Terrific. I'm not dead. I can't move and my bladder is maybe five minutes from rupture, but where there's life there's a lesson to be learned: Relax. Breathe in, breathe out. In . . . and out . . .

A piercing ring from the telephone on the night table shattered my transcendental hangover cure and cracked the shell of my coma. I bolted straight up, swung my feet to the floor, and grabbed the side of the bed with both hands. The second ring arrived with equal shrillness. I grabbed the receiver and calmly said, "Call back in ten minutes." I replaced the receiver and stumbled into the bathroom.

The phone rang again in exactly ten minutes. "Hello . . ."

"Jamie?" a tentative female voice inquired.

"What's left of him . . . Who's this?"

"Juliet."

"Juliet Franklin-Rossini, influence peddler and purveyor of fine bribes? The gorgeous lady to whom I'm forever indebted for bailing me out of Club Fed?"

"Well," she said, laughing, "I never thought of myself as gorgeous . . . and as it turned out the bribe was small. How are you?"

"Hung over. What time is it?"

"A little after ten."

"And what day is it?"

"Saturday. Do you remember leaving a message on my answering machine last night?"

"Sure. I never get so drunk I can't remember what I did. I have occasionally wished I *couldn't* remember, but no such luck."

"Do you remember the message you left?"

"I said, 'This is Jamie Hawkins . . .' I don't remember exactly what else. The hotel?"

"You said, 'Hi, this is Jamie Hawkins. It's high noon and I'm in Philadelphia. Or it's Tuesday and I'm in Belgium. Or, it's about eight o'clock Friday night and I'm at the Christian Mission for dope smokers and renegade reporters. If you don't hear from me by Monday check the jail. 'Bye.' "

I could tell by her tone that I had made her laugh. Lucky for me. "So how did you find me?" I asked while I desperately searched for some indication of where I actually had crashed. I spotted a matchbook while she was talking. I had landed at the Market Street Ramada.

"I called a few places. Actually, this was only my fifth or sixth call. What's on your schedule today?"

"After I manage to reattach my head to the rest of my body, I'm pretty much out of scheduled activities. You want to get something to eat?"

"How about lunch around one? I'll pick you up."

"Okay. I'll meet you out front so you won't have to park."

" 'Bye . . ."

I hung up, then lifted the receiver and called room service for coffee, o.j., and a shot of tequila. While I was waiting for the tools to jump-start my heart I considered all that had happened since I had first encountered Juliet Franklin-Rossini. And for perhaps the hundredth time I decided that either she was free-lancing as a guardian angel or none of what I knew made any sense at all.

━━　━━　━━　━━

Juliet had found me the first time in the Mexican Federal Prison in Mérida, capital city of the Yucatán. She had come into the prison with three middle-aged American couples shopping for hammocks. The prisoners have a reputation for making some of the best and selling them for half the price charged outside the jail. I was one of three gringos in residence, each of us having found his way into the heart of the Mexican judicial system independently. All of our problems began with varying amounts of marijuana, my four ounces being the least.

The three couples, who looked like members of the Sioux City Rotary Club and Ladies Auxiliary, nervously made their way around the enclosed quadrangle as though they were expecting one of us to grab them as a shield and shoot our way out of the place. Five of them were seriously overweight, and all of them were dressed in K-Mart Blue Light specials and sensible shoes. The sixth member of the troupe, a guy about fifty, was board-thin, with hollow cheeks, dark circles under his eyes, and a hacking cough. Cancer city, I thought as he walked by where I was sitting with my back to a wall.

Their conversation was suitably moronic. Five people discussing the relative

merits of something about which they knew next to nothing were pure enter-
tainment for me.

And then Juliet walked into the yard, escorted by a member of the U.S.
consul's staff. Clifford Pace, the designated friend of American prisoners. I'd
seen him once during my six weeks in Club Fed. He had showed up, as protocol
required, informed me that there was absolutely nothing the American consul
could do to help me, and offered to find me a Mexican lawyer and/or notify
anyone of my choice that I had been dumb enough to get busted. He had wished
me luck as he left. The whole exercise had taken less than ten minutes of his
time and I'd have bet six months to sixty pesos that he couldn't remember my
name five minutes after he was out the door.

The hammock weavers had their wares on display in the quadrangle, having
been alerted to the expected contingent of Rotarians. Once each week, usually
on Thursday, two to a dozen American tourists would show up, look at the
hammocks, butcher several Spanish phrases, haggle with the weavers over a few
pesos, and leave with one more piece of excess baggage they'd rarely, or never,
use.

Occasionally one or two of them would chat with the American prisoners,
tsk-tsk at appropriate intervals when told the story of setup, bust, and slam time,
and ask if there was anything they could do to help. They meant well but we
presented an awful dilemma. On the one hand, we were Americans in a Third
World prison: suitable fodder for their sympathy. On the other hand, the charge
was *drugs!* And we all know that drugs are at the heart of all that's gone wrong
with the American Dream. Sixty-five percent of all those Americans polled may
admit to having once tried marijuana, but the operative word is *once*. Or maybe
twice. Of all those surveyed, probably fewer than ten percent would say they
still use it.

Pace was like smoke over a poker table, hovering over Juliet, watching her
every move, desperate to impress her. His Spanish was excellent, and he knew
some of the Mexican prisoners by name. He chatted with them in rapid-fire
exchanges, smiling at her from time to time, translating what he thought she
might find amusing.

I stared at her, a half-smile on my face, delighted to see anyone so beautiful
in such a bizarre place. She wore a cream-colored two-piece silk suit with a
navy-blue silk blouse and low-heeled sandals. Her strawberry-blond hair was
medium length and pulled back in a thick braid. She had blue eyes full of
sparkle and intelligence. I guessed her age and her bust size at about 38.

She finally arrived at the corner where I was sitting and glanced down. I
smiled. She smiled, held my gaze for a moment, then resumed looking at the
hammock being offered to her for a song. The guy selling it was equally en-
thralled.

"He's offering you an excellent buy," Pace told her.

She smiled, amused by the attention she had attracted, and seemed ready
to move on when one of the other shoppers called across the quadrangle, "Mr.

Pace, can you help us? We've got a language problem. This man simply doesn't understand proper Spanish." Pace rolled his eyes, excused himself, and left Juliet alone.

"If you really want a hammock," I said to her, "his are as good as any and the price is right."

At the first sound of my voice she looked surprised, then smiled. "You're an American."

"Right now I'm a prisoner," I said as I stood up. "It's kind of like being an army private. Race, creed, and country of origin don't mean much." I held out my hand. "I'm Jamie Hawkins."

"Juliet Franklin-Rossini. Have you been here long?"

"Six weeks. Long enough to lose fifteen or twenty pounds and get one hellava suntan."

"How much longer do you have to be here?"

"Who knows? The Mexicans' idea of due process would make great stand-up comedy material. I'm not even sure that I've been charged with anything, and if I have they haven't told me what."

"What do you *think* the charge might be?"

"I had about four ounces of their principal agricultural export in a little brown bag when I was busted." I shrugged. "Who knows, it may be related to that."

"Four *ounces?*" She laughed. "Why don't you post bail and get out of this prison while you wait?"

"No bail until after you're sentenced, if at all, and the trial probably won't happen for a year, at least."

"My God!" she said with dismay.

"From your mouth to His ears."

She laughed. "I'm amazed that you can make jokes about it."

"I've had some bad moments, but some of this really is funny if you look at it in the right perspective. Anyway, it's just more grist for the mill, and writers live on grist. It's all we can afford most of the time."

Her eyes showed surprise. "You're a writer?"

"I'm a newspaper reporter when I get tired of being broke and I write books when I've got money."

"Have you ever published anything?"

"A novel, about Vietnam. Nothing you would have read."

Pace walked up as I mentioned Vietnam. "So you've met Mr. Dawkins," he said to Juliet. "How's it going, Jim?"

"Great! I'm learning a lot of new Spanish words, losing weight, and gaining remarkable insight into the culture of Mexico. And this place has the best dope this side of 'Nam."

"This guy's got a great sense of humor," he said to Juliet. "Doesn't complain, doesn't ask for any special consideration."

"Can't you do anything to help him?"

"Our policy is strictly one of monitoring his welfare and ensuring that his rights, under Mexican law, aren't violated. He broke the law and he's going to have to wait for them to decide on the disposition of his case." He served up a bureaucrat's bullshit smile for the two of us. "Anyway, Mr. Dawkins's case doesn't appear to be too serious. Possession of a pound of marijuana isn't necessarily prima facie evidence of intent to traffic in drugs. He should make out okay at the trial."

Juliet looked from Pace to me, confused. "My name," I said to Pace, "is Hawkins, not Dawkins. My first name is Jamie, not Jim. And I had four ounces of the wicked weed, not a pound. But other than that I'd guess you've got a grip on the case."

"Sorry." He shifted his gaze from me to Juliet. "Have you decided on a hammock? We really should be going soon."

"I think I'll pass on a hammock. I'm tired and it's so hot out here . . . could you drop me at the hotel?"

"Of course. Let me round up the others and we'll be on our way." He hurried after the Rotarians.

"Are you allowed visitors?" Juliet asked as soon as Pace was out of earshot.

"Thursday afternoon and all day Sunday."

"If I can't get back this afternoon I'll stop here Sunday. Can I bring you anything?"

"A bottle of tequila, a pack of Camels, and a slab of prime rib, medium rare."

"Why don't I just take you out for dinner?"

"Fine with me. If you tell them we'll be back in time for bed check there shouldn't be any problem." I took her hand. "Thanks for the offer, but other than the Camels and something decent to eat, I can't think of anything."

"Juliet, we're ready," Pace called from the far side of the yard.

"I'll be back," she said with a smile.

"That's what they all say . . ."

— — — —

I spent the next four hours thinking about her, asking myself ridiculous questions that God Himself couldn't have answered. I probably would have spent the next three days doing that, but she showed up a little before five, followed by a cute young Mexican girl who carried several containers of food and fresh fruit. The Mexican prisoners whistled and made the usual assortment of mindless male comments, in Spanish, which Juliet didn't understand and to which the young girl responded with giggles.

"No prime rib available for carryout," Juliet announced as the girl lifted the lid on a huge, perfectly broiled lobster split down the middle. It was still steaming. "Sorry."

The girl was busy unpacking plates and flatware from a straw basket. She handed me a napkin.

"Well, I'll tell you what . . . let's do the best we can with what we have. How do you feel about premarital gluttony?"

"Will you still respect me in the morning?"

"Did you bring butter and lemon?"

"In the small tin, by your plate."

"You've earned my undying, everlasting respect. Let's eat."

We ate. And we talked. Or I should say she asked a lot of questions and I answered, willingly and cheerfully. I stopped periodically, stopped eating, stopped talking, and just stared at her. A classic, I thought. She'll be beautiful when she's sixty and if her skin holds up she'll be beautiful when she's seventy. The first time I did that she stopped in mid-question, looked uncertain for a moment, then said, "I'm sorry. It's probably very rude of me to ask so many questions."

I laughed. "I don't care how many questions you ask."

"Well, even so, since I'm not interviewing you for a job I should at least give you the option of declining to answer."

"Have you got a job that's open?"

"Perhaps. My brother and I own a newspaper, and I could probably arrange a job for you. I'm on the board."

"Well, I'm in the slam. Unless you're looking for a prison correspondent in Mexico I'm going to have one hellava time doing rewrites and obits from here. And I wouldn't bet much on my chances of getting out before the spring thaw."

"If you were out, would you consider working for the *Philadelphia Call?*"

"I'd consider working for the *Hoboken Herald* or the *Walla Walla Wednesday Gazette* at this point."

"If you'll come see me when you're out I'll make sure you get on the staff."

I tried to look beyond the eyes, or through the eyes. She didn't flinch and she didn't look away. "You don't even know if I can do the job. And if I gave you references I'd be hanging myself. There's only one editor I know who might say something nice about me, and he likes everybody."

"I'll take a chance. Call me when you get to Philadelphia."

An hour later she was gone. She left me with a carton of Camels but without any promise to return or any indication that she wasn't gone forever.

— — — —

Room service arrived with my minimum daily requirements for facing the world, and a nine-dollar tab. I gave the guy a ten and paused to consider the purchase. A pot of coffee, a pygmy-sized glass of orange juice, and an ounce of tequila. I wondered if Ramada was Spanish for robbery? Probably not. And these prices aren't peculiar to the Ramada, I reminded myself. The cost of service is ridiculous no matter where you are. At least they remembered the salt, bless someone's tequila-loving heart.

I downed the shot with a slightly painful twinge and chased it with the o.j. The Mexican connection of tequila and orange juice reminded me of Clifford Pace and I laughed aloud as I headed for the shower. My last meeting with him was one of those totally satisfactory events that will linger long after I've forgotten the crazy sonofabitch who arrested me and the absurdity of the Mexican judicial system.

— — — —

Wednesday, a day short of two weeks after Juliet had left me wondering if I would ever see her again, Pace showed up at the jail. I was sitting in the cantina, drinking coffee bought with what little remained of a hundred-dollar bill the *Federales* overlooked when they searched me at the jail. Their idea of a body search consisted of a quick frisk above the waist, after which they said to empty my pockets. I gave up everything except the hundred. They kept the pesos and a pocketknife, and returned my comb.

"*Buenos días*, Señor Pace."

"Good morning."

"Have a seat. I'd offer to buy you a coffee but I'm quickly coming to the end of my meager funds." I picked up my cigarettes and offered him the pack. "To what do we owe this unexpected visit from the Man Who Would Be Consul?"

He waved away the Camels and glanced around, as though checking to ensure no one would overhear him. "A rather substantial bribe would be my guess." His tone was a reasonably suitable mix of accusation and disapproval.

"Well, that certainly clears up the mystery." I lit a cigarette.

"You are being released." He looked offended. "And deported, I might add." That prospect evoked a tight little humorless smile.

"Me?" If it had come from the mouth of almost anyone else I wouldn't have believed it. "Who the fuck bailed me out?"

"I haven't been made privy to that information, but I think we can safely presume it was Ms. Rossini. Why she would bother is beyond me." He centered his attaché case on the table in front of him, snapped open the locks, and pulled out a 5 × 7 envelope, which he handed to me. It had my name written on it.

I opened the envelope and peeked inside. I saw my passport, a stack of money, and another envelope. "No shit!" I emptied everything on the table.

"I've been instructed to give you that envelope, and to accompany you to the airport and see you on the plane. It leaves in"—he checked his gold Omega—"ninety-two minutes."

"Has anyone informed the guards of this new development? I think they'll want to see a note from the warden before they open those gates."

"Two members of the federal police are attending to your release."

"Even as we speak?"

"Don't be a wiseass, Mr. Hawkins. You aren't out of here yet."

"Two weeks ago you were telling Ms. Rossini what a great sense of humor I have. Now I'm a wiseass. Tact, Mr. Pace. Tact at all costs." I exhaled the last drag of my cigarette in his direction and killed the butt on the floor.

Behind him two very large members of the Mexican Federal Police, in plain clothes, arrived at the door. I nodded in their direction. "Frick and Frack are here."

Pace turned in his chair and spoke to them in Spanish. They came over and one of them pulled out a pair of handcuffs. "Your arms, Señor."

My heart turned to ice. I looked at Pace. "Cuffs? Where the fuck are we going?"

He asked the guy in Spanish, then translated. "It's the required procedure." He grinned with obvious delight at my concern. "Don't worry, I'm here to ensure that you are on the next plane to Miami."

I surrendered to the cuffs and stood, hoping that would speed up the departure. "By the way, where's my pack and my typewriter?"

"In the van."

At the airport I was kept in an office of the immigration police, still cuffed. "Where in the name of Christ do these brain-damaged examples of Latin bureaucracy imagine I would go if I weren't wearing these bracelets?" I asked Pace. "What would I do? Run away? You can tell them that I'm overjoyed at my deportation."

"They are simply adhering to proper procedure, Mr. Hawkins. And you might bear in mind that you are still a criminal in the eyes of the Mexican authorities."

"Yeah, yeah, yeah. Big-time dope dealer. I can accept their eagerness to bust me and their reluctance to let me go. They need to justify their jobs like everyone else. But why have you got the righteous rag on for me?"

"I simply am not prepared to condone this type of behavior. I would have thought that someone of Ms. Rossini's caliber and experience would have seen through you and whatever pitiful story you told her. After all, she is half-owner of a very large and influential newspaper."

"And I'm a reporter, Mr. Pace. Employed by the *Philadelphia Call*." That set off a little chain reaction of doubt, dismay, and confusion. "You want to take a guess as to why I've been a guest at Club Fed for the last two months?"

"You were arrested while in possession of slightly more than one pound of marijuana. A rather serious offense in Mexico."

"It was four ounces, or less, not half a key like those shit-dipping *Federales* said. Enough to get me in here, but not enough to make it really difficult to get me out. Right?"

"Are you suggesting that you arranged your own arrest?" That particular prospect no doubt opened up all kinds of unhappy possibilities for him.

"Mr. Pace, in the last two years I've done short terms in more foreign prisons than you've seen since you joined the silk-panty corps. Greece, Turkey, Germany, South Africa, Japan—you name the place and I've seen their idea of justice up close." I smiled. "It's going to make one hellava story. How the ordinary American citizen who gets into trouble in another country is treated by the legal establishments of our reputed friends. How we're treated by members of the American diplomatic corps. Who was helpful and who wasn't. Who showed their concern with action and who sat on their collective ass."

"Well, I certainly have no concerns about my role in all of this. I adhered to proper procedures as set forth by the U.S. State Department's guidelines. There's really nothing we *can* do in these types of cases—"

"Bullshit! But, compared to some, you've been a prince."

"What exactly do you imagine I could have done in your particular case?"

I smiled. Now he wants to know what specific complaints I intend to print regarding him. Christ, I'd love to have him in a poker game. "I'll tell you one thing: You could have made the effort to remember my goddamn name. Jim Dawkins?"

"An unfortunate oversight, but hardly significant."

"Hardly significant to whom? Don't be an asshole. How would you feel if you were dependent on some mindless bureaucrat to defend your meager rights and he referred to you as Chuck Mace? Would that inspire confidence? And you accepted without question that I was arrested with half a key of grass. Not only did you accept it, you repeated it as fact."

"Those charged with crimes have a long history of attempting to minimize the offense."

"And there's an equally long history of unfounded accusations. The problem is, you've never been caught outside the perimeter of your sanitized little world where the rules are all written down and everyone stays in step with the music. Out here no one gives a flying fuck about the rules and the name of the game is changed to survival." I held up my hands. "You ever been cuffed?"

"Certainly not."

"It's a strange experience. And at the moment totally without cause."

He gave me a long look, then crossed the room and spoke to the chief clerk, who went into another office and returned with permission to uncuff me.

"Thanks." I rubbed my wrists. "Now when I do my story I'll have at least one positive thing to say about you and the staff of the American consulate in Mérida." He snorted somewhat disdainfully and walked away to chat with a cute young female clerk who had been watching us and him in particular.

With the cuffs off and a modicum of privacy I quickly went through my pack. Everything was there, including almost seven hundred dollars in American Express traveler's checks. I opened the larger envelope Pace had handed me and pulled out money and my passport. I counted twenty dollars in pesos, and five hundred in U.S. currency. I'm particularly fond of fifty-dollar bills, and along with the ten twenties there were six pictures of General Grant. Not bad.

The second, letter-sized, envelope had my name written on the front in feminine script:

Jamie Hawkins
The Philadelphia Call
c/o U.S. Consul, Mérida, Yucatán, Mexico

I opened it and found a note from Juliet.

Dear Jamie,

Everything has been arranged for your release. Please behave yourself, at least until the plane lands in Miami.

I've enclosed enough money for you to buy a ticket to Philadelphia, or almost anywhere else if you've changed your mind. I trust you'll keep your promise to at least visit me in our fair City of Brotherly Love.

Looking forward to seeing you in a few days. Call when you arrive. If I'm not home leave a message.

— — — —

I came out of the shower with a grin on my face, feeling good. The hot water had washed away the grime, and remembering the look on Pace's face was as good as a second wind.

I dressed and sat on the edge of the bed to reread Juliet's note. What the fuck does she want? I wondered as I poured myself a cup of coffee. She had to have expended a good deal of energy and influence to get me out. The money didn't amount to much in her league, but rich people don't make a habit of throwing the stuff away. As an investment I was over the counter, at best. Maybe over the hill. And I can't be bought. I can be rented for a while if the price is right, but she looked like an owner.

— — — —

Even better, she looked like a million dollars when she rolled up to the Ramada in her black Mercedes 450-SL. I wasn't sure it was her until she smiled and waved. She wore creamy beige leather slacks, a silk pullover, and an oversized tobacco-colored leather jacket. She still wore her hair in a thick braid and her eyes were hidden behind a pair of Porsche sunglasses. *Sheee-it!* A gorgeous strawberry blonde in a black Mercedes with big sunglasses.

I walked up to the car and looked down through the open sunroof. "Hi . . . and welcome to the Ramada. Will you be staying long?"

"Not if you'll get in the car. You want to drive?"

I opened the passenger door and climbed in. "Nope. You got me this far all on your own." She gunned the car onto Market Street, ran a yellow light, and shifted into third at about forty miles an hour. I took a deep breath and exhaled loudly. "On the other hand, if you get tired of driving . . ."

"Hungry?"

"I could eat. I'm not absolutely positive, but I think my last meal was turkey tongue on rye somewhere around Richmond."

She laughed. "Airline food is bad, but 'turkey tongue on rye'?"

"I came up on the train."

"From *Miami?* Why on earth would you do that?"

"I always thought it would be fun to get ripped and ride a train for a couple of days. So I got ripped, got on board, and here I am. Famished."

"We should be at the place I've got in mind in fifteen or twenty minutes." She hit the on ramp of the Schuylkill Expressway at something close to fifty and shifted into a higher gear. I tipped my head to the side and watched the speedometer climb past seventy. "What do you mean when you say you got 'ripped'?"

"I had some magic mushrooms in my pack that the Mexican narcs missed. You ever trip?"

"God, no! I'd be terrified. You actually had drugs in your pack? And you brought them through customs? What would you have said if the customs officer found them?"

"Who knows? I probably would've told them that I had been in jail in Mexico for the last two months and that the narcs were all pissed off because I was released, so they must have planted the stuff in my pack. I didn't have that much. Those guys in Miami would have laughed me out of the terminal."

"Jamie, you spent two months in jail for possession of marijuana. I get you out and you get on a train and trip all the way home?"

"I don't have a home, and I didn't worry about getting caught. I had a couple of paranoid moments on the train when the psilocybin and the tequila lit up at the same time, and some mindless retard from the Delaware County Sheriff's auxiliary police force wanted to play the part of Dirty Harry."

"What happened?"

"I scared him with my Dogs of War routine." She had no idea what I was talking about and it showed in her expression.

"Tell me about your 'Dogs of War' routine."

"There's a movie called *The Dogs of War*. It's about mercenaries, and Christopher Walken plays a whacked-out merc given to outrageous fits of temper."

"He seems very strange to me."

"Right. And that, mind you, from an obviously beautiful woman of means who meets an American prisoner in a Mexican jail, spends ten minutes talking to him before deciding to cater dinner in the prison *cantina*, then decides after two hours of dinner conversation to use her influence and money to bail him out. She gives him money to fly to Philadelphia for a job which he may or may not be qualified for—and given that sentence, I'd say I'm not even qualified to sit at the obit desk."

She was laughing. "So you think I'm strange."

"Yes, and lucky for me. I was getting real tired of having to choose between starvation and eating boiled black beans and bread. The bread was good but the beans were a disaster. They weren't even half cooked, and they served them out of a five-gallon can that looked exactly like the cans roofers use to carry hot tar." I lit a cigarette, remembering the first and last time I made an attempt to eat the beans. "I couldn't eat that crap."

"Couldn't or wouldn't?"

"Wouldn't, probably. I've heard people say that you can eat anything if you're starving. Maybe."

She took the City Line Avenue exit at close to seventy miles an hour, downshifted, ran another yellow, and settled down to a speed closer to the limit. "So where the hell are we? Is this still Philadelphia?"

"On our left it is. On our right is Montgomery County."

"Is this the famed Philadelphia Main Line?"

"Not yet," she said. "This is Bala Kinwood, spelled C-Y-N-W-Y-D for reasons known only to the Welsh."

"That's the problem with letting riffraff immigrants name their own towns. They can't spell in English." She gave me a quick, disapproving glance. I laughed. "See why I wouldn't give you any references? I make fun of everyone, including myself."

"Why?"

"Because we're all ridiculous creatures, weighed down with pretensions about our own self-importance. And it gets worse all the time. Too many people are convinced that whatever they want, whatever they're doing, wherever they're going is the focal point of all creation at that instant. And the truth is, if any one of us fell off the face of the earth, now or next week, not much would change."

She pulled into a parking slot next to a restaurant and turned off the engine. "Would you describe yourself as a cynic?"

"Nope." I opened the door and got out. She did the same and I leaned on the roof, looking across at her. "But you can, if that makes it easier for you to deal with me." I winked at her and she made a face. "Actually, I'm a romantic."

As we walked toward the front door of the restaurant I draped my arm over her shoulder. She didn't pull away, but she didn't move any closer, either.

The place had a maître d', which didn't surprise me, and a waiter who introduced himself as Aaron, which did. It didn't seem trendy enough.

"Listen," I said as she opened her menu, "don't mistake my humor for indifference. I say what a lot of people think, but I say it with humor. I make a lot of people smile and a few of them laugh."

"Comedians are rarely taken seriously," she said without looking up.

"I'm not a comedian. I'm an observer, and a commentator on the absurdities of life."

She looked up, peering over the top of the menu. "Not to mention a romantic."

"Cynicism, to quote an anonymous observer, is the last retreat of the idealist, and the idealist is invariably a romantic. I'm skeptical, and maybe a little sardonic, but I can't really qualify as a genuine cynic because I'm still struggling to make things better." I stood and she looked up, confused. "Relax. I'll be back in a minute."

"Can I order for you?"

"Sure."

"What would you like? The eggs Benedict are excellent . . . and the bartender makes a very good Bloody Mary."

"Get me a shot of tequila with a piece of lime, and poached eggs with hash and toast, crisp. Tell *Aaron* to nuke it if he has to, but no limp toast."

Coming out of the bathroom I stopped at the bar. They had two bartenders, neither of them unduly busy. The younger one came over. "What can I get you?"

"Is there a flower shop around here, somewhere close?"

He thought for a second, then nodded. "Yeah, new place just down the block a couple of doors."

I took a ten off the top of my bankroll and laid it on the bar. "Could you find a waiter who's having a slow day and ask him to bring one yellow rose to that lady at my table?"

He grinned. "A yellow rose for Miss Rossini? Sure."

"Tell him to keep the change, but pick the best of the lot, okay?"

"You got it."

The bill disappeared and I went back to the table. Juliet was absentmindedly stirring her Bloody Mary, lost in thought. I sat down and lifted the shot glass. "A toast to someone who cared enough to help. Thank you."

She lifted her glass with a warm smile that showed in her eyes. "You're welcome." We drank. I bit into the slice of lime.

She eyed the empty shot glass. "It's over so quickly when you drink it like that . . . and aren't you supposed to do it with salt?"

"Yes, but I checked the place out and I didn't see any signs of undercover tequila police, so who's to know? You aren't going to turn me in, are you?"

"Probably not. I went to a lot of trouble to get you out."

"How did you manage that, anyway?"

"Friends of friends with the right connections. And some money discreetly distributed to the right people." She took another sip of her drink. "How did Mr. Pace react?"

"He was sorely disappointed that you didn't 'see through my pitiful story.'

I think he was a lot more disappointed by the thought that I would be in the same city with you while he bakes what's left of his brain in the Yucatán."

"Clifford?! He's such a weenie." She laughed.

"How did you get hooked up with him, anyway?"

"Whenever I travel out of the country my secretary contacts the American consulate to let them know my itinerary and I usually get the low-level VIP treatment. Clifford came with the deal."

"Jesus! I spend my life trying to avoid notice and you send out announcements."

"The way you've described your travels that's probably a wise decision. I don't have anything to hide."

Aaron arrived at that moment and I avoided saying something unkind, like 'How boring'. The food was good, as nine-dollar eggs go. For her, fifteen dollars for eggs Benedict probably didn't set off any alarms. In Mexico, before I got busted, I could eat for a week on fifteen dollars.

About halfway through the meal she suddenly looked up with a big smile and asked, "Are you still interested in a job on the *Call?*" I shrugged. "I spoke to one of the editors and there's a position as feature writer on the dayside staff. It's yours if you want it."

"Just like that? No interview with some putz from Personnel and no battery of psychological tests?"

"Not unless you want all that."

"I can probably struggle through without it." I chewed on a piece of toast for a while, thinking about work and all the bullshit that goes with a straight-time job. Stuck in an office all day, surrounded by people I'd rather not know, let alone have to deal with or answer to. Worse still, editors.

"Are you considering the offer or daydreaming?"

"Probably a little of both."

"The editor to whom I spoke about you, Daniel French, has read your book." She concentrated for a moment. *"Throwaway Soldiers,* right?"

"That's it." I searched her face for some clue to his reaction.

She smiled. "He really liked it. In fact, he said it might be the best pure fiction he'd read about Vietnam. And he said that even if you don't want a job with the *Call* he'd like for you to come in so he can meet you."

She was positively beaming. I had been legitimized. Not to mention pigeonholed, and maybe hamstrung. Shit!

"You don't look too happy about the news," she said. "Is something wrong?"

"Not with the news." How the hell could I explain to anyone like her what I felt? Or worse, why I felt anything other than delight? I looked up from the empty shot glass at which I had been staring and there was the bartender with one perfect yellow rose.

"From an admirer, Miss Rossini . . ."

"Oh, Stephen, how beautiful." She looked around the room, searching for a familiar face. After a moment it dawned on her and genuine delight displaced the artificial look of pleasure. The bartender gave me a look that said we'd scored one for the proletariat and left grinning. "Thank you, Jamie. That's really very sweet."

"And romantic."

"And romantic," she agreed. She reached across the table and touched my hand. Her long, elegantly tapered fingers were soft and surprisingly warm.

"So, what now?"

"Are you up for a tour with a native guide?" She signaled Aaron for the check. "I've got all afternoon free and you should see something of the city if you're going to work here. Right?"

"Right." *If* is the key word, I thought as I took the check from Aaron and dropped two twenties on top of it. "You bought dinner, remember?"

Holding the rose, she stood and curtsied slightly. "Your chariot awaits, sir."

— — — —

At 6:30 we were standing at the corner of Second and Locust. "Where are we now? Other than Philadelphia, I mean?"

"Straight ahead, more or less, is Penn's Landing." She waved at the concrete congestion on our right. "That's Society Hill."

"Where's the hill?"

"It's slightly elevated."

I laughed. "And highly inflated. High rises and high rents. Undoubtedly preceded by low-rent slums. It's got that urban-renewal look to it."

"It was pretty bad down here."

It was still pretty bad as far as I was concerned. One slum exchanged for another, one physical and one spiritual. "Is there a saloon around here, some place that hasn't been shot full of terminal quaintness?"

"Not really," she said after a moment's thought. "But there is a nice little bar about a block from here that you might find interesting. Want to take a chance?"

"Why not?" We walked toward the Delaware River and made a turn on Front. "What bridge is that?"

"Ben Franklin."

"And across the river?"

"Camden." If she had said "cod liver oil" the tone would have been equally appropriate.

"New Jersey?" She nodded. "Not one of your favorite places, I take it." Even in the shadows it looked grimy and decayed. Cinderella sitting by the embers while Prince Charming chases around the big city.

"This is it," she said. We were standing in front of the Cock'n'Bull Pub. The door was planked oak held together with iron strap hinges and old iron nails. A crest displayed over the door showed a fighting cock astride the shoulders of a huge black bull.

"That's a great name," I said laughing. "Is this where all your editors hang out?"

"It is, actually." She stood aside while I opened the door. "How did you guess?"

"It figured."

As I followed her in I glanced down at the floor, to be sure I didn't trip over the threshold. When I looked up my eyes were about four inches from some of the loveliest female flesh I had seen in months. The barmaids were all dressed like English wenches from some eighteenth-century London pub, with laced bodices over low-cut cotton blouses, and full skirts . . . only these skirts had been slit to the hip, revealing some gorgeous legs in black cotton stockings. The one standing directly in front of us smiled a welcome. "Good evening. Would you like a table or a seat at the bar?"

I looked at Juliet, who was grinning. She shrugged, so I said, "We'll park at the bar, thanks."

"I trust she's not too 'quaint' for your taste."

"I suppose I could make some allowances." I signaled the bartender. "You want to try a shot of tequila with me?"

"Thanks, but I think I'll have a dry white wine."

"How veddy veddy. At least you don't drink spritzers and smoke Virginia Slims."

"I rarely smoke anything, but when I do I'm partial to small cigars called Whiffs. Have you ever tried them?"

"No, but I sure hope I'm around the next time *you* do. I can't wait to see you with a low-fat stogy." I downed my tequila, chased it with some Mexican beer, and signaled the bartender for a refill.

"So, were you impressed with your tour?"

"In a way. I haven't seen so many towns with names I couldn't spell since I left Vietnam. Wynne Wood . . . Bryn Mawr . . . Villanova . . . Paoli. Christ on a bike. I always had trouble spelling Philadelphia."

"Wait until you try the Schuylkill River."

"The Schuylkill River . . . School-kill R-I-V-E-R. Easy."

"Close, but no Corona. S-C-H-U-Y-L-K-I-L-L. Dutch."

"Clever. Were you born here? In the, excuse the expression, Greater Philadelphia area?"

"Yes."

"Was your father in the newspaper business, too?"

"He owned the *Call*, which he inherited from his father."

"Is he still living?"

"No. He died several years ago. My brother and I inherited the paper from him."

"How about your mom?"

"She died when I was born."

"What do you do at the *Call?* Do you have an office?"

"I have an office. I attend board meetings. I make public appearances representing the *Call.* I occasionally attend newspaper conventions, or speak at seminars . . ."

In other words, I thought, you haven't got shit to say about the way that paper is run.

"You're right," she said, obviously reading my mind.

"About what?"

"My involvement is somewhat limited . . ."

Right. Well, that is a nicer way of putting it.

". . . but I can still guarantee you a job as a feature writer. I do have allies."

"Daniel French being one of them, I trust." She nodded. "What's his position?"

"Managing editor."

"And I'd work for him?"

"Well, you would be assigned to the city desk as dayside feature writer."

"And you know what happens to so-called feature writers assigned to the city desk?"

"They write features."

"They write obits, and make filler from handouts sent in by the Kiwanis Club, and rewrite pseudo–news releases from every self-serving corporate PR flack within fifty miles . . . and once in a while, if they haven't made the city editor's shit list or totally pissed off one or more of his assistants, they are assigned to do an in-depth report on teenage suicide, or the newest treatment for cancer or senility, or the revitalization of some previously defunct entity of some kind. That's always filler material, something to flesh out Sunday's collection of classified and display ads."

"And if I tell you it won't be that way . . . ?"

I licked the spot on my left hand between my thumb and forefinger, sprinkled some salt on it, and picked up my second shot of tequila. "Here's to innocence, and innocence lost." I licked the salt, knocked back the shot, and bit into a slice of lemon.

"Whose innocence are we toasting?" she asked as she lifted her glass.

"Your choice."

She sipped from her glass, looking at me over the rim. "I got you out of prison, didn't I?"

"You did."

"Isn't that worth something? A modicum of confidence, some degree of trust?"

" 'A *modicum* of confidence . . .' Anyone who can properly fit that word into such a simple sentence deserves something." I looked around the bar, watching the wenches, checking out the new arrivals. "Tell me something . . ."

She tilted her head to the side slightly. "What the fuck do you want from me? Feature writers, reporters, and rewrite men are a lot like lemons: a little sour, usually, but very plentiful and relatively cheap. You could buy as many as you want with one ad in *Editor and Publisher*."

"But not like you."

"How so?"

"You're different."

"Or indifferent."

She laughed. "You're one of the most arrogant and opinionated people I've ever met. You *are* funny, like you said. And I don't necessarily disagree with a lot of your observations, although I probably wouldn't say what you do even if I had your wit. You're a lot of things, Jamie Hawkins, but indifference isn't your strong suit."

"So make me a columnist. I've got perfect credentials."

"That possibility was discussed, but it would bruise too many egos and I'm not sure I could pull it off, even with Daniel's help. Let's consider that a mid-range goal."

"What's the short-range goal?"

"*My* short-range goal is getting you to accept the goddamn job." Her expression was a mix of exasperation and amusement.

"You too can have an exciting new career in personnel recruitment," I said in my best late-night-TV announcer's voice. "The Philadelphia School of Slipshod Recruitment teaches you all the little-known techniques used by successful recruiters in the armed forces! The Foreign Legion! *And* the Chrysler Corporation. Slipshod teaches *you* to spot out-of-work bozos in cheap cafés, Christian missions, and Mexican jails. . . ."

"Are you enjoying yourself?" She sipped her wine.

"Thoroughly." I laughed as I reached over and took her hand.

"I wish you would be serious about this."

"Okay. Seriously, what kind of salary?"

"Five hundred a week, plus any expenses you incur."

"Seven-fifty. The Guild minimum for a journeyman reporter must be over six by now and I'm a certified novelist, to boot."

Big sigh. "Seven."

"I don't have a car and I don't have money to buy one."

"You can rent one if you need it, or take cabs locally, and the *Call* will cover the expense."

"I'm going to need an advance to buy some clothes. I don't own anything acceptable to a city editor."

"I'll take care of that."

"I'll need a place to live, something furnished since I don't own any furniture."

"I've got something in mind."

"And I don't work on Sundays."

"You can work Tuesday through Saturday, eight to five, with an hour for lunch."

"All right, but I rarely talk to anyone before ten o'clock. The truth is, I rarely talk to anyone before noon, but I don't want to make your job any more difficult than it already is."

"How thoughtful. We've got a deal? No bullshit? You won't call me in two or three days and say you've changed your mind?"

I looked long and hard at her, then smiled. "One more condition, and the deal is done. And when I give my word I keep it, come hell or high water."

"What else?"

"We seal the deal with a shot of tequila."

She made a face. "Jamie, don't be mean. I can't drink that stuff." She shuddered.

"One shot. C'mon, it's good for you. I hate it, but since I started drinking it I haven't had a cold, menstrual cramps, or lower back pain." I waved the bartender over. "Two shots of cactus juice and another beer."

"Do I have to do that nonsense with the salt and lemon, too?"

"Hell, yes. It's all part of contract validation."

The bartender poured two shots, put a saucer full of fresh-cut lemon wedges between them, and placed a fresh beer and clean glass next to Juliet's wine. He was grinning and Juliet looked from him to me as though she had just discovered proof of the so-called male conspiracy.

"I think he's looking forward to this."

"Probably," I said. "Okay . . . salt." She watched me, then licked the spot on her left hand and wrinkled her nose. "How tacky."

"Never mind. Now, hold the lemon between the thumb and index finger of your left hand and pick up the shot with your right."

"I think I can handle it without the Arthur Murray chart, thank you."

"Nice to see I'm not the only wiseass in the group."

"My apologies. Okay, first the salt, then the tequila, then the lemon. Right?"

"Right." I raised my glass. "Hell or high water . . ."

She licked the salt, downed the tequila, and bit the lemon, all in one fluid series of moves. And for about five seconds she didn't wince or groan or make a face. I chased mine with a slug of beer. "What are you, a ringer?"

"Noooo!" she gasped as she grabbed my glass of beer and drank half of what was left. She burped. "Jesus! That stuff really lights a fire." She shuddered slightly, then smiled. "Actually, it feels good once it's down."

"Welcome to the club," the bartender said and poured two more shots. "On the house."

"Oh no!" Juliet exclaimed. "No, no, no."

I pushed the saltshaker toward her. "Come on, one for the river. Otherwise they'll bar me from even coming in here." I looked to the bartender. "Right?"

"Right you are, sir. Once poured, a drink must be drunk."

"And a drunk in the drink is worth two in the tank, or something like that."

She giggled. "Okay, but this is absolutely it. I'm not a drinker. Two of these and I'll be lucky if I can find the river."

"Pour yourself one, innkeeper," I said. "This is history in the making."

He poured a shot and we all clinked glasses, licked the salt, downed the booze, and bit the lemons. This time she casually poured a little beer into her own glass and drank slowly, watching me, laughing with her eyes. The bartender walked away to take care of another customer.

"Good stuff, huh?"

She shook her head. "I can't believe you would drink this while you were eating those mushrooms. You must have made the entire trip in another world."

"Well, I remember parking myself in a geosynchronous orbit over Neptune as the train was rolling into Savannah. That worked well enough until I hit Washington. After that it was touch and go."

"Speaking of go," she said, and checked her watch, "I have a dinner appointment."

"*Sheee-it!* You're gonna leave a great place and a warm-hearted guy like me to keep a dinner 'appointment'? Not even a date, mind you. An 'appointment'."

"I'd probably have more fun if I stayed, but I'm expected at a dinner party and if I don't go there'll be questions asked that I would rather not answer under the circumstances."

"You ever heard the expression 'What the fuck's it to ya?!' It's an all-purpose response to uninvited inquiries regarding one's activities." She closed her eyes and shook her head, the pathetic parent confronted with the hopeless child. "It usually works for me," I added as an afterthought. "Although it did get me fired once."

She slid down from the bar stool. "I'll be back in a few minutes."

"Telephone?"

"Ladies' room."

The great escape. If things get uncomfortable, hit the head. I turned on the bar stool to watch her walk away. A fine-looking tush, nice hips . . . my employer. Shit.

"So how's it going?"

I turned back to find the bartender leaning against the bar, his eyes following Juliet. I shrugged. "Hard to say."

"Say it's hard and see if that helps." Stupid joke, but we both laughed. "I've seen her in here from time to time. Who is she?"

"Juliet Franklin-Rossini, with a hyphen, thank you."

"Whoa . . . big time. Her brother owns the *Call*. We get a few of their editors in here. On a bad day, we get a lot of their editors in here." He mopped up a few water spots. "You a news guy, too?"

"Off and on."

He nodded. "Well, if you can hook up with her you may be on for a long time. I mean, she must have some influence at the paper, right?"

"So she says."

"The least she could do is introduce you to her brother. He's a powerhouse in Philly. I've done some bartending at the Alliance Club and he's in there a lot. Hangs out with the mayor and that bunch." He picked up the empty shot glasses. "Want another one?"

"Why not?"

He poured a shot into a fresh glass. "See the barmaid near the door, the one with the short black hair who's always kidding around with the customers?"

"Yeah. She was at the door when we came in."

"Her name's Sheila Wolinski. She asked me if I know you." He raised his eyes to the ceiling for an instant and grinned. "I don't know what you've got planned with Miss Rossini, but if it doesn't work out you could probably do okay with Sheila. She's my dinner relief between eight and eight-thirty."

Sheila looked about twenty-five, five-five, maybe 35C, and stacked like a crooked deck. Nothing was straight but everything was in place. "I should be so lucky," I said. He went down the bar to take care of a customer and I looked longingly at Sheila. After two months of sleeping with Little Mary Five-Fingers in Club Fed, Ms. Wolinski could be manna from heaven falling into the lap of a randy monk. I watched her flounce across the room to the bar and hoped that she didn't routinely change into street clothes before she left for home. I was in the midst of a fantasy that involved peeling off the bodice when she looked down the bar, grinned, and stuck out her tongue like a ten-year-old who knows she's being watched.

"Having fun?" Juliet asked from behind me.

"Not as much as I was before you disappeared into the nether world of the Cock'n'Bull's powder room. I've never understood why it takes women so long to accomplish something so basic."

She laughed. "You don't miss a beat, do you?"

"Everybody misses once in a while, but I never let it become a habit. So, what's the story? Are we going out to celebrate my new status among the gainfully employed?"

"Tomorrow night. I really do have to attend this dinner, and I'm already behind schedule. Will you walk me to my car?"

"But of course," I said in my best Clouseau-inspired accent. "Permit me to settle the debt and we'll be on our way."

━━ ━━ ━━ ━━

"Can you find your way back?" Juliet asked as we approached her car. "I'm really pressed for time."

"Go. If I get lost I'll ask for directions." I took the keys from her and opened the door. "You mentioned tomorrow . . ."

She took the keys. "I'll call you in the afternoon." She made a move to slip into the seat, then stopped and straightened up, looking at me across the top of the door. "I'm very pleased that you've accepted the offer."

I leaned as close as I could get, searching her eyes for a signal. I wanted to kiss her. She smiled and slid behind the wheel. Well, I thought, that's clear enough. She started the engine, closed the door, and opened the window. "See you tomorrow?"

"If I'm lucky."

"If you're lucky I may not see you for a week."

"If I were to get really lucky you could call me from across the room."

"Behave yourself." She pulled away and disappeared into the night.

— — — —

My eyes opened at seven o'clock the next morning. The part of my brain which insists on waking me up is half-witted and linked to some ridiculous metabolic clock that knows little and cares less about my desire to sleep. Sometimes I go back to sleep, only to wake an hour or so later, then back to sleep again. If I'm lucky. Another legacy of 'Nam, is my guess. Probably one of the many unre-searched side-effects that results from eating too many C rations.

For the first few seconds I didn't have a clue to where the hell I was. The mattress was soft, the sheets were a floral print, and the bed was too crowded for me to be alone. The room was filled with rattan furniture, green plants, and early morning sunlight, which was pleasant. Kind of like waking up in a commercial for Wamsutta. Or Jamaica. Sure as hell it wasn't my room at the Ramada.

Very slowly I raised my upper body onto my elbows and looked to my right. Sheila Wolinski. Ah yes. My Polish serving wench. I put my head back on the pillow, closed my eyes, and waited for sleep. No way. Not in a strange bed with a woman whose name I could barely pronounce and definitely couldn't spell.

An image from the previous night flashed into my semi-conscious mind: Sheila in bikini briefs and the lace-up bodice, wearing a black flat-brim bolero hat and black high-heeled boots. I was on the bed, propped against the wall, completely nude.

As she leaned over so I could unlace the bodice she said, "I haven't been laid in almost a month . . ."

And I had said, "I haven't been laid in almost three months."

I was lying there with a big grin on my face. I couldn't remember the last time I'd smiled like that before noon. Christ, what a night. Which, as I thought about it, hadn't ended until amost four o'clock. What in the name of Mary's mule was I doing awake at the crack of dawn? A sudden craving for a cigarette and a cup of coffee pushed the erotic thoughts into the background. I climbed out of bed, taking great care not to awaken Sheila, and stepped directly onto a loose plank in the floor. The squeak could have been heard in hell.

"Good morning," Sheila said in a voice muffled by sleep and sheets. "You always get up so early?"

"There's chores to be seen to, woman. Llamas to be milked, goats to be fed. And you'd best be gatherin' up the eggs 'stead of lyin' abed."

"Eggs are in the fridge. I put 'em in one of them funny looking designer boxes marked Grade A." She turned over, opened one eye for a moment, and said, "By the way, you talk in your sleep."

"Yeah, and you stole the blanket. Go back to sleep." I pulled on my clothes and left her in the arms of Morpheus.

What now? I wondered as I stirred sugar into my coffee. It's seven-fifteen on a Sunday morning in a strange city and I'm sitting in the kitchen of a stranger wondering what to say to her when she gets out of bed. 'Morning after' small talk with a *gringa* hadn't been required for months. Too many months.

A loud thump at the door brought me to my feet in a flash. I took a couple of steps toward the kitchen entrance, wondering if the door into the apartment would suddenly fly open to reveal Sheila's irate boyfriend. Hell, I didn't even know if she had a boyfriend, but I had no difficulty picturing a brain-dead linebacker from Penn State who had driven all night to get here because he couldn't reach her on the phone. Another thump down the hall evoked a sigh of relief. That's either a Saturday night drunk or the Sunday paper, I decided, and went back to my coffee.

— — — —

I was standing at the sink, staring through the narrow kitchen window into an air shaft while I considered my options, when two warm hands slid under my shirt and Sheila's husky voice filled my ear.

"Can I watch you milk the llamas?"

"Absolutely not!" I turned around and looked straight into her blue eyes. "I made a promise to your mom, and promises I make, I keep."

"To *my* mom?"

"That's right. She called last night while you were in the bathroom. I answered the phone, and she said, 'Young man, I know how Sheila is, so she'll probably have her way with you before the night is over, but promise me, whatever happens, you won't let her watch you milk the llamas.' " I shrugged. "I could tell it meant a lot to her, so I promised."

She stepped back and sucked in a chestful of air, which set all sorts of muscles in motion. "Thanks a lot, Jimbo!"

"Jamie."

"Fine. I don't even know your name and you've already made a promise to my mom to deprive me of the one thing that might have made you different from all the other dirty old men in the Cock'n'Bull."

"Well, your mom sounded frantic . . ."

"What about *me?* Do you know how long I've waited for the man of my dreams, my mighty white knight, to show me the erotic secrets of llama milking?"

"A week?"

"Exactly! Seven days today."

I put both hands on her breasts and pulled gently on her nipples. "It's still early in the day." I slipped my left hand behind her head and pulled her face close. Our mouths were inches apart. "Maybe you can talk me into a change of"—she put both of her hands between my legs—*"heart."*

▬ ▬ ▬ ▬

I walked into the Ramada a little before noon and the desk clerk gave me a telephone message from Juliet. It was marked ten-thirty P.M. and dated the previous night.

Call me if you get this before midnight. JFR.

Interesting, I thought as I headed for a hot shower. The same old female bullshit. Yes, no, maybe . . . and meanwhile, where were you when I called? Why weren't you waiting by the phone, just in case? If I could add to my life all the hours wasted by all the women I've known who waited for some man to call I'd live to be as old as God. I'd rather not, if it's all the same to the guy keeping the books, but the mathematical possibilities are there.

I was sleeping when the phone rang a couple of hours later.

"Did I wake you?" Juliet asked.

"Not yet, but keep talking. Something will break through in a few minutes."

"I've found you a place to live. Would you like to see it?"

"Sure, why not? You want to pick me up or should I meet you?"

"I'll be out front in half an hour if that's okay."

"Half an hour is fine. 'Bye."

She arrived in the Franklin-Rossini Sunday chariot, an old E-type Jag, fully restored of course, inside and out. New leather seats, door panels, and headliner. New carpets and floor mats. The walnut dash gleamed. And neatly tucked under the dash was your basic fifteen-hundred-dollar stereo system. The only problem with the car, other than the fact that it was a Jag, which meant it wouldn't run most of the time, was the color. Icebox white. I almost laughed out loud.

Fortunately, she attributed my smile to my enchantment with life outside Club Fed, or maybe she assumed it was a reflection of my delight in seeing her again. I *was* happy to see her, and I was also about to piss my pants to keep from laughing at the Jag. She looked for all the world as though she was driving a fucking igloo.

"Well, you certainly look cheerful today. Did you enjoy yourself last night?"

"Fun for one, fun for all. How was your dinner for a dozen?"

"Worthwhile, but not a lot of fun."

"Where's this place you found for me to live? And how could you find something between last night and this morning?"

"It's an apartment on Rittenhouse Square. It belongs to a friend of the family, an older woman who's going to live for a year in Greece, with her sister. She's been looking for someone to take care of it while she's away."

I can't wait to see this, I thought, but I kept the thought to myself. Maybe the old lady's in love with stark modern.

— — — —

Rittenhouse Square fits right into that peculiar illusion I think of as intercity chic. It's overrated, overpriced, and not all that exclusive. Too many nouveau yuppie riffraffers take up all the parking spaces. Even so, it's touted as one of *the* places to live in Willie Penn's Greene Country Towne. And in season, the square *is* green, more or less. Big fuckin' deal. Only those souls fortunate enough to live in the apartments that face the Square can actually look out on spindly trees, park benches, patches of grass, and geraniums. Just about everyone else looks out on an air shaft or into the neighboring living room.

I hated the place on sight. The trees were bare, the grass was dead, and the benches were empty. It was overcast, which is a way of life in Philadelphia, and the wind was whipping through the streets at close to fifteen knots. Saturday's Indian Summer had been displaced by Sunday's Puritan autumn—a cold front and a falling barometer.

Juliet had to settle for a parking spot almost two blocks away. As we walked back I studied the streets and the buildings and the people we passed. Every place I've ever been has a feel to it, a combination of elements I've never really identified. Some people call it vibes, which is a word I dislike. Resonance is a word I do like, but it's equally inept as an explanation of the sensation I feel when I allow whatever it is to pass through all the mindless bullshit that occupies my senses during the great majority of my waking hours. And whatever was there to be felt couldn't get by the distractions, the strongest being Juliet. She was chattering like Chatty Cathy.

"This is one of the best areas in Philadelphia, good housing, walking distance to a lot of shopping, and easy access to transportation . . ."

"Not to mention a real mix of ethnic groups." She gave me a sideways glance to let me know I had once more offended her.

Our arrival at the building, an eighteen-story remnant of the Age of Solid Construction, was duly noted by the two geriatric doormen decked out in Ritz-on-the-Square uniforms fashioned from wool heavy enough to stop a small-caliber bullet. They both tipped their visored caps to Juliet. "Good afternoon, Miss Rossini," said the one who opened the door. "Mrs. Wiggins left instructions for us to give you the keys to her apartment." The second one handed Juliet a key ring. They both, in turn, cast a curious eye on me.

"Thank you, Thomas," she said as she took the key. "How's your mother these days?"

"Oh, she's still kicking," Tom said. "Eighty-seven and giving everybody a bad time because we don't want her out alone."

Sweet Mother of the Baby Jesus. I took a quick look around the lobby. Of the half-dozen breathing beings I could see, five were females with blue hair and all of them were old enough for Medicare. The Sunday Afternoon Society of Coupon Clippers meets here.

I followed Juliet onto the elevator. The door closed and she pushed the button for the fifteenth floor. "Who owns this building, Clairol or Geritol?" I asked.

"Don't be rude."

"Rude, crude, and tattooed. I can tell you right now the day I move in here Qaddafi will get an invitation to a White House tea for B'nai B'rith."

It took a moment for her to envision Colonel Q. in the Rose Garden. Even then, I suspect, she didn't really want to laugh but a smile slipped through despite her best effort. "Wait until you see the apartment before you make your decision."

Apartment 15-B, home of Mrs. Emily Wiggins, proved to be a testament to velvet-covered Victorian taste and senile paranoia. She had three dead-bolt locks on the door, and every window was sealed tighter than the bung hole on Ahab's rum keg.

"Two large bedrooms, a library, living room, dining room, two baths, full-sized kitchen with a breakfast nook . . ." Her voice trailed off. "It would be rent-free."

I was standing next to French windows that had once opened onto a balcony overlooking Rittenhouse Square. "Jesus H. Christ! Look at this."

"What?"

"She had these welded shut."

"C'mon, Jamie . . ." She came over to where I stood.

"That silly-looking metal seam is a weld."

She looked from the weld to me. "Maybe the apartment was burglarized. She *is* in her sixties . . ."

"We're on the fifteenth floor! How the hell would a burglar get onto the balcony?"

"So are you saying you aren't interested?"

"Do I look like someone who could live comfortably in an old lady's velvet-lined tomb? I'd have to break a window to get a breeze in here." She looked disappointed. I couldn't wait to get the hell out of the place. "Thanks for the effort, but I wouldn't last three days in here." I started moving toward the door. "Walking over here we passed a place that claims to make cappuccino. Let's give it a try. I need caffeine."

"Okay," she sighed.

On the elevator she finally saw the humor in her effort and grinned at me. "That *was* dumb. I apologize."

"You've been generous and thoughtful and kind in everything you've done for me," I said. "You sure as well don't owe me an apology for trying to help. But I couldn't live there unless my only alternative was a few months in one of those refrigerator boxes the upscale winos have taken to lately."

— — — —

We found a small table in the coffeehouse and ordered cappuccino. The waitress directed Juliet to the ladies' room while I studied the patrons of the Rittenhouse Café. They were all painfully trendy and to my eye they looked incredibly fragile. Fear of failure with their lives and with Life. And here was *another* goddamn empty Sunday afternoon in the city with nothing better to do than read the boring *New York Times*, eat an overpriced Sunday brunch, and watch the Eagles lose another boring game. The whole fucking room was a seedbed of depression and if you looked close you could see the roots taking hold, the sprouts breaking through.

Juliet returned in time to rescue me from the morbid abyss. "Want to look at another place?"

"Jesus, you go to the bathroom like any ordinary mortal and come back with a rental listing? What do you do with your free time?"

"Bake bread and knit warm socks. This place is close by and I can guarantee you it won't be decorated in velvet."

"Sounds promising. We got time to drink the coffee?"

"Sure."

The waitress served us two steaming cups of cappuccino. I added sugar; Juliet drank hers plain.

"Listen, what's the deal with the *Call?* Am I supposed to go in there for an interview or something? I know I asked you basically the same thing yesterday, but I'm still not clear on how all this is supposed to happen."

"Tomorrow morning, at ten A.M., you have an appointment with Daniel French, the managing editor, in his office. It's semiformal, so wear your best jeans."

"What's the address?"

"We're on Callowhill, between Seventh and Eighth. You can't miss the building. He's on the eleventh floor, and you're on his calendar. Please don't be late. He gets real grumpy when anyone is late for an appointment."

"Okay. Does he know anything about me?"

"I told him you had had a misunderstanding with the local police in Mexico and that I found you in jail." She smiled.

"Nice intro. Did you follow up with a summary of my sterling war record?"

She blew into the layer of foamy milk and sipped her coffee. "I don't know anything about your war record, but Daniel commented that a few of our better writers had seen the inside of more than one prison."

"When he said 'our better writers,' was he referring to employees of the *Call* or writers of American literature?"

She frowned for a moment, then said, "Actually, I don't now. Isn't it interesting that I would just assume he was referring to writers of novels or plays, and you would raise the possibility that he was referring to our reporters?"

It's more ordinary than interesting, I thought, but I didn't think she would appreciate my observation so I shrugged. "The Second Law of Hawkins: Assume nothing."

"And the first law is?"

"Love many, trust few, and always cut the cards."

"That says a lot about you," she said with a laugh.

"Succinct and cynical . . . ?"

"And probably a real good poker player."

"I do okay. Where's this apartment you've got a line on?"

"Twenty-first Street between Walnut and Spruce. Not far from here."

We finished our coffee in silence. When she had drained the last of hers she looked at her watch. "Shall we?"

"I'm with you, Magoo."

"You're the one with the glasses, *Magoo*," she said and took my arm.

— — — —

Two twenty-two South Twenty-first Street had once been one hell of a town house: three stories of leaded glass, oak floors, mahogany panels, walnut mantels, and marble fireplaces. Probably owned by some fuckin' robber baron who moved on to bigger crimes and even more expensive housing. The house, Juliet said, had fallen into disrepair. I took that to mean that some low-rent families had trashed the place for a number of years.

And then, she said, it had been bought by an architect, a wonderfully sensitive man devoted to restoring inner-city town houses built during the latter half of the 1800s. I took that to mean that some guy good with a T square and a calculator figured he could buy these places at a cut rate, cut them into half a dozen apartments, and thus bring cheer to the tax assessors, bank loan officers, neighborhood businesses, and trendy couples who couldn't deal with commuting.

As it turned out, the apartment was nice. One large room, 24 × 20, with an eighteen-foot ceiling. It had a separate bath and a small kitchen. What had once been a porch was now enclosed, with three arched floor-to-ceiling windows. That room was only six or seven feet deep, but it was the width of the main room, and I decided as soon as I saw it that if I moved in that was my place to read and write and watch TV. The sleeping area was on a 10 × 18 platform loft built over the center of the main room.

I climbed the open, polished oak stairs to get up there and stood at the low railing, looking down at Juliet and Rob, the rental agent, a warm, friendly cherub who had mentioned several times that he lived just a couple of blocks away on Spruce Street. "How much is this place?" I asked.

"Five-fifty per month, plus utilities."

"Lease or month-to-month?"

"Either way, although most people prefer a lease."

"Most people probably have more illusions about their future than I do. How much to move in?"

"Two months' rent and a one-hundred-dollar cleaning deposit."

I came down the stairs and stopped at the door into the hall. "I'll let you know."

"He'll take it," Juliet said. "I'll write you a check for the first month now, and he'll give you the balance when he moves in."

"We'll need a completed application, of course, with credit references," Rob said. "Mr. Rondazzi has very specific employment and credit criteria . . ."

"Mr. Rondazzi," Juliet interrupted, "was a very close friend of my late husband, Antonio Rossini."

"And of course we'll want references from two previous landlords," Rob continued.

"Rob," I said, "cut the crap. You may be light in the loafers but you're not altogether stupid. This lady will have your ass sliced, diced, and jammed between pieces of white bread which she will feed to the rats like finger sandwiches if you don't cool it with the power trip."

He stared at me for a moment, then looked at Juliet with a fair amount of loathing. She was busy writing out a check, which she handed to him with a smile. "Please tell Ted it's a lovely place and I'll call him tomorrow." She walked to the door.

"And who may I say sent the message?" he asked in his best snide tone.

"Look at the check, putz. Her name's printed in the upper left corner." I opened the door and waited for Juliet to make her exit. When she was in the hall I looked back at Rob, watching his face. He looked up, still not really sure who she was but fairly certain that anyone with the name Franklin-Rossini who referred to his boss as Ted should be treated with a good deal more respect than he had shown. He looked pathetic. I shook my head from side to side, very slowly. "Nice going . . ."

Outside on the front steps, our eyes met and I cracked up laughing, for a moment. The laughter stopped when she said, "How dare you!"

"How dare who?"

"Who do you think you are?!"

"Let's go back to the first question."

"I am perfectly capable of dealing with those persons who affect my life in any way, large or small, without intervention from my escort, thank you very much."

"What the fuck are you talking about?"

The Fifth Law of Hawkins   41

"I am talking about your eagerness to 'rescue' me from Mr. Rondazzi's representative." Her eyes were ice-blue pits of fire.

"And you were the one who decided that I'd take the apartment after I told Rondazzi's dimwit that I'd let him know. Just who the fuck gave you the right to decide where I'll live? You're lucky I don't hand you your goddamn head and leave you to figure out how to get Tab A in Slot B." I stomped down the steps, steaming.

"Where are you going?" she called.

"That's none of your fuckin' business." I was walking south toward Spruce Street without a clue to where I was, or which way I should head to get back to the Ramada.

"Jamie! You can't just walk away."

I kept walking, listening to her heels clicking on the sidewalk behind me, half running. I turned to face her. She stopped a foot away.

"You arrogant, thankless bastard. You'd still be in a Mexican jail if—"

I filled my left hand with her lapels and jerked her up on her toes.

"—I hadn't bailed you out," she finished in a squeaky voice.

With my right hand I raised my sunglasses up on top of my head and looked her straight in the eye. "Don't fuck with me. And don't delude yourself that being a female is like wearing a flak vest. I don't give a flying fuck about your money, your power, or your gender. I can't be bought and I can't be bossed." I let her back down on her feet and released her jacket.

"I could have you arrested for assault."

"*That* you can do, and that's about all you can do—yell for help and let someone else handle it." I laughed at her. "Proving that you can't really handle everything, large or small, all by yourself . . . thank you very much."

I left her staring in disbelief and continued walking toward Spruce Street, wondering if she would start screaming for a cop. Just what I needed to round out another fine fucking sunless Sunday. I hate Sundays, especially U.S. Grade A Sundays. They always come boxed in expectations and gift-wrapped in melancholy. I'd cheerfully wager the last year of my life against a case of Corona that if records were kept of all the stupid, mindless fights that erupt between males and females, married or not, at least three times as many occur on Sunday as any other day of the week.

The walk back to the Ramada was long and unpleasant. I wasn't dressed for an overcast October day in Philadelphia and the wind had picked up as the temperature fell. One bank thermometer read fifty-one, another forty-nine. It felt colder, and no matter which way I walked the wind blew in my face. City wind should be classified as a meteorological phenomenon all its own. In the winter, at a major intersection, it can and does blow from four directions, simultaneously. In the summer the wind doesn't blow at all unless it's raining or you're walking by a construction site.

My mood didn't help, either. I was pissed, mostly with myself. I had broken the Third Law of Hawkins: Never let emotions rule. I'd fucked up. Never let emotions rule, goddamn it. And *never* prolong the moment. Forget it and keep moving.

Of course, the Fourth Law of Hawkins is: Never say Never.

— — — —

The red message light on the telephone was blinking as I came into the room. I covered the phone with a pillow, slipped off my sneakers, and rolled up in a blanket. I slept from about five-thirty until a little after seven.

Dinner at eight consisted of a Burger King char-broiled crime against humanity, fries and a Coke. I ate in my room, sitting on the bed, working the *Call's* crossword puzzle. I didn't get far. The yutz who created it had come up with a wonderful new innovation in stupidity—intentionally misspelled answers. Not only was I required to remember that 'those famous off-shore islands' are Quemoy and Matsu, but I was also required to figure out his spellings, which turned out to be Keemoy and Matsoo. Fuck you too.

I smoked half a joint of some wicked shit I'd brought back with the mushrooms, turned on the TV, and found *Shampoo* on a UHF channel. It had been edited for TV, as they say. Cut with a knife and fork, I'd say, but even with all the blips and edits, it's funny. Considering my fucked-up state of mind, anything that would amuse me was a welcome distraction.

The phone rang at eight-forty-five, during a commercial break. I didn't answer. It rang again at ten-fifty. The movie was over and I was typing my latest entry in the Jamie Hawkins Journal of a Misspent Life. I ignored it and kept typing:

PHILADELPHIA
Sunday, Oct. 15
     So, here I am in this Quaker haven without a friend in sight. The Ramada is better than the Club Fed, but I can't sit here for the next six months working out what to do with what's left of this life. I've got maybe 100 pages of another book ms, but no title, no editor, no agent, and no inclination to play the role of starving writer. I can't work when I'm hungry.
     I've got enough money to live for a month or six weeks if I don't spend much on transportation or eat a lot.
     And if tension could be turned into lettuce leaves I could serve salad to the entire City of Philadelphia.
     The fucking telephone is ring, ring, ringing . . . shit!

I glanced at my watch as I reached for the phone. Eleven-thirty. I picked up the receiver none too gently. "Hello."

"Jamie . . . ?"

"No, but you may leave a message after the Bronx cheer." I made an unpleasant noise.

"Please tell Jamie that Juliet called to apologize for being a horse's ass and hopes that he will overlook the momentary lapse in her normally acceptable behavior."

"Ask Ms. Franklin-Rossini if she considers pomposity to be 'acceptable behavior.' "

"No, but she's in a forgiving mood, especially considering her own regrettable pose earlier today."

I laughed, grudgingly. "Funny. Let's call it even, and quit."

"I can't sleep."

"And I can't dance worth a damn. But there's still time for both of us to recover from the disappointment and get on with our lives."

"Can we talk without you being a wiseass?"

"I'm not sure." I leaned back against the headboard and looked for my cigarettes. It sounded like a long conversation in the making. "What's on your mind?"

"You. Would you consider coming out with me, to talk? I dislike telephones except for gossip and 'news flashes' . . ." Her voice trailed off, waiting for reassurance, a verbal smile, some sign to continue, or best of all, immediate agreement.

"Okay."

Immediate agreement might be best, but getting it was what she least expected. A long pause was followed by "Really?"

I was on the verge of saying, No, it was a trick, when the better part of my nature reminded me that foolish responses don't always have to be answered with an insult. "If you know someplace where I can get a shot of tequila and a double espresso chaser, I'll listen to whatever you've got to say."

"Meet me out front in twenty minutes. I'll be in the Mercedes."

"With the heater on, please. It's freezing and I don't have a heavy jacket. 'Bye."

—— —— —— ——

"Do you realize," I asked as I settled into the passenger seat, "that this is the third time in less than thirty-six hours that you've picked me up in front of the Ramada?" I lit a cigarette and she opened the sunroof an inch or so to let out the smoke.

"I thought about that while I was driving over."

"Your reputation's probably shot."

"Long before I met you, Jamie. *Long* before."

She headed out on the Schuylkill Expressway, in the direction of all those towns with names I couldn't spell, pronounce, or remember. I leaned over, to peek at the speedometer: seventy-five miles per hour.

"I'm an excellent driver," she said without taking her eyes off the road.

Ah yes . . . Famous Last Words, brought to you by White Star Lines.

She drove with a silent intensity that I admired. She really was a good driver as far as technique was concerned. But that don't mean shit when your only hope for seeing another sunrise rides on instinct and reflexes.

At City Line Avenue she headed west, as she had on Saturday, but a few minutes later she turned north on something called Conshohocken State Road. She slowed to a respectable fifty.

"Where the hell are we going?"

"For tequila with an espresso chaser."

"Right." Her face was illuminated by the lights from the dash and I saw a brief smile blink on and off. "Do you have some particular place in mind, or should I be looking for a piece of flashing neon?"

"We'll be there in a few minutes."

She hooked a left on Bala Cynwyd Avenue, then a right on Fox Run Lane. Every time we made another turn the price of the real estate escalated and the driveways got longer. By the time we reached Fox Run Court all the driveways were guarded and the houses barely visible, if at all.

Juliet abruptly turned into a drive and stopped before a pair of huge black wrought-iron gates anchored in stone gateposts set back from the street maybe twelve or fifteen feet. She aimed what looked like a remote control at some magic black box I couldn't see, and spoke into the device she was holding. "The bitch is back." The gates opened, rolling noisily on a track set into the asphalt drive.

I tried not to laugh, and to some degree I succeeded. The noise that did come out was probably no less offensive, but she had only finished apologizing for her last outburst so she stayed calm.

"It's a long story," she said. "And probably not without its humor if the joke's on someone else."

"Probably," I said and looked out the side window so she wouldn't see me smiling. "How does it work?"

She eased through the opening at a sensible speed. "It's a VIP system. Voice identification program."

"I didn't know that kind of shit was available in the real world, all things being relative."

"My husband didn't live in what most of us would consider the real world." Her tone was as flat as the driveway, and almost as cool. I didn't get the feeling that she missed him a whole hell of a lot.

The gates closed behind us with a thunderous sound that had a familiar, unsettling ring. As we rolled to a stop in front of chez Franklin it came to me. Club Fed. The sound of prison gates closing, I suspect, is very similar in every part of the world.

She stopped the Mercedes directly behind the Jag, killed the lights, and shut off the engine. "Welcome to Fox Lair. There's a sign to the right of the gate, in case you missed it in the dark." She opened the door, got out, and smiled with a good deal of amusement. "Tequila and espresso will be served in the library . . . unless you'd rather we sat on the hood of the car."

"Too cold." I got out and took her arm. "I'm with you, Magoo."

— — — —

The library looked less like a library than a room decorated with books, brass, Tiffany glass, marble, and custom-made leather furniture. There wasn't a crooked spine or a speck of dust among the two thousand or so books arranged along the two walls of floor-to-ceiling shelves. I ran my hand across a few of them, curious to see if touch could turn them into something a little more real.

"Take one down," Juliet said from somewhere behind me. I turned around and there she stood, an unopened bottle of Sauza Conmemorativo in one hand, a couple of shot glasses in the other. She had changed into an old, oversized black sweatshirt, a pair of soft, baggy cotton pants, and sneakers. "Edward will serve the espresso in a few minutes."

"Edward? Let me guess . . . you've got a butler."

"I do. And a maid, but this is her night off. I also employ a gardener."

"Damn!"

"What?"

"There goes my fallback. I figured with a place like this I could always hire out as the gardener if I couldn't cut it at the *Call*. How about a houseboy? I look great with one of those little white towels draped over my arm and a silver tray balanced on my hand."

She laughed. "Five minutes and Edward would fire you. He runs a tight ship, as he says."

Edward came into the room carrying a large silver tray by the handles. It was decorated with a silver creamer, a sugar dish, two cups, a silver coffee server, a couple of limes, a knife with a bone handle, spoons, a silver saltshaker, and a couple of chocolate dessert things. Tortes or some such. Perfectly arranged. Still life, with limes and chocolate.

"Edward, this is Jamie Hawkins. Mr. Hawkins is soon to be a reporter with the *Call*."

Edward placed the tray on a low table near a huge pale-gray suede sofa, stood at attention, and bowed ever so slightly. "My pleasure to make your acquaintance, sir. If I can be of service, please call on me." He shifted his eyes slightly. "Will there be anything else, Miss Franklin?"

"Thank you, Edward, but I believe that will be all for this evening. Please have coffee ready at eight."

"Very good, madam. Good evening."

I watched him leave the room, as upright and proper as a Beefeater at the door to the queen's chamber, and I wondered how anyone could actually pull off an act like that with a straight face. "I admire your taste in stone masks. What is he, King's Cross, circa '37?"

"Buckingham Palace, '33."

"You've gotta be kidding. Edward the Upright actually worked for the king?"

"He was born in the palace. His mother and his father were both in service to the queen. He left when he was in his early twenties, I believe he said."

"No shit." For whatever weird reason, I wanted to laugh. I opened the tequila instead and poured two shots into the tiny crystal glasses. I couldn't stop grinning, and I let the blade of the knife slip while I was slicing one of the limes. Almost cut myself.

"Careful," Juliet said.

"Tough to type without all my fingers."

"Where did you learn to type?"

I looked up, distracted by the question. "In school. Why?"

She shook her head, a half-smile making her already sexy mouth even more inviting. "I just wondered. I find it difficult to picture you in a high school typing class."

"Well, paint the picture with seventeen healthy young females, at least three of whom could have made *Playboy* in a flash, and me. I was the only guy in class. For all I know, I may have been the only virgin in class when it started. I was stuck in a small-town Georgia high school where the third and fourth years of English lit were electives and shop class was required to graduate. Took me about three weeks to learn to type. I spent the next eight months enjoying myself. Beat the hell out of algebra."

"I can imagine." She came over and picked up a piece of lime and one of the shot glasses. "I think I'll skip the salt, if you won't be offended."

"Fine with me." I raised my glass. "To peace on earth and goodwill toward women who rescue *gringo* dope smokers from the clutches of Mexican jurisprudence." We drank.

She poured steaming espresso into a large coffee cup. "Sugar?"

"Couple of teaspoons, and some cream or half-and-half, or whatever you've got. Unless it's skim milk. That stuff looks like unstirred off-white latex paint and probably tastes about the same." I parked myself in a large overstuffed chair and leaned back, wishing it was a recliner so I could get my feet up. A double row of buttons on the arm caught my attention.

"Chocolate?" She bit into a piece of the torte. When she licked a little of the icing from her bottom lip I offered a deal to the devil: one kiss and I'll vote for Reagan in '84.

"No," I said, "but you can pour us another shot of cactus juice, as long as you're up." I pushed one of the buttons and the chair began to vibrate moderately. "I can't wait to find out what happens when I push these other buttons. Does any of them eject the seat-ee?"

She put the coffee on a side table, leaned over slightly, and pushed another button. The chair tilted back about five degrees. "Would you like music? Heat? A reading light?" I closed my eyes and sighed. "There are eight different functions you can select."

"Which button do I push to find out what the fuck I'm doing in this house in the middle of the night with you, your butler, and a bottle of tequila?"

She collected the bottle and the shot glasses and placed them on the table with the coffee. "We're going to talk."

I filled both glasses and handed her one. "Okay, two shots and a cup of espresso was the deal. Drink up."

"The 'deal' was a shot of tequila and a double espresso chaser, as I recall. However, I won't hold you to that part. But I don't really think I should drink any more."

I waited a moment, then lifted my glass. "In the desert, a fountain is springing . . . in the wilderness there stands a tree . . . and a bird in the solitude singing speaks of my love for thee . . ."

That, I'd guess, was the last thing she expected. For a moment she just stared at me, watched me down the shot, then she lifted my sunglasses to the top of my head. Her eyes searched mine for an explanation, a clue, anything that she could use to reconcile poetry with the persona of Jamie Hawkins. The eyes are supposed to be windows to the soul, and sometimes that's true. Sometimes it's bullshit. It depends on who's sitting at the table, and what game they're playing.

Whatever she saw satisfied her for the moment. She leaned forward and kissed me. Her breath was hot; her mouth was warm and had the faint taste of tequila masked by chocolate. Her hands caressed my face. My glasses disappeared somewhere in the first few moments. I dropped the shot glass on the rug and raised my hands, circling her head, pulling her toward me. She pulled away and sucked in a chestful of air. I closed my eyes and shuddered. "Sweet Mother of the Christ Child," I sighed, and not altogether without reverence. She kissed like an angel. Or like Jessica Lange in *All That Jazz*.

"I shouldn't have done that." She stood and looked around as though she needed to reorient herself, then looked down at me. "I can't even say I don't know what came over me."

"Well, that's a relief. Because if that wasn't a pure, deliberate, and unmitigated exhibition of lust I don't know that I could endure the real thing." I held out my hand.

She ignored it and with her own unsteady hand she retrieved the fallen shot glass, filled it, filled hers, and put the bottle down. Then she collected the lime wedges I had cut, and the saltshaker. I sprinkled a little salt on my tongue, which made her smile, and touched my glass to hers. We drank without benefit of a spoken toast. I lit a cigarette while I pondered the questions of the moment: Who makes the next move? And what happens when I don't vote for Ronnie? "Can you stop this damn chair from vibrating? I can't remember which one I pushed to get it started."

She pushed the top right button, then found me an ashtray and took a seat on the sofa. Two or three minutes passed in silence. Finally she asked, "May I ask you a question, something very personal? It may help me to deal with all of this."

"I like your other approach better, but go ahead. The worst I can do is tell you something you don't want to hear. I have a real skill with that."

"What do you think of me? If I call you, what goes through your mind when you hear my voice?"

"That's two questions. First, I think you're full of shit."

She winced. "Why do you think I'm . . . full of shit?"

"Most people are."

"And you think I'm like most people?"

"You want me to believe you're an exception?" I could feel my head moving from side to side, as if I was looking at one more version of J.C. with his .30-caliber ammo and his M-16. "Look at what happened this afternoon. That was stone fuckin' ridiculous. You presumed to obligate me to an apartment that I might or might not want, but you lost it when I stepped on your feminist sensitivities. You have the right to decide where I'll live *and* you have the right to be offended when I butt into what you believe is strictly your business? If you believe that, you *are* full of shit. And if you don't believe that, if that seems real stupid, then you tell me: What are you?"

She laced her fingers together and locked her elbows for a moment, then raised her hands to a level with her chin, peering at me over the tips of her fingers. "I'm sometimes very difficult to deal with."

"That sounds about right."

"And I'm overly sensitive to male encroachment, due to a lot of very negative experiences."

"That sounds like so much bullshit."

"You don't always have to be so tactless and impolite . . ." Her hands were suddenly tight little fists, and her eyes were on fire. I laughed.

"Juliet, I'm an outlaw. A misfit. A fuckin' malcontent. I have very little tolerance for gratuitous displays of power, sanitized conversation, or slow dancing with a bullshitter. Why don't you just ask Edward to drive me back to the Ramada and let's go our separate ways."

"Because . . ."

I poured another shot and downed it, staring at her. She's either real stubborn or real stupid, I thought, and sometimes that's the same thing, and sometimes it isn't. I filled the two shot glasses and carried one to her. She looked as though she might refuse, then shrugged and held out her hand. "Let's drink to a lowering of the barriers and a loosening of the inhibitions," I said.

"And a lessening of the competition," she added.

An interesting observation, I thought, as the tequila burned a path down my throat.

"My God," she gasped. "How can you even stand on your feet after—how many, four?"

"It's an acquired taste and an acquired tolerance." I leaned over and kissed her. This kiss didn't have the urgency of the earlier one, but it was nice, and she responded instead of resisting. "Have another one and you'll start to feel better."

"In a few minutes, maybe."

"Okay." I sat on the end of the sofa opposite her. "Let's say I apologize for saying I think you're full of shit." She smiled. "And let's say that in exchange for that you tell me, no bullshit, why you bailed me out of jail. How's that for openers?"

"I'll try." She inhaled slowly, and let it out slowly. I know the trick. "The moment I saw you I was struck by something. I felt a rush, a jolt of recognition." She held out her hands, open and empty, as if to say, This is all I have to offer and I know it probably sounds weird. "I'd been looking for you, and when I saw you it was as if I'd gotten what I'd been promised before I was ready."

"What you had been 'promised'?"

She shrugged. "Maybe forewarned would be a better way of putting it. *I don't know.* Jesus Christ, you are so goddamn difficult to deal with."

"Juliet, as tactless and impolite as you believe me to be—"

"As you *are,*" she fairly shouted.

"—as I am . . . I'm going to tell you something that seems fairly obvious to me: Sexual tension is eating us alive and we're both unwilling or unable to do anything about it. Kissing me like you did while I was sitting in that chair is like opening an artery. Being competitive is just another dimwitted way of dealing with the frustrating fact that we should be fucking instead of talking."

"What I felt when I saw you in jail wasn't *just* sexual."

"So what? It's mostly sexual now."

"Do you believe in psychic visions and past lives?" Her hands were in her lap, and her eyes were unwavering. She looked tired but she also looked determined.

"I've never felt a need to decide about past lives. It wouldn't surprise me, but I've got all I can do to handle this one."

"What about precognition?"

"I've had some dreams that sort of came true, but who knows what that means, if it means anything?" I wasn't being altogether truthful, but I wasn't sure where she was headed with this conversation.

"I . . ." She stopped, squirmed a bit, then produced the shot glass from between her thighs and held it up. "Maybe I should have another one."

I got up and poured two more shots. Hers went down easily and I grinned. "It gets easier and tastes better as the evening wears on."

"Right." She handed me the shot glass. "That's enough for me.

"Anyway, a few months ago I had a session with a psychic. I go twice each year, and have for several years. He has told me some amazing things over the years and I have a lot of confidence in his visions.

"The last time I saw him, at the very end of the session, he asked me if the name Jamie meant anything to me. I said no. He asked me if I knew of a reporter, or writer, perhaps on the *Call*, with the last name of Hawk, or Hawker. I didn't, and later I checked with Daniel. Nothing even close to that name.

"He said, 'I see those two names. They could be the names of one person, or two. I think it's one and he needs help.' I asked him what kind of help this person needed and he said, 'He needs someone to get him out of jail. If he doesn't get out before his trial his future . . .' He sort of shrugged."

"Did you ask him what jail I would be in?"

"Yes. He said he couldn't see anything to identify the location, but he 'felt' warm and the face he saw was tanned. He described your face, your build. He said, 'He's wearing sunglasses . . . he smokes cigarettes without a filter . . . and he has a very expensive cigarette lighter. Gold.'

"I didn't know anyone with either of those names, and I couldn't imagine how I would meet anyone in jail. When I found out we didn't have any reporters named Jamie or Hawk or Hawker, or anything close, I shrugged it off.

"And I didn't have any plans to visit Mexico. I had had an invitation to visit some friends in New Zealand and I had planned to go, in October."

"So how did you end up in Mexico, in Mérida?"

"I'm on the board of the Philadelphia Art Museum, and for the last few years I've been working on the acquisition of Mayan artifacts. I've been drawn to Mayan art and Mayan culture since I first saw pictures of their pyramids. I was ten years old and I remember the day and the pictures as if it had happened this morning.

"Anyway, about six weeks ago I got a letter from a contact in Mexico City, an assistant curator at the museum there. We met a few years ago, and we see each other from time to time at various conferences. He wrote that he had had some conversations with a wealthy Mexican collector of Mayan art who was willing to part with some very nice pieces, for a price."

"Taking that stuff out of the country is illegal. I almost got sucked into a deal down there once. I backed away just before the shit hit the fan and even then I heard that the fuckin' *Federales* were looking for me. I sneaked into Guatemala and flew back to the States from there."

"It *is* illegal to buy the art on the black market and take it out of the country. But one can arrange, with suitable amounts of dollars deposited in the appropriate accounts, for a permanent loan." She smiled.

"So, you went in search of precious treasures and came back with a pain in the ass. In a manner of speaking." I laughed. "It's the curse of Hunab Ku."

"Actually, your 'bail' and the 'loan' of the Mayan art were arranged by the same gentleman." She tilted her head slightly and looked at me as though she had discovered a facet of my being that qualified as a pleasant surprise. "How did you come to know of Hunab Ku?" she asked with a half-smile.

"Buddy of mine." I retrieved the bottle of tequila, poured a couple of shots and held one out to her.

She surprised me by taking it. "Someone you met in prison?"

"Hunab Ku? Not bloody likely, now is it?" I touched her glass with mine and poured the tequila down my throat. "He's the Mayan god of all that is. Those guys rarely get busted."

I had her off balance. "What *are* you talking about?"

I filled my glass again. "You asked me how I came to know of Hunab Ku and I said he's a buddy of mine. Drink." We drank together.

"You're impossible." She giggled. A few drops of the tequila dribbled down her chin. "And I'm drunk. How can you even stand up?"

"Practice."

"What time is it?"

I looked at my watch. "Two forty. A.M. Jesus . . . what time am I supposed to see what's-his-name?"

"Daniel French. Ten o'clock. You should leave here by nine at the latest. The traffic is terrible."

Right. That traffic would be midnight on Main Street in Altoona, PA compared to the crowd of thoughts leaping around in my tequila-soaked frontal lobes. If I wasn't expected to leave before nine o'clock, then, *ipso facto*, I was invited to spend the night. Choose carefully what you wish for, sayeth the proverb. You just may end up with it.

"Are you okay?" she asked. "You suddenly looked as though you were a thousand miles away."

"Yeah, a thousand would just about do it. I was thinking about the first time I saw you, in the prison yard." I was also rummaging through the thirty-one flavors of sexual fantasy I had created since that first meeting.

And clamoring in the back of my sodden, erotic thoughts was the voice of my objective self, asking for nothing more than a moment of my attention directed to the practical consequences of fooling around with anyone so far removed from the world I ordinarily inhabit. It was a reasonable request and I got as far as reminding myself that she had been born into the true Protestant position: White Anglo-Saxon Power. She held the deck and owned the table. I was just another player. It should have been a sobering thought. It would have been a sobering thought, but before it could sink in she took my hand.

"Come with me," she said, and she led me through the house, up a wide set of stairs, to the doorway of her bedroom. I stopped at the threshold while she continued into the room and disappeared to my right.

Her bedroom was huge and furnished in a mix of Oriental and Art Deco. The bed was a rosewood four-poster centered under a ceiling fan whose blades had been cut from African mahogany. The sheets, pillowcases, and satin comforter were what decorators call peach and matched the fabric on the chairs, whose design and wood matched the bedstead, dressers, end tables, and armoire. She had added dried flowers, a large fan palm, and a couple of Chinese or Japanese prints. I still haven't learned to tell the difference, although some people insist there is a discernible distinction. I took a few steps into the room.

"Do you like it?" she asked as she came back into view.

"It's nice," I said. Faint praise, but what the fuck do I know? In my family, the benchmark of good taste was floral prints.

She lit some candles on the dresser and two more on a chest at the foot of the bed, then stretched out on her side, smiling, arm bent, her head propped on her hand. She was wearing a black silk camisole, the bust of which was meant to be held together with a lace that she hadn't bothered to tie. Her right breast was two-thirds exposed. Smiling, she reached behind her head and twisted a dimmer control. Satisfied with the light, she shifted into another position, leaning against the headboard, and the silk cup overflowed. The nipple was the size and color of a medium-sized ripe plum. The skin was the color of fresh cream. I took an extra-deep breath. She smiled and opened her legs, bending the right one at the knee. Her long, elegant fingers found the sweet spot and she stroked herself, all the while watching me.

I wondered if this was how the Rubicon looked to Caesar. Conquer or perish. I peeled off my shirt, thinking that's a hell of a thought to take into bed with anyone. But five minutes later I had her pinned to the bed, her arms over her head, and she was moaning, "Don't let me move . . . hold me tight, hold me tight and make me come."

━━ ━━ ━━ ━━

PHILADELPHIA
Monday 16 Oct. 4 p.m.

I am, as they say, 'gainfully' employed. For the princely sum of $700 per week I will make daily, if not hourly, contributions to the continuing myth of a well-informed American public. I start tomorrow, and work Tuesday through Saturday.

Regrettably, I start at eight A.M. What the fuck can they possibly want from anyone at that time of day? Eight to five, with an hour for lunch. Maybe I should buy a hard hat and a lunch bucket.

My meeting with Daniel French, our esteemed managing editor, seemed to go well. I was in and out of his office in less than fifteen minutes. I wouldn't take any bets that he will even recognize me the next time we pass each other, but he has a nice way of dealing with people and I probably could get along well enough with him. He's likable, and he did have a couple of nice things to say about Throwaway Soldiers. He may actually have read it.

I wonder what time he starts work?

I also was introduced to the city editor, Ivan the Terrible. That motherfucker probably never leaves the city room. He's tall, almost bald, with no taste in clothes and no sense of humor. Reminds me of Ichabod Crane with a mean streak.

He exists on the power of his position, looking down from his lofty editor's chair on the lesser life forms who inhabit the city room. The asshole actually has his desk perched on a twelve-inch riser. Even from my lowly position I can see trouble writ large and I'd bet my first week's pay against Marybeth's collection of Neil Diamond albums that he and I are head-to-head before Halloween. He's going to test me.

I wonder how he would respond to my Dogs of War routine?

For that matter, I wonder if I'll last long enough to collect a week's pay.

I drank a little of the warm beer remaining in the bottle and shifted my butt, looking for a more comfortable position. I might as well have been looking for flaws in Kathleen Turner's face. Anything's possible, but finding either seemed unlikely.

I hate typing. How many hours and days and weeks and months have I spent hunched over a goddamn keyboard? And never once was I physically at ease. Now and then I get so involved in whatever I'm writing that I don't notice the strain, but I cannot remember ever feeling relaxed and comfortable.

What a way to make a living.

And what a waste of time, I thought, but I didn't type it. Instead, I got up and wandered around the hotel room, carefully. One slip, one careless step, one fucking nanosecond of despair and the Beast would drag my sorry-ass self into that goddamn dung pit of depression. And that, I suspected, would be the last Willie Penn's Greene Country Towne would see of me.

I opened another bottle of beer and parked my butt at the typewriter. The sense of foreboding was like an overcoat in July. Very uncomfortable, and possibly stupid.

"Okay," I said aloud, and sat up straight. I inhaled as deeply as I could, held my breath for a few seconds, then slowly exhaled. When my lungs were practically empty I made a mental picture of my other self floating in space, bobbing like a mooring buoy in some cosmic cove far from Philadelphia. I opened myself to whatever thoughts might come.

Culture shock.

The thought came through the gloom like a Huey loaded with cold beer and ammo. Sal-*vation*. No shit, dimwit.

It occurs to me that a large part of my immediate problem is simply defined, if not easily solved: I haven't had to cope with the Urban American Dream in a long, long time. No shopping malls, no supermarkets, no drug-addled retards willing to kill you for loose change . . . no expressways that look like a Honda ana- conda snaking its way into suburban oblivion . . . no city editors, no obits, no fucking need or reason to wear a tie. I hate ties.

The best tequila for two dollars a bottle, not two dollars a shot.

I hadn't even read an American newspaper for six months, and that made absolutely no difference to me or to the 'world.'

Except for my time in Club Fed, I made my own hours, my own routine, and my own way through my day-to-day exis- tence. No one to whom I had to answer, no expectations, no real need to dress for the occasion in proper demeanor, freshly pressed each day.

I am, very simply, nothing more than another reject without a cause, a fucking refugee from the Great Ameri- can slam dance we're all doing to the music of Neo-Tech and the Consumers.

I was hammering the typewriter keys, typing quickly.

My attitude, as always, is my biggest problem. I can't say it's wrong, but it sure as hell isn't right for these circumstances. I already know this job is another exercise in mind-fucking boredom, occasionally relieved by brief moments of black humor. I hate being a reporter.

The phone rang. I ignored it. After five rings it switched back to the hotel operator and a few moments later the message light began flashing.

And my options? All things considered, they suck. Maybe I should just surrender to the centurions of the Information Age and embrace the perceived need for so-

called news. Ninety percent of it is <u>useless</u> information
and/or an unnecessary intrusion into the private lives
of people who would be better off left alone, but I don't
have the energy to finish the book and I can't find the
strength to fight with the pagan mavins of publishing.
What's a mutha to do?

The phone rang again. Sometimes I think about the people who made, or
at least were given the credit for making, such enormous impact on what we
describe as civilization, and I wonder how they would have dealt with this shit.
Imagine, if you will, Buddha with a beeper on his hip.

The phone stopped ringing.

Ms. Juliet Franklin-Rossini would be my guess. She would no doubt like
to hear from me, to be reassured that I am, in fact, still physically present in
the city of Philadelphia. After that she would want to know how my interview
with Daniel French went, even though he almost certainly reported his version
to her before I cleared the building.

And then she would ask me to some restaurant that charged more for a
single entrée than I would pay for fifty grams of good grass in Mexico, to celebrate
my newly acquired status as dayside feature writer for the *Philadelphia Call*.
Nothing unreasonable in any of that, but I wasn't ready to deal with her or her
world.

What I need most is a friend, someone who knows me well
and cares enough to convince me that this job isn't either
a total sellout or a total setup. But I don't have one.

Nowhere between the Pacific and the Atlantic is there
a living being to whom I can confide my misery or confess
my doubts, least of all here, in the midst of what's left
of the Society of Friends. I don't know anyone who truly
gives a flying fuck.

I poured myself a shot of tequila from the bottle I had bought after leaving
the *Call*. The glass was at my lips when the phone rang again. I downed the
shot and picked up the receiver, expecting the caller to be Juliet. "At your
service, m'lady."

"The last time I saw you," Sheila said, "as you were walking out the door,
you slapped my ass and called me a strumpet."

Damn. "Same thing. 'Strumpet' is a Middle English title of respect for
working girls. So to speak."

"Something you learned reading Chaucer, no doubt."

Another fuckin' ambush. "Yeah . . . so what's all this? Are the serving
wenches at the Cock'n'Bull required to recite *The Canterbury Tales* before they're
hired?"

"Beats me. I only go in there dressed like that so I can meet newspaper reporters. I love being with guys who have their hands on the *pulse* of the city." The inflection in her voice made the last half of the sentence sound like something from a porno movie.

"Forget it," I said with a laugh. "Most of the reporters I've known spent so much time playing with their pud they couldn't get their own pulse. That's why so many people think we're jerk-offs."

"So I've heard."

"What else have you heard, little girl?" I asked with a growl.

"I heard you're now working for the *Call.*"

"How the fuck would you hear about that?"

She laughed. "So it's not just another cock'n'bull story?"

I couldn't fucking believe it. "Who told you?"

"Listen, they spelled your name right. What does it matter where I heard it?" I didn't answer. "Jamie?"

"Yeah."

"I'm not working tonight."

"I think I'm expected elsewhere for dinner."

"Stop by after, for dessert. I'll 'serve.' "

I thought about it, my thoughts lavishly colored by intense visual images of Sheila in various states of passion. "That's a great offer for me, but it doesn't sound like much of a deal for you."

After a beat she said mockingly, "Lame. Definitely not one of your better lines."

"Why do so many lit majors grow up to be critics?"

"Disillusioned romantics. Fiction rots the brain, you know."

I grinned. "Funny. What was your specialty, Woody Allen screenplays?"

"Henry Miller."

Well, now . . . a kindred spirit. "Do you like Thai food?"

"Yeah."

"Is there a good Thai restaurant in Philadelphia?"

"There's one that I know, not too far from my place. Why?"

"You hungry?"

"Yeah."

I checked the time. "It's twenty to six. How's seven o'clock? Do you own a car?"

"Seven is good. But let's walk. It isn't far and it's hard to find parking."

"Tell you what. I'll get a cab here, pick you up, and we'll walk back."

"I'll be waiting . . ." She hung up with a chuckle.

And now what? Call Juliet, or just go about this evening's adventures and talk to her tomorrow? If she's expecting to see me this evening and I tell her I've got other plans she'll take it as rejection. If I don't tell her she'll take it as indifference. And if I call her and lie she'll know I'm lying and be hurt.

I was pondering those three meager choices when the phone rang again. "Mr. Hawkins?"

"Speaking."

"Good evening, sir. This is Edward, Miss Rossini's butler. I hope I haven't disturbed you."

"Not at all. What's up?"

"Miss Rossini asked me to contact you after she was unable to reach you earlier. She wants me to tell you that she was called away suddenly on a matter of some urgency. She also asked me to deliver the keys to the apartment on Twenty-first Street, as well as the keys to the Jaguar, which she's lending you until you can find a vehicle more to your liking."

"Did she say what the problem is, or how long she'll be away?"

"I'm afraid not, sir. When would it be convenient for me to deliver the keys?"

"Do you need a ride back?"

"No sir, I have arranged for transportation home."

"Well, whenever you're ready. I'm going out for something to eat, but you can leave the keys with the desk clerk. I'm at the Ramada on Market Street. Room seven-fourteen."

"Very good, sir. I will see to it forthwith."

"Thanks. Good-bye."

Forthwith? Jesus, who but a butler, or an editor, would use the word 'forthwith' in ordinary conversation? Forthwith, my ass. And what the hell is 'a matter of some urgency'? I tried to imagine saying to someone, "Terribly sorry, but I'm afraid I must leave immediately. A matter of some *urgency* has come up."

Sounds like bullshit to me. On the other hand, I wasn't stuck with my three meager choices.

I was, however, stuck with the igloo. Not to mention an empty apartment.

— — — —

"If you think about it," Sheila said in answer to my question, "my choices were very limited." We were walking west on Pine Street, stuffed on some of the worst Thai food I've ever eaten from a plate. Once, in San Diego, I ate something from a sidewalk barbecue that the cook claimed was Thai chicken on a stick. That was worse.

"At least you had a choice . . ." I said and burped quietly.

"Right. I've got a lit degree, no interest in teaching, and no tolerance for an office." We stopped for a red light at the corner of Fifth and Pine. It was still overcast and too chilly for my blood.

"So you settled for being a barmaid? Picking up beer-soaked tips and smiling at guys whose first and last thought is how to get you in bed?"

"Like you . . . ?"

"I didn't tip you." She grinned. "And that's not the point, is it?"

"I happen to like working in a bar," she said with a fair amount of exasperation. She was undoubtedly tired of defending her choice. I know the feeling. "I'm good at it, my customers enjoy themselves, and some old fart copping a feel once in a while doesn't bother me. It's all a game and most of them don't even care who wins."

"So why spend four years in college if all you wanted was to work in a saloon?"

"That's not *all* I want."

The light turned green. I took her hand and we crossed the street, continuing along the south side of Pine. "What else, then? A husband, a house in suburbia, and a station wagon filled with little Polish refugees from the inner-city school system?"

She laughed. "I'm going to be a writer."

Oh, sweet Jesus. Another fuckin' gonna-be-writer. "When do you think that's going to happen? Maybe I can do a feature for the *Call*. 'Philly filly finds fame and fortune with Cock'n'Bull stories.' Whatta you think?"

"I think you're being mean without a reason. I didn't ask for your approval and I didn't ask you to support me while I do it."

"You're right, and I'm an asshole, for which I apologize. The sweet and sour monkey feet curdled my otherwise sweet disposition." I draped my arm over her shoulder and gave her a hug. "Have you written anything since you left school?"

"Some short stories, and I've started a novel."

"Have you tried selling any of it?"

"Yeah." Her tone was one I knew well, the sound of pent-up frustration, confusion, and probably a little anger. "I've had a lot of rejections, but an editor at *Cosmo* said she really liked one of the stories I sent her."

"Did she buy it?"

"No. She said it wasn't a *Cosmo* story. Whatever that means." I laughed. "I mean, if you're an editor and you like the work, why wouldn't you publish it?"

"Sheila, I've never come close to understanding editors, no matter who they worked for. Once, in Oaxaca, after I'd been eating mushrooms, smoking dope, and drinking tequila for three days and nights, I had a vision of *Alice in Wonderland* as the perfect allegory for publishing. We're all like Alice."

"Weren't you afraid?"

We had arrived at her building and she sat on the steps. "Of what?" I asked as I lit a cigarette. "A puny little allegorical vision? It wasn't as though I had a conversation with Lewis Carroll." I smiled. "Although that might be interesting."

"I mean weren't you afraid of losing your mind?"

"No. I enjoy it."

"What? Being drugged into oblivion?"

I tried to picture Sheila suspended from a psilocybin glider, soaring into that space where all our carefully nurtured perspectives of a shared reality and shared values suddenly become nothing more than a silly façade as thin as broth made from compressed beef flakes or chicken lips or whatever the hell they pack in those little foil-covered cubes. She would love it. "I haven't been drugged into oblivion, as you call it, since I left Vietnam."

"So what happened? Did you suddenly 'see the light'?"

"Nope. Have you ever read *Alice in Wonderland*?"

"Truthfully?" I nodded. "No. I started a couple of times but I couldn't get involved. I'm too literal to identify with the ten-year-old heroine of a fairy tale."

"There's time to learn not to be so literal. And if you have any real ambition to be a writer, learning that may be your only hope for salvation."

— — — —

My problems with Ivan the Terrible started thirty minutes after my scheduled arrival at the *Call*. I was twenty minutes late. I came in with a cup of espresso in one hand, the October issue of *Esquire* in the other, and a sour knot in the pit of my stomach. Ivan had delegated one of his desk assistants to find me a desk the day before, so I didn't have to hunt for a place to sit.

I put the magazine on the desk, uncapped the coffee, lit a cigarette, and started flipping pages, looking at the ads for all the essential elements needed to construct the masculine American Dream: British and German cars, French wines, Italian suits, Swiss watches, South African diamonds, and Japanese high-tech toys. A large, possibly diabolical smile spread across my face. I had an idea for a hell of a feature story. I was still smiling when Jay Simpson, a rewrite hack and part-time desk assistant, leaned over my desk and waved his hand between my eyes and the page.

"Ivan would like to see you at his desk," Simpson announced as I looked up. He dropped three or four news releases on the desk. The top one was from a local bank announcing the promotion of Ms. Cynthia Pryde to the position of assistant vice president in municipal bonds.

"Now, that's exciting," I said with what I hoped would sound like genuine surprise.

He copped a quick look at the news release. "You know her?"

"Cindy? We had sex this morning on the uptown bus. But I wasn't talking about her. I don't believe a gentleman should talk about his exploits."

He gave me a look that fairly shouted "Jerk!"

I stood up to answer my summons to an audience with the pope of the City Room. "What time do the copyboys start?"

"We've got two on now, and two more come on at nine o'clock. Why?"

"I need one of them to pull some information for me. Does the *Call* have a research staff?"

"Is this for an assignment?" His tone suggested skepticism.

"It will be soon enough."

"Reporters are required to pull their own clips from the morgue unless they're working on deadline."

"No shit." I glanced over his shoulder at the far wall, which was constructed largely of dirty glass. "And, pray tell, what do the copyboys do? Windows?" I walked away, shaking my head.

"I'd ditch the coffee, if I was you."

I stopped and turned back, frowning as though I had just discovered that Simpson was retarded. "If I were you I'd give some thought to how illogical and unlikely that is, because if you were me you'd be doing exactly what I'm doing . . . right?" I let him stare into his confusion for a moment, then added, "But thanks for the tip." I made my way to Ivan's desk, coffee cup in one hand, *Esquire* in the other. I wondered how long it would take him to figure out that what I just said made absolutely no sense, because if I *were* him, I would undoubtedly have said exactly what he had said. I was grinning as I approached Ivan's demi-throne. Christ! I said to myself, I'm actually enjoying this bullshit.

Ivan was on the phone as I stepped up on the riser and came to a stop on the opposite side of his desk. He waved me to a chair. I sat down and casually checked out the room. A lot of curious and nervously expectant glances greeted me. No one smiled. I counted seventeen people, all but three of them at their desks. To my eye, not one of them was actually busy, but they made damn sure they looked like they were working. Welcome to the fun house, Jamie m'boy.

"Mr. Hawkins, if I can have your attention . . ."

I turned to look at Ivan. "You may."

"Excuse me. *May* I have your attention?"

"You've got it." I sipped my coffee and waited.

"Mr. Hawkins, I believe in teamwork and I believe in playing by the rules of the house." He made 'rules of the house' sound like the title of a pamphlet: "How to Get More from Your Stay at Camp Hoodwink."

"I'm a team player," I said with a straight face. "And so far as the rules of the house go, as soon as I know what the rules are I'll do my best to conform to them." I sipped my coffee. "You can count on me."

"Rule number one, Mr. Hawkins, is be on time. And rule number two is respect for your editors." His voice, I realized, had very little bass. It was moderately pitched when he felt he was in control, but the pitch tended to rise as the level of stress increased. It probably wouldn't take me more than five minutes to turn him into a choirboy. So to speak. The idea flashed before me and I know he caught at least the hint of a grin.

"All things being relative and all judgments being subjective, I don't think rule one or rule two should present any real problems." I dug out my cigarettes. "Do you have these rules written down? A pamphlet, maybe? Something like a guide to getting along at the *Call*? It might come in handy." I tapped the end of the Camel on my lighter and glanced up at Ivan.

His phone rang. "I don't permit smoking around my desk," he said with some annoyance, and grabbed the receiver. "Blum!"

Well, that figures, I muttered to myself. Is there anything else? Spit-shined shoes? Short-arm inspection? Polygraph?

Ivan hung up after a few seconds and returned his attention to me. "Mr. Hawkins, I realize that you have a strong connection to the *Call*'s upper management, and Daniel French will protect you to some extent. But don't let your attitude screw up an exceptional career opportunity. The *Call* is a great paper, the best in Philadelphia, one of the best on the East Coast. I'd like to see you do well." He picked up a copy pencil, examined the point, and put it down. "I need good rewrite men, guys who can crank out clean copy under deadline pressure, and then when things are slow take an ordinary, boring news release and find an entertaining hook to hang a good story on."

"Actually, I was hired as a feature writer."

"And you will be assigned features from time to time, but I don't have enough staff to dedicate any *one* reporter to features." He made a dismissive gesture and continued, "Of course anything is possible . . ."

"But not very probable, I suppose."

"Who's to say? But for now I'd like to see you join the dayside team. Arrive on time, make constructive contributions to our effort . . ." He paused and gave me a fast once-over. "And dress more appropriately. Your clothes don't really meet with our dress code."

"Really? You've got a dress code? Like high school? No hard-soled shoes on the gym floor and no sneakers in the city room? No smoking at the city editor's desk?"

"Are you trying to provoke an unpleasant confrontation, or is that your idea of wit?" His voice was peaking in the soprano range.

"I'm trying to tell you," I said in a nice level tone, "that all of this is unnecessary. I don't need to be indoctrinated. I know who has the power in the city room. I know you'll still be here long after I'm gone, and I know it's possible that you may have a hand in my departure. I also know how to do my job and what I like best is being left alone to do it."

"I'm not convinced that you should be left alone under any circumstances, least of all in my city room."

"And I'm not sure you should be let out of the house without a note from your mother, but here we both are. You didn't hire me, and you can't fire me without permission. Let's have a truce and see how it works out. You may come to appreciate my talent."

His tight, self-satisfied little smile went south and he stared at me in disbelief, despair, and anger. In all his years on the desk, from his first assignment to fill in for some hung-over hack to this very moment, never, not once, had anyone had the goddamn gall to speak to me as I had.

"Let's talk about an assignment for me, a feature." I held up the copy of *Esquire*. "I think I could do an interesting piece on the irony of having to import the majority of our most revered status symbols."

"That's not really a *Call* type of story. And while I'm always receptive to good story ideas from reporters, as a rule feature assignments will come from either myself or Ed Prescott, my assistant city editor."

"Listen, this story ties into the U.S. trade deficit, the diminished role we play in producing status goods, the declining value of our dollar, loss of prestige in world markets . . ."

He was shaking his head, no, no, no way, before I was halfway through my list of reasons why the story would appeal to a wide readership. I could have guaranteed him a Pulitzer Prize and he would still have said no. Not that it really mattered to me. I'd already decided to write it anyway and give it to Daniel French.

— — — —

Tuesday 17 Oct. 8:15 p.m.

Last week at this time I was in Club Fed with no idea of when I would see the outside again.

Today I surrendered myself to Ivan the Terrible and resumed my rightful place in the grand scheme of things.

I can only be here in this peculiar place, dealing with these ridiculous people, because it was ordained by those who plan our fate. Or those who fuck with our ten-uous hold on what passes for reality.

I read what I had typed, and thought, Maybe I really have lost contact with the left side of my brain. Is it the left side that supposedly deals with logic? I can never remember. And that, quite possibly, is the final bit of evidence needed to prove that the word "maybe" isn't at issue here. Chasing my tail again: Right side, left side, who gives a fuck? This whole society is stone strange and it takes time to adjust. Buy a tie. Buy some clothes. Buy some furniture, move into the apartment and settle down for a year or so. Buy some time and see how it develops. Sheila's a pleasant distraction. Juliet is a pleasant mystery. And Ivan is the perfect self-centered asshole.

Well, now that we've heard from the rational self, what's left to do but make a few adjustments and get on with it? Buy a tie, buy some clothes, buy furniture, buy time. Buy this and buy that, and if I buy enough maybe I'll become a fully certified, card-carrying member of the Establishment.

Remember: You are what you and your creditors own.

I went back to typing my latest entry in the Jamie Hawkins Journal of a Misspent Life:

```
I was twenty minutes late and not suitably dressed,
or so I was told by Ivan. He also turned down my idea for
a feature, and then assigned me to a steady stream of
bullshit rewrites and obits. Big surprise.
    I'll give it a week and see what happens.
    Juliet is out of touch for a while. She had her butler
deliver the keys to her Jag (which I really would rather
not drive), the keys to the apartment that set us at odds,
and a message that she had "been called away on a matter
of some urgency." Sunday we fought, fucked, and finally
fell asleep about 5 a.m. Monday I got the goddamn job she
wanted me to take. And then she disappears. She's as
fuckin' weird as all the other people I've met at that
rag.
    Last night I was with Sheila. Again. She should be
added to the DEA's list of controlled substances. She's
definitely addictive and I don't need another bad habit.
```

I leaned back against the headboard and stared across the room at the far wall. The wallpaper was a pale color of no distinction and appeared to have no discernible pattern. I squinted. *Nada*. I knew goddamn well there was a pattern—pinstripes, or windowpanes, or something. Shit. I need new glasses. The thought came and sat there for a moment, then gave way to thoughts about age and purpose and how fuckin' pointless most of life seemed to me. One toke over the line, sweet Jesus . . . one toke over the line . . .

I was, in truth, totally straight, so the lyrics didn't have any relationship to my sobriety. As to their relationship to my state of mind, maybe. A toke could be purely symbolic. Shit, Ronnie Ray-gun has been two or three tokes over the line for so long not many people seem to notice. Talk about a poor sonofabitch without a clue. I'm convinced that he still thinks he's rehearsing for a movie, and I can hear him whining to Nancy about all the time they're spending on preproduction. I wonder if he ever wonders why he's never seen a completed script?

— — — —

. . . Pulaski Day came close to being my undoing. Or, I should say, Pulaski Day *Observed*. Whatever the fuck that means.

At any rate, someone had determined that Pulaski Day Observed was to be observed on Saturday, my fifth day at the *Call*. I showed up thirty minutes late, tired from too little sleep, shivering from the cold. It was raining a little and the wind was howling through the streets. After three days of foul weather, four days of Ivan, and a week in Philadelphia, I was in desperate need of an attitude adjustment. A couple of weeks in Cabo San Lucas would be about right.

Other than my attitude, my biggest problem was also my most constant problem with working for a living: I was bored. Obits and rewrites, rewrites and obits. Another week or two and I'd be on a first-name basis with every fuckin' undertaker in the Philadelphia area.

I put my butt in my chair, my feet on my desk, and pried the lid off my coffee. The steam from the espresso rose toward the ceiling and I inhaled the aroma of strong coffee mixed with half-and-half. I love that smell. I love it even better when it's laced with cognac, but the *Call* city room didn't seem like the kind of place where I'd find someone with a flask of Courvoisier.

Across the room, Ivan was already seated on his perch. When I had been introduced to him on Monday, after my meeting with Daniel French, I had assumed Ivan worked Monday through Friday. Turned out he was in for only an hour or so, and his regular routine was the same as mine: Tuesday through Saturday. Wonderful. Maybe we could play golf on one of our days off.

From the corner of my eye, I saw Sammy Fox, the copyboy, making his rounds, dropping assignments on the desks of the few reporters who were working. Roughly one-third of the dayside staff had Saturday and Sunday off, and most of the others split the weekend, taking off Friday and Saturday or Sunday and Monday. Only a few were required to show before ten o'clock.

Sammy and I had established a bond of sorts on my second day at the *Call*. I had taken some drivel issued as a press release by the Philadelphia Chamber of Commerce and turned it into a funny commentary on the difference between official fantasy and the facts of life. For reasons known only to God and Ivan, one of them had let it pass and it was printed. I was the most surprised person in the room when the first edition came up from the pressroom and the story was set in a box on the first page of the Metro section. Ordinarily I wouldn't have been in the building that late, but Ivan had left and I had hung around to work on my story about status symbols.

Sammy had brought me a copy of the first edition, with the Metro section on top; there was a big grin on his face. "Nice job."

"Thanks." I went through it quickly, amazed to discover no one had fucked with the story.

"So, you want to get into the pool?" Sammy asked.

I looked up from the paper. "What pool? Football?"

"Naw, the pool on how long it's gonna take Ivan to get you fired." He grinned again. I cracked up, and the sound of my laughter seemed to rise above all the other noise in the room. A few people looked our way, then went back to whatever they had been doing.

"The probation period is ninety days," he said. "After that you're sanctioned by the union and it's a little tougher to get rid of you. But for the first ninety days you can be canned for almost anything.

"So we made a chart, y'know, with thirteen weeks, and whoever makes a bet picks one of those weeks and puts ten bucks in the kitty. There's only maybe half a dozen slots left, so if you want one let me know."

I was trying to imagine how I appeared to all these people if they were already wagering on when I'd be sent back to the minors. I hadn't even said hello to probably ninety percent of them, hadn't bitched to anyone, hadn't received another summons to the throne since that first morning. And still they were making bets. Jesus. What next? "I probably shouldn't bet on my own dismissal, since I could make it happen without a lot of effort."

"I picked the third week."

"I'll keep that in mind. Did anyone bet that I'd survive the probation?"

"No."

"Is that a possibility? As a bet, I mean."

"Probably, although it didn't come up."

"Take the bet."

"I've already got you out the third week."

"How old are you?"

"Twenty-five."

"I'm almost ten years older than you, so consider it advice from an older brother: Don't bet against me."

He smiled and I smiled in return. "Let me know if you need help with anything," he said, then went on his way.

— — — —

Watching Sammy make his rounds, I wondered why I'd been so emphatic when I'd said "Don't bet against me." Why had I said anything at all? Considering my doubts about being here under the best of circumstances, which these weren't, what I had said to Sammy didn't make much sense unless I'd been reduced to trying to impress copyboys. With Ivan holding the deck and dealing whatever he felt was suitable at any given moment, my chances of anything better than obits and rewrites were roughly equal to my chances of winning a Pulitzer. Slim, fat, and no fuckin' way. Surviving the probation seemed a long shot. *Real* long.

On the other hand, what I had said would get back to a few people and give them something to think about. If they were going to talk anyway I might as well put some grist in the mill.

Sammy was moving in my direction when Alexis Cabot waved him over to her desk. I already had mixed feelings about Alexis, and we hadn't even been introduced.

On the positive side, she was cute, a sexy elf with thick auburn hair, a wicked smile, and a bust that could have been fitted into a couple of teacups. I thought she'd make a great model for Playtex training bras. She looked to be about five three in her three-inch heels; she was close to thirty years old, and trendy in her dress and speech. Of course, by the time whatever it is becomes trendy in Philadelphia it's ancient history almost everywhere else.

In the one brief moment that she and I had been almost face to face, while we were waiting for an elevator, I'd seen enough spark in her hazel eyes to suggest at least some intelligence, and enough lines creeping out from the corners of her eyes to make me think she lived hard. It wasn't difficult to picture her in ten or fifteen years, aging and angry, still married to the business, drinking too much, finally ending up as a midlevel editor with little power and almost no one to talk to after the shop closes.

But for the moment, if what I had read of her work was an accurate indication of her talent, she wasn't anything more than another fuckin' city-room princess with a cute ass and more ambition than ability. She should have been moved over to what's known as the "Society Page," where her gushing accounts of debs and antique auctions would be appreciated.

And worst of all, she was obviously tied to Ivan. Or maybe Ivan was tied to her. I wasn't sure, but she was the only person of either gender I'd seen generate any outward expression of human warmth in our leader. She walked up to his desk as she pleased, and he unfailingly smiled and put aside whatever he was doing. If he happened to step down from his demi-throne he usually found some excuse to stop by her desk. And twice in the four days I'd spent regurgitating rewrites, she had had a bylined story. Fluff, for sure, but still a byline.

Which led me to believe that Ivan hadn't been altogether truthful when he said he didn't have enough staff to assign any one reporter to write nothing but features. Unless she was working double shifts and writing obits after I left, she was, like it or not, the designated prima donna, and I was in for a long run playing the proverbial second fiddle. Actually, if I couldn't shake things up, I was more likely to be relegated to fiddling with my fingers between obits. I needed something to amuse me and advance my cause, whatever that might be, or bring about my departure to a warmer climate, ASAP.

That thought and Sammy arrived at the same moment.

"Hey-hey, big break for the Dealer," Sammy said as he waved a two-page press release from the opposite side of my desk. "That's right, sports fans, it's feature time." His grin was not without obvious malevolent satisfaction.

What the fuck is Ivan up to? I wondered. It's Saturday, so he's gonna need a shitload of three- and four-paragraph fillers to jam between the ads a lot more than he needs a feature. "Tips for a Safe Halloween." "Civic Clubs Urge End to Inner-City Neglect." "Life on Mars 'Unlikely,' Say Scientists." I could write them in my sleep. Sometimes I *did* write them in my sleep, when things were really bad.

"What precious nugget of mindless, self-serving excreta have you fetched up for me this morning? And what's this bullshit with calling me the Dealer?"

"Aw, it's nothing. Just, a couple of the guys were saying you look like a dope dealer or an undercover narc working on a bust. It's the sunglasses. I mean, when you come in out of the rain wearing sunglasses at eight-thirty in the morning it looks a little strange, y'know?"

I took the press release from his hand and glanced at the first paragraph while I considered what Sammy had just told me. Personally, I think it's a little strange to wear a suit and tie on a rainy Saturday morning, even more so when you know before you get out of the shower that the odds are about a million to one against your leaving the city room for any reason more exciting than lunch and the trip home.

"So whatta you know about Pulaski?" he asked when the silence became uncomfortable.

"He's dead. May he rest in peace."

"I think Ivan's gonna want a few more paragraphs than it will take to say that."

"Probably." I looked up. "Sammy, what the fuck is Pulaski Day, Observed? Was there another one that wasn't observed, a day that just slipped by without any mention on the six o'clock news or any notice in the *Call*?"

"Beats me. Want me to have the morgue send down the clips?"

"I suppose." I read the brief note Ivan had attached to the first page: "Give me 1000 to 1200 words for 2nd edition. Cover the ceremony. Add some historical info and a little color. Ivan."

The second-edition deadline for Sunday's paper was five or five-thirty, as I recalled. That should be plenty of time.

"Ivan says he wants a thousand words, with color, before second-edition deadline . . . what time is that?"

"Five-thirty."

"See if you can find me an extra copy of the Random House dictionary and gift-wrap it. That way he can choose the words *he* wants and arrange them any way he likes."

Sammy walked away chuckling. "I'll get the clips."

Not only didn't I know much about General Casimir (properly spelled Kazimierz) Pulaski, I didn't have a clue to his connection to Philadelphia. He didn't sound like a local boy who had made good. I remembered him, vaguely, from some high school history class, just the name and some connection to the Revolutionary War. I also remembered a Fort Pulaski, somewhere near Savannah.

But I would have been hard pressed to name even one other dead general about whom I could honestly say I cared less. Ah, yes, I sighed. One more fine example of Sunday journalism.

There was a rarely used Encyclopedia Britannica in the far corner of the room. I read the entry on the general. Not much. I did find out he was in Paris, dodging the Polish secret police after he fucked up a kidnapping of the Polish king, old Stanislaw II, when he met Benjamin Franklin. Who knows what kind of song and dance those two did for each other?

Six months later, Pulaski turned up in the Colonies, fought a few battles, did well, and died somewhere around the tenth or eleventh of October 1779. Evidently he took a round during a firefight in or near Savannah and died on a ship somewhere between there and Charleston. He was thirty-two years old. That's what I would call a first-rate argument for either giving up war or using choppers to evac the wounded.

I also figured out his connection to Philadelphia. He was a hero at the Battle of Germantown, once a separate village not far from Philadelphia. It has since become another sterling example of inner-city decay. Old Casimir probably wouldn't recognize the place.

"Here's the dirt on Count Cashmere," Sammy said as he put two thick manila envelopes on my desk.

I picked up one of the two envelopes and blew away a couple of layers of dust. "Where do they keep these, in his coffin? Jesus. The guys in the morgue must belong to the same union as the window washers."

"Teamsters." He laughed.

"Right. And the secretaries belong to the IBEW."

"Nope, they're Teamsters too." He sat on the corner of the desk. "Anything else I can do to protect my bet? You know the easiest way to get from here to the art museum?"

"Chopper, but that's probably out of the question." I checked the press release for the time of the ceremony. Eleven A.M. It was only nine-twenty, according to the wall clock.

"Listen," Sammy said. I looked up. "You know Ivan gave you this assignment to bust your chops, right?"

I shrugged. "He hasn't given me anything worth a fat rat's ass since I walked in here Tuesday morning. Why should today be any different?"

"He's testing you."

"Ivan wouldn't make a small cyst on the crotch of some people who've tested me."

"I heard you wrote a book about Vietnam. That right?"

"Yeah, that's right. Where the hell did you hear that?"

"Never reveal sources." He was smirking. "I also hear you're real tight with Daniel French."

"Tell your sources being half right isn't any better than being half-assed. I've spent fifteen minutes, at the most, with French, and I don't know that he would remember me if he walked in right now."

"What's the name of the book?"

"*Throwaway Soldiers.* Jesus, Sammy, I hope you aren't paying a lot for your information. You sure as hell aren't getting much for your money."

"You've only been here a week. Give us some time." He was enjoying himself. "How you getting to the museum?"

"Who knows? Ask your sources, maybe they can tell us." I stood up. "I'm going down to the coffee shop to get a refill. You want one?"

He glanced over his shoulder, found Ivan staring at us, and looked back at me. "I'll meet you down there in ten minutes."

I watched him hustle away. He stopped for a minute to talk to another reporter, checked the wire machines, then disappeared into an alcove fashioned from an arrangement of four-drawer file cabinets. I waited a few minutes, until Ivan was distracted by one of his desk assistants, then left my desk and walked out of the city room.

— — — —

I was sitting on a narrow stone step near the rear of the Philadelphia Art Museum, staring into drizzle, thinking about Juliet, when I heard the first faint, off-key sounds of bugles, followed by the thumping of a bass drum. The sounds seeped through my thoughts and gnawed at my awareness, insisting on my attention. And then, as soon as I changed focus, the sounds stopped. I couldn't hear anything other than street noise.

Weird, I thought. This town is weird, the *Call* is weird, and this is a weird place to put a statue. Way weird.

The copper-coated likeness of Pulaski, green from years of oxidation, crusted in pigeon shit, and unseen by ninety-nine and nine-tenths percent of Philadelphia's citizens, was anchored to a stone pedestal surrounded by a flowerbed overrun with weeds. The small garden in which it had been planted was encircled by hedges. It wasn't a place many people were likely to discover. My guess would have been that Casimir spent most days alone, staring toward whatever lay beyond the hedges. Germantown, maybe.

I heard the bugles again, a little louder, but no closer to being on key. And field drums, played raggedly. From the top of the stairs on which I'd been sitting I stared over the hedges and up the street opposite the garden. I could see two or three blocks, to the top of the hill where the street disappeared. The "music" was coming from the reverse side of the slope. Here we go . . . a V.F.W. drum and bugle crops that hasn't rehearsed since Memorial Day. An honor guard. And a dozen or so members of the local Pulaski Historical Society, led by the chapter president. I raised my eyes to the heavens, which were obscured by a five-hundred-foot ceiling of black clouds. Why me?

And I swear I heard a voice, a cross between a grumble and a growl, say, "Why not? You're available."

The sound of car doors being slammed shut crashed into the moment of what I suddenly feared might be Truth. Or one of the many Truths. I couldn't, or wouldn't, believe that my own subconscious would be so blatantly indifferent. But if it wasn't my subconscious I was surely in deep shit.

I put the questions aside for the business at hand, that business being a full bird colonel in winter greens, obviously hung over and quite possibly still a little drunk from a night of making merry with the local Polish community, accompanied by a striking blonde bimbette wearing a low-cut black dress that didn't quite reach the knees and a damp, slightly matted rabbit wrap. They were surrounded by half a dozen of the Polish community's leading citizens, and two flaxen-haired nymphets with baskets of flowers.

All the men were dressed in double-breasted wool suits that almost without a doubt had been cut by a Warsaw tailor, or a tailor from Warsaw. The women wore overcoats fashioned from material of the same weight and cut by the same hand. Every coat was like a coffin, buttoned from neck to shin. The flower girls, who looked fourteen or fifteen years old, were somewhat more stylish.

Now that, I thought, is truly a picture of mediocrity come home to roost.

And then the Germantown Avenue Pulaski Club Drum and Bugle Corps came over the crest of the hill, just as it started raining again.

— — — —

A few minutes before three-thirty I typed the last sentence of my feature on Pulaski Day and leaned back in my chair. Sammy showed up a minute later with another cup of espresso and whispered in my ear as he leaned over to hand me the cup, "Ferris is giving thirty to one that your piece never gets printed. If you want some of the action, I can get the bet down without him knowing it's your money."

"Who the fuck is Ferris?" I asked as I uncapped the coffee.

"The Prince of Darkness."

"The *what!?*"

"He more or less runs the nightside staff."

"He's an editor and he's takin' bets? Fuck him."

"No, no . . . he's not an editor, he's—" Sammy shrugged.

"He's what?" I sipped my coffee.

"He's Ferris." Sammy grinned. "You have to meet him to understand."

"Fine. You tell Mr. Ferris that I've got five hundred dollars *I* want to bet, thirty to one."

Sammy looked at me as though I had launched a first strike against an ally. "You crazy, or what?"

"Is he taking fuckin' bets, or what?"

The expression on Sammy's face went from disbelief to despair. He desperately searched mine, looking for some hint of humor. This had to be a joke, right? And if not, he didn't want to be the one to take the news to his hero.

"Sammy, either tell Mr. Ferris that I want the bet, or go pull wire copy and let me finish my editing."

"You sure about this?" I nodded. "Oooh-kay."

I went to work on the story, changed a couple of words on the first page, took out a sentence in the first paragraph of the second page, and was almost through the third page when I caught a glimpse of Sammy and a guy I presumed was Ferris walking across the city room toward me. I put the story in computer limbo and lit a cigarette.

Ferris was easily three inches taller than Sammy, probably six one, and well-muscled. I guessed his age at thirty, maybe thirty-one, and his weight at one ninety. I also guessed his suit probably cost as much as my entire stock of clothes. And he was black, but he definitely was not the Prince of Darkness.

Watching him stride across the room, I pigeonholed him as another tangible token of the *Call*'s compliance with federal E.E.O. programs. One more warm body to flesh out the charts needed to feed Big Brother's appetite for statistical equality.

"Jamie Hawkins," Sammy said. "Leon Ferris."

"I hear you want to make a bet," Ferris said without any trace of humor. "Five hundred?"

"At thirty to one, I believe you said."

"You finished writing the story?"

"All done." I let him look into the face of innocence.

"Let me see it," he demanded.

"Tell you what, for a hundred dollars a page I'll let you read it."

He glared at me. "You've got the money?"

I pulled a stack of folded fifties and twenties from the back pocket of my jeans, peeled off ten fifties, and held them up. "And you've got the fifteen thou?"

"Not on me. What are you, a clown?"

"I'm a man with the price of the bet, willing to wager." He made a face. "Y'know, it seems a little odd to me that you'd insist I produce such a piddling sum, yet take such unreasonable offense at my asking you for proof that you can pay if you lose. I'd guess fifteen grand is about two-thirds of your salary for a year. Right?"

"You are one arrogant sonofabitch." He smiled without any warmth. "But I can spend a sonofabitch's money as easy as I can spend my own. I'll have it by midnight."

"By midnight, Mr. Ferris, I hope to be wrapped in the arms of some wench with loose morals and long legs. However, if you've got the money here before Ivan starts screaming for copy, I think we probably can do business. Let me know how you make out." I turned my back to them and picked up my coffee.

"Bullshit!" Ferris grumbled and walked away.

"You are one crazy fucker," Sammy said over my shoulder.

I turned around, laughing. "No, I'm not. Not really. Look at it from my perspective. You tell me this guy's taking bets on whether my story's gonna be published, and he hasn't even read it? He's a fuckin' hotdog."

"Well," Sammy said in a slightly plaintive tone, "what are *you*?"

"An arrogant sonofabitch with five hundred dollars and nothing much to lose. I don't give a shit about the money, and I don't let people mind-fuck me."

"Can I read what you wrote? Not so I can make a bet. Just because I know something about Ivan and Pulaski Day stories."

I stared at him for a few seconds, then turned back to the screen and pulled up the story.

Saturday's ceremonies at the Philadelphia Art Museum, intended to highlight a city-wide celebration of Pulaski Day Observed, were, in fact, observed by fewer than fifty people.

The highlight of the ceremonies would be hard to pinpoint, but most votes undoubtedly would be cast for the moment when the Irish colonel representing the United States Army's Air Cav. Division stumbled as he approached the statue raised to honor a Polish mercenary horse soldier—and dropped the wreath he had meant to place at the base of the memorial.

Being a soldier with almost 30 years' experience, Col. Sean F. O'Brien was not at a loss for words. Those few choice words, however, cannot be printed here.

"*Holy shit!* Ivan will have a fucking stroke."

"So what are you saying? I was too hard on the colonel?"

Sammy cackled, and I smacked his ribs with my elbow. "Keep it down, dipshit. I don't want to tip my hand before I'm ready."

"Ready? Ready for *what?* Ivan's gonna personally write up your pink slip."

"Pink would be about the right color for Ivan."

"Can I read the rest of it?"

"If you keep your voice down to a low roar." I advanced the page on the screen.

The tone of the official ceremony, which began at 11 A.M., might be said to have been set with the sound of off-key bugles and badly played drums, courtesy of the Germantown Avenue Pulaski Club Drum and Bugle Corps. Like rowdy children and elephants on a rampage, they were heard before they were seen by those who had gathered in the secluded and neglected garden that hides in the shadows of the Museum.

Colonel O'Brien arrived in an official olive-green U.S. Army Chevrolet four-door sedan with an official olive-green U.S. Army driver bearing the rank of corporal. Two more vehicles, crowded with dignitaries from the Polish community, arrived with the colonel's car.

All eight passengers quickly joined the colonel under a
huge patio umbrella emblazoned with the Cinzano logo,
thoughtfully provided by the colonel's escort, Sasha
Kubasak, a former Miss Allentown, 1981.

"*Fox!*" Sammy snapped upright as though his spine was spring-loaded. "Get
over here." The command had come from one of the assistant editors I didn't
know.

"Better move it, boy," I said with a laugh.

"In a sec. Move your hand." When I didn't react fast enough he pushed
it from the keyboard, tapped in a series of commands so quickly I couldn't follow
him, then backed away, grinning. "Catch you later."

For a couple of minutes I sat there, staring at the words on the screen,
wondering what he had done. I scrolled through the pages, searching for some
clue to his mischief. And then it dawned on me: He'd made an electronic dupe
of the story and parked it somewhere in the mainframe, probably in a locked
file to which only he had the password. That's a *serious* reader.

— — — —

At four-twenty I delivered my story to Ivan, told him that I had missed lunch
and that since I hadn't had time to eat I'd like to leave ASAP. He was surrounded
by the usual bullshit and bullshitters who feast on first-edition pressures. "Take
off," he said, barely looking up.

I was out of the city room in thirty seconds, and out of the building, headed
for the Ramada, in under three minutes. Walking toward the Ramada, I thanked
the gods that be for their generosity. As tired as I was, I didn't really want to
listen to Ivan rant and rave. I needed a couple of hours of sleep. And something
to eat. And after that, maybe a couple of shots of tequila and a Corona at the
Cock'n'Bull. Tuesday would be soon enough to bang heads with Czar Ivan.

— — — —

Ferris showed up at the Cock'n'Bull a few minutes after nine o'clock, about
fifteen minutes after I gave Sheila a pat on the butt and seated myself at the far
end of the bar where Juliet and I had sat one week earlier. I was having a problem
dealing with the last seven days as a standard earth week. It had seemed a lot
longer than the usual seven days. My last seven days in Vietnam went faster,
and I had spent those in the stockade, in isolation.

The Cock'n'Bull was only moderately busy. It was still raining off and on,
which meant a lot of people would stay home. I liked that. Fifty people in the
bar would make a nice atmosphere and still leave me enough room to feel

comfortable. I liked the Cock'n'Bull even though the decor was pure bullshit. Too much brass and glass, but at least the brass was real, not that tin plate crap coated with three microns of pseudo-brass finish. The lighting was subdued, which I liked. No glare, but bright enough to let you read the check without difficulty. No background music. And thank you, merciful fathers, no fucking piano, which precluded the sing-along shit. There was also a fine assortment of female flesh and a wonderful walnut bar, two of the three hallmarks of a good saloon.

The most intriguing element of the decor was the fifty or so framed photostats of front pages from a dozen different newspapers dating back to the turn of the century. Wandering around the room with cold beer, you could read an eighty-two-year history of man's follies and fuck-ups. One of those old Hebrews warned that the end of the world would arrive with the Four Horsemen of the Apocalypse: Pestilence, War, Famine, and Death. That's about all we've had for most of the twentieth century. Maybe this is it. Maybe the world as we know it is ending as we all sit around and try to figure out how to save the whales.

I didn't notice Ferris until he took his seat. I don't know if he saw me, although I would guess he had since he had to walk in my direction to get his seat in the middle of the bar. He sat next to an empty stool and ordered a Molson Ale. We made eye contact as he raised his glass for the first long swallow. He drank, put his glass on the bar, and glared at me for a few seconds, then shifted his gaze back to the rows and rows of bottles.

John, the bartender who had indirectly introduced me to Sheila, came down the bar with a bottle of Conmemorativo and a fresh Corona. He refilled the shot glass and put the beer on the counter. "Maybe I should just leave the tequila here. None of my other customers order it."

"Most of them probably don't drink straight tequila of any kind, and not many bars carry Conmemorativo. It's up to you to spread the gospel. Let them know that God has given his blessing to the producers of Conmemorativo. It's your duty as a good Christian *and* a connoisseur of well-aged cactus juice." I downed the shot.

"How many did you have before you got here?"

"None, actually." He refilled the glass. "I'm just a little crazed from a week of bullshit."

"Things'll get better," John said as though he really meant it. "New guy on the block's gonna have to take a little shit."

"I wish it was that simple. Listen, there's a black guy at the bar . . ."

"Ferris? The guy with the three-hundred-dollar suit?"

"Yeah. Give him a shot of this and put it on my tab, okay?"

"He doesn't drink much of the hard stuff, and when he does it's Scotch. Black Label."

"He's a fuckin' spearchucker, what does he know? Give him a shot and tell him I said I hope he didn't lose too much money today."

John's expression went from startled to amused. "Okay. It's your money."

He started a turn, stopped, and turned back. "How you and the Polish Princess getting on?"

"So far, so good. Did she talk to you about the wedding? She wants you to work the bar at the reception."

For a fleeting moment he had the hook in his mouth, then he spat it out with a laugh. "Fuck you." He collected a clean shot glass from the back bar, put it in front of Ferris, and poured the shot. He said something I couldn't hear and jerked his head in my direction. Ferris looked down the bar, then back at John. John shrugged, and wandered up the bar to fill an order.

I wasn't sure what Ferris would do, but I was curious enough to waste a couple of dollars. I hoped he would relent, because I was curious about him. Of the people I'd met at the *Call*, he was the most compelling.

After a minute or so of studying the shot glass, Ferris picked it up and walked to where I was seated. His face was a cool ebony mask.

"We've got to stop meeting like this, Leon," I said with a straight face and raised my tequila. "It's sure to get back to Ivan."

After a beat, he snorted, we clicked glasses, and the tequila disappeared. "Now that's a thought that I can dwell on with pleasure," he said with a hint of a smile. "Anything that will add to Ivan's list of worries is worth two bucks." He waved at the bartender. "John, two more of these Mexican bullets." He turned back to stare at me. "So what's your story?"

"Just passing through. Life on the run."

"Yeah, and Jesse Jackson is just another pretty face. You don't cut nobody no slack, do you?"

"What goes around, comes around. Or so I've heard. I also heard some people on the eleventh floor think I might be a dope dealer, or a narc. That right?"

"Could be. I know a guy on the copy desk who's stone-cold convinced that Rudolph Reichmann is a great cop. People swear by all kinds of shit."

"Who's Rudolph Reichmann?"

"Commissioner of Police." His face was as cool as ever.

"Oh well, of course, that goes without saying. Any man with the fortitude, intelligence, and integrity to rise to the rank of *Commissar* . . ." I shrugged. "How could there be any question?"

"Like I said, you don't cut no slack for nobody."

John arrived with the bottle. "If you two gentlemen don't have any late-night plans, there's a party starts about midnight at Debs 'Я' Us. Andrea called earlier and said I should pass the word to any interesting unattached males I thought were sober enough to make the drive."

"Debs 'Я' Us?" Cracked me up. "What the fuck is that?"

Ferris looked at John, laughing. "We should take this honky fucker out there. Probably wouldn't see him for a week."

John found that idea equally hilarious. He'd been filling my shot glass and didn't stop in time. Still laughing, he said, "Oops," lifted the glass to his lips, and the tequila was gone. "That one's on me," he announced as he mopped up the excess.

"What a sport," I said. "Now see if you can pour three more into the glasses rather than on the top of the bar. On Mr. Fun, here." That also set them off, and finally I was laughing just because they were having such a good time.

"Listen," John finally managed to say, "it's sort of an inside joke." He filled our glasses and got one for himself. "Debs 'Я' Us is the name three very rich young ladies from the Main Line gave to the mansion they live in, and when they throw a party *nobody* goes home for at least a couple of days." He put the bottle on the bar and pulled a couple of Coronas from the cooler. "Andrea, Michelle, and Muffie."

I caught a glimpse of Sheila as she turned the end of the bar and circled behind me. She put her arm over my shoulder and looked from John to Ferris and back to John. "Looks like you three are having a lot of fun." She picked up the shot John had poured for himself. "Is this for me?"

"John just invited this pilgrim to a party at Debs 'Я' Us, and we had to explain who they are."

"He's got a date tonight." She downed the shot, flashed a smile and gave me a squeeze. "Anyway, none of them are his type."

"Oh, I don't know about that," Ferris said with a grin. "Little Miss Muffie might find him very appealing. She likes to mix in the occasional 'artist' with her curs and whey. And the Hawk here, who knows what he likes?"

"Other than tequila and Camels," John said.

"Curs and whey?" I laughed. "I like that. I probably wouldn't like her at all, but that's funny."

"Don't encourage him," Sheila said. She wasn't smiling and I had the feeling that she was a little nervous about the three of us being together having a good time. I hadn't seen her since the night of the Thai-tanic disaster, and I'd only talked to her once, for about ten minutes on the phone.

John looked over his shoulder, to check the bar. The second bartender was leaning on his elbow, bullshitting with a customer. "Slow night. I probably should go out there. Pour a few drinks and pick up a couple of bills. Whatta you say, guys?"

"Not me," I said. "I've got to be up by five and that party isn't gonna happen until at least three or four, right?"

"You're off tomorrow and Monday . . . where you going at five A.M.?"

"It's my job to milk the llamas." I stood up. "Excuse me. My bladder runneth over."

I was standing over the urinal when Ferris's comment about the copy editor flashed through my thoughts. "I know a guy on the copy desk who's convinced

Rudolph Reichmann is a great cop. . . ." What was interesting, as I thought about it, was that something had lit up in his eyes when I asked who Rudolph Reichmann was. If I was a narc, I should know Reichmann, and I shouldn't be swift enough to ask the question with such total innocence.

The thought stayed with me for a few seconds, and then the whole idea seemed absurd. Playing guessing games based on subjective projection, along with writing and rewriting hours of internal dialogue, are two of the most pointless exercises in the amazingly wide range of ridiculous human mental activities. I do both, but only if it's fun or my survival seems to depend on it. And since I'm not a narc or a dealer, I don't truly give a fat rat's ass who on the *Call* thinks I may be.

— — — —

When I got back to the bar, Ferris looked as though he still needed some reassurance that I was nothing more than what I had said: just one more wandering scribbler who happened to have landed at the *Call*. "How did you come to have over five hundred in cash on you today?"

"I haven't had time to open a bank account, and I didn't think to leave it in the hotel safe. Why?"

"You bullshitted me about wanting to make a bet. You *knew* there was no way Ivan would print that story." He laughed, shaking his head. "I can't believe you got the balls to write something like that and turn it in. Maybe half an hour after you left, Ivan got around to reading it. He was *pissed*."

"So you don't think he printed it, huh?"

Ferris raised his beer. "It was a hellava story, though. And Sammy has a copy tucked away in the mainframe. I think he's selling the password for five bucks a pop."

I chuckled. "Listen, speaking of Sammy, he said something about knowing something about Ivan that I didn't, if you can follow that."

"I don't know what he had in mind"—he took a slug of his beer, and I followed suit—"unless it had something to do with Ivan's mother being Polish."

I almost spat my beer into his lap. "*What?*" I managed to swallow the beer without giving either of us a bath. "Do you mean Warsaw-Pact, pickled-eggs, and my-favorite-barmaid Polish?"

"You got it."

"I can't wait until Tuesday."

"What are you doing tomorrow?"

"I don't have a clue. I probably won't be moving into my new apartment, since I may well be unemployed by Tuesday at lunch."

"You may well be unemployed as of this moment. Ivan was on the phone practically foaming at the mouth after he read the piece. My guess is he called Daniel French."

"Well, French didn't call me and I was in my room for three hours. And I'll tell you something else: I don't really give a shit."

"We noticed."

— — — —

About five after midnight Sheila came over and sat on the stool Ferris had vacated an hour earlier. John came down the bar with the tequila bottle. "Buy me a drink, sexy?"

"How about a tutu from Frederick's of Hollywood?"

She frowned at John. "Can you make one of those?"

"What's in it?" he asked as he poured the Conmemorativo.

"Whatever's available."

Sheila slapped my arm. "You better be a little more specific than that."

"Well," I said, "there's the Polish Princess version . . . you mix a couple of shots of tequila, two or three grams of grass, and a prize-winning pair of bazongas . . ."

"Stirred, not shaken," John added in his best James Bond accent.

"With him," Sheila said to John, "I've had some of both." She put her arm around me and pulled me toward her, leaning in until our cheeks were touching. "Don't we make a cute couple?"

"I'll drink to that," John said, and hoisted his beer.

"You'll drink to anything," Sheila said.

We finished off the shots and chased them with beer.

"You guys want to come out with me to Debs Are Us?"

Sheila glanced at me, then said, "No way. Mr. Hawkins and I have early morning chores."

John looked from her to me, and I shrugged. "I'm teaching her to read, and she seems most attentive in the early morning hours."

"Interesting," John said. "Any particular topics? Cooking? Care and feeding of newspaper reporters? Stuff like that?"

"Actually, I started her out with *Story of O* . . ." Sheila hit me in the ribs with her elbow. "Then we moved on to *Tropic of Cancer*. And after that I think we'll try *The Autobiography of a Flea*."

"Well, that's it for me," Sheila announced as she stood up and grabbed her purse. "You two are disgusting."

John looked at me as she walked away. "Is she really upset or just messing around?"

"I don't know." When she didn't stop I called her name. She stopped, waited a second, then turned slightly and looked over her shoulder. I still couldn't tell if she was serious. "Come here." She stood where she was. "Come *on*. I just want to tell you something, then you can go back to being pissed off, or whatever it is that you are." I beckoned and she walked over, slowly. I thought I caught a hint of a grin about to break through.

When she was at my side, I leaned close and whispered a short, graphic story about a Chinese girl and a string of pearls, the pearls' placement within a specific body cavity, and what happens when they're removed during orgasm. As I described the last phase of the event her fingernails dug into my arm and I swear she shuddered.

Then she backed up, staring at me. *"That* is disgusting." My smile said, Maybe . . . but wouldn't you really like to try it? "God!" She shuddered again. "Did that really happen to you, like that?"

I nodded. "But I know how right and proper you are, so I wouldn't even think of suggesting anything like that."

"Thank you. You're a real gentleman. Can we go now? I know I've got a necklace somewhere."

"Just let me take care of the tab and we'll be on our way."

— — — —

It was still drizzling as we came out of the Cock'n'Bull, and I was jolted by the sudden reminder that I had driven Juliet's Jag to the bar. It was parked on a side street a block away, forgotten while I was enjoying myself. If there had been a cab at the door I might have left the car parked and avoided what I saw as inevitable. But there wasn't a cab in sight, and the wind drove the light rain sideways into my face. I hate that. I had enough fucking cold rain in 'Nam. Looking up and down the street for a taxi, Sheila opened an umbrella she'd picked up as we left.

"C'mon," I said, and took her arm.

"Where? If there's a cab cruising the area it'll pass here."

"I've got something quicker."

She stayed in step, looking up at me a couple of times, but she didn't ask any questions and I used the time to search for something I could say if she got bent out of shape when she saw the car. What the fuck, maybe she'll just get in and navigate.

"You fucker," she said as I put the key into the passenger-door lock.

"Is that a question, or a one-word summary of some inner secret just revealed to you?" I opened the door but she didn't move. "Are we gonna stand here in the rain like refugees, or what?" She still didn't move and she didn't say anything. She just glared. "I'm good at reading faces, but all I can see in yours is 'pissed off.' Let's try words. Tell me what your problem is."

"You fucked her."

Well now, that certainly is to the point. I almost laughed. The air was ready to roll out of my mouth in a thoroughly raucous explosion. Somehow, I stopped it. I shook my head and turned my face away. I didn't want her to see even a hint of mirth in my eyes. This was serious shit to her. When I looked back a few seconds later she was ready to explode.

"You fucked her!" She was maybe half a db below screaming.

"So what?"

She blinked as though I had slapped her with something she couldn't see. "Whatta you mean, so what?"

"So what? So I fucked her. Or she fucked me. So what?"

"I can't believe you would stand there and say 'So what?' "

"You're stalling. It happened last Sunday night. Tell me, in terms as concise as you used when you said 'You fucked her': What would have been different if I *hadn't* fucked her? What would have changed, how would you have been different? How would I have been different with regard to you?"

"You seduce me Saturday night, fuck her Sunday night, spend the night with me again Monday, and you . . . you . . ."

"I know the chronology. But the point is, you can't answer my question because the only sensible answer is, It didn't change anything."

"I hate you!" She slammed the door and started up the street.

I started after her at something between a quickstep and a trot, and the image of Juliet chasing me down Twenty-first Street flashed in front of me. I stopped dead in my tracks. Sheila kept walking while I stood there, replaying the scene of last Sunday.

I was still standing there when she turned and started back. She was about to walk by me, her eyes fixed on some angry point on the horizon, when I spoke. "Listen, did you ever hear the story about the yuppie who wanted to be a Buddhist monk?" She kept on walking. "It's an interesting story, and if you don't see any relevance you can always tell me to stuff it and go home alone."

"I don't have to choose between you and going home alone," she said. But she stopped and slowly turned around to face me. I moved over and sat on the fender of the Jag.

"You fucked her," she said again, this time with less anger but more anguish.

"I did. So, you want to hear the story?"

"You're getting soaked."

"You don't know soaked until you've spent a week in the bush during monsoon season. I'll survive a few more minutes, and I won't complain if you'll stop yelling at me and let us talk."

"Well, I'm not getting in that car."

"Fine." I locked the door. "Now, do we walk, call a cab, or stand out here?"

"Come under the umbrella with me and let's go back and call a cab."

I accepted the invitation, all the while wondering what the fuck I was going to do when she and I got back to her place. What could I say that would mend the rip and help her get rid of the pain? I wasn't going to say I was sorry, because I wasn't. I wasn't going to apologize, because I didn't believe I had done anything wrong. I wasn't going to lie and say I wouldn't ever do it again. Given the right circumstances, I knew I would.

The possibilities were still dwindling when we arrived at her apartment.

"You want to know how I knew?" Sheila asked as she came into the living room. She'd changed into a pair of faded jeans and a yellow sweatshirt on which a Cock'n'Bull University emblem had been silk-screened. Her hair was damp. Thick yellow cotton socks covered her feet.

I watched her closely as she crossed the room and sat on the end of the sofa where I was stretched out, wrapped in an afghan. I was just beginning to warm up. "Probably not as much as you want to tell me."

"Don't you care? You should at least care enough not to want to make the same mistake again."

"You saw me with her the night you and I met, you saw the CALL 1 vanity plates tonight, and you very quickly added one and one, so to speak."

"You really don't care, do you?" The disappointment she felt at having me take away her opportunity to feel superior in at least this one thing turned to tears. Not only had I fucked another woman, I was accused of the even more heinous crime of *not caring*. In the emotional arena of relationships, that's treason. Infidelity may be forgiven after due process, but not caring, failure to feel guilty, insufficient display of emotion . . . Only a person of mean spirit could behave rationally in a time of such intense, meaningful confrontation.

"I care about you. I *don't* care that you now know I fucked someone else."

Tears flowed, and she sobbed a little. At that moment, I would have wagered my full week's wages to a wax apple that within the next five minutes she would ask me, "Aren't I enough for you?" Someone had to be blamed. She, Juliet, and I were the only candidates. It was safest to blame herself. That tack was also the one most likely to lead to reconciliation. She'd plead the helpless inadequate child and I would rush to reassure her that she was wonderfully adequate, wonderful in every respect. I would then plead that I hadn't meant to hurt her. By then we would be touching and kissing and nothing said would matter until she had to spend her first night alone. Then she would replay every word, examine every nuance, freeze every fucking frame of the picture, looking for the most minute inconsistencies, all the while wondering if I was with *her*.

"Aren't I enough for you?"

Jackpot. Three fucking lemons. I thought about leaving. No long good-bye, no speech, no nothing. Give her a kiss, wish her well, and get the hell out. The problem was, I liked her, a lot. She was bright, she had a good sense of humor, she had ambition. And she was fun in bed. "You are enough," I finally responded, "if you're asking me whether I'm satisfied sexually when we're together. If I had an inclination to search for one woman with whom to spend my life, with whom I could share the burden of living and find solace in her comfort, you would be a very real possibility. I don't know why in the name of Christ and Casimir Pulaski you'd want to have me around, but that isn't the point.

"The point, in fact, is simple: I'm not so inclined. I'm not going to limit my options, sexual or otherwise, to one way of living, one job, one city, one area of the country, or one woman. Not you, not Juliet, not fuckin' Kathleen Turner who has broken my heart so often she should send me a case of Conmemorativo and a bottle of Elmer's Glue so I can drown my sorrows and put myself back together every time I see one of her movies."

"Kathleen Turner? Oh my God!" She got up and stomped out of the room, into the kitchen. The sounds of the refrigerator being yanked open and slammed closed were sandwiched around a loud, emphatic, "Shit! Fucking Kathleen Turner I've got to compete with." She yanked open a drawer, rattled some utensils, opened a beer.

"You want a beer, Hawkins?"

"Coffee. Would you make some coffee?"

"Fuck you. It's beer or nothing."

"Nothing will be fine. Could you wrap it to go?"

She came back into view, drinking from a bottle of Miller Lite as she walked, her focus shifting from me to the beer to me to the beer. Finally, she pulled the bottle down about a third less full. "I should wrap you to go," she said and burped.

Her vulnerability was very appealing but I missed the cheerful, assertive, impish expression she usually wore. For an instant I felt sad, and then I mentally stepped around that trap and concentrated on the possibilities and probabilities, asking myself what I wanted from her. Could I define it?

"What the fuck do you want from me?" she asked as though she had read my thoughts.

"I don't know. What do you want from me?"

She stared at me and the seconds ticked by. I could have looked a hole through her but it seemed ridiculous.

"The other night, Monday, before you called, I was sitting in my room at the Ramada, really fucked up. I had a lot of doubts about working for the *Call*. I had a lot of doubts about being in Philadelphia. I've still got a hellava lot of doubts about playing this dumb-fuck game. . . ."

"What game? I'm a *game* to you?"

"Not you. Life in America. Get a job. Get married. Get laid. Get a car. Get *ahead!*"

"Well, you sure don't have to worry about buying a car, do you? You've got someone else to do that for you. And she'll probably see that you get ahead. Does she give head?"

"Are you interested in what I want to tell you, or are you only interested in hearing your own voice? This isn't fucking responsive reading."

"I'm sorry . . . I'm trying real hard not to start crying again, not to lose my temper. . . ."

"And not to listen because if you really listen, mostly to yourself, you're going to be even more disappointed in yourself than you were in me."

"How so?" She had switched from defensive to defiant.

"Because you don't have any claim to my fidelity, for one. I was out with you twice in one week, the one week that I've known you. That doesn't give you a right to dictate whose bed I can sleep in.

"Supposing, last Monday after dinner, I had said that I wanted to move in here with you and I wanted you to quit your job at the Cock'n'Bull because half the guys who come in there are trying to get their hands up your skirt or down your blouse? How would that sit with you?"

"That's not the same thing!"

"Bullshit."

"How? How can they be the same? I'm not fucking those guys and I'm not telling you where to work, or how to live. I'm not trying to take away your space."

I laughed. There wasn't a lot of real humor in the sound but I could see humor in the situation. "What we're talking about has nothing to do with who I fucked or where you work or what car I drive. It has to do with approval and disapproval, with presuming the right to dictate to other people how they will live, how to think, what's okay and what isn't okay, who they can fuck and who they can't fuck, and when and how often, and in what goddamn position, when none of those things has any effect on the person or persons doing the dictating." It was all oversimplified, but her whole emotional outburst was pure bullshit as far as I was concerned.

"We've been programmed to manipulate the behavior of others by giving or withholding approval for behavior that a lot of times doesn't concern anyone, and I mean *anyone*."

"Well, there's such a thing as moral values, which two people who're sleeping together should share."

"And you think I'm immoral because I fucked another woman?" I sat up, tucked the afghan under my legs, and lit a cigarette. She found an ashtray for me and sat back on the end of the sofa. "I asked you a question. Can you give me an answer?"

"Well, it's not right."

"You never did that, huh?"

"Only once, and I hated myself afterward."

"Why?"

"Because I felt cheap."

"Why did you feel 'cheap'? Because you made it with two guys in a week, or whatever time it was? Or because you knew that some people, probably people you care about, would *say* that you're cheap or easy or promiscuous?"

She stared at me for a few seconds. I wasn't sure if I had opened a door to a new thought or closed another one to any possibility of communication. She finally shook her head, either unwilling or unable to risk a different way of looking at herself.

"Let me tell you a story, something that happened to me that might help you to understand why I don't have a lot of regard for other people's values. It's kind of a long story, so be patient, okay?"

"Okay. You still want the coffee? I'll make it."

"Sure." I followed her into the kitchen.

"The first months I was in Vietnam I didn't kill anyone, as far as I know. I couldn't shoot someone who hadn't done anything to me. Least of all from ambush. I just couldn't do it.

"Can you understand that, or is it too weird for you?"

"I understand it. I don't think I could kill anyone unless it was to save my life, or the life of someone I loved."

"Okay. Now, there I am, ass-deep in paddy water and pig shit, surrounded by guys who've been armed and primed, guys who were labeled, packaged, and shipped thousands of miles for one basic purpose—to kill people who had never even given them a reason to leave home. We were pulled from the stockpile, just another hundred and fifty or so interchangeable parts, tossed into the shit together, and the only hope in hell we had for survival was to stick together. To do that each of us had to be there when the shit hit the fan."

She was busy with the coffeepot, and I wasn't sure she was even listening. "You with me?"

"Yes." She lit the burner under a kettle of water and turned around. "I'm listening."

"I was taught that it's wrong to take the life of another human being except in self-defense. The Bible says, 'Thou shalt not kill,' and it doesn't even mention self-defense. Of course, there probably are more deaths recorded in the Bible than there are on the list of KIAs from 'Nam. But be that as it may, killing people without a damn good reason was not acceptable.

"I lived with that idea for eighteen years and the army gave me about eighteen weeks to come to my senses and accept that killing the *enemy* was sanctioned by law and quite possibly could lead to a promotion, medals, and veteran's benefits.

"The idea didn't take. But the guys I was with needed to know that I'd protect them and myself, that I would participate in the scheme of things. I said I would but I didn't fire a round. My attitude was considered very unprofessional, and there were those who took exception. One of them threatened to kill me if I didn't start killing the bad guys.

"Then, one day, I was out in a village, away from the base camp, with a buddy. He was a country boy who did his job, kept his mouth shut, and got promoted. He carried a ten-gauge shotgun.

"As we came into the village a little girl, maybe four or five years old, started running toward my buddy, laughing, trying to say his name. He'd been in there a few times and he thought he'd made friends with the people.

"When the kid was maybe twenty, twenty-five yards from my buddy she lifted her arms, like kids do when they're running to an adult . . ."

"I don't want to hear this," Sheila said. She turned her back, killed the flame under the kettle, and started pouring the water through coffee into a glass pot.

"He threw the shotgun to me and started toward the girl . . ."

"Jamie, please . . ."

"Listen! Listen to me. The spoon from a grenade fell out of her dress and I fired. My buddy only carried buckshot. The kid's middle practically disappeared. The grenade exploded, and my buddy was hurt, seriously hurt. There wasn't enough left of that little girl to fill a sandbag."

Sheila turned around, trembling. "Jamie, *please* . . ."

"So the kid's dead. I grab my buddy and some fuckin' VC opens up with an automatic. I drag him inside a hooch, which is made out of palm fronds and some tin sheeting—Vietnamese armor plating. I'm so fuckin' scared I can barely breathe or stop myself from pissing in my pants.

"There's an old, old woman in the hooch, God, probably seventy years old, and she's pissin' scared, too, and she won't shut up, yammering and pleading in that fuckin' nasal noise they call a language. I screamed at her and one of the AKs fires about half a clip through the wall. I emptied both barrels into her and the wall and the VC.

"Then I went out the door, looking for the second guy. I found the one I'd lit up and took his weapon. I couldn't find the second one and I pissed away the ammo left in the AK. I went back to the first one to see if he had another magazine, and he was lying on his back trying to hold his guts in. I shot him once, with my rifle."

She reached for a cup and her hand was shaking. I put my hand over hers for a moment, then filled the cup myself. She turned on the sink faucet, and wiped her face with her wet hands. I stirred some sugar in my coffee and opened the fridge, looking for half-and-half. She had it, which made me feel good. She drank her coffee black.

When she had a little more control she turned to look at me. I was suddenly a real stranger, rather than another lover with an untalked-about history and a forgivable lapse in 'morals.' The few stories I'd told her about my travels and travails, anecdotes that had amused and surprised her, were timid cover copy compared to this flash.

"So, one minute I'm a virgin, an apprentice to the low art of violent death, and the next I'm a hero." I tasted the coffee, watching her over the rim of the cup. "No shit, a certified medal-carrying hero. Wounded in action, heroism under fire."

She tried to say something. Her mouth opened, but the mechanism failed her. All she managed was an expulsion of hot air.

"More important, having proven myself, I was accepted by my platoon. I was one of them. I had become the thing I most feared. I won their acceptance by killing a child, an old woman, a VC grunt who wasn't any older than me, and quite probably another one I never saw.

"So, here's the point of all of this. A lot of shit happened after that, which I won't bore you with, but finally, one day, I said 'I quit' and I did. And I got away with it, which is another long story, but while the final chapter was being worked out I was sent to see a psychiatrist. Actually, I saw several of them. I may even be a fuckin' footnote in a couple of their books.

"Lotta talk, talk, talk. And in all that talk, this one guy, a major, maybe thirty-five, never fired a shot in anger, never been shot at, never walked point, never even been close to having to make decisions like we made every goddamn day—he says to me, 'Private Hawkins, you have yet to come to terms with something very basic in our society, in our world. It's a universal truth: Self-esteem is rooted in acceptance by our peers, by our superiors, even, one might argue, by our subordinates. Our self-worth, how we see ourselves as individuals, how we rate ourselves at any given moment, is all determined by how others see us. If they have a positive image of us, and convey that to us, then we see ourselves as worthy. And how do they convey that information? Through love, through desire to be with us, to share with us, through promotions and raises and gifts, through verbal approval and willingness to forgive our mistakes . . . through acceptance.

" 'If, however, they do not accept us, if we are rejected and scorned, then we unfailingly come to see ourselves as unworthy, unfit for the company of our fellow human beings. And from there we either lose our sense of self, or we compensate, often with arrogance and defiance.

" 'You have no sense of self-worth. You hate yourself for abandoning your buddies, for failing to live up to your sworn duty as a soldier, and for failing to fulfill your duties to yourself, for not living up to your own image of what you should be.

" 'You have failed yourself,' he said. And then he said, 'Not one person I interviewed in your behalf had one good thing to say about you. Not one.' And this asshole, mind you, was supposed to be the psychiatrist for the defense."

Sheila's face was filled with the pain of imagining how it would feel to hear that said about herself. She believed the pain was for me, but it wasn't. She was projecting, and it was painful for me to contemplate. "What did you say to him? Anything?"

"I told him to fuck off, because the only people who might have had a kind word to say about me were dead, and I had carried back the body of the one who came closest to loving me."

I finished my coffee, rinsed the cup, and put it in the sink. "The other night, in the Ramada, before you called, I was sitting there thinking about the *Call*, and my doubts and my attitude, and it occurred to me that there was no one I could talk to who knew me well and cared enough to listen. Not one person."

"I certainly would have listened!" she protested

"Maybe, but you don't know me well, and I can't imagine you saying, 'I'd get the hell out of here if I were you.' "

"I wouldn't want you to leave."

"Thanks, but that kind of proves my point."

She sighed with genuine fatigue. "Can we go to bed? I'm exhausted."

"You go. C'mon, I'll tuck you in."

"What about you?"

"I'll be awake for a while." I took her hand and led her into the bedroom. Her uncertainty was evident in every move, every glance. She peeled off her jeans, and her bikini panties came off in the process. For an instant I was tempted to stay. The curve of her ass was as smooth and perfect as I can imagine. She crawled under the sheet and blanket and I tucked them in around her, leaned over, and kissed her gently.

"I made myself a promise," I said as I pushed her hair away from her eyes and stroked her face. "I promised myself that I would do my best to find the truth within me, my truth, and be faithful to that truth, whatever it is. I don't care anymore what anyone thinks about the way I am or what I do or why I do it. That's why I've spent so much time out of the country. When you can't speak the language well enough to discuss anything more basic than your needs for survival—a place to sleep, something to eat, the next bus to Puerto Vallarta— it's easier to stay out of discussions about values." I kissed her on the forehead. "Sleep well."

"I love you," she said. "Please stay."

Would that you could, I thought as I left the room.

———   ———   ———   ———

I poured myself another cup of coffee, picked up a joint from the kitchen table, and sat on the sofa, smoking dope and thinking. After I was discharged, I'd never talked to anyone about the kid and the old woman and the VC grunt. A couple of times I'd tried to talk to Marybeth about 'Nam and why I had so many problems accepting the routine bullshit of life. It hadn't started in 'Nam, but what had already taken root leaped from the fertile earth of my childhood and stood like a grove of oaks. I fell asleep on the sofa thinking that I would much rather be like bamboo than oak. I just didn't know how to bend with the wind. And if ever I couldn't absorb the pressure I'd end up face down for some totally stupid reason that everyone would misunderstand.

Two hours later I woke with a jolt, sweating, my heart pounding from the anxiety of some dream I couldn't recall. I left Sheila sleeping, walked over to pick up the Jag, and drove back to the Ramada. After a few shots of tequila and half of another joint, I went to sleep holding my pillow, hoping it would cushion my fall if I rolled into the Pit while I was unconscious.

———   ———   ———   ———

The first time I saw Charlie Patton was Christmas Eve. He was standing in front of his battered yellow VW, off Quaker Plaza, staring at the red tongue of a parking meter that, he later told me, had just swallowed his second quarter and still refused to raise its little arrow to indicate to passing meter maids that the fare had been paid. Patton was looking at the red tongue but he was seeing a parking ticket.

At that moment my attention was primarily focused on the long legs of a stunning young female who was leading me around Quaker Plaza in a game of catch me if you can. When I'd first seen her, a few minutes earlier, her rich copper–colored, shoulder-length hair streaming in the wind, dressed in tight jeans, knee-high tobacco-colored boots, and quilted jacket, I'd thought it was Marybeth. Just for an instant. This girl, though, was taller, and she wore her clothes better than Marybeth. She'd also given me a big smile, which I doubt Marybeth would have done at that point.

Sitting on a cold bench, holding the uneaten half of a fatty pastrami sandwich I didn't want, sipping cold coffee from a Styrofoam cup, I had been considering the possible consequences of taking off for the afternoon, the first five minutes of which I meant to spend ripping out the cassette player hidden somewhere in the Salvation Army mobile unit parked around the corner. It would be a gift to all those who, like me, were fighting melancholy on Christmas Eve.

If I did that, I wondered, who on the *Call* would have to write the story of the lunatic reporter who split his seams and allowed all his Christmas misery to spill into the dirty snow? My guess was that Ivan would assign the story to Alexis. That way they could both enjoy my momentary lapse in good behavior. Ivan still hadn't come to terms with the fact that he needed Daniel French's permission to fire me.

Thinking about Ivan was enough to ruin my lunch even if the pastrami hadn't been fatty. Being unable to get away from the bullshit that went with Christmas, especially the stories Ivan assigned me to write about all the hungry children and homeless old people, was more than enough to ruin my whole goddamn perspective on Christmas, which was none too charitable under the best of circumstances. One each day for the last two weeks. Plus, I had to write extra stories to cover my days off.

Fatty pastrami, Ivan the Terrible, and seasonal concern for the plight of the unfortunate was a mean combination.

And then she had come bouncing along, carrying a bright red shopping bag from Wanamaker's crammed with gifts and streaming ribbons. I caught her eye and she returned my smile with a lingering glance and a hint of a grin. Killer by-God legs, I thought as I dumped the remains of my lunch in a wire basket and plowed into her wake.

The plaza was crowded with shoppers roaming between credit card terminals. Some of them looked cheerful enough, and some of them looked as though they'd been stretched to the emotional limit. I steered clear of them. Twice the girl turned to see if I was still there.

My first glimpse of Patton distracted me from my pursuit of Legs Galore. The image of a large black male dressed in combat fatigues, with greasepaint on his face and an M-16 cradled in his right arm, struck me as something other than another bit of big-city weirdness. I stopped and stared for a moment. Patton was across the street, probably thirty yards away, and even at that distance I could see his boots gleaming. His posture was rigid.

I watched him, waiting, waiting . . . What the hell could he be doing here, on Christmas Eve, dressed like that and carrying a weapon, I wondered? Patton just stood there. I glanced to my right, looking for the girl. She had stopped to say hello to a wandering Santa. She glanced back at me, then moved on, a little slower maybe, but I was going to have to decide between the guy with the M-16 and the girl with the killer legs.

I took a couple of steps in her direction, stopped, and looked back. Charlie Patton raised the M-16 and fired a single round into the glass bubble that encased the red tongue. The noise wasn't much. A "pop!" An explosion of glass that barely carried across the open space between us. A couple of people looked shocked, but before anyone could say anything, Patton was double-timing toward the plaza. I stole a quick look at the girl. Our eyes met and she cocked her head slightly, as though to say, Well, have you given up already?

Damn! I moved along, trailing her and trying to keep Patton in sight. Then she disappeared into a crowd and Patton came into the plaza, running directly toward the Tourist Center, a low, round, glass-sided building that catered to lost souls looking for directions to the monuments. Or the highway to Manhattan. I veered toward the building, jogging a few steps, walking a few, watching Patton. He went through the swinging doors like an MP busting an off-limits saloon. Maybe two seconds later I heard, barely, what must have originated as a bellow—"HIT IT!"—followed by the sound of twenty rounds fired on full automatic.

I stopped abruptly a few yards shy of the building and watched Patton stomp the length of the counter that ordinarily separated the pilgrims from the employees, using the rifle barrel to rake an assortment of baskets, maps, phones, and who knows what onto the floor. Glass from the ceiling fixtures fell in a shower. Only one person, a middle-aged male, was visible behind the counter. Everyone else was on the floor.

Patton pulled the empty magazine out of the M-16 and jammed in a new one. The man who had declined to join his sensible co-workers on the floor seemed to be lecturing Patton. I could see his mouth moving and he was gesturing with his right index finger. In the few seconds Patton used to reload, the man seemed to be working up to a fury. He even took a step away from his position behind his desk, as though he intended to get in close and hammer his point home. Patton fired two three-round bursts in the man's direction. A picture frame went to pieces, a lamp shattered, and a large painting on the wall hit the floor. The man froze, mouth open, eyes wide with indignation, then shock. He backed up to the wall, then slowly slid down until he was seated on the floor.

"Move it! MOVE IT! *MOVE IT!!!*" Patton's repeated commands followed a small group of hysterical people running for their lives through the Tourist Center's doors. He squeezed off another half-dozen rounds, firing into the ceiling, but never, I noticed, actually aiming the weapon at anyone. An older, obese woman, the last one out the door, tripped as she cleared the building. Her two shopping bags of Christmas gifts spilled across the sidewalk, and she slid eight or ten feet on the light crust of ice before she crashed headfirst into the legs of a young guy in a business suit and overcoat. He lost his balance and ended up on the ground with her.

I went over to help untangle them and to see if she had a clue to what the gunman wanted. She was borderline hysterical, as big as a whale, and as dumb as an ox. "He's crazy!" was all she could get out for the first minute. "He's crazy. He's shooting everywhere. Glass is flyin' and stuff's breakin' and he said he's gonna kill a bunch of people if he don't get to talk to the mayor."

The guy she had flattened was on his feet. With both of us tugging, she managed finally to stand up. Her knees were skinned and bleeding and I think she had a broken nose, but she hadn't been badly hurt.

"Has he actually shot anyone?" I asked her.

"I don't know, I don't know what he's doin' in there. He run us out, and I lost my Christmas presents for my children." The tears were streaming and she wiped at her face and nose with her coat sleeve. When she touched her nose she screamed, and for a moment I thought she might faint.

I looked at the guy, who was a little rattled himself. "Can you keep her standing up? I've got to make a call." He nodded and I sprinted to the closest pay phone to call Ivan.

"City desk. Bell speaking."

"Bell, this is Hawkins. Tell Ivan—"

"Ivan's in conference, and you were due back here an hour ago. Where the hell are you?"

"Tell Ivan, when he gets out of his meeting, that I've got a goddamn fruitcake armed with an M-16 who just shot up the Tourist Center or Convention Bureau or whatever the hell they call this fucking place. Send me a photographer, and get me a goddamn editor on this phone."

"Hang on," Bell sighed.

I paced up and down on the short tether, mumbling under my breath while I watched for some sign of Patton. I saw him once, for an instant, but he wasn't showing a lot of himself.

The seconds ticked by and finally I screamed into the phone, "Are you totally incompetent, or just brain-dead? Get me a goddamn editor."

"This is Ivan. Who the hell do you think you're talking to?"

"That retard you pay to answer phones and lose messages."

"Listen, some black guy all dolled up in combat fatigues and greasepaint just lit up the inside of the Tourist Center, then let a shitload of potential hostages loose. But he's still got a few inside."

"Anyone hurt?"

I could barely hear him over the sound of sirens. Five police cars and two ambulances were within a block, and off in the distance I heard what sounded like a fire truck. "No gunshot wounds that I could see," I yelled. "Few cuts and scrapes probably."

"I'm sending Alexis over with a photographer. Give her what you've got on the situation, then get back here and do a sidebar for first edition."

"*Sidebar?* Sidebar on what?"

"Vietnam syndrome. Post-traumatic stress."

"Fuck you, Ivan, this is *my* goddamn story." I would have continued with a few more choice words, but I realized I was yelling into a dead phone. The sonofabitch had hung up.

Vietnam syndrome, my ass. I had no more interest in writing a sidebar on wigged-out vets than I had in giving this story to Princess Alexis. No fuckin' way.

While I was trying to cool my anger enough to ward off an emotional melt-down, the mobile units from all the local TV stations arrived. Cameras, equipment, and people came out of the vehicles with the precision of a well-rehearsed ballet. I was surveying the ranks of would-be Rathers and Rather-nots when I saw Rudolph Reichmann for the first time since my arrival in Philadelphia.

A lot of people talked about Philadelphia's Commissioner of Police, some with reverence, some with awe, and some with language as profane as any I had heard in 'Nam. He was not beloved by all. Physically, he was big, but not as big as he appeared. I doubt that he measured a full six feet. He probably weighed two hundred, maybe two ten. He had bulk. He wore a nicely tailored wool uniform, with a long jacket that flared out at the hips to hide a little of the bulge that came with all the years of sitting on his ass in police cars and precinct offices. On his right hip he wore a nickel-plated .44, undoubtedly a Magnum. And with his visored, military-style hat he had enough gold braid to qualify for Admiral of the Fleet.

The thing about Reichmann that intimidated so many people couldn't be seen at first, if at all. For all the thought I've given to it since I first saw him, I still can't describe it better than to say he was one mean, merciless sonofabitch, totally without compassion.

It showed in his face, which was squared off and a little fleshy, with a lot of broken capillaries in his cheeks and nose.

It showed in his eyes, dark and relentless. If there was an inner light to shine through from the soul, Reichmann had the shades pulled.

And it showed in the way he moved. He seemed only to move forward, rarely sideways, and never backwards. If he wanted to move in a new direction he turned, and then he went forward. A step to the side or a step back might have been easier, but he would pivot and move forward.

If he had ever been graced with a sense of charity toward mankind, and the ability and willingness to empathize, it was an experience forgotten, probably by the force of his own will.

The local precinct watch captain met Reichmann as the Commissioner stepped from his car. They were surrounded by TV and print reporters, still photographers, cameramen, cops, and a couple of guys in suits and black overcoats. The media people couldn't shut up, but Reichmann ignored them, listening to the watch captain's briefing.

"Chief, apparently there's one gunman, guy with an automatic rifle, dressed in cammies. He's black. Sounds like he might have a modified AR-15 or an M-16. He's got five or six hostages, as far as we can tell."

"Injuries?"

"None that we know about."

"Demands? Deadlines?"

"We haven't had any direct contact with the gunman, but one of the people he let go says he's demanding to see the Mayor by fifteen hundred hours. I've notified the Mayor's aide. Should I ask for a hostage negotiator from the Feds?"

"Negative." Reichmann stared at the front of the building, possibly looking for a glimpse of the gunman, possibly trying to figure out how to resolve this mess. More cops arrived, most of them wearing black fatigue-style clothes and field jackets with SWAT TEAM stenciled on the back. I counted twelve, and at least four of them were armed with sniper rifles. Two of them were showing what looked like M-79 grenade launchers, probably for tear-gas shells. The others carried M-16s and all of them had sidearms, commando knives, and Christ only knows what else hidden in the folds of their combat clothing.

Not a pretty sight. They were members of an elite club and they had death and destruction written all over them. They had come to kill some poor bastard who had lost everything *but* his life, and law enforcement in the traditional sense was the last thing on their mind. Reichmann had already made his decision. No negotiations. No explanations. No fucking around.

I was on my way to the phone to call Ivan again, when I saw Alexis and two *Call* photographers closing in on Reichmann, who was already surrounded by reporters and cameramen. Reichmann stepped up on a bench as I joined the circle, waving at Alexis.

"Gentlemen . . ." Reichmann's baritone boomed across their heads like the voice of a battle-hardened old centurion with ambitions to be Caesar, rather than just serve him.

"The next mayor of Dell-a-philthia," Ferris would say every time Reichmann grabbed another headline or his picture turned up in the *Call*.

"Gentlemen, gentlemen . . ." The watch captain raised his voice above the level of self-important media chitchat.

"And Miss Cabot," Reichmann added with a nod to Alexis.

Alexis smiled and tossed an offhanded wave in his direction as she picked her way through the crowd. She reached me just as Patton let go with another long burst and two of the huge windows disintegrated, crashing to the cement in a shower of fragments.

"Ivan said for you to brief me, then get back to the *Call*," she said. "He's a little pissed with you, by the way."

I looked from her to Allen Dark, one of the photographers sent along with

Alexis. He grimaced and shook his head from side to side. Dark is a tall, bony guy, probably in his mid-thirties, with thinning hair and dark eyes, one of which is usually looking at the world through a viewfinder. He's okay, as news photographers go. They're all a little strange, if you want to know the truth.

"So what's the story?" she asked.

"It's long and sad, but it ends happily when I tell you to go fuck yourself, and if it'll make Ivan happy, let him watch. This is my goddamn story and I'm not going anywhere." I caught Dark grinning just before he looked away.

"If the members of the *Call* staff can stop bickering about their differences, whatever they are," Reichmann said, "I'll give you the information available to us at this time.

"You all know my feelings about negotiating with terrorists. I will not talk to anyone holding a weapon or endangering the lives of hostages."

"Has the mayor been notified?" one of the TV reporters shouted.

"The mayor is vacationing in San Juan," Reichmann replied. "I'm in charge."

"San Juan, Puerto Rico?" another voice yelled.

"Unless it's been moved." Reichmann was annoyed. A few of the people surrounding him laughed.

"This being Christmas Eve," he continued, "I know you're all anxious to get home to your families. So are we. I expect to have this business wrapped up in time for all of you to make *your* deadlines. The gunman's deadline is of no interest ot me."

No shit! "Alexis . . ."

Standing beside me, she turned her head to the sound of my voice, and as she did Dark took our picture. I still have a copy, which I come across from time to time. Looking at that picture of Alexis and me, not quite face-to-face, and a long way from being eye-to-eye on what we saw and how we saw it, I always wonder if there's some clue in that photograph, something that foreshadowed the misadventures and mistakes that were about to unroll like a bloody red carpet. If there is, I've never found it. But I keep looking.

"Yes . . .?" She was smiling. I think she thought I was going to yield the story to her and she was already gloating.

"You can stay or go, as you please, but I'm here for the whole show."

She said something, probably something meant to remind me of my place in all this, but the sound of a chopper at two hundred feet obliterated her voice.

I looked up, expecting to see a black Corba gunship with a death's-head painted on the nose, something meant to intimidate the 'enemy,' and there was one of the Philadelphia police department's helicopters painted to look like Santa's sleigh. Rudolph the Red-nosed Reindeer was arched in flight on the nose of Santa's chopper. Dark was shooting as quickly as he could focus. I walked away, laughing.

The chopper moved off and began circling about two hundred yards to the west.

Reichmann took a bullhorn from one of the cops standing at his side. "Now hear this," Reichmann said. "You in the Tourist Center. This is Rudolph Reichmann, Commissioner of Police. Release your hostages and surrender. You cannot escape." He paused, then repeated himself. "You cannot escape. Free . . . your . . . hostages. You have five minutes."

— — — —

As I walked toward the phone I replayed the scene in my head, laughing at the absurdity of a police helicopter painted to look like a sleigh and the Commissioner of Police actually saying, free your hostages, you cannot escape. What is this, fuckin' "Dragnet"?

I got Ivan on the first ring. "Ivan—"

"Hawkins, if you're not back here in ten minutes you're fired."

"Right. I think you said that earlier. Somebody did. So, listen . . . Reichmann is here, acting like he's Joe Friday or Eliot Ness, giving ultimatums to another escapee from Looney Tunes Farm who's holding hostages. The gunman said if he doesn't talk to the mayor by three o'clock he's gonna fry a few people, and Rudolph the Red-nosed Chief-o says the gunman's only got five minutes."

"Five minutes until what?" another voice asked.

"Who the fuck knows? And who am I talking to now?"

"Atlee Hearn, night city editor. Since this standoff is probably going into the night I'd like to be kept posted on the situation."

"You probably should talk to Alexis since Ivan keeps threatening to fire me."

"Not a threat, Hawkins. A promise. I want you back here and I want a sidebar before first edition."

"We'll see how it goes. 'Bye." I hung up before either of them could make any more promises and started walking back to the enchanted circle around Reichmann.

Outside that "inner circle" thirty or forty cops were standing around with little or nothing to do but keep the media at bay and the crowds behind the barriers.

Beyond them and the barriers they had erected was a mixed crowd of the curious, the bored, and the bloodthirsty. Three very distinct groups, although the bored and the bloodthirsty were thoroughly mixed.

The curious gave themselves away by moving along after a moment's pause, or a couple of questions and a disbelieving shake of the head.

The bored, for the most part, just stood there like cattle waiting to be let into the barn. They were quiet, didn't ask many questions, and were among the first to start buying pretzels and coffee from the vendors who started working the crowd.

The bloodthirsty ignored the refreshments and vocalized a lot, screaming for "that nigger terrorist's blood."

In the background, a scratchy, static-filled rendition of "Sleigh Bells" ended, and the first, equally scratchy strains of "White Christmas" descended on us, along with a few very large and wet snowflakes. Everyone was waiting for the play to continue.

Charlie Patton opened the second act by sending out two more hostages, a young black woman with her child, a little girl no more than two or three years old. They came out cautiously, stepping carefully through the glass, the mother so frightened she could barely force one foot in front of the other. The girl rode on her mother's hip, clutching her mother's neck with one arm and holding a candy cane in her hand.

When they were clear of the glass, Patton fired a few rounds into the ceiling, and the woman, shrieking, bolted toward the crowd. "Don't shoot, dear God, my little girl . . . don't shoot, don't shoot." In the few seconds it took her to reach the illusion of safety she lost what little control she had over her emotions and motor functions. Two of Reichmann's cops caught her as she pitched forward maybe five feet from the Commissioner.

Dark was there, winding film and snapping shots. Alexis pushed her way into the swarm of reporters and cameras. The cops pushed back. The watch captain bellowed, "Get back. Give this woman a little room, f'Chrissake!" He took the little girl from one of the two cops who had caught the woman. The kid was sobbing, and she'd lost her candy cane.

Reichmann, following the keeper of the bullhorn, reached the woman. "All right," he barked, "back up and give us some room here." He reached to take her arm and she pulled back.

"She's about to lose it," I said quietly to Alexis. "She's going into shock."

"What are you, a doctor?"

"No, but I've been scared half out of my mind, and I've seen shit that makes this look like bad community theater."

"Why don't you tell someone, then?"

"I don't think it would be real smart to tell these cops anything, least of all their leader. But she's maybe thirty seconds from losing it."

"Ma'am," Reichmann said, moving closer. "What does the gunman want? Did he give you a message for us?"

She was sucking in air, hyperventilating a little, trying to stay out of that void yawning in front of her. She wobbled slightly, then steadied herself with the last of her will. "He said, 'You tell old Tuna Belly that Charlie Patton wants to see the mayor in the next fifteen minutes or Christmas gonna be late this year.' "

Reichmann's face went from pasty to pink. "How many hostages does he have left?"

"I don't know," she sighed. "Maybe five or six . . ." She reached blindly for something to support herself and grabbed the arm of a cop. "I don't feel so good . . ."

A police medic elbowed his way through the crowd. "Let me in here." He took one look at her and yelled, "Yo! John! Get the gurney, couple of blankets, and break out the IV. She's going into shock."

"Shit!" Reichmann glared at the medic, then stomped off about ten feet, followed by a dozen questions, all of which he ignored. When he stopped he was actually a little closer to Alexis and me. His blood pressure was in the red zone.

The watch captain, minus the little girl, caught up with Reichmann. "Chief, you want me to tell the chopper to put a SWAT team on the roof?"

"Yes. No, let's wait on that. Get me a status report on the snipers. And get the SWAT team commanders over here. I want that sonofabitch out of there, dead or alive, and I want to be home in time to watch it on the six o'clock news." He turned and walked toward his car. The watch captain summoned his lieutenant to pass the word.

I walked a little closer to the building and stared at the open front. I couldn't see Charlie Patton. I've been here before, surrounded by too many people with too many guns, all too ready to eliminate the manifestation of our real problems. We are all addicted to the quick solution. And it rarely works.

"I'm going in," Alexis said from my side. Scared me. I hadn't heard her walk up, and that isn't like me.

"Good. Tell Ivan that I'll call in a story if this gets too close to deadline."

"Hawkins, I didn't mean that I'm going back to the office. I'm going in there and trade myself for one of his hostages."

"You've been watching too many movies."

"I'm going." She took a step and I grabbed her arm. "Alexis, listen to me! Don't fuck with this guy." I lowered my voice and took the hard edge out of my tone. "He'll waste you before you can make an offer. You can't get close enough to even call his name. If he hears you, everyone out here will hear you and you can kiss it good-bye.

"If he doesn't hear you, you're gonna look like a well-dressed tomato strainer."

"*Tsk!* He wouldn't dare shoot a woman, especially a woman reporter who might be able to help him."

I looked at her in disbelief. She sounded as though she had talked herself into believing that being a female reporter was more than adequate compensation for a lack of good sense, and my first thought was of Marybeth. As different as they were in most respects, they shared a simple-minded view of reality that would rival my vision of Valley Girls.

If I want it, I was meant to have it.

I pictured her striding into the building like some latter-day Katharine Hepburn, certain that her destiny was on the front page. I wanted to laugh but this wasn't the time for me to bait her. She was set on doing something that I was certain she'd be lucky to survive with regret.

She was about to walk away when we both saw Ferris closing in on us. "Alexis," I said as Ferris joined us, "you better check your caulking. Your brains are seeping into your bowels."

"That's a disgusting thing to say," she snapped.

"Hawkins," Ferris announced, "Ivan wants you back in the office, *immediately*."

"Now, *that's* a disgusting thing to say."

"I'm just delivering the message."

"And a job well done. But I think I'll wait until little Miss Stoutheart here slips into her John Wayne costume and gets her ass shot off. After that, Ivan should be overjoyed to have me at the scene."

Ferris looked from me to Alexis, frowning. "Hey, girl, what's honky boy talking about?"

"I'm going in and trade myself for a hostage. I'm going after an exclusive."

"You do that, while I call Ivan and dictate your obit." I left them and went to the phone, raising my eyes in prayerful thanksgiving when I saw that it was free for the third time. If the rest of my luck was as good, I'd have a page one byline tomorrow. Of course, nobody reads the paper on Christmas Day. And, if the truth were told, I'd probably be lucky if I still had a job. Forget about bylines.

Ah, what the fuck, I thought. This is the first real run-in I've had with Ivan since Pulaski. We've butted heads a few times, but nothing worth a good rage.

It took a minute for Ivan to get on the phone. I told him everything was still at a standoff, and that I had a great idea that would let us both off the hook. "Let me do a feature, or sidebar, or whatever you want to call it, on overkill. Reichmann has enough firepower out here to put down a rebellion. And the chopper the cops sent is painted like Santa's, with a fuckin' reindeer on the nose. It's great."

"Have you seen Ferris?"

"Yeah, he's here. You want to talk to him?"

"I want *you* to talk to him. I gave him a message to deliver."

"Yeah, yeah. I know. Five minutes or you're fired. Write a sidebar on fucked-up vets. Forget it. No one knows if this guy's ever been further east than the Jersey Shore for Chrissake. Have you thought about that?"

"Listen, Hawkins, *I'm* the city editor and—"

"Holy shit!" I yelled into the phone.

"What? What?"

"The fuckin' little space cadet's going in."

"Who? Hawkins, goddamn it!"

"Alexis!" I bolted after her. "*Alexis!*"

She marched on, and no one seemed to notice. She was two-thirds of the way to the door when Patton popped up from behind the counter.

"Hit the deck, dummy!"

My voice and the slugs arrived at about the same instant. He sprayed the ground around her with at least a dozen rounds. One round, probably a ricochet, clipped the heel from her right boot. Another one grazed her knee. She was dumped on her ass without ceremony. And Patton disappeared behind the counter.

"Oh, my God, I'm shot," she wailed.

I was running low, trying to keep my balance on the icy crust. I grabbed the collar of her coat and dragged her fifteen or twenty feet to a piece of stone sculpture. Once we were there I pulled her behind the base and sat down heavily, momentarily exhausted.

"I can't believe he shot me," she cried. "He tried to kill me." It must have been the first time she'd ever confronted the possibility that she wasn't the center of the known universe and, indeed, was nothing more than another mortal being in a dangerous world. Being a female reporter didn't offer any real protection after all. She seemed somewhat astonished by the realization. Or maybe she really was astounded that someone, anyone, would actually shoot at her. With live ammo and intent to inflict grievous bodily harm.

It *is* a little unnerving the first few times it happens.

I was busy giving her a quick once-over when it occurred to me that I probably looked as though I was feeling her up. I laughed at the thought and she slapped at my hands.

"Relax. I was checking for wounds. You're okay. You've got a flesh wound on your knee, and you're missing one boot heel."

She looked down and saw the blood on my hand. "My God, I'm bleeding."

"Purple Heart and a Band-Aid. The fuckin' tetanus shot will hurt worse."

Two medics, the watch captain, at least ten cops, and a lot of our brothers in alarm surrounded Alexis, jabbering like the proverbial flock of magpies. Ferris drifted over, as though one of his co-workers being shot was an everyday event, nothing worth a hurried step.

"That was your big chance to say 'I told you so,' " Ferris said. "And you chose to pull her ass out of the fire. Why is that, Jamie-boy?"

"It was in the script." Over Ferris's shoulder I saw two cops talking to the watch captain, and all three of them casting glances in our direction. "Cover for me. I'm going to call Ivan."

From the phone, I watched Alexis being loaded on the gurney, chattering all the time with reporters, looking into the cameras when directed, waving to her fans. They pushed the gurney toward the ambulance, and all the TV cameras followed, all of them shooting exactly the same mindless footage. "Local news reporter shot by gunman under siege at Quaker Plaza . . . film at six."

They haven't had film for ten years, or close to it, but saying "video at eleven" or "pictures at six" doesn't have the same sound of importance. And *sounding* important is the bedrock of TV news.

— — — —

"You're fired," Ivan yelled into the phone.

"Yeah, yeah, yeah. I know. Disrespectful, disagreeable, and occasionally disgraceful. Not to mention full of bad attitude. Listen, Alexis is on her way to the hospital with a flesh wound."

"What happened?" Ivan shrieked. He was about to lose it, and I probably wasn't the most helpful element in his life at the moment.

"She tried to walk into the Tourist Center and the gunman sprayed a few rounds at her.

"Now, you still want me off the staff, or would you rather wait until this shit is wrapped?"

"Which hospital!?"

"I don't know, Ivan. I don't give a shit. What do you want me to do now?"

After a long silence, Ivan said, "Call the story in if it's not wrapped before five o'clock. And I'd like to have a sidebar written by you on her heroic attempt to resolve the standoff. We can go with that as late as the third edition."

"Whatever you say." Grinning, I hung up. The phone's bell jingled once as I slammed the receiver down.

"Round three. Racing from the sidelines to replace a fallen comrade, Jamie Hawkins leads the *Call* troops to victory," Ferris said from behind me. "I didn't hear you mention bad work habits in that tidy summary. I'd give you a five-point penalty for that."

"He wants me to write another sidebar, about Alexis's 'heroic attempt to resolve the standoff.' Quote, unquote." I started walking back toward what passed for the command center.

"Too bad Ivan's afraid of blood. Otherwise he could spend the night licking her wounds instead of her feet, or whatever it is submissives do under the cover of night."

"You've got a little bit of dirt on everyone, don't you?"

"I am the Mayor of Nightside."

"I thought you were the Prince of Darkness."

"Fuckin' Sammy. He likes to be poetic. Anyway, I'm their protector, *and* the shop steward. It pays for me to know who's doing what to who."

"Whom," I said automatically.

"Them, too." He looked at the milling crowd. "She had a good idea, y'know. But the execution was all wrong."

I stopped dead in my tracks. "What good idea? Going in there and trading places with the hostages?"

"One hellava story, hey? You and me?"

"You want to get your ass shot off? That guy's not fuckin' around."

He dropped his arm over my shoulder and started walking away from the crowd. "Listen, Hawk, you're a better writer right now than I'll be in twenty years if I practice every day. You got the gift. All I've got is the basic J-school jive education that begins and ends with the five Ws. And better manners."

"Why does this feel like a shuck?"

" 'Cause you don't trust *nobody*. And I do mean nobody." He stopped walking. We'd ended up back at the phone.

"The First Law of Hawkins," I said. "Love many, trust few, and always cut the cards." I slid out from under his arm. "So cut the crap, and tell me what weird shit you've got in mind."

"We go in and bring that guy out, under our protection, so Reichmann's Special Weapons and Tactics teams don't *swat* the poor bastard. He's got to have a story, right? Shit, even lunatics like to be home for Christmas. This guy's got to be desperate."

"Damn sure he's desperate, but I'm not. I wouldn't try to walk in there on a bet." As I recall, that was the moment when I first came face to face with the Big Idea. The kind of inspired madness that later, usually after it's too late to change course, leads to the question "Whose big idea was this, anyway?"

I called information for the number of the Tourist Center, dialed it, and got one of those nasal computer voices that informed me the number had been temporarily disconnected.

"Disconnect," I shouted over the roar of the helicopter, which was making low passes over the crowd. "You think Reichmann's gonna send in a SWAT team?"

Ferris surveyed the activity. "Not yet. None of the TV cameramen are moving." He grabbed the receiver and punched 0 on the dial. "Operator, this is Deputy Chief of Police Francis X. Fisher. Connect me to your chief operator immediately, please."

A few seconds later he said, "Chief Operator McCall, this is Deputy Chief of Police Francis X. Fisher. I'm at the scene of the hostage taking. My apologies for shouting, but as you can hear, one of our Special Weapons and Tactics choppers is in the area." He paused.

"Thank you for your concern. Now, I want you to open one line into the Tourist Center. ASAP. Lives are at stake, and one of the hostage negotiators suggested we try to talk to the gunman. How soon can you reconnect?" He winced.

"As quickly as possible, and call me at this number." He read it off the pay phone. "I'll be standing by."

He hung up with a sigh. "Ten minutes, probably. I don't know if we've got that much time."

"You try to get in there without his permission and I'll guarantee you won't last ten seconds. You look too much like a cop."

"Fuck you, cops don't wear suits like this."

"Well, *excuse me*. But I'd bet the distinction goes right over that guy's head."

The disconnect left me disappointed. And relieved. I hate that. It's as if I don't know what the hell I want. And that may be true, but this wasn't the time for indecision. I was also nervous, afraid the phone would ring and afraid it wouldn't.

I moved off a few feet and watched a group of black kids behind the police baricades, ten of them on skates and skateboards, whirling and prancing to music blaring from a pair of boom boxes that two of them carried on their shoulders. All of them could skate well, and a couple of them could have made the Olympics if all it took was talent.

"Let's say we do get inside," I yelled back to Ferris, who was bopping in place to the music and smiling. "What happens then? We just sit there interviewing him until the cops break in?" The idea seemed more and more ridiculous as the minutes ticked by.

That's when the phone rang. Scared the hell out of me. Ferris grabbed it and I heard him say, "Thank you very much," as I walked up. "Ring that number, please." He winked at me as he covered the phone.

"He's a brother, so I got a better chance of talkin' him into a face-to-face meeting. I get us in, you get his story, we walk him out, I give you the other information I already picked up, you write the story, and we share a byline."

No shit, here we go.

"Thank you," Ferris said to the operator. "Now, please clear the line. We can't afford to antagonize this man and if he hears anything that makes him think someone is listening in . . ." He was grinning.

"It's ringing," he said to me. Then he inhaled and started his rap. "Hello, who's speaking, please?" Pause. "Okay, Mrs. Washington, listen carefully. Tell the gunman, Mr. Patton, that Leon Ferris and Jamie Hawkins, newspaper reporters for the *Philadelphia Call*, want to help him. And we'd like to start by talking to him on the phone."

Ferris shifted from one foot to the other while he waited. The grin was gone and he looked totally serious.

"Mr. Patton, this is Leon Ferris of the *Call*. Listen, man, you have got yourself one hellava big audience out here, but most of 'em are cops, including two SWAT teams, you dig? Yo' ass be jammed between a rock and a hard place, and it ain't gonna be long till they start pushin' from both sides." Pause. "Yeah, I can dig it, but the mayor's in San Juan, it's Christmas Eve, and Reichmann's lookin' for blood. He don't give a shit 'bout them hostages. They just loose change and this is a high-stakes game.

"But I got my buddy here, he's one hellava writer, and we got a plan that'll get you out alive, get your story told, and maybe stir up some sympathy for you. Right now, with just one side of the story bein' told, you got pretty much the whole city of Philadelphia pissed off. They think you're just another whacked-out junkie or a terrorist. That ain't gonna help you, and if we don't get you out of there you ain't gonna live long enough to tell anybody anything different. Dig it?

"So, why don't you let me and my buddy in, tell us what this is about, and we'll walk you out between us. Cops ain't gonna shoot no reporters in front of all the TV cameras. Whatta y'say?"

Ferris was quiet for maybe fifteen or twenty seconds. Then he said, "Shit, you still got the gun. If you don't like what you see you can always shoot us."

I turned away and looked up at the skyline, wondering if numb-nuts had just signed our goddamn death warrant.

"Okay," Ferris said. "Look for us. I got on a gray suit, black overcoat, and I'll be the lead man. My buddy's wearin' jeans, sneakers, and a sheepskin coat. He looks like a fuckin' narc with sunglasses, but he's cool.

"It may take a few minutes, so sit tight and stay low. There's at least ten snipers around the area." He hung up and looked at me.

"You ever been in a firefight, Ferris?"

"Nope. I managed to stay out of 'Nam."

"You won't like it."

"Ain't gonna be no gunfire. He might shoot one of us, if we didn't have an invitation, but the cops won't. They hate us, but they won't shoot us, least not out in the open."

The chopper flew over us just as I was about to tell him it wasn't a great idea to suggest to anyone that the easy solution to not liking us was to open fire. The sound of the chopper churned up a lot of memories and my heart turned to ice. This was 'Nam, with spectators.

"Did you know that a few hundred of the so-called upper crust of Washington took picnic lunches to the First Battle of Bull Run?" He just looked at me. "Forget it. How do we get in there? We need something to distract our audience."

"How much cash you carrying?"

"Probably three or four hundred. I was planning to buy a couple of presents."

"Give me what you've got."

I pulled a wad of bills out of my pocket and counted off six fifties, four twenties, a ten, and three ones. I put the ten and the ones back in my pocket. "Three hundred and eighty bucks."

He plucked it from my hand, withdrew his own money, and counted one hundred and eight dollars. "That should do it. We'll get it back after we get this story. Promise."

"Who or what do you plan to buy?"

"Just hang loose while I do some business."

I watched him circle the crowd, which was close to five hundred people; he was cruising through the outer edges. A couple of minutes passed. I looked from Ferris to what I could see of Reichmann's inner circle, back to Ferris, and he had one of the skaters in a huddle. Another one joined them, and then another. Money changed hands. Ferris came back.

"Okay. We are now official sponsors of the Quaker Plaza Community Skate

Club, whose members have agreed to perform for this festive holiday crowd gathered here. When everyone's busy looking at them, we go in. Just like Woodward and Bernstein."

"More like Smith and Murdoch would be my guess."

The leader of the skate squad blew a couple of sharp bursts through a whistle suspended from his neck and all ten of them came into the DMZ from different points.

"Who the fuck are Smith and Murdoch?" he asked as he took my arm and led me into the chaos.

"The captain and the first officer of the Titanic."

Laughing, he let go of my arm. "You are one cheerful sonofabitch."

Two skaters whizzed between us, chased by half a dozen cops. We ducked out of the way. We were dancing a little, anyway, trying to look as though we were part of the posse, not part of the problem. I wondered if we looked more like plainclothes cops or plainclothes lunatics.

My spine was wired directly into that little cranial multiplexer that converts thought to low-voltage electrical impulses, which as I understand it allows us to transmit all kinds of high-voltage shit through our system and react accordingly. Thought is transmitted sort of like an analog signal and directed to the multi-plexer, which converts it to digital impulses and sends it out like laser bursts. The stuff I was getting made my spine contract like a coil spring carrying a heavy load. My whole system was running on afterburner, sucking up adrenaline like I drink shots of tequila. I fully expected to hear gunfire, and unlike Alexis, I wouldn't have been surprised if I took a round or two.

What a dumb-fuck, dumb-ass place to die, I thought.

I was still waiting for something or someone to stop us in our tracks as we crunched through the broken glass and entered the building. Apart from Patton, there were seven people left, all of them on the floor.

Patton peeked out from behind the counter. "Step in here where I can see, an' shuck them coats."

Ferris and I peeled off our coats and waited.

"Raise up them pants legs."

We did, and then we turned a full circle, and then Ferris had to take off his suit jacket and make another turn. Finally, Patton seemed satisfied.

"You two is crazy. What you want?"

"Tell us your story," I said. "We can do more for you than you can do for yourself talking to the mayor, who isn't here anyway."

"Then what?"

"My buddy here says we'll walk you out so the cops don't waste you. We may all get wasted, but it's about the only real chance you've got."

"*You* could be the law for all I know. Jus' cause you ain't holdin' no heat don't mean nothin'. Right?"

"You're right. We could be."

"But we're not," Ferris said. "An' you gonna have to trust somebody or this may be your last Christmas."

"I like yo' style," Patton said to Ferris, "but I got to think about it."

The chopper, which had been making passes back and forth over the roof, came in directly above us and hovered for a few seconds, then moved away. I thought I heard a thump, something being dropped.

"What's your full name?" I asked Patton.

"Patton. Charles Winston Patton, Jr., but my friends call me Charlie."

"Well, Charlie Patton, I'd say you've got maybe five minutes to tell us whatever you want the world to know. Maybe five, maybe less, 'cause I think Reichmann just put a couple of guys on the roof. If you plan to talk to us you better make it quick." I brought out a 3-×-5 spiral notebook and my pen.

— — — —

It took me less than ten minutes to get what I needed to report Charlie Patton's tale. It was the same old story about power and lack of power, bad faith and broken dreams, deceit and despair. It had a beginning, a middle, and an end, all of which I promised him I would write, if and when we managed to get out of the building.

About nine minutes into my interview the chopper came again, and I said to Ferris, "Methinks our time is just about up, Mr. Murdoch."

Patton's grip on the M-16, which he had cradled loosely in his lap, abruptly tightened. He looked at me with hard eyes. "What's that you called him?"

"Who, Ferris? I called him Murdoch. It's a joke. I hope." I also hoped that fucking multiplexer didn't go into the red zone. I'd had about as much of this adrenal rush as my nervous system could handle. "He calls me Smith, I call him Murdoch."

"The captain and the first mate of a ship that sank," Ferris added. "C'mon, let's get these people over here. You people ready to go home?" he asked. The response was unanimous. "Then gather around, and we'll all stand up on my command. Okay, move over . . . C'mon, let's go. We all got better places to be."

They crawled across the room until everyone was huddled in a circle around Patton. I reached for the rifle. "Leave it, Charlie. It's the only way we'll convince them that you've surrendered."

He handed it to me with a sigh. I put it on one of the counter shelves, and looked at Ferris.

Ferris grinned. "Ready, Smith?"

"Ready when you are."

"Everybody up!"

"They're coming out, they're coming out!" Dark's voice boomed through the air, and before I could offer a prayer for our safety to the lunatic gods that arrange these events we were surrounded by the media mob, cops, cameras, and a fucking firestorm of questions from the reporters. I didn't say anything.

Laughing, Ferris kept saying, "No comment, gentlemen. Sorry, no comment at this time." He was having the time of his life. After years of listening to that shit, he could finally give it back.

We'd been steadily moving forward, but everything abruptly came to a halt in front of Reichmann. He didn't look happy to see us.

"Maybe, Mr. Ferris, you've got a comment for me. Maybe you can tell me what the hell you two goddamn smartass hotdogs think you've done."

"Got a hellava story. And maybe saved a life or two."

Reichmann jabbed his finger at Patton and shouted to his watch captain, "Get that scum out of my sight. I want him cuffed, searched, and booked into the Roundhouse."

"He's got a lot to say, Chief. Give 'im a chance to speak."

"Ferris, when I want advice from the media on how to do my job I'll call a press conference and give all of you a chance to talk." He caught the attention of his watch captain.

"Get these hostages checked out. Get their statements. If they need medical help, see they get it. If not, see they get a ride home in a patrol car."

"Yes sir."

"You," Reichmann said, turning his angry gaze on me, "what's your name?"

"Jamie Hawkins. I'm with the *Call*."

"No shit. How long have you been on the staff, Hawkins?"

"Two months and a week, give or take a few hours."

"Well, Mr. Hawkins, that's time enough for you to have figured out that I don't put up with a lot of bullshit from the media, and more than enough time to realize that I don't like reporters screwing up a police operation. Wouldn't you agree?"

I nodded.

"*Speak up, Mr. Hawkins!*" He was livid. "Or I can have your ass in the lock-up with that fuckin' terrorist from now 'til the Christ Child comes to make your bail."

Ferris cracked up, and made no attempt to hide it.

"What the hell's so funny, Ferris?"

"This has not been Jamie's day. Ol' Ivan the Terrible is pacing up and down the city room, waiting to tear another hole in my buddy's ass, and now you want to lock him up. If you bust Jamie, Ivan will have his bail ticket paid before the photographer finishes the head shots. I think Ivan's intent on serious conversation with my man. Hawk may not even have a job after the last edition goes to bed."

Reichmann looked from Ferris to me. His expression would have curdled frozen yogurt. "Get the fuck out of here, both of you." He shifted his gaze back to me. "And don't let me see you around town if you don't have a job." He spun around and stomped away.

Ferris and I looked at each other, both of us grinning. Dark came up with Sammy the copyboy.

"You guys want a ride? Ivan sent me over to pick you up."

"I guess I better go write a story. I need the money."

■— ■— ■— ■

The shootout between Ivan and me began when I turned in my second story on Charlie Patton, the story I'd been writing since I'd first seen Patton blow away the parking meter. It was, in the words of Daniel French, a fine piece of writing.

Ivan's praise was faint by comparison. He called it half a ream of subjective drivel, which surprised me. That was a nice turn of phrase and I'd never considered the possibility that Ivan might have a little of the poet in his twisted psyche.

As I stood in front of Ivan's desk with what I hoped would be my last page of copy, I finally admitted to myself that I was exhausted. When Ivan hung up his phone I pushed the pages in front of him.

"What's this?" he asked in the face of the obvious.

"It's slugged 'sidebar' and is, in fact, exactly that."

He pushed it away. "I don't have any more room."

"Then pull something. Jesus, *that's* the story. That who-what-when-where-and-why shit I wrote isn't anything more than our readers will have seen ten times before the ink's dry on the third edition. 'Television news,' excuse the expression, has one advantage we can't overcome. It's already being seen while the page-make-up editor is still trying to figure out if he should move the bra ad away from the story on breast cancer."

Ivan picked up the pages and glanced at the first paragraph. Unless he was speed reading, he was shaking his head no, no, no before he finished the third sentence.

"I don't see anything here that would further inform or be of interest to many of our readers."

I blew up. "How the fuck would you know?!" I bellowed. "You didn't even finish the first fuckin' page."

Ivan came out of his seat like a tracer round, his face flushed with anger. "I've had enough of your insolence, Hawkins." He charged from behind his desk, a knight riding out to repel the heathen threat. "Come with me."

He stormed off the riser and as he hit the floor where lesser mortals tread, he yelled, "Ferris. Over here."

Ferris and I followed Ivan, making faces at each other like a pair of five-year-olds. As we approached French's door I whispered to Ferris, "You better make damn sure I get my expense money if I'm fired tonight."

"If you're *not* fired you should give that money to the Church of St. Jude, 'cause you are *the* most hopeless cause I've seen in a long time."

"Thanks. Let's get a drink after we finish this song and dance."

"We're both broke, remember?"

"I've got credit."

Ivan was standing at the corner of French's desk, tapping his foot, when Ferris and I entered. I looked up from his foot to his face, which was filled with outrage, to French.

Daniel French looks like someone Norman Rockwell would have created. The country doctor or the small-town editor. Except I've never cared for Rockwell's peculiar handling of colors. French looked a lot healthier than Uncle Norman's characters. He had a round face, blue eyes, a small mouth, an adequate nose, crow's-feet, and a pleasant manner. Although his hair was gray, I could easily picture him with a blonde granddaughter, three or four years old, bouncing on his knee.

"Daniel, I trust you remember Mr. Hawkins . . ."

"Indeed." He smiled at me. "You did a fine job with that hostage situation." He shifted his attention back to Ivan. "Is there a problem, Ivan?"

"Several problems, not the least of which is Mr. Hawkins's attitude. He often ignores specific instructions, he's insubordinate, and he routinely displays contempt for any and all authority."

French turned his gaze from Ivan to me. "Jamie, can you explain?"

"I believe so. What Ivan's trying to say is that I wouldn't give up my story to Alexis when he sent her over to the plaza. He has difficulty with simple sentences and conversational English but we're all working with him."

"I strongly recommend terminating Mr. Hawkins's employment, forthwith."

"That means he wants to fire me in the next sixty seconds."

"I got that," French said. He looked beyond me to Ferris, who was leaning against the doorframe. "And Ferris," he said to Ivan, "is he involved in this disagreement?"

"I brought him along to verify my charges against Mr. Hawkins. Several times today, Mr. Hawkins refused my specific instructions to return to the city room. I even sent Ferris to the location with a follow-up directive, which Mr. Hawkins ignored."

French frowned slightly and scratched the back of his head as he spoke. "Ivan, it's a little unusual for the deacon to plead his case and ask the Devil to back his hand."

"Ivan's like God," Ferris said. "He works in truly mysterious ways and no one understands him."

"I've had enough insults, Mr. Ferris."

I looked away, trying not to laugh. French laughed without sound. I saw his stomach jump.

"Jamie was the one who got us into the place."

"I don't need to ask who procured the disco skaters. How much is that going to cost us?"

"You mean how much did I donate to the Quaker Plaza Community Skate Club?" Ferris said. "Five hundred dollars for ten performers."

"That seems a reasonable price for an exclusive."

"Daniel," Ivan snapped, "I cannot and will not work with Mr. Hawkins on my staff. If you won't authorize termination of his employment I will insist that he be transferred to the nightside staff. Immediately."

French's focus shifted from Ivan to Ferris to me, then back to Ivan. "Thank you, gentlemen. Ivan, if you and Leon will leave us alone, I'd like to discuss this with Mr. Hawkins."

"I'm leaving for home," Ivan said. "Have a merry Christmas." He was out the door before anyone could reply.

I turned to Ferris. " 'Have a merry Christmas'?" I glanced from Ferris to French. "I have to fight with the sonofabitch for my ordained right to cover my story"—I turned my eyes back to Ferris—"we give him a fuckin' exclusive"—back to French—"he thanks me by trying to have me fired"—I looked straight ahead, at the wall—"and then he says 'Have a merry Christmas' on his way out the door?" I looked from French to Ferris to French. "Doesn't he know I'm Jewish?"

I thought Ferris would piss in his pants. He laughed so hard he had to leave the room, which he'd been asked to do, anyway.

I closed the door and turned around, not sure what French would have to say. He was sitting with his forehead resting on the palm of his right hand, elbow on his desk, laughing quietly as he shook his head. At that moment I knew I had the advantage because I knew the thought running through his mind:

What the fuck am I going to do with this one?

"So, am I fired or can I go home to the hearth and kids?"

Sighing, he leaned back in his chair, a huge old leather relic scuffed and stained from years of use. "This is one of those times," he said after a long pause, "when I wish I smoked a pipe. I've seen men faced with difficult decisions kill five minutes fiddling with their pipe and tobacco. I tried one a couple of times but I really dislike the taste. And it burns my tongue."

"Life's a bitch. May I sit down? I'm beat."

"Please. I didn't mean to be ill-mannered." He leaned forward with both arms on his desk, and a slight, very slight, smile played around the corners of his mouth.

"I tried a pipe a couple of times," I said, "but I couldn't keep the damn thing lit."

"Perhaps that had something to do with the substance you were smoking," he replied, doodling on a pad he had retrieved from the corner of his desk. The desktop was pitifully neat.

"It was dry cornsilk, if you want to know. And you may be right about the substance being part of the problem."

"You did a damn good job today, from all I've heard. The reviews weren't unaminous in their praise, but you got three out of four."

"Well, a hung jury is better than a hanging jury. I guess."

"It is, but it does leave me in something of a bind. Ivan is outraged."

"Ivan made the wrong calls from the beginning. He wanted me to give the story to Alexis and come back here to write a sidebar on the so-called Vietnam syndrome. Charlie Patton was never in Vietnam. He did six years in the army, two at Fort Knox, four in Germany."

"That's not in your story."

"The story you read wasn't the only one I wrote. The real story of Charlie Patton is on Ivan's spike."

"I'll give it a look before I leave." He added a couple of strokes to whatever he was drawing, then looked at me. "The way I see it, I'm left with very limited options. Either I fire you, or I shift you to nightside to keep you away from Ivan."

"Tough choice, but you left out the possibilities of shifting Ivan to the society page or firing him. I know I'd be willing to chip in for a going-away present."

"The problem with that is I need Ivan more than I need you. Or, perhaps I should say, the *Call* needs Ivan more than it needs you."

I stood up.

"Sit down, please."

"I don't want to keep you from your family," I said, but I sat down.

"There's only my wife, and she's used to me being late." He put the pencil down and leaned back. "If we're lucky, you will bring us one or two good stories in a month, a great one maybe once every three months, and I'll be lucky if I can print fifty percent of them.

"Ivan, on the other hand, is constant. Not nearly as bright as he has let his wife, and probably his mother, convince him that he is, but his intelligence is adequate to the job. His personality leaves something to be desired, but a city room isn't a place to hold popularity contests. He's tough, he's more fair than you would give him credit for being, and he's *there*. Five days a week, six days a week . . . whatever I need, whenever I need it, Ivan's there, on the job."

"Sounds like my kinda guy. I don't see how I could have misjudged him so terribly."

"He's *not* your kinda guy," French said with a smile. He was not going to let me push his buttons. "He's not even my kinda guy if I want to go drinking, or go to Veterans Stadium to watch the Eagles lose another game. But he's my city editor."

"And I'm your problem."

"No, you're Ivan's problem, and one of the very few I've seen defeat him."

"I can't say that I see how I defeated Ivan."

"Well, that's not really important. What's important is what happens next. I'm not going to fire you, but I've got to get you out of Ivan's domain."

"Ah yes, I see the horns of a dilemma lurking here."

"But there is a way around those horns."

"You know, working for Ivan, ninety percent of what I do is obits and rewrites of PR bullshit. Why not wire a computer terminal into my apartment, let Sammy drop off the press releases, and I'll work at home. Put in a special telephone line: 976-OBIT. I can send them to the desk on a modem."

"That would be a little too much like a transfer to the Riviera. What I had in mind might be more analogous to the Russian front."

"Nightside."

He picked up the pencil and added something to the sketch. "When I was a young man working as a general-assignment reporter I rather enjoyed night-side."

"Well, let's just trade jobs."

"I'll give it some thought. But in the meantime, what will you choose?"

"Suppose I work for you? You and I come up with story ideas, I write, you edit, and Ivan is off the hook."

"That would create more problems than it would solve—for me, anyway.

"Jamie, I would hate to lose you, but . . ." He made a face. "As soon as it's feasible to make you a columnist, if that's what you want, and if you're still around, I'll do it. But in the meantime . . ."

"The Russian front." I stood up. "Merry Christmas. And thanks for not firing me. It's too fuckin' cold to be unemployed and I'm too tired to go on the road again."

He was happy enough with my decision. He smiled as he signed his name to the sketch, pulled it out of the pad and handed it to me. "And a Happy Chanukah, Rabbi."

He had titled it Casimir Hawkins at the Battle of Quaker Plaza. There I was, astride something that looked like that strange beast Don Quixote rode. Rosinante, as I recall. I was dressed in jeans, sneakers, a bomber jacket, and a Russian-style fur hat. A large Star of David hung from a chain around my neck. The 'horns' of my dilemma were protruding from the forehead of the horse and I was looking down through the horns at an 'authority figure' which I had impaled on a spear styled like an old fashioned pen.

"This is hysterical," I said, laughing. "You draw really well. Do you do editorial cartoons?"

"Not any more. Now I draw for fun."

"Thanks. It's great. And it's late. I'm going home." As I reached the door I remembered the story Ivan had spiked. "Will you read my sidebar on Charlie Patton? I made him a promise and I'd like to keep it."

"I'll read it because I enjoy your writing. Whether your promise is kept or not depends on a lot of things."

"At least you'll give it a fair reading. That's more than I got from Ivan. Good night."

— — — —

The lobby clock read 9:11 as I stepped out of the elevator. That's about right for this day, I thought. 9–1–1. Help. It was snowing, if just barely. The same kind of slushy wet stuff that had been falling at the plaza. None of it had stuck.

I pulled up my coat collar and looked around for a cab. Not at nine-fifteen on Christmas Eve, at least not around this neighborhood. It was a long walk to Twenty-first Street, but I didn't have anything else to do. Nowhere to go, no one to see. Sheila was in Allentown to spend Christmas with her parents. She had tried, several times, to talk me into making the trip Christmas morning. She even offered to take a bus and leave her car for me. Cars were a touchy subject with us, since I still had Juliet's Jag, which I rarely drove, and never when I intended to meet Ms. Wolinski.

I hadn't seen Juliet since the night we fucked. She hadn't called, and I didn't call her. She did send me an occasional post card, from Hawaii, from New Zealand, from Sydney, and one from somewhere else. Singapore, I think. The "matter of some urgency" upon which she had been called away evidently was scattered over half the globe.

The day after my fight with Sheila about Juliet, I piled my meager possessions into the Jag and drove to the Twenty-first Street apartment thinking I'd dump my knapsack, typewriter, and assorted junk, then buy the barest of bare necessities and camp out until I decided where to go next. I even considered the possibility of hanging around until I was evicted, working on my novel. Six weeks, two months . . . who knew how long it would take for the landlord to get me out?

When I arrived at the apartment I walked straight into what must have been Juliet's image of how I would live if I had a sense of belonging and a desire to own furniture. She did a pretty good job, all in all. The furniture was a clean design, moderately expensive, no more and no less than what the room needed. A sofa covered in a heavy cotton fabric that was mostly the color of sand with a few cobalt-blue highlights. A recliner, covered in the same cotton as the sofa. Rattan-and-glass coffee table, end tables, and an étagère. A cotton rug. Two lamps. A vase with dried flowers. A couple of harmless Oriental prints on the wall.

In one corner there was a black lacquer table and two chairs set with two place settings, flatware, glasses, and napkins on place mats. Here, too, she had an Oriental print that complemented the others.

Upstairs was a platform bed and triple dresser in teak, or teak veneer. If it was veneer it was done exceptionally well. There wasn't room for anything else.

In the narrow room with the floor-to-ceiling windows she had installed a small desk, a comfortable chair in which to work, two bookcases, and another large leather chair in which to read or watch the nineteen-inch NEC color TV with remote control and VCR that sat atop a teak stereo cabinet.

She had also had a telephone installed, utilities connected, and the windows washed.

My first thought, as I stepped through the door for the first time, was that I had fucked up, misunderstood the message, and this place had been rented to someone else. I called "hello" a couple of times, then ventured a little further into the room, leaving the hall door open. Something was missing, and it took me a second to realize that there was absolutely no clutter visible. No living being can inhabit a place without *some* clutter. Then I noticed that the shelves of the étagère were empty. I closed the hall door and stood just inside, amazed, wondering what went on in her mind while she was doing all of this. Or maybe she had had it done. Here's a check for ten thousand and a list of his personality disorders. Do your best, and keep the change.

After I parked the Jag and came back I found cheese, fruit, and half-and-half in the refrigerator. Two kinds of crackers, a box of Frosted Flakes, coffee, and sugar in a cabinet, and on the kitchen counter a bottle of Conmemorativo with two shot glasses.

I found her note the next day. It was on the pillow, and I had fallen asleep on the sofa so I never got into bed the first night. I can sleep anywhere, and it isn't unusual for me to sleep on the floor once or twice a week.

Oct. 18
Jamie,
    This is all yours for as long as you're here. Rearrange it, add to it, do as you like, but enjoy the comfort for a change. It won't hurt you. Nor will I.

    J.

━ ━ ━ ━

. . . At Broad and Chestnut I waved off a cruising cab that slowed while the driver gave me a look. The cold air and the long walk seemed like a fitting end to a long cold day. I was filled with sadness, part of which was for Charlie Patton and part of which was for me. Thinking about the note, and Juliet, it was clear even to me that I missed her. The fact that she and I were still far from being in the same game didn't affect my lust for her physically, or my fondness for her company when we weren't battling each other.

I felt sadness for Sheila, too. She'd gone from the *Joy of Sex* to "Over the Rainbow."

After our fight about the Jag, I'd waited a few days to call, and when I did she seemed delighted to hear from me. She'd called the Ramada, she said, only to be told that I had checked out. She knew about the Pulaski Day story, so she assumed at first that I'd been fired and left town. Then she saw Ferris at the Cock'n'Bull and he told her I was still working, so she leaped to the conclusion that I'd moved in with Juliet.

That I hadn't was reason enough to return me to her good graces. I invited her over, thinking the sooner the better. Let's get this bullshit finished, one way or the other.

The moment I opened the door I knew the problems had just begun. She was in love with me. It showed in her eyes, which lacked the good-humored sparkle and wit I had found so appealing that first night. And she had that look of emotional uncertainty that takes root in one-sided love and calves separated from their mothers. In less than a week she had changed the nature of her relationship with me, and what she wanted now was to see if I would go along with the change.

I was not happy with what I saw, and I knew that the only possibility of anything being resolved depended on my willingness to free us both from whatever projections she was using to flesh out the fantasy.

She kissed me as though we hadn't seen each other for a month, and as I held her, hugging her, stalling, she whispered, "Please don't be upset with me about the other night. I was afraid of losing you to her. I won't make problems for you, I promise. And I won't cry if you want to yell at me."

Suppose, I had wondered, just suppose I said very quietly, "Get the fuck out of my life." Would you? Would you go quietly? Or would you cry, and plead for 'one more chance,' and call me five times an hour until I finally said we can talk, and then would you cry instead of talking?

I didn't ask, nor did I tell her to go.

I found myself wishing that I had, and happy that I hadn't. In the two months that had passed since that night we had had some good times. We also had had some ridiculously emotional moments, angry confrontations, futile attempts at compromise, and incredibly consuming sex. Fight and fuck. She was using sex as a weapon. Lucky for me, I heal quickly.

With my thoughts on Sheila I slipped on the icy steps that lead to the entry of my apartment. I tried to catch my balance, and in the process I turned about ninety degrees and ended up being slammed into the hard edge of brick on my right side. The fall knocked the wind out of me and pain turned everything in sight to a splash of bright red.

"God-*damn!*" I moaned, gasping for air. Three or four minutes passed before I managed to sit up by pulling on the railing. A middle-aged couple passed and I glanced up. The man eyed me with suspicion. The woman chirped, "Merry Christmas."

Eventually, the pain from the cold exceeded the pain of moving. I forced myself into a standing position and limped inside, still hurting, but reasonably sure nothing was broken. Only a fuckin' moron would do that, I said to myself as I poured tequila into a highball glass. I drank a couple of ounces in a single swallow and every nerve ending in my back and right leg lit up like one of those animated neon billboard advertisements. "*Mother*-fucker," I moaned. My last thoughts before I fell asleep were reruns of conversations I'd had with Ferris in the last two months. Bits and pieces of himself and myself lay on the table— answers to questions, and questions unasked. . . . How had he managed to avoid 'Nam? Where did he hope this low-rent version of Woodward and Bernstein would lead? Why hadn't I gone out for a drink with him, rather than coming back here to rummage among the bittersweet memories of a life pissed away? Why couldn't I fall sleep?

The telephone woke me a few minutes after nine o'clock. More asleep than awake, I tried to sit up. The pain that shot through my back and leg gave me a sharp, single focus that probably can best be described as a strong desire to be unconscious.

I managed to crawl to the telephone and answer it on the fifth or sixth ring. Ferris started chattering as soon as I said hello.

"Merry Christmas, Mr. Smith. We made page one."

"Brenda Starr would have made page one with that goddamn story."

"You also made page one in the final edition with that second piece you wrote."

"As Scrooge should have said, 'Who gives a shit?' "

"Is there anything that makes you feel good? Other than the Polish Princess with her head in your lap?"

"I fell on the steps last night, and I'm fuckin' dying. Everything hurts, and I'm too crippled to even stand up long enough to piss. You got any more good news or can I crawl back to my bed?"

"Charlie Patton is dead."

I didn't say anything. What was there to say?

"You hear me, Scrooge?"

"I don't think I'm ready for the details."

"In fifteen minutes or less I'm gonna be pounding on your door. You'd do well to open it."

"I'll do well to have my eyes open in fifteen minutes." I hung up, rested my head on my arm and tried to go back to sleep. The phone rang again.

"Hello . . ."

"Merry Christmas," Sheila said.

"Thanks. How was your trip?"

"Okay. You sound strange. Are you hung over?"

"I just woke up. And Ferris is on his way over so I've got to make some coffee and jump-start my heart before he arrives."

"I'm driving back tomorrow. Are you busy tomorrow night?"

"I'm gonna be busy most nights from here on. I've been transferred to nightside."

"What time will you get off work?"

"I don't know yet. That wasn't part of the discussion."

"Did you have another fight with Ivan?"

"A little disagreement. He was just looking for an excuse." I was dying for a cigarette and a cup of coffee. Wincing and groaning, I pushed myself up on my knees and looked around for my Camels. They weren't close enough to reach.

"Why are you groaning like that? Are you okay?"

"I'm fine. Listen, I've got to go. I'll call you after you're back."

"Okay. My mom's sending you some cookies. She says you're the best-looking guy I've been out with since I left home."

"Hard to believe."

"If it will make you feel better, my dad says you look like a bum."

"My kinda guy. I'll call you in a couple of days. 'Bye."

" 'Bye . . ."

Wonderful. She shows them one underexposed Polaroid and I become the topic of conversation and character assassination, and my potential as a husband is evaluated, tacitly or not. I don't have the patience to cope with that kind of mentality. I don't even understand it.

— — — —

"**A**mong my people," Ferris said as he poured fresh o.j. into the shot glasses, "this is an ancient tribal custom associated with Christmas."

I was sitting on the sofa, watching him as he poured the juice and uncapped the bottle of Conmemorativo. "What tribe is that?" I asked.

"The Negrito Apache."

"Never heard of them."

"You ever hear of a prisoner, supposedly under constant observation, hanging himself with a mattress cover?"

"It's possible. Not bloody likely, but possible."

He sat down and handed me my orange juice. "This is called an Apache sunrise." He upended the bottle of tequila, drank an ounce or so, and chased it with the o.j.

I took the bottle and did as he had done. "If I drink a few more of those I may feel human by sunset."

"Don't be bashful." He refilled the shot glasses with juice and we did it again. "How the hell did you manage to fall on your ass climbing steps? You drunk?"

"I hadn't even had a drink. Thinking about bullshit instead of paying attention to what I was doing."

He filled the shot glasses with tequila and handed one of them to me. "To Charlie Patton, and Charlie Swinburne, who thanked whatever gods there be that no life lives forever, that dead men rise up never, et cetera, et cetera, and so forth."

"Et cetera, et cetera, and so forth?"

"It's a long poem."

"I know the poem. 'The Garden of Proserpine.' But I don't remember reading any et cetera, et cetera in it. Doesn't rhyme."

"Drink."

We drank to Charlie Patton, and I made a face.

"In my tribe, man who drinks and makes face must spend four moons on the copy desk," Ferris announced.

"Christ, you're a lucky charm. First it's the Russian front and now the fuckin' copy desk. Another week with you and I'll be in the basement learning to set type." I stood up, slowly. The tequila made the pain manageable, but the floor tilted slightly. I guess all wonder drugs have some side effects.

"You want some coffee?"

"I want to know what we're gonna do about Charlie Patton."

"Well, I don't see that we have a lot of opportunities to do anything." I corrected for the incline and limped into the kitchen. "Coffee, or not?"

"Yeah, if you can handle it." He followed me into the kitchen. "We promised him that we'd be his voice, that we'd tell his story."

"We did. He's dead. I'm drunk. And life goes on. Whatta you want?"

"Black with sugar."

With a slightly unsteady hand I poured two cups of coffee. "I wonder if it's time for me to move on . . .?"

"You just got here. And where the hell would you go? Back to Mexico? You can't spend your life in Mexico, y'know."

"So it seems. I keep coming back."

"Listen, on nightside you won't have to come in before three in the afternoon. Atlee Hearn is a lot easier to deal with than Ivan. And *I* think Uncle Dan's got big plans for us."

"Atlee the Hun . . ."

"Atilla the Hearn. Get it right."

"Whatever. Our night city editor doesn't have any reason to deal with me any differently than Ivan did. Obits, rewrites, and long hours of abject boredom. I can't handle much more of that."

"You haven't seen the nightside staff in action. You won't be bored with us."

I made my way slowly back to the sofa and lit a cigarette. "So what kind of wishful thinking led you to believe French has something in mind for us? Just because he didn't fire me?"

"Shit, I knew he wasn't goin' to fire you."

"Yeah, right. That's why you said I should give my expense money to St. Jude."

"You *are* fuckin' hopeless, man." He laughed, shaking his head. "And stone by-God strange.

"But that's one of the reasons I think Uncle Dan will give us a different track to run on. He wants to hold onto you, and we *all* know that's gonna take something more than the ordinary routine most of us follow."

"Last night he gave me two choices: nightside or Sayonara City."

"He was bluffing."

"Maybe, but the truth is I've had enough of Ivan and all those drones he has working the desk."

"We noticed. Anyway, you belong on nightside." He stood up. "You want another cup of coffee? I'll pour."

I looked into my cup, surprised to find it almost empty. I couldn't remember drinking it. "Yeah. Please."

From the kitchen Ferris said, "By the way, you've been invited to the twentieth annual Anton-French Christmas Day to-do. I think Daniel wants to talk to us privately. And Sally's parties are a lot more fun than hanging around here like an orphan."

"How would 'Sally,' whoever she is, know I even exist, let alone want to invite me to a party I don't want to go to?"

"Sally is Daniel's wife. Daniel made the invitation, last night after you left. Do you know your phone number isn't in the city desk file?"

"Imagine that. I only gave it to them three times. How do you think Hearn will react to my reassignment?" I asked as Ferris came back with the coffee.

"In some ways he's smarter than Ivan. He won't give you a bad time about wearing sneakers and jeans, or not wearing a tie, or all those fuckin' cigarettes you smoke. He don't give a shit if you put your feet on your desk. That's all petty bullshit to him. And he'll give you more slack with what you write."

"So why was he dubbed Atilla the Hearn?"

"As a joke. He knew we all called Ivan 'Ivan the Terrible,' so we came up with a name for him because he's okay and we didn't want him to feel left out."

"Life as a city room sitcom."

"The party starts at two o'clock. Want me to pick you up?"

"I'm not really interested in going to a company Christmas party. I can barely walk, anyway. And I'm drunk."

"It's not even ten o'clock yet. Listen, go back to sleep, sober up, take a hot shower, and I'll pick you up between three and three-fifteen. We'll be there by four, stay a couple of hours, see what Daniel has in mind."

"Why don't you go and take notes. You can tell me about it later."

"Miss Franklin-Rossini is on the guest list," he said with a sly smile.

"Oh, well, in that case I think you should videotape the fuckin' thing and I'll look at it tonight. Send it over by messenger."

"What's the story with you two?"

"There isn't any story. Where the hell do you come up with your shit?"

"I heard from John, the bartender at the Cock'n'Bull, that you were in there with her right before you started working."

"So . . .?"

"C'mon, Hawk, you've got a guardian angel with some heavy connections. She's supposedly half owner of the *Call*."

I stared at him, trying to decide what, if anything, I should tell him. "There isn't much to tell."

"Tell me how you came to know her?"

"She got me out of jail in Mexico and gave me a job on the *Call*."

"Get outta here. Out of jail? In Mexico? What was she doing in a Mexican jail? Social work?"

"You know, you could make my life even more difficult if you pass this shit around."

"Swear on the blood of my ancient tribal chief, I won't say a word to anyone."

"Thanks, I feel so much better."

He got up and shrugged into his jacket. "By the way, KSAY, the all-news station, otherwise known as Radio Reichmann, is carrying reports that Patton confessed to membership in the covert-action group of the National Front for Radical Action."

"The bomb squad!?" I laughed, the first crack in the gloom since I'd been jarred from sleep. It may have been the shortest laugh of my life. "*Jesus.*"

"You think you maybe broke a couple of ribs?"

"Naw, it doesn't hurt to breathe. But I must have bruises that go all the way through. So where did they get the story?"

Ferris imitated a radio newsreader: "Sources in the Philadelphia police department's intelligence division raised the possibility that Patton, having confessed his membership in the NFRA, killed himself rather than face almost certain retribution at the hands of his fellow terrorists."

"Great copy. Written by the Red Queen and delivered by the White Rabbit."

"A spokesman for the NFRA contacted KSAY all-news radio to deny that Patton would have met with anything but high praise for his heroic actions," Ferris continued. "The terrorist spokesman then charged Philadelphia police with, quote, negligence, end quote, and called upon the director of the City's human rights agency to appoint a special investigator to look into Patton's death."

"The director," I added, "could not be reached for comment. She's on vacation in San Juan."

Ferris opened the door to leave. "Three o'clock."

"Call me when you're ready to leave. If I'm sober and still breathing, maybe I'll go."

"Okay. Later."

— — — —

Daniel and Sally French's house was a two-story, ten-room Tudor, designed and decorated by romantics with money to spend. The stonework, the landscaping, the interior paneling, the bay windows, and the planked wooden floors were as I would have described them if I had "created" the house and grounds for a story I was writing. Except the people about whom I write never seem to live in houses like Sally and Daniel French.

Surrounded by the better part of two acres in Chestnut Hill, it was built, Sally French told me, in 1930.

"Most of the work," she said, "was done by Italian laborers who probably thought Stradivarius was a little slipshod."

What I liked best about the house was what I liked best about Sally French. They both exuded warmth. Sally was a giving soul with an easy smile and a love of life that showed in her blue eyes and her genuine enthusiasm for the joy of living. Sometimes, at totally odd moments and for reasons I've never understood, I am suddenly saturated with joy or filled with contentment. The feelings are completely different, and they are as rare as rain in the Sahara. Maybe rarer, since I really don't know how often it rains there. In my life I've known those feelings maybe eight or ten times, never for more than an hour or so.

Her delight in seeing Ferris was so obvious and unaffected I wished I could slip out of the picture, or beam myself to the bar and pretend I had been there for hours.

"You are in trouble, my friend," she said, looking up at Ferris. She was easily a foot shorter than he, measuring maybe five foot two. "You haven't been here since Thanksgiving, and you haven't called even to say hello."

"I wish I had an excuse," he said as he hugged her.

She gave him a look that said, with good humor, You're full of shit, and we both know it. Then she looked at me, and with a grin that would have bought her anything from emeralds to a bail ticket, she said, "You've got to be Hawkins."

"If you'll consider adopting me," I said, holding out my hand, "I'll be anyone you want me to be, except him. I don't eat much and I'll do the gardening."

She stepped past my hand and gave me a hug, laughing softly. The moan came despite my best effort to keep it bottled up.

She stepped back and gave me a curious look.

"He's one of the walking wounded," Ferris said.

"Were you injured yesterday? Daniel only mentioned Alexis."

"I fell on the steps last night, after work. Nothing broken but I'm bruised a little."

"I need to find you a good woman who'll take care of you," Sally said. "And if that doesn't work I'll speak to Daniel about the adoption."

"I've got enough problems with women as it is." I laughed. And as the words left my mouth I caught sight of Juliet. She had come toward us from an angle that kept her hidden behind Ferris. She smiled and continued walking.

Sally caught the movement of my eyes and cast a quick glance over her shoulder. When she looked back she said, "You have very expensive taste."

"Plus he's rude, and has no respect for authority," Ferris said. "You gonna offer us a drink or do we have to mug a couple of kindhearted strangers?"

"That's Tennessee Williams rewritten for the ghetto," I said. "Don't even think about adopting him."

"The bar is in here," she said, pointing toward the living room, "and this year I hired a bartender." She took us each by the hand. "Come along."

There were at least fifty people in the living room, which was large enough to accommodate the whole lot and still leave lanes for those on the move. At least half of them were seated, on sofas, on chairs, on window seats that overlooked the gardens. I counted seven people, aside from Ferris, whom I knew to say hello to, all of them from the *Call*. Juliet wasn't in sight.

"I heard you almost got yourself fired," Alexis said from behind me.

I turned around, surprised to hear her voice. "Not close enough to call it almost."

"I'm glad you didn't."

That surprised me more than hearing her voice. "Why?"

"I don't know. You're kind of interesting to have around."

"I've heard that about everything from tropical fish to bimbos. How's the knee?"

"Sore." She was wearing a long, flared skirt, which she raised a few inches so I could see the bandage. "You were right about the tetanus shot."

"Did they keep you overnight?"

"No way." She sipped from the glass she was holding. "I never thanked you. Thanks. I owe you one."

"You don't owe me anything."

"You saved my life."

"He never intended to shoot you. If he had, you'd be dead or in the ICU. Believe me. M-16 slugs make an ugly wound. He just wanted to warn you off, and you caught a ricochet."

"Were you ever wounded, in Vietnam?"

I laughed. "Actually, I got hit in just about the same place as you. They gave me a nice white bandage, a Purple Heart, and a ride back to my company."

"I can't believe he would hang himself after what you guys did to get him out of there."

"Ferris and I are having a little trouble with that, too."

"Terrorists should all be shot, on the spot. They put everyone in jeopardy, women, children, babies for God's sake."

Since it was the birthday of the Baby Jesus, I decided my contribution to peace on earth would be my silence. Why argue with a displaced Valley Girl whose little world had been turned on its head? I lifted my glass of eggnog. "Here's to your health."

"And your new assignment," she responded, grinning.

"Well, what's this? Jayne Wayne and Dudley Do-Good? How's the old backside, girl?"

"Fuck off, Ferris. I was wounded in the leg."

"Maybe, but I'll bet that's not where they put the needle."

Alexis finished her drink in a swallow. "I'm going for a refill. See you around, Hawkins."

"You are certainly the ladies' man, aren't you? Ivan would have fucking heart failure if he ever saw her smiling at you like that."

"Well shit, man, take a goddamn Polaroid and send it to him. Let's strike a blow for freedom of the press." I held my glass of eggnog up and wrinkled my nose. "This is a real wussie drink. Speaking of which, where the fuck is Ivan?"

"Working."

"You're kidding. He's in the city room?"

"He may have left by now, but he comes in on Christmas so the Christians can take the day off."

"I'm impressed. 'Course, I've always been a sucker for superficial gestures and meaningless compliments."

"Sally sure took a liking to you."

"I'm a likable guy. Anyway, you don't really want to be the only person in the known universe who might answer yes when God asks if I had any friends in Philadelphia, do you?"

"Who said I like you?"

"You did, about a month ago. Admittedly, you were drunk, so I won't hold you to it."

"I hope not. You already ruined my reputation with the Commissioner of Police and the watch captain of that precinct." He touched my glass with his. "Daniel wants to talk to us in a few minutes. He's in his library, end of the hall where we came in. There's a crest with a lion on the door."

"Where are you going?" I asked as he started to leave.

"To the bathroom, if it's okay with you."

"To quote one of your favorite female reporters, 'Fuck off, Ferris.' "

I looked around the room, wishing I was somewhere else. I was hurting. Alexis was flirting with me. Juliet was avoiding me. And Daniel was in the lion's den, waiting.

It seemed a good time to get serious about my drinking. I asked the bartender to pour two shots of tequila, which I downed one after the other. My ribs stopped hurting, and I felt better. I thanked the bartender, took a beer, and turned to look directly into Juliet's eyes.

"Hi," she said.

"Greetings, Pilgrim. Have you traveled far? Would you like some refreshment? Coffee? Tea? Me?"

"I'll take door number three, please."

"Awww, too bad, Miss Franklin. Door number three opens up a room filled with vile foot-long worms, leeches, and slimy little creatures we can't mention by name."

"You said, 'Coffee, tea, or me.' You didn't mention worms and stuff."

"Yeah, I know. Life's a bitch, and then we get fucked over by a game-show host."

"Do you have any plans for this evening?"

"Nothing other than smoking dope and drinking. Why?"

"I thought I'd invite you to dinner."

"Fine, we'll eat, then I'll go home and smoke dope and drink. I can do that on a full stomach."

"Are you going in to see Daniel? He's waiting."

"Oh, right. Well, let me get my earnest-young-reporter face out of my pocket and be on my way. See you later."

— — — —

"Come in, come in," Daniel said as I pushed open the door to his den. Ferris was already seated near French windows that overlooked a grassy slope studded with chestnut trees. "Take a seat and let's drink a Christmas toast. Leon tells me you're partial to tequila."

"When it's available."

He opened a wood-paneled bar and brought out a bottle of Cuervo. "I only have rocks glasses in here. . . ."

"About half of one of those should do it."

He poured maybe three ounces into the glass, neat, and handed it to me. "Leon, a toast. You two guys did a fine job yesterday."

Ferris extended his glass and French poured it half full of Scotch. "One for the road," Ferris said.

"Are you leaving?" French asked.

"Sooner or later. Meanwhile, I'll take care of the details."

"To a job well done, and the two guys who made it look easy."

We clinked our glasses and drank a little. I was already closer to being drunk than I wanted to be. What I needed was food, not more booze.

"Knowing her as I do, I don't imagine that my wife is going to give us a lot of time to hide in here while her party's going on out there, so let's talk about a story I want the two of you to work on.

"Right after the New Year, the U.S. Department of Justice is going to begin an investigation of the Philadelphia police."

"Anything in particular?" I asked, looking around for an ashtray. I found one on a shelf in the floor-to-ceiling bookcase that covered one wall of the room.

"Civil rights violations, kickbacks, illegal and improper handling of confiscated weapons and explosives, and improper use of federal law-enforcement funds. Among other things."

"It's too bad they weren't around last night. Charlie Patton might still be alive."

"You and Leon seem convinced that they had a hand in the death of Mr. Patton."

"Two hands, actually. Around his neck."

"Would you two be interested in trying to make a case for your suspicion?"

"You've got to be kidding," I said. "How the hell would we ever do that?"

"Entrapment," Ferris responded. "We sell 'em some guns or explosives and photograph the whole thing. Hell, we can videotape it."

"Right." I sipped a little of the tequila. "Two reporters employed by the *Philadelphia Call* were found early this morning floating in the Delaware River. Police suspect foul play."

"You're reporters," French said. "Or you claim to be. Dig out the story with legwork. It's a time-honored tradition."

"Shee-it! The only people who know enough to make a case against the cops, are cops. And probably not more than two or three of them. Without a confession, or an eyewitness, we've got *nada*."

"Make a circumstantial case and let's see what happens when it's printed."

I looked from French to Ferris. I needed a reality check. Are we on the same planet here? Are we both speaking American Standard English? Am I more fried than I thought?

"Ferris, are we talking to the same person who supported Ivan the Chickenhearted's decision to spike my story on the Casimir Pulaski Drum and Bugle Corps?"

"Same guy," Ferris nodded. He swirled the ice in his vodka and sipped. "But maybe's he's gotten more liberal as he's gotten older." He grinned at French. To him it was a joke.

"Gentlemen, if you two will restrain yourselves from speaking of me as though I were elsewhere, and make a serious effort to concentrate instead of sharpening your alleged wit, I would like to talk seriously about making a case, a strong case, that Rudolph Reichmann is unfit to be the Commissioner of Police."

"Why not simply tap the U.S. Attorney's staff and get what we need from them?" I suggested. "Their resources are a lot better than ours. Or mine, at least. I don't know anyone in the police department, any lawyers, or any victims who're still breathing."

"Ferris?"

"The only information they'll give us that they haven't given to everyone else is what they want to see published without attribution. *If* we make the right contact. I think we have to run our own investigation."

I yawned. The tequila, the warmth of the room, and my lack of interest in the investigative process were enough to put me into a coma. Investigative reporting, especially on the scale French envisioned, is too much like working for a living. It's depressing.

"I'm offering you an opportunity to make a name for yourself and a contribution to the improvement of a city about which I care a great deal," French said, directing his comments much more to me than to Ferris. "You could generate enough attention with this one story to ensure you'd never have to look for a job again. The editors will be coming to you."

"They do that now," Ferris piped in. " 'Course, they usually have a complaint, but what the hell?"

"Mr. French, the truth of the matter is I hate being a reporter most of the time. I don't mind calling a dozen people in an afternoon to get what I need for a story I can finish before my shift is over, but this kind of stuff, weeks and weeks of asking questions that no one wants to answer so I can write an article that's as likely to get us into a libel suit as it is to get us in the Sunday editorial section . . . that's not my style."

"Tell me something, Jamie. What do you plan to do with what's left of your career?"

"Write a lot of obits and do a lot of rewrites, probably. Unless you're willing to give me the kind of assignments that allow me to do what I was hired to do."

"Why work for newspapers if you hate being a reporter?"

"It's a living, for a while." I stood up and moved over to the French windows. "I need some air. Is it okay for me to open these?"

French nodded, and Ferris moved so I could step through onto a pebbled path. I left the window open, and I heard Ferris say, "We had tequila for breakfast."

"You don't need to apologize for him. He hasn't done anything wrong. He's obstinate, but that isn't an altogether negative trait, especially in reporters."

I walked down the slope to a rock ledge and sat on one of the boulders that overlooked a small frozen pond surrounded by leafless plum or cherry trees. A koi pool, I guessed. Very Oriental. I wished it was spring.

So, I thought, here I am again, with my ass in the deep freeze, staring at another goddamn fork in the road, without a clue to which route to choose. Hell, I don't even have a clue to where I want to be, other than someplace warm, so how can I choose a route?

Insufficient data. I could hear the phrase, from some old science-fiction TV show. Probably *Star Trek*. In my head it sounded like it did when I first heard it, a slightly speeded-up playback, very nasal. Someone's strange idea of how a computer would or should sound if it could speak. When computers are given voices they're much more apt to sound like the one in *The Andromeda Strain*. Or like HAL. As reassuring as technology allows. That will make them less threatening, and the less threatening they are the more they'll sell. I went from insufficient data to guessing the circumference of the koi pool, trying to remember how you determine the diameter of a circle. Pi times r-squared? And a radius? It was all gibberish.

I tried to recall the image in my geometry book, all those precise little lines intersecting with this and that, and the only image that came to mind was Janis Tanner's legs. I always sat behind her and to her right, and she *always* spent half the class stretching her legs, which were long and perfectly shaped. I don't think I saw more than five percent of the stuff the teacher was scribbling on the blackboard. And the final exam, which I failed, was the last time I had tried to recall the formula.

Ferris and French interrupted my meditations.

"My wife said to tell you that you have exactly five more minutes to contemplate the nature of the universe. After that she's sending out the Anton-French SWAT team, which consists of three yapping poodles who at the moment are locked in the garage."

"It's less the nature of the universe than the error of my ways, but I get the message. You think she might have a can of soup in the kitchen I could heat up?"

Ferris burst out laughing. "Sally has more food set out for this party than three times these people could eat. You ask her for a can of soup and you'll be the chopped meat entrée for the poodles."

We came back into the house through the French windows, which made me smile. It was as though I had a part in some French film comedy. And that thought cracked me up. It *was* a 'French' film comedy, without the cameras and lights. Hell, life is a goddamn comedy. I wish I had a better sense of humor.

— — — —

Ferris and I left the party after Juliet whispered to me that she would stop by the apartment around eight o'clock. Discretion, she informed me, was a vital part of fooling around with the boss. Her sense of humor seemed to have improved with her travels.

Ferris was unusually quiet on the trip back to the city, and when we stopped in front of my apartment he looked troubled. When I opened the door to get out he asked, "So, are we gonna dig up the dirt?"

"You dig," I said, "and I'll spread it around."

"We've got possibilities here, Hawk. French is onto something. He's been in this business for close to forty years and he was the m.e. when I got to the *Call* seven years ago. He's no dummy."

"What's in it for him? He didn't mention that."

"Jesus Christ, he gets the applause at the executive level. Can't you see him standing in front of five hundred editors at a meeting of some newspaper association, describing how he put two reporters onto a trail that started with a terrorist who supposedly committed suicide? We could win a fuckin' Pulitzer and he'd still get the credit with the publishers.

"It's like the manager of some goddamn assembly line who gets two hundred workers to work faster. They do the work, he gets the credit. Right?"

"Maybe, but French isn't Pulitzer or Hearst. He's not a crusader. And if he isn't on a crusade, what's he get out of it?"

Ferris shrugged. "He really does love this city . . ."

"You don't cross swords with somebody like Reichmann because you love the city or you're looking for accolades from five hundred rum-soaked old fucks with blue pencils hanging where their cocks used to be."

"Now that's a goddamn graphic image of our leaders." He laughed despite himself, shaking his head. "You are one mean, suspicious sonofabitch."

"Love many, trust few, and *always* cut the cards. We don't have any leads to anything or anyone, so it's all a moot point for now. This morning you asked me about my connection to Ms. Juliet Franklin-Rossini. Have you ever wondered about the relationship between her and French?"

He shrugged. "She's half owner, right? He works for her."

"The half she owns ain't shit to a swan. Who runs the paper?"

"The city editors, if you mean who makes the wheels go around."

"But who do they answer to? Who do they run to if they think there's the least chance of offending some politician, or activist group, or one of their advertisers?"

"Daniel."

"And to whom does Daniel answer? Juliet or her brother?"

"Brother James. He's the power."

"Think about it," I said as I got out of the car and shut the door.

He stared at me for a few seconds, then drove away.

— — — —

At three minutes past eight I answered the buzzer and opened my door about three inches. A few moments later Juliet was standing on the other side, peeking in, puzzled.

"Hi," she said. All I could see was her face and hair, and a sable coat that cost as much as a cottage in the Poconos.

"Oh be still, my heart. 'Tis Juliet, my sun, looming out of the East."

"Are you going to open the door?"

"I gave at the office."

"So I heard."

"Ah, she speaks, yet she says nothing." I opened the door. "Shake-a-spear bids thee enter."

She came in just far enough to allow me to close the door. When I turned she was so close I could smell the eggnog. We kissed, and then kissed again, and then again. In the midst of the third one I opened her coat and almost came in my jeans. She was wearing pink G-string panties, a matching bra, and a touch of Shalimar between her breasts. That was it.

She slipped her arms around my waist and pulled me toward her. I stopped short of screaming, but only barely.

"Jamie?! What's wrong?"

"God has finally gotten around to punishing me for all my carnal sins."

That threw her. "We haven't done anything, yet."

"Exactly. One of my most constant and erotic fantasies delivers herself to my door, dressed like a slut, and I'm so bruised and beat up I can't even lean over to tie my shoes without pain."

She looked into my eyes with a half-smile playing across her sweet, full lips. "Try kneeling."

— — — —

I awoke to the smell of French roast and Shalimar. The scent of the perfume was in the pillow. The aroma of the coffee wafted up from the kitchen. Juliet was up and about, humming. I was aching. The second day is always the worst.

Well, I thought as I maneuvered myself into a sitting position, at least you've got someone to make the coffee. Too bad she can't pee for me. I could stay here for another hour.

"What's it take to get a cup of coffee in this place?" I yelled as I descended into the living room. "Man could die for lack of caffeine around here."

"If anything could kill you, that probably would be the right approach," she yelled from the kitchen.

As I came out of the bathroom she was standing at the far end of the room, holding two cups of steaming coffee and wearing my Baja T-shirt. It's about the size of a one-man tent and ripped from neck to breastbone.

"Why don't you let me call my doctor, or at least let me take you to a hospital for X rays."

"I've seen doctors work. Most of them do okay with frag wounds and bleeding bullet holes, but when there's nothing to stitch or cut, they're mostly bullshitters with a large overhead to cover." I sat down with a groan. "Nothing's broken, and they don't have anything to cure a bruise." I lit my first Camel of the day and inhaled deeply. I really am an addict.

She handed me my coffee. "You should have been born two hundred years ago."

"Maybe I was." I tasted the coffee, and sighed. She wasn't a stranger to rocket fuel.

"Listen, I can see you as a Russian princess, back when Ivan the Terrible was really Ivan the Terrible. And me as a cavalry officer busted out of the corps.

I'm hanging around the palace and you get me a job as stable hand. Then one day, one of the horses runs away with you only half in the saddle, and I catch up on another horse that no one has ever been able to ride."

"Except Ivan the Terrible was the czar in the fifteen or sixteen hundreds. Have to have been born more than two hundred years ago."

"You believe in reincarnation?" She looked as though she might giggle.

"Hey, I'm a Buddhist without a rice bowl."

"Right." She was smiling. "That's a very romantic fantasy, you know."

"A Buddhist without a rice bowl? You must read some pretty dull fiction."

"No, *not* a Buddhist without a rice bowl, you turkey." She finished her coffee, sat back, and curled her legs under her. "Can we talk for a while?"

"The last time I agreed to that you fucked my lights out, then disappeared for three months. Is this gonna be a preflight check for another trip?"

"No. I had to get away from you. I needed time to sort through my emotions without you hovering in the background. And I did try to provide for you before I left."

"You did a nice job. Thanks for all of this . . . and the car, which I drove maybe three times."

"You're welcome. So, can we talk?"

"If you'll bring me the bottle of Conmemorativo and another cup of coffee."

"Jamie, it's barely eight o'clock. In the morning."

"Mother's work is never done. Just get the bottle, and some more coffee so I can treat my injuries. I've never felt compelled to regulate my vices by a clock."

She put the bottle and a shot glass on the coffee table, along with a fresh cup of coffee, and started to sit.

"Whoa, wait."

She stopped, frowning.

"I never drink alone before noon. You want me to turn into a lonely, undernourished old alcoholic?"

"Well, I'm certainly not going to drink that stuff before I'm even dressed."

"You don't have any clothes here, remember?" I filled the shot glass and handed it to her. "What price conversation?"

She took the glass reluctantly, then shook her head and grinned. "You're probably the most seriously demonic sonofabitch I've ever had the pleasure of knowing."

I raised the bottle. "Live long, love many, and remember the words of Jamie Fortune Hawkins the First: Boy, when you find yo'self up a creek without a paddle, always go with the flow."

She choked on the tequila, and made a face that would have landed her in a permanent seat at the copy desk if she hadn't owned the fuckin' paper. "My God!" she gasped.

"Amen." I took a second slug from the bottle, replaced the cap, and leaned back smiling. Sail on, Cap'n Smith, sail on. "So, whatta you want to talk about?"

"Do all of your women have to endure this kind of abuse, or is this something special for me?"

"*That's* what you want to talk about? What the hell do you think I am, an Arab sheik with a harem?"

"No, no no no. Forget it." She was shaking her head, enjoying herself. "No, that's not on the list of topics I had prepared. Just curious."

"I'm practically a virgin, a victim of fast-talking women who've robbed me of my innocence and left me to find my way in a wicked world."

"You liar!" she laughed. "How can you sit there and say that with a straight face?"

"Well, it was something like that. I think. Or maybe I read that somewhere."

"I can imagine." She pushed out her bottom lip, the way people do when they want to appear deep in thought. "Daniel said you didn't seem real happy with his ideas about Reichmann and the federal investigation . . ."

"Is that an ellipsis on the end of your sentence? Kind of like an implied question? Or is there more to it?"

"Jamie, please don't. I want to talk, not get beat up with words."

"Okay. I'm a little touchy but I don't have to be an asshole all the time. No, I wasn't overwhelmed with Daniel French's agenda for what remains of my checkered career. I was hired, if you remember, as a feature writer, and you didn't believe me when I told you what would happen. 'A modicum of confidence,' you said. Is that how Main Line mavins say 'Trust me'?"

"Has it been that unbearable?"

"Probably no worse than having someone staple my underwear to my pelvis. I'm still here."

"God in heaven, where do you find your images?"

"I majored in metaphors at the Hallmark School of Tabloid Journalism." I was laughing at myself as I unscrewed the cap on the tequila. "Listen, you wanna smoke a joint? And don't tell me what time it is. I feel like getting ripped to the tits and having a good time."

"Well, I'm certainly dressed for it," she said, tugging on the loose flap of material. "How did you rip this shirt like this?"

"I don't remember," I lied. I remember very well, but some stories are better left untold in the company of sheltered souls. I brought out the grass and rolling papers from my desk and cleaned enough dope to roll a couple of joints. She watched me closely, as though she had never seen anyone roll grass.

"You do that like it's second nature. Who taught you?"

"I taught myself. It's easy. I can show you."

"Thanks, but I probably won't ever really need that skill."

"Suit yourself." I lit the first joint and handed it to her. "This stuff isn't what I'd call killer weed, but it will get you stoned."

She inhaled, and coughed.

"Tsk, tsk, tsk. Here, take a shot of this. It'll clear your palate, sort of."

"Not on your life. I can't believe I'm sitting here drinking and smoking marijuana at eight o'clock in the morning."

"Gimme a break. You probably haven't had this much fun since our first dinner date at Club Fed. C'mon, inhale slowly, and hold it for a few seconds."

She tried, and coughed. I took the joint and filled my lungs. I figured she probably was already stoned. Coughing with a lungful of marijuana smoke is a lot like inhaling it through a carburetor. It goes straight into the bloodstream and reaches the brain a hell of a lot faster.

"How you feel?"

"A little lightheaded, I guess . . ."

"A little stoned would be my guess." I finished my coffee. "We better talk quickly. Lord only knows what you'll be trying to convince me to do in another ten minutes."

"I'm *not* stoned." She giggled.

"Right. I knew that. So, what's the topic for today's adventure in language? Daniel French's crusade? I told you, I'm the wrong reporter for the job."

"You talked your way into the Tourist Center and sat face to face with a terrorist, and you say you're the wrong person for the job? Who would you recommend? Alexis?"

"The only thing for which I might recommend Alexis is liposuction. She's got chubby thighs."

I lit a Camel, wondering what I could say that would return me to my rightful place in her ambitious plan, whatever it was. Seeing me as a hero, she would be inclined to expect heroic behavior. I liked it better when I was just talented and difficult to control. That I could handle, for a while anyway.

"I didn't mean to upset you," Juliet said.

"I'm not 'upset' but I'm not going to cast my vote for Hawkins as a hero. That's bullshit.

"First of all, Charlie Patton was not a 'terrorist.' At least not in the radical-political-activist sense of the word. He scared the shit out of a few people, but I don't believe for a minute that he had any connection to the NFRA. From what he told me I'd say he got fucked over by a lot of people, including three or four agencies of the state and city governments. He came unglued.

"Second, it wasn't me who talked my way into the Tourist Center. Ferris did that. I just went along for the ride.

"Also remember that Alexis had the idea first. And it was Ferris who ran the scam on the phone company. Deputy Chief of Police Francis X. Fisher, f'Chrissake . . ." I said, laughing.

"Well, for someone who was 'just along for the ride' you wrote an excellent summary of what happened, and a very sensitive piece about him and his background."

"Thanks, and I mean that. You went to a lot of trouble to get me here and a lot of expense to keep me here. I wouldn't want you to feel you'd made a bad investment. But I'm not a hero. And I'm not a reporter. I'm a writer. The story French wants to do is something for an investigative reporter, a muckraker with strong local connections and at least one well-placed inside contact with the cops. I don't, as the saying goes, fit the profile."

"Can we smoke a little more of that stuff?" She was grinning and probably more stoned than she realized.

I lit the joint, took a hit, and handed it to her. "How do you know Alexis has 'chubby' thighs?"

My laughter was so abrupt, and I laughed so hard, that I choked on the smoke I was holding in my lungs, which started me coughing. "Jesus Christ! That hurts. Don't make me laugh like that."

She tried to stop giggling, which made it worse. "I don't even know why we're laughing," she finally confessed. "Why are we laughing?"

"I'm laughing because you listened to all my reasons for not wanting to turn myself into one-half of a low-rent Woodward and Bernstein act, then asked how I know Alexis has chubby thighs. *You're* laughing because you're stoned."

"Oh . . . I knew there was a reason, but I couldn't figure it out." She lit the joint, inhaled, and managed to hold it for a few seconds without coughing.

"Where the hell did you ever find those panties, anyway?" I was looking directly into the thin pink panel of nylon that barely covered her crotch. And I mean, barely. "Looks like Frederick's of Philadelphia."

"Why? You thinking of getting a pair for yourself?" She tugged on the tail of the shirt, stretching it until it covered her knees, which pretty well eliminated the view, then took another hit from the joint.

"Not until after the operation. But I'm surprised that you would shop in a place that sells anything that, ah, revealing."

"What operation?"

"Never mind," I took the joint from her. "So what else is on our conversational agenda?"

"Oh!" The reminder that she had said she wanted to talk, presumably about topics a little more important than chubby thighs and underwear, left her momentarily confused. "Oh, right. I wanted to ask you to do a feature story on the Philadelphia Art Museum's special Catacombs by Night tour."

Somewhere toward the middle of her request I closed my eyes, probably trying to hide my distaste for the idea. When I opened them she smiled.

"For me."

"What the hell is a Catacombs by Night tour?"

"It's a hokey appeal for new subscribers. The museum needs donors, and every year they take prospective members on a tour of the catacombs for a look behind the scenes. They get to see where the restoration work is done, and look at some of the pieces we've set apart from the public viewing areas."

"All the crap that's too ugly, too insignificant, or too fucked up to put on display."

"You do have a way with words. I hope that won't be the tone of your story."

"You can probably count on Attila the Hearn deleting any offensive or unkind comments. When's the tour scheduled?"

"There's three of them, actually. The first one is January fifth, which is the one I hope you'll attend. Every year someone from the *Call* writes another story and none of them is the kind of story that would get me interested in membership if I was reading it on a train into the city."

"That may owe something to the nature of the material. What's exciting about wandering around in the basement of the Philadelphia Art Museum?"

"It's how you present it, isn't it? Any story can be made to sound boring. Or it can be made interesting."

"If you ever need a job you should think about working for the *Call*. You sound exactly like an assignment editor. 'Here's a pig's ear. I want to see a little silk purse before first edition.' "

"I read *Throwaway Soldiers* while I was away."

"You were gone long enough to *write* the book." She shrugged and lowered her eyes. "Why did you do a disappearing act?"

"To get away from you, like I said." She smiled. "You are very difficult to leave behind. You were always popping up like one of those shooting-range targets." She stopped and shook her head. "That's a terrible analogy, isn't it?"

"I get the picture."

"I'd lose track of what was being said in the middle of a conversation, or lose my place in a book I was reading, or lie awake for two hours listening to your voice."

"Well, I must have said something that impressed you. You came back and had your way with me again."

"That was fun. I never did it wearing my sable."

"I don't remember ever being that close to a sable, let alone fucking on one."

I went to the kitchen to make a pot of coffee and think about what was implied, or maybe just inferred, from her confessions. I didn't get far because she followed me.

"How much of what you wrote in *Throwaway Soldiers* really happened to you?"

"I made up page nineteen, and page one thirty-seven. Everything else is 'true.' "

"Do you have any plans for New Year's Eve?"

"I could be working, for all I know. On nightside there's a deadline every minute, and nobody goes on holiday."

"I think I'll give you the night off. I'd like to spend the evening with you in a special place."

I pulled her against me, pulled up the tail of the shirt, and gripped the smooth round cheeks of her butt with both hands. "How about the Admiral Wilson Motel in Camden. Six bucks an hour, thirty-five for the night."

"You know, one of the things that disturbed me about you was the incredible sexual attraction I felt. I couldn't see how we could be together and you work for the *Call*. Sooner or later someone would find out and that would probably hurt you more than it would help."

"The word, as it were, is already out." I let go of her bottom, pulled the torn neck of the shirt open, and peeked in. "Ferris heard from John, the bartender at the Cock'n'Bull, that you and I were in there drinking together. God, you've got one hellava body for an old lady."

She slapped my hand. "What did Ferris say?"

" 'What's the story with you and Ms. Franklin-Rossini?' I told him there wasn't any story. He doesn't believe me, but he may keep it to himself."

"I was very impressed with your book. I don't know how to say what I really felt. The pain and the emotion and the comical scenes. I hadn't read any novels about Vietnam, so some of it was a shock. I kept wondering how any of you survived, how you managed not to lose your minds and your will to live."

I wasn't altogether certain that I had managed, but I didn't want to open the door on that possibility with her. "I survived because I quit."

"I think I understand you a lot better since I read it. Your experience has been a lot different than mine. But, in some ways, we've both been fighting a war for a long, long time."

"Do what I did. Quit. Tell 'em it's over and declare a victory for yourself."

"Does that work?"

"Not as well as I had hoped." I poured the boiling water into the coffee pot and washed the dirty cups and glasses while she watched. She was smiling.

"I'd never have guessed that you have latent domestic abilities."

"And I wouldn't have guessed that you'd be a *latent* smart-mouth observer of man and his mundane efforts to keep a neat kitchen." I pushed down the plunger on the coffee pot. "You want some of this?"

"What else have you got?" She opened the fridge.

"If you're looking for food you're wasting your time."

"You've got eggs. And cheese. I could make an omelet."

"Go ahead, but keep in mind that those are the eggs you left here before you went on your trip. And while you're in there, hand me the half-and-half. Please."

She grabbed the carton and shut the door. "That was three months ago!"

"Yeah yeah, I know. I counted the days." I took the half-and-half from her.

"Liar. Don't you ever cook for yourself, or have one of your girlfriends cook for you?"

"I don't eat breakfast, and I don't have girlfriends in the plural. If you're hungry, let's go out."

"I can't go out like this," she laughed. "Are you still going out with the girl from the Cock'n'Bull?"

"Yeah, but I don't want her cooking breakfast for me." I stirred sugar into my coffee. "You can wear a pair of my jeans and a shirt. You've got shoes and a damn fine-looking coat."

"Jeans and a sable?!"

"It'a all the rage in New York and LA."

"If that's the strongest recommendation you've got to give it, I'll suggest something else."

"What?"

"You go to the deli down the street and get us some food."

"You'll have to give me some money. I donated all of mine to the Quaker Plaza Community Skate Club."

━━ ━━ ━━ ━━

Juliet left at eleven. Sheila showed up at ten after eleven. She rang the buzzer and I thought it was Juliet coming back for something she'd left behind, although I couldn't imagine what it could be.

"Hi," Sheila said, peeking through the open door. She pushed a package through the opening. "I can't stay, but I decided to stop here on my way home and leave these with you. My mom threatened to disown me if I didn't deliver them tonight. 'While they're fresh.' "

I leaned forward and kissed her lightly on the mouth. "Tell your mom thanks. You want to come in long enough for a cup of coffee and a couple of these?"

"No. I mean, I'd love to, but I've got to go home tonight and if I come in I won't want to leave. Samson's probably pacing up and down, yowling every fifteen seconds. My cat sitter could only stay until Christmas morning."

"Okay, I'll call you tomorrow."

She gave me a quick kiss and started down the hall, then stopped abruptly. "Oh, I almost forgot. My uncle read your book, and he read your articles about the guy you captured. He wants to meet you."

"Yeah, well . . . Listen, I'm not big on meeting family or fans. I'm always embarrassed by the fans and I don't have much to say to family. And I didn't capture anyone, not that it matters." Jesus Christ, the next thing I'll hear is I shot Patton to save Reichmann's life.

"You'd like Uncle Angelo. He's cool."

"*Angelo?*" I laughed. "You've got an Uncle Angelo Wolinski?"

"No, dummy. Angelo Finori. My mom's brother." She grinned. "I'm half Italian. Didn't you know that?"

"How the hell would I know? You don't have a map of Italy on your bottom, or *mangia* tattooed on your top. Do you?"

"Don't I look Italian to you?"

"More Italian than Oriental, I guess, but you could be second-or-third-generation anything from around the Mediterranean and anyway, your dad's Polish so I'm not looking at the face of Rome."

"Well, I gotta go. Think about it. He comes in the bar sometimes. Maybe you could just have a drink with him."

"If he's there, then sure. I'll buy him a drink."

I watched her until she was out the street door, then closed my apartment door with a sigh of relief. She hadn't mentioned Juliet, for which I was grateful. I'd had enough serious sex to last me a couple of days, and enough meaningful conversation to last me until somewhere around Memorial Day. Juliet Franklin-Rossini was as much as I could handle in one twenty-four-hour period, and Sheila could fuck my lights out any night of the week.

I'm convinced that all things being reasonably equal—stamina, present state of relative fatigue, inhibitions or lack of inhibitions, lust quotient, etc.—nine times out of ten the woman will have a lot more drive left after a couple of hours of fooling around than the man who thinks he's behind the wheel.

— — — —

Ferris called at ten the next morning. "You're back to work today, starting at one. How's the ribs?"

"Better. You making up the nightside duty roster for the week?"

"I get a copy of the schedule, since I'm the nightside shop steward. And I've got your first assignment. You cover the coroner's hearing on Charlie Patton's death."

"C'mon, Ferris, that's bullshit. You think the coroner's gonna tell us anything different than what the cops had to say?"

"Probably not, but go anyway. It'll make Daniel happy and Atlee's already got you penciled in. I'll see you back in the office later."

"Where the fuck are you off to?"

"Fishin'," he said as he hung up.

I was writing my third obit of the afternoon when Ferris waltzed in at three-thirty. Some things, if they change at all, change very slowly.

"What's doin'?"

"Obits, what else? Where've you been, all dolled up like the loan officer of Sharks'Я'Us?"

"These are my working clothes. To some of us, a professional appearance is important."

"Then I should dress in black, since I seem to be the *Call*'s designated obit writer no matter who I work for. So, where've you been?"

"Out, talkin' to people. We have an appointment, sort of, at the Round-house. This afternoon."

"What time?"

"When we get there. So quit screwin' around and let's stroll over to see where the other side works."

"These are the last words and testament to someone's dearly departed, so give me time to do the job right. I'll be with you in a minute."

"How'd you make out at the coroner's hearing?"

"Shit! I got there at one, as scheduled, and it was over. They held it this morning. But I did bring back some delightful photographs, suitable for framing." I yanked open my desk drawer, then went back to Miss Ruth Metzenbalm, age seventy-two, beloved sister of David and Samuel Metzenbalm, member of Hadassah, B'nai B'rith, and the ACLU.

"Jesus God," Ferris whispered when he got a look at the top photo of Charlie Patton, a close-up of his face from a head-on view. It wasn't pretty. Ferris slammed the drawer shut without looking at any of the other photographs.

I typed -30- at the end of Ruth's obit. "Let's go."

— — — —

From the eleventh-floor city room, looking south, the Philadelphia Police Administration Building, known to most of the citizens, criminal and otherwise, as the Roundhouse, is clearly visible near the southwest corner of Franklin Square and next door to the federal office building.

The Roundhouse is round. Weird-looking building to be a police station. If it was pink and turquoise it would fit right into Miami. But in Philadelphia it looked like a misplaced museum of second-rate modern art. Why anyone would design a circular police-headquarters building seems to be a mystery, at least to everyone I ever asked about it. The answer I got most often was "It's less threatening." That's the same answer I got when I asked why the cops' cars were all painted baby blue and white.

From the *Call*, the Roundhouse is a rifle shot, a straight-line walk south on Seventh, across Vine, and along the western edge of Franklin Square that takes ten or fifteen minutes, depending on how many times you're stopped by winos and panhandlers, and how much traffic there is on Vine Street. The best way to get there is by cab.

Ferris said he wanted to walk. I fell into step with him rather than argue. The sun was out, and it had warmed up to a sultry thirty-seven degrees, or so the outside thermometer on the *Call* building claimed. With the ten-knot wind blowing off the Delaware River, I wouldn't have argued if someone had said it was seven degrees.

We walked almost to Vine Street, two blocks, before Ferris spoke. "I did some checkin' on Charlie Patton today. I doubt that any of the people I talked to would swear to what they said in court, but 'off the record' they confirmed just about everything he told us. He was promised a lottery ticket outlet, which didn't happen. He was promised a zoning variance, which he was denied. He was promised a beer and wine license, and at his hearing he was creamed by the same developers who were tryin' to force the original owners to sell. They knew he had a criminal record. They even had a copy of it."

"He said all that shit was twenty years old."

"It was," Ferris said. "But it was on record, and that was all they needed. The developers probably dropped a bundle of cash on someone."

"So he was set up, burned, and buried. Who did it?"

"Who knows? At least one guy on the zoning commission, couple of ward-level politicians, someone with enough influence to impress Patton . . . There's always a lot of players in the game."

"Spread enough money around and the sharks come out to feed."

"So," Ferris said, "he lost everything, came unglued, and tried to change things with a rifle."

"Bullshit. The fuckin' rifle was a prop. Think about it. Christmas Eve. He's got a wife and a kid at home, the home is about a week from foreclosure, the kid is sick, Patton's been shafted by half the agencies in the city, and nobody gives a shit. He doesn't even have money to buy his kid the bicycle he's been waiting for all year. Empty stockings on Christmas Eve. Poor Tiny Tim.

"Then, suddenly, out of the overcast . . ." I dum-dum-de-dummed my way through a few bars of the theme from *Superman*. "Look, up in the sky, it's the defender of the underdog . . . it's the will of God . . . it's *Supermedia!*

"Faster than a fiber optic light wave . . . able to leap from satellite to satellite in a single bound . . . stronger than the first ten amendments and commandments combined . . . Why the fuck are we going to the Roundhouse?"

Ferris was laughing. "You are one cynical sonofabitch."

"Fuck you. You think I'm wrong? Christ, every time you turn on the TV some fuckin' gaggle of pissed-off Arabs has grabbed another goddamn airplane or boat or public building. The antiwar people did it. Pro-abortion, anti-abortion, pronuke and antinuke, the JDL, the PLO.

"Man, every day is Howdy Doody Time for TV news. The writers of wrongs and purveyor of justice to all, or all whose story can be told in ninety seconds or less, including stand-ups and bridges.

"Nothing's changed since Hearst and Pulitzer except the time it takes to get the 'news' to the subscribers.

"And you never answered my question: Why are we going to the Round-house?"

"We're not. I wanted to get us out of the city room to tell you what I found out. Too many eyes and ears in that place."

For a few seconds I just looked at him. "Excuse me," I finally said, "but aren't we all on the same team? Except maybe for Ivan?"

"Trust me."

I cracked up. "You're the one who's paranoid and you say 'Trust me'?"

"Yeah, well, trust me. Keep this stuff we're doing' between you'n'me."

"*We're* not doing anything. You may be doing something. All I'm doing is freezing my ass off in Franklin Square. You think Granddaddy Franklin picked the *Call's* location because it's so close to Franklin Square? I wonder if they were related?"

"My mama's maiden name was Jefferson. You think we were related?"

"Hard to tell, but old Thomas was a man of many and varied tastes, from what I've read. I heard he was makin' push-push with a 'colored girl.' "

"I read that somewhere, too. You think it's true?"

"I hope so. Sure makes him seem a lot more human." We'd stopped at the corner of Race and Franklin. "Isn't Chinatown over there a couple of blocks?"

"You hungry?"

"Well, we're out here with nothing to do. How about some dim sum? There's got to be at least one Chinese restaurant that doesn't serve Chung King fried rice."

"Let's go," he said with a know-it-all grin.

Philadelphia has some of the worst Chinese restaurants on the face of the earth. It's a problem for people who appreciate good Chinese food, a problem compounded by the surprising fact that almost everyone you ask knows a great place that serves the best egg rolls or fried wonton or mu-shu pork in the city. They always name something that I could get from Stouffer's, and it probably would taste better if I did. The Five Happiness dinner for two at the Lotus Flower Inn is not my idea of happiness or dinner, but that was all I'd found until Ferris took me to Mama-san Yin's.

"It's a damn good thing I don't work for the Board of Health," I said as we entered the place. "I'd close this place in five seconds."

"The kitchen's clean, the plates are clean, the chopsticks are—"

"If you've got any word other than 'new' in mind . . ."

"New. Almost, anyway. C'mon," he said, laughing as he led the way through the narrow, dingy room where a dozen or so Chinese males were sitting around in twos and threes, drinking tea. Except for a sugar cookie or some rice, no one was eating anything. It looked more like a greasy-spoon café than a restaurant.

We were the only two round-eyes in the place, which I would ordinarily take as a positive sign. Most Americans don't like authentic Chinese cooking. The herbs and spices are too weird. And in Philadelphia, if it's even semi-authentic, it's probably Cantonese. As a rule, American Cantonese cooking is to Chinese cuisine what chopped chicken liver is to pâté de foie gras with truffles. Not even close.

At the rear of the room through which Ferris was leading me was a narrow doorway covered with a plastic shower curtain suspended from a wood pole. He pushed it aside and stepped into the kitchen, which was, in truth, as clean as mine, and as big as my apartment. At least.

A huge Chinese male, dressed in kitchen whites, was haranguing everyone in sight, slamming pans and pot lids with admirable abandon, jabbing the air with chopsticks, and occasionally joining Mick Jagger for a few lines of "Satisfaction," which was blasting from four bookcase speakers placed haphazardly around the room.

"This must be the kitchen equivalent of a mortar attack. Who the fuck is the fat man?"

"Best damn cook in Chinatown. I think his Chinese name is Ling, or something like that, but everyone calls him Mick. He loves Jagger and all he plays all day and all night is the Rolling Stones."

Aside from Mick there were five or six women, a bunch of kids, and Mick's assistant, a young Chinese man, probably thirty years old.

Mama-san Yin, who Ferris said owned the place, was bustling around the huge stove, tending the soup or something. When she saw Ferris she beamed. "Lee-on, where you been so long?" She wiped her hands on her apron and hustled over. She was barely five feet tall and hefty, with a huge gleaming smile highlighted with several gold crowns. Every child born to this sorry world should have a mother like Mama-san. We'd all grow up a lot happier. She hugged Ferris as though he was one of her own.

"Long time no see," she said with a sudden frown. "Mama-san think maybe you mar-rhee girl who no like Chinese food."

"I'm waiting for Sue Lin. Then we'll eat with you every night."

"Sue Lin only nine year old . . ."

"Plenty of time," Ferris said. "Five or six more years."

She glanced at me, and went on talking to Ferris. "You bring friend to eat? I fix first-rate dinner for you. Some soup, so you be warm. Have fresh fish today . . ."

"How about something light?" I suggested to Ferris.

"You tell her you want something 'light' and she'll give you a can of Bud and a pork bun, and put you in the front room." He pointed to a large table that had been shoved into the corner. "Sit over there. I'll order."

I sat and watched the two of them jabbering. I think half of what was said was said with their hands. The other half was with smiles and affection. When he sat down he was grinning and rolled his eyes to the ceiling. "She said you're too skinny."

"I can't wait."

"This may be the best meal you'll eat in Philadelphia, unless I decide I like you enough to take you to a neighborhood chicken-and-ribs joint I know."

"How'd you ever manage this? Eating in the kitchen?"

"About five years ago, I was walking along the street looking for a place to eat, and Sue Lin, who was four years old, was standing in the door waiting for her father. He was across the street, parking his car.

"As I came even with the door one of the customers, a big-time Chinese Mafia guy, came out, and at the same time two punks, a hit man from one of the local gangs and a driver, rode by on a motorcycle and opened up with an Uzi.

"I saw it happenin', like fuckin' slow motion. I grabbed Sue Lin and hit the sidewalk, all at the same time. I don't even know why. Just instinct, I guess. The guy went down, Sue Lin and I both got skinned knees . . . and Alexis got a byline.

"So I was a hero, and they made me family."

"Well, no shit. And you were on my ass about pulling Little Miss Muff out of the line of fire."

"Not the same. Sue Lin's gonna grow up to be a great cook. Alexis ain't never gonna grow up."

Mama-san brought us a pot of steaming, spicy corn-crab chowder with a loaf of crusty Italian bread, and two bottles of icy Chinese beer. Ferris ripped off one end of the loaf and dunked it into the soup.

"The Chinese can't make bread worth a damn, but Mama-san knows how much I love it, so she sent one of the kitchen boys out. She always finds bread for me unless I come in here at midnight."

"Oh, you mean this isn't Hunan whole wheat?"

"Baked this morning in South Philly. Eat."

He was right about one thing: It was the best meal I'd eaten in Philadelphia.

"So tell me how Alexis got a byline out of your story."

The piece of bread he had level with his mouth stopped in midflight. We stared at each other, then I went on eating and he said, "I told you Christmas Eve, I'm not a writer. Five years ago I could barely put together a sentence. The only reason I got the story was because it happened to me." He dunked the bread into the soup and held it over the bowl, looking at me, his eyes boring into mine.

"For my first seven years at the *Call*," he said, "I was a beat man. I covered the police beat with an old-timer, Frank Unruh. He was an alcoholic, a horse player, a three-pack-a-day smoker, and a bullshitter beyond your wildest ambitions—and you, *amigo*, are one of the best I've met in a long time.

"Frank knew every goddamn desk sergeant, watch captain, precinct commander and prosecutor in the Delaware Valley. State cops, county sheriffs, township and borough cops, city cops, the Feds. He never forgot a name. He could be so drunk he couldn't hold the phone and still get a burglary report out of Toms River, New Jersey, at two A.M. before half the guys on the *Call* could get a badge number off a cop they were talking to face to face." He dipped the bread again and chewed.

"So why did they send you to cover the cops?"

"I was hired because I'm black. Pressure from the EEOC. Couple of black community groups were grumbling because the *Call* didn't have any black street reporters. There's always racial tension in Philly, and the *Call* didn't have anyone to send into the combat zones when they heated up. And my journalism advisor knew Ivan. They were roommates at Temple."

"Didn't you have to write in school?"

"I worked out a deal with a guy." He smiled at whatever image flashed before his mind's eye. "Andy Rigatoni. Reminds me of you. Fuckin' wise ass. Funny guy."

"C'mon, Ferris. Nobody's named Rigatoni. That's fuckin' pasta."

"His real name was Peterson, but we all called him Rigatoni because he ate pasta at least four or five times every week. I mean *every* week, for three and a half years. He lived on pasta and whatever. Meat sauce, shellfish, sausage, butter. I saw him eat pasta and tuna, more than once.

"And he could flat-out write. He could take any ten facts you gave him and write three different articles, all true reports of whatever, and all three of 'em would sound like the truth, but they'd all have a different slant.

"The thing was, though, he hated to go to class. He loved to hang out with black women. And he was a world-class dope smoker."

"So you pimped your way through school?"

His look said, in no uncertain terms, that I was obviously an idiot as well as an asshole. "Hey, whatta you want? You tell me you made a deal with a guy who likes dope and black women, and you want me to leap to the conclusion that you fixed him up with Mensa candidates from West Philly who got him high on life?"

"I delivered grass, I covered for him in class, and I introduced him to a few black female students, and a couple of black women who worked in the dean's office. I don't call that bein' a pimp. I don't know if he got laid or not. We never talked about it. He had so many white chicks promising him anything and everything if he'd write their papers, I doubt that he needed a pimp."

"What happened to him? Did he graduate and go to work for the *National Enquirer*?"

"He didn't graduate. 'Bout six months before cap-and-gown time he dropped out, enlisted in the army. He got killed in 'Nam. One of our classmates who graduated went into the army public-information department. He must've run across Rigatoni because he wrote Rigatoni's obit and sent it to the school paper."

"And Unruh? He doesn't work for the *Call*, right?"

"Dropped dead of a heart attack. I went on nightside about a month later, and I've been there since."

Mama-san cleared away the soup bowls and brought out a plate of pot stickers, which Ferris called fried dumplings.

"And now what? You want to make a deal with me?"

"Yeah."

We ate the pot stickers without talking. He was waiting for me, and I was thinking about another black guy from Philly, one I'd known in 'Nam, and what a sorry fuckin' end that friendship had come to.

"Did you ever read *All the President's Men*?" I asked Ferris after he took the last pot sticker.

"Yeah." He cut the dumpling into two roughly equal parts. "You want half?"

"No, lucky for me since it's on your plate. What's the biggest story you ever broke? Other than the one you told me about Sue Lin?"

"It's all been pretty routine. How about you?"

"Nothing that ever won me a Pulitzer nomination. Which is my point. We don't know shit from a Chinese checker game about the fine art of muck-raking. Those guys were damn sure better reporters than we are, and they fucked up almost as often as they were right.

"Plus, unimportant as it might seem to you and French, they had Deep Throat. We've got *bubkes,* and half a pot sticker. Which is about the same thing." I speared the last half of the pot sticker with one chopstick and laughed at him with my eyes as I chewed.

"You said you didn't want that half."

"I don't know what came over me. Maybe it's the MSG."

"She don't use MSG."

━━ ━━ ━━ ━━

"**S**oon big fish ready, okay?" Mama-san announced as she stacked the dirty plates.

"Great," Ferris said. "This honky boy stole the last half of my fried dump-ling."

"Nooo. Maybe we don't give him rice with fish."

"No, no, that's okay." He waved one of my chopsticks in front of her, grinning. "He won't be eating a lot of the next course."

"There's an old Chinese saying: Give a hungry man a fish and you've fed him for a day. Teach a hungry man to fish and you've fed him for life. But give a hungry man a fish after you've taken away one of his chopsticks and he will display execrable table manners as well as a bad attitude."

"What is 'ex-cree-abrul'?" Mama-san inquired.

"Number ten," Ferris answered.

"Actually, we always called it number two, but I was raised in a different part of the country."

"Ahhh!" she sighed, nodding her head, understanding only that we were screwing around with a language she undoubtedly found difficult to fathom under the best of circumstances. Still nodding, she left us, mumbling under her breath in Chinese.

"Whatta you think she was saying?" Ferris laughed.

" 'Why rhee-dic-u-lous round-eye running dogs eat here? Better they go Burger King.' "

He tore off another piece of bread and chewed on it, seemingly deep in thought. "You know," he said after he washed the bread down with beer, "I keep thinking that you're lyin' to me about something. That something isn't right with you."

"What?" I could feel the frown spreading across my face like a dark cloud.

"I don't know. Something. Not even a lie, like I ask if you like Chinese beer and you say yeah but you actually hate it. I mean, that's one kind of a lie, which you probably wouldn't do. Right?"

"Not about Chinese beer."

"It's more like you're hiding something. You know? All that bullshit about *All the President's Men*, Woodward and Bernstein being better reporters, the only people who know for sure if cops murdered Charlie Patton are cops. Dead end, ipso facto."

"Ipso facto? Ipso facto, my ass." I laughed. "Listen, what you told me about J school warrants something from me. What would you like to know? Ask me."

"No bullshit?"

"Truth, straight up."

"What are you hiding?"

"Nothing. I haven't told you my life story, but it's mostly boring anyway. I don't know what you sense, so I don't know what to tell you."

"Well, let's start with Charlie Patton. Why don't you want to work on it with me? Hell, you'll get the writing glory, all I'll get is second billing."

What the fuck can I tell him that he'll understand when I don't know any more than he does? I wondered. "You said that you think I'm lying, like lying by omission. I'm not telling you something that must be important because it's bugging you, right?" He nodded. "Well, in a sense, that's how I feel about this story. None of this shit is what it seems to be."

"None of what shit?"

"Charlie Patton, Daniel French, Rudolph Reichmann, the federal investigation, the un-assigned assignment.

"Leon, there's too much that *we* aren't being told. Daniel French wouldn't open this can of worms on a bet if the only prize was peer-group adulation. Not French. Someone else, without a doubt. Ivan, if he had the balls, which he doesn't. French has the balls, and he's smart, but the reward would have to be something big. Something worth the risk."

"What risk?"

"Reichmann is a dangerous man. He's wrapped too tight. If Patton was murdered, Reichmann was the one who said do it."

Mama-san came then with the 'big fish' which was steamed sea bass covered in a spicy sauce and bamboo shoots, and wrapped in foil. Smiling slyly, she slipped me a new pair of chopsticks. On rare and fortunate occasions, I've had fish as good as hers, but never better.

"Maybe," Ferris sighed after a long pause, "Patton didn't hang himself."

"Right. Can we get another beer?"

Ferris waved his bottle at one of the kitchen helpers. The boy nodded enthusiastically. He brought two beers a couple of minutes later. Basic sign language is almost universal. Waving an empty cup, bottle, or coconut shell signals a need for a refill. A "writing" motion with the index finger will bring a check in every place I've ever been. The fact that I've rarely been able to read them, and usually had no idea how accurate or inaccurate they were, didn't change the motion or the result. Any culture that has motor vehicles seems to understand the extended thumb. But the extended middle finger doesn't mean anything unless the action was preceded by a few years of Western influence, or a few weeks of American military presence. One of our cultural legacies.

"Okay," Ferris said a few minutes later, "Reichmann is dangerous. You were in 'Nam. Wasn't that dangerous?"

"Leon, I went to 'Nam when I was nineteen years old. I wouldn't do that again. I turned down an assignment in Salvador two years ago. I don't go looking for trouble. I've had my share for this life." I took a slug of beer, watching him digest what I'd said.

He laughed, a great, rumbling belly laugh that almost drowned out the sound of the Rolling Stones. "Hawkins, you don't have to look for it. You *are* trouble."

"The trouble I cause, if that's what you mean, is like happy hour at the Cock'n'Bull compared to what Reichmann could bring down on us." I pushed away my plate and lit a Camel. "Listen to me, Leon. We are small-time turkeys and this is a high-stakes game."

"I don't understand why you make it sound like we're after a Supreme Court justice or the governor."

"Shit, those people would be very unlikely to put out a contract on us. But if Reichmann wants us dead, half the Dellafilthia police force is gonna be on our ass."

"C'mon, Jamie, this ain't El Salvador. Reichmann's not crazy enough to hit two newspaper reporters."

"That, oh Prince of Nightside, is just about the sum of what Alexis said to me two minutes before Charlie Patton put her on her ass. 'He wouldn't *dare* shoot a woman, especially not a woman reporter . . .' She a graduate of Temple, too? Or is that a fantasy you two created after you started working on the *Call?*"

"Captain Chickenheart," he grumbled without looking at me.

I laughed, which pissed him off a little more. And then Mama-san came over, followed by a kitchen boy who cleared the table. She sat down. The boy returned with a pot of hot tea and cups, which he filled. I hate hot green tea but anyone who would put a meal like that in front of me deserved my respect.

She lifted her cup without a word, waiting. Ferris and I did the same, and we all drank a little. I did my best not to make a face, and failed.

"You do not like Chinese tea?"

I looked into the cup, considering several bullshit answers, then shook my head. "No. But I like you, and I'm honored to be here." I gestured with the cup. "To your health and good fortune. In the words of my favorite alien, 'Live long and prosper.' "

"Thank you."

I couldn't think of anything else to say to her, and I didn't know what to say to Ferris. The only thing he wanted to hear was yes and the word wouldn't have come from my heart even if I had made it come out of my mouth.

"There is trouble, Lee-on?" Mama-san asked.

"A little disagreement," I said with a smile.

"You like Mama-san to cast *I Ching?*" she asked him.

He brightened up and grinned. "Yeah, let's do it."

She left the table and Ferris looked at me with the kind of confidence you might feel if you suddenly discovered a pair of aces in the hole.

———

It was dark by the time we started back to the *Call*. We'd been gone for over two hours, which didn't seem to concern Ferris at all. I said I'd pay for a cab, he said he wanted to walk, so we walked, neither of us talking. It was too damn cold, and getting colder. The traffic was typical big-city "outta my way" nonsense, loud horns and loud mouths racing to the next red light. The winner's prize is a longer wait for the green. We stopped so I could pick up an espresso to go.

Atlee glanced up when we walked in, nodded, then went back to butchering someone's copy. Ivan would have had a fuckin' posse after us, or at the least we'd have been expected to volunteer some long-winded explanation of where we'd been and what we had accomplished. Nightside, I decided, did have a few good points to recommend it.

I poured my espresso from the Styrofoam cup into a mug I found on my desk. Sheila must have dropped it off as a Christmas present.

The mug had been a special order. On one side it read YOU GET IT ALL WITH A CALL—the *Call* advertising slogan was "You get it all with the *Call*"— and on the other side was her phone number. I'm always impressed by subtlety. I wondered what would happen if I left the cup in the men's room. For that matter, what would happen if I just left it on top of my desk?

"A very attractive young lady," Atlee said. I almost spilled the coffee. "Does she work at the Cock'n'Bull? She looked familiar."

"Yeah."

He squinted at the type on the cup. "She almost got it right. Should be 'You get it all with *the Call.*' "

"I'll mention that when I see her." I kept the phone number turned away from him. It was, from my point of view, bad enough that my 'boss' knew I was dating someone from the Cock'n'Bull. If he saw the phone number Christ only knew what strange conclusions he would joyfully jump to.

"You got a minute?" he asked as he pulled a chair over and sat down.

"My time is your time, until ten o'clock anyway."

"I've been made aware of the special circumstances covering your transfer to nightside, and although I don't have as much information as I'd like, you and Ferris will have my complete cooperation. I'd like to be kept posted, as much as possible, on your whereabouts and availability, but I realize you won't always be able to do that. Just do your best and I'll cover for you when you're away."

"That's great," I said with total sincerity and absolutely no idea what he was talking about. But it sounded too good for that kind of response, so I added, "I really appreciate your help. I was concerned about possible conflicts."

"No problem. After the way you handled the story on Patton, I can't wait to see where all of this leads."

"Me either."

He flashed a knowing smile and stood up. "By the way, although I never had an opportunity to tell you, I thought that piece you did on Pulaski Day was right on the money. I'd have liked to see it in print. We've got too many sacred cows in our barn." He smiled again and left.

If I'd never experienced psilocybin, I might have thought Mama-san added a little magic to the mushrooms that accompanied the fish, but I was stone sober and straight. Or dead and in newspaper heaven. Talk about a transfer to nightside.

I got up, thinking I'd have a little talk with Ferris, and the phone rang. Nickelson's Funeral Home had another obit for me. After that it was Goldstein's, with two, and finally Avia. I started laughing, which didn't go over too well with the guy. I couldn't help it. *Avia*, in Italian, means 'to go.' He pronounced it differently, but it took me a minute or so to settle down.

Sammy the copyboy stopped by my desk as I finished the last obit. "What the hell are you doing on nightside?" I asked.

"Three months on dayside, three months on nightside. French wants to see you in his office."

"For how long? The three-on-three-off business, I mean."

"Year, unless I get lucky and dig up a big story, which might get me an early promotion. But that doesn't seem like much of a possibility when I'm stuck in the city room all the time. It's the copyboy's version of Catch-22."

I stood up and put my arm around him, walking him in the direction of French's office. "The key to success in this business, Sammy, is a polite manner and a positive attitude."

"Like yours, Mr. Hawkins? If I may be permitted to call you Mr. Hawkins."

"In private moments, Sammy, I think that's an acceptable alternative to addressing me as God, but in circumstances where others can hear you, I think 'Yo, Shit-for-brains' would indicate an approach more suited to our chosen profession's manner of dealing with those who have attained heroic stature.

"We in the media, Sammy, have a spiritual obligation to create and destroy heroes, to unseat those whom others have put on a pedestal, and to hold up to the unforgiving light of public opinion the flawed fabric of human nature. Provided, of course, that there's little or nothing of importance or substance in our revelations and/or their sins. If there's substance to our criticisms then we run the risk of actually doing some good, and that's *not* what we're here for, or here after, if you can follow that."

"Not really," he laughed. "What are we here for or here after?"

"Beats the shit out of me, but I've heard it said that our primary responsibility is to create the sensations necessary to keep our publisher in business." I shrugged. "That has a certain ring of righteousness, don't you think?"

"You're much too abstract and philosophical for me, Mr. Hawkins, but will you tell me something, or perhaps I should say, may I ask you a question?" His tone shifted from pseudo-admiring to semiserious.

"Seriously?"

"Well, sure, I guess. It's just that I heard you were, ah, good friends with Miss Rossini, and I was wondering if that's true?"

"Actually, I shouldn't answer any question that personal, but you're obviously a serious-minded journalist, in pursuit of information you not only don't need but information which is none of your fucking business, and I want to do what I can to help you get out of the slime pit you copyboys occupy. The truth is, Sammy, Miss Rossini is my mom, and I'm her illegitimate son. By Daniel French." I patted him on the shoulder. "I've got to go talk to Dad now. See you later."

French was doodling when I entered his office. "Come in, Jamie. And sit down, please." He seemed cheerful enough.

I parked myself in a well-preserved wing chair and, for a fleeting moment, I was shrouded with the scent of Shalimar. Juliet had been sitting in the same chair, probably within the hour. "Am I on the carpet, so to speak?"

"No, no, nothing like that," French said with a smile. "Why, is there a problem?"

"Beats me. I was out for a little better than two hours with Ferris, but Atlee didn't seem upset. He did say a few things, though, that made absolutely no sense, and I didn't say anything to change his impressions."

"You must be referring to my instructions to let you come and go as you please."

"He seems to think Ferris and I are working on a covert assignment, and that I was transferred to nightside because of that assignment."

"Does that bother you? It leaves you with a great deal of latitude to dig up the kinds of stories you said you want to do."

"Mr. French—"

"You may call me Daniel. I'm the managing editor, not the editor emeritus."

"Well, since I just told Sammy the copyboy that you're my father, and I'm the illegitimate son you and Juliet produced in a moment of unbridled passion, I suppose calling you Daniel would be acceptable." About halfway between dismay and disbelief the absurdity cracked his shell and he cackled with laughter. "I mean, I could call you Dad, but the guys in the city room might have a problem with that. What do you think?"

"Let's stick with Daniel," he answered, shaking his head. "May I ask what brought about the need to give us away?"

"Rumor, I'd guess. He wanted to know if I was, as reported, quote, good friends, end quote, with Juliet."

"Well, you've certainly given him something to think about."

"Isn't that great? The lie is so outrageous that he'll fuck with it for a week because there just might be some truth in there somewhere. That's good training for a young copyboy." I wished I had a cigarette, but mine were on my desk and French didn't smoke.

"I suppose you'd like to know why you've been summoned to my office . . ."

"Well, either that or we can talk about the Eagles' chances of making the Super Bowl."

"They didn't even make the playoffs." He looked confused.

"Imagine that. I guess we're down to one subject then. Sir, why have you called me to your office?"

"I'd like for you to read that," he said, handing me a photocopy of an official-looking document. "Then come back and talk to me."

I had to leave my chair to retrieve it, and as I did I checked the time. It was already after seven. "You mean tonight?"

"No, over the weekend." He flipped open his appointment book. "Sunday is New Year's Day. Monday I'm out of town. Let's plan to get together Tuesday afternoon." He made a note. "You're my first entry for the New Year."

I glanced at the manuscript, forty-two pages of single-spaced type. The title page was printed on U.S. Department of Justice letterhead.

"Preliminary findings, summarized," French said. "The full report, I'm told, runs close to five hundred pages."

"Does this very large CONFIDENTIAL stamp on the front mean anything? Like unauthorized possession is a felony?"

"Probably. It's certainly confidential and I trust you'll treat it as such. As James Bond used to say, 'For your eyes only.' When the time is right you can share it with Leon."

I sat down again. "Daniel, what the hell is going on?"

"I think you'll find the material interesting, and the basis for an excellent story at the appropriate time."

"You ever hear the expression 'slow shuck'?"

"I don't believe so."

"This business feels a lot like a slow shuck. A con job run at a snail's pace."

"Put that aside for the moment," he said without any sign of annoyance. He'd be a tough fuckin' poker player. "Tell me, what do you think of Reichmann?"

"Dangerous."

"Fit to be the mayor of Philadelphia?"

"Is that the agenda here? Is he running for mayor?"

"The election is some time away, but sooner or later, yes, Rudolph Reichmann will run for mayor. Do you want him for mayor?"

"To tell the truth, I don't care who's mayor. Anyone who'd want the job probably isn't qualified to have it, and if they think they've got a chance of having it, damn sure they've already sold their ass to the special interests. And yes, I've been told I'm a cynic."

"I'm more inclined to think of you as a realist. And you, no doubt, think of yourself as a romantic. Most good writers are romantics. Not all of them, but the majority, I'd say."

I hoisted the confidential report. "What's in here?"

"A fascinating study guide to the sins and errors of the Philadelphia Police Department."

"Top to bottom, or bottom to top?"

"Do you play poker, by any chance?"

"Not with you. So it's bottom to top, with the emphasis on the bottom. Right? And that isn't going to stop ol' Rudy Reichmann's quest for power."

"I haven't read the full report . . ."

"I don't think you've even read this, never mind the whole thing."

He cracked a little, just a hint of surprise, but I smiled to myself. Fuck you, D.F. You're not as cool as you've got all of us convinced you are.

"Why do you say that?"

"Just a lucky guess." I got up again, satisfied that I'd left a little food for thought in that cooler he used for a brain. And then he surprised me.

"You're right, and I'm impressed. I'd like to know what tipped it, but I've played enough poker to know better than to ask." His smile was one of genuine admiration—or just more of the slow shuck. "You are a thoroughly entertaining young man, Jamie. Full of surprises. Almost impossible to predict."

Bullshit. The word was banging around, desperate to get out. "I'm an open book, Mr. French. Just a little ol' country boy tryin' to make my way in the wicked city."

"I'll expect you Tuesday, about two-thirty."

"I trust you've got your own copy of this."

"Indeed," he said with a grin. "And I'll read it before our meeting."

— — — —

I was sitting in the *Call* library, staring at the Assistant U.S. Attorney's confidential summary of the Philadelphia PD's zealous crime-fighting tactics when Ferris wandered in and put a double espresso in front of me. He put my new mug next to the Styrofoam cup. His grin was roughly the width of the mug.

"Where the fuck did you get this?" I asked as I uncapped the coffee.

"Sammy had to make a run, so I told 'im to stop and pick up a cup for you. I won't ask where you got that," he added with a snort.

"Why not? I mean, as long as you're prying."

"It was on your desk, in plain view." He waved his hand, fanning the air. "You ever think about what all that smoke does to your lungs?"

"Thanks for the coffee, and fuck you very much for your concerns about my lungs. Open the window if it's too much for your tender self."

"You've been in here two hours."

"It's a quiet place to read. I kinda like it in here at night. No phones, no obits, nobody yapping in my ear about how much I smoke. At least 'til now." I emptied the coffee into the mug. "What time you get off?"

"I'm off now if I want to be off. Why?"

"We need to talk."

"So talk."

"Tell you what, I'm off the clock in a few minutes. Meet me at the Cock'n'Bull sometime around ten-thirty, eleven."

"Okay," he agreed with a shrug. "Whatcha got there?"

"A war story. Interesting stuff." The document was face down and could have been anything except a glowing appraisal from Ivan of my dayside tour. That probably would have taken fewer words.

Sammy stuck his head into the room. "Leon, phone."

Ferris grumbled and started toward the door.

"Leon." He stopped. I put my finger to my lips. He looked for a long second, then nodded.

After Ferris closed the door I put my feet up and surveyed the room, looking at the rows of books and bound magazines, most of which hadn't been opened in years. Most of them, I'd wager, hadn't been off the shelf since they were installed. There's rarely time to research anything unless you're writing a column or some long, tiresome feature. Too much of the work is down and dirty.

The room was about 20 × 30, with what I think of as old-boys'-club furniture: leather and oak, all dark brown. It was reassuring to sit there alone amid all the books and imagine that I had all the time I'd ever need to write columns and entertaining features. For a moment, the library became my private domain, my office, where I could sit in solitude and comfort.

The moment ended quickly enough. Philadelphia, as a city, was already one of my least favorite places. It was cold and wet and shot full of decay. The new buildings were like dental crowns. What the city needed was full-scale root canal. From everything I'd read and heard, before and after my arrival, its politics were among the most corrupt in the world.

And the *Call* was just one more big-city newspaper that survived on the need of retailers to reach consumers with display ads. Even though most of its three-hundred thousand subscribers paid for the paper to read the sports, the comics, and the obits.

Time to get the fuck out of here. I picked up the forty-odd pages of summarized misery and misconduct, and the mug. It wasn't until I was in the elevator that I realized I wasn't sure if 'out of here' was something as simple as leaving the *Call* building or if I was ready to leave Philadelphia. Depression was hovering over me. What I wanted was a cool sea breeze off Cabo San Lucas. I settled for a brisk wind off the Delaware River. By the time I walked into the Cock'n'Bull I'd changed clothes, made peace with myself, and remembered to bring the present I had for Sheila.

— — — —

"God, what a night," Sheila said, leading me down the bar to my favorite spot. The Cock'n'Bull was almost empty. "The place was packed from five-thirty to seven-thirty, and we were two girls short. Then, at seven-thirty, the place empties out and the two missing girls show up. I haven't had a new customer in the last hour."

"Oh, woe is me. Here." I handed her the gift I'd brought, a black coral necklace and matching earrings set in silver.

"Oh, Jamie . . . they're beautiful. My God, where did you ever find something like this in Philadelphia?"

"Oaxaca."

"Is that a new store? I never heard of it."

"It's in Trenton," I lied. "So, do I get a drink?"

"Better." She kissed me full on the mouth, a lingering searching kiss that made me wonder, for a second, if I wouldn't have been smarter to give her a sweater from The Urban Girl. "I love you," she whispered, and I knew without a doubt that the sweater would have been a better choice. "Back in a minute."

She hustled behind the bar and pulled down a bottle of Conmemorativo. John popped off the cap on a bottle of Corona and put it in front of me. "Merry Christmas. Where the hell have you been?"

"Working nightside and trying to negotiate a separate peace. You have a nice holiday?"

"Yeah, I guess. I can't handle too much of that Yuletide joyous family crap. And I hate turkey."

"Maybe we should get married and live happily ever after," I said. "I feel the same way."

"Forget it, John," Sheila said. "He's mine. Why don't you go wash glasses or something so I can have a little privacy here."

John made a face and wandered down the bar. With only two other customers at the bar he didn't have anything to do or many glasses to wash.

Sheila checked the necklace and earrings in the bar mirror, preening with a smile. They did look good on her.

"Is that tequila bottle a prop, or can we have a drink?"

She poured two shots and we drank to a merry Christmas past and a great New Year upcoming. Then she leaned over the bar and kissed me again.

"I can probably leave early," she said as she poured my beer into a glass. "Sure isn't anything to keep me here."

"I'm meeting Ferris here sometime in the next half-hour. After I talk to him we can leave, if you don't get a better offer." I lit a Camel. "Sheila, I want to tell you something and I don't want you to get all bent out of shape."

"Okay." She took a napkin from the bar and began shredding it.

"The cup was cute, and I appreciate it, but don't come to the *Call* looking for me unless I invite you. I do my best to keep my work and my personal life separate, and the only reason I hang around where you work is because it's a bar. In fact, if you were uncomfortable with me being here I would be happy to drink somewhere else."

"I like for you to come here," she said. "Why wouldn't I want you to drink here?"

"Who knows? I'm just saying that I'd understand if you didn't want me to. I don't want you in the city room unless I ask you. Okay? No offense, it's just me."

"Well, if you don't want me there I'll stay away."

I knew she was offended, but better that than her popping in whenever she hadn't seen me for a couple of days, or didn't have anything better to do.

"Listen, I want to ask you something," Sheila said.

"Not if it's going to provoke a fight. I'm too tired to fight with you."

"No, no, nothing like that. I just wondered if you know John's gay?"

"That's funny," I laughed. "No, I didn't know. Couple of times I wondered, but he isn't obvious at all, at least not to me."

"Well, I heard you say that maybe the two of you should get married, and . . . I don't know . . ." She made herself busy, pushing the bits of napkin into a neat pile.

"You thought I might be a closet case?"

"No!" She laughed. "I thought he might think you were ridiculing him, or something."

"I hope not, but he should know better." I was looking past her, at the back of John's head, when a new customer walked in. He was about my height, with a dark complexion and black hair, and he was dressed in a suit, tie, and overcoat. He checked out the room before he actually came through the door, and once inside he stood for a moment with the closed door behind hm. Satisfied, he came toward us as Sheila turned to see what had taken my attention from her.

"Uncle Angelo," she called down the bar.

Oh shit, I sighed under my breath. My first meeting and I get the family badass. "He looks like Mafia," I whispered to Sheila.

She slapped my arm, scowling. "That's a terrible thing to say." And then she giggled. "Especially about Uncle Angelo. He's a lieutenant on the Philadelphia police force."

Fuck me. Next, she'll tell me her brother's a goddamn copy editor.

Angelo kissed Sheila hello, then turned his attention to me, extending his hand. "Angelo Finori."

"Jamie Hawkins, Lef'tenant."

"Sheila told you? She was worried about you knowing I'm a police officer."

"I screwed up," she said, trying not to giggle. "He said you looked like Mafia, and I said that was a terrible thing to say, especially with you being a policeman."

"I've heard worse," he said to me. "Let's have a drink here, if you can stop giggling long enough to pour a couple."

"Vodka?"

"Wod-ka," he smiled. "With ice."

She poured a sizeable sum into a rocks glass and handed it to him, then refilled our shot glasses. "To a happy and prosperous new year," Angelo toasted.

A pair of shivering would-be customers came in and took a table. "Sheila," John called, "You want Annie to cover your tables or what?"

"I'll get 'em." She gave us a smile. "Back in a minute."

Angelo slipped off his overcoat and hung it on a coat tree, then returned to the bar. He took a pack of Marlboros from his jacket, stuck a cigarette between his lips and lifted my lighter. "Nice. Dunhill?"

"Yeah. What precinct are you in?"

"I'm a sector commander in the department's Intelligence Division." He had a pleasant baritone voice and an easy manner, confident without seeming arrogant.

"Really? How many sectors are there?"

"Six."

"How many officers per sector?"

"It varies, but there's never enough. We have a hellava time trying to keep up with everything."

He drank a little of his vodka and I played with my glass of beer.

"Interesting possibility, huh?" he asked. "But you wouldn't get much co-operation from anyone beyond the PR level."

"Is mind-reading a prerequisite for the job or is that a hobby?"

"If I were a reporter talking to a cop in internal affairs or intelligence or counterterrorism, my first thoughts would be how to get a story out of the conversation. Isn't that a prerequisite for your job?"

"Depends. On some papers the only prerequisite is a pulse and a basic understanding of the five Ws. But I am curious."

"Well, there isn't much I can tell you. By the way, I liked your piece on Charlie Patton."

"Why? It wasn't a flattering picture I painted of your associates."

He shrugged. "My associates don't always merit flattery. The biggest problem I see with reporters and cops is that neither one of them has ever done the other guy's job. The second problem is that most reporters are predisposed to deal with us as either heroes or villains. It's one extreme or the other."

"We're supposed to come to some understanding of your job by working the police beat."

"That makes about as much sense as expecting us to come to an understanding of your job by reading the paper."

"What was your major in college?"

"English literature, with a minor in sociology, and four semesters in journalism."

Well, now, how about that shit. "Are you the 'spokesman' KSAY radio quotes as their unidentified source in police intelligence?"

"No," he said with a laugh.

"Who is?"

"I can't tell you that." He smiled.

I was fascinated. I wouldn't have any trouble liking this guy, I thought. If he weren't a cop. Which is stupid. There have to be at least a few cops you can like.

"You look like you're debating something with yourself. Are you always wrapped this tight?"

"You're the first member of Sheila's family I've met," I said. "Maybe I'm overreacting to that."

His laugh was barely audible. "Maybe . . ."

"When you were explaining the mystery of your psychic ability earlier, you said, 'If I were a reporter talking to a cop in intelligence, or counter-terrorism, or internal affairs . . .' Does the Philadelphia PD have a counter-terrorism group?"

"Not as such," he said, swirling the vodka and ice around in his glass. He drank most of what was left. "Commissioner Reichmann has made repeated requests for the funds to establish such a division but so far he hasn't received the approval."

"Not as such." Now what the hell does that mean? I wondered.

I was still working on that when Ferris came in and waved. "Angelo, that's a friend of mine I asked to meet me here."

"Ferris?"

"Yeah. I should've expected that you'd know him. Anyway, we've got to work out some stuff on a story, so I'm gonna leave, but it was nice meeting you. And I apologize for the comment about the Mafia."

"No problem." He slipped an elegant brown calfskin wallet out of his jacket pocket and handed me a business card on which were embossed his name, his rank, and two telephone numbers. No mention of the fact that he was a cop. "Keep that with you, in case you need to reach me. The second number is a locator. If you leave a message they'll get it to me."

"Thanks. Never know when I'll need help with a parking ticket."

"Since you don't own a car, I hope to hear from you before then. Call me and let's get together for dinner, or a couple of drinks. I might be able to soften your view of the police without compromising your journalistic integrity.

"And I meant what I said about the piece on Patton. The mere possibility of an urban terrorist in Quaker Plaza on Christmas Eve let loose a lot of fears . . . but that doesn't justify the overkill and the very real possibility that we might have done a lot more harm than good by overreacting."

"I'll call," I promised, holding out my hand.

— — — —

"I still don't get it," Ferris said, and drained the glass he was holding.

"You're not listening," I insisted. "You don't want to hear what I'm saying because you don't like what I'm saying."

He took his feet off the coffee table and sat up straight, leaning forward with his elbows on his knees. "Tell me again, and go slow. Maybe I'm missing something."

"You want another drink?"

"Yeah, and give me some ice."

I filled his glass with ice and handed it to him, then opened a Pepsi for myself. "Okay, listen: Juliet gets me out of jail in Mexico and gets me a job on the *Call*. She does that without knowing if I can write my name."

"You could shuck the pants off Pulaski's statute," Ferris said and poured Scotch into the glass. "What did you tell her?"

"Nothing. Swear to God. But let's say you're partly right. She admitted a strong sexual attraction. She has money and the right connections. For whatever reason, she's smitten with me and thinks it would be fun to rescue a *gringo* from a Mexican jail and bring him to Philadelphia. She's a dilettante, and I'm a sex object to play around with for a few weeks. Good for a few giggles with her girlfriends."

"She's not in real tight with the society crowd, from what I hear. Her connections are more political than old hardcore Main Line money like the Biddles and Pughs."

"Whatever, they're all a little bent.

"So, I show up riding a ticket for which she paid, in cash. I could have gone anywhere with that money, but I came here. And she provokes a fight."

"Well, you were a little severe, from what you said."

"Agreed. But only after she came out of nowhere with that feminist bullshit. I tell her to go fuck herself and leave her standing in the street. End of story, right? I mean, she may be smitten but she isn't gonna put up with that kind of crap. Hell, *I'm* the one on the leash. If I don't behave properly, sayonara. Right?"

"Hawk, I've never understood why a woman does what she does or doesn't do what she doesn't. Some women like abuse."

"I didn't abuse her. I just told her I wouldn't put up with her shit."

"Maybe that turned her on, a guy that didn't care if she's rich and owns half a newspaper."

"Okay, maybe. So she fucks me through the mattress and then she disappears for almost three months, but before she goes she arranges for this apartment, the furniture, and leaves me one of her cars."

"*She* did this place?" He glanced around, shaking his head. "Man, you must have some kind of magic in your dick."

"It's standard issue. And don't get distracted by some bullshit fantasy." I lit another Camel and waited.

"Okay. That's an interesting story, but so what?"

"So, I go to work on the *Call* and I piss off Ivan on a daily basis. I'm his worst nightmare—a fucking maverick he can't control and can't get rid of. Why can't he fire me?"

"Daniel French. He likes you, and he has a lot of respect for you."

"Bullshit. Juliet Franklin-Rossini. French told me, after the Patton story, that he, or I should say the *Call*, needs Ivan a lot more than it needs me. And I agree. But I still didn't get fired. *He* can't fire me without approval from Juliet. So I get invited to a Christmas party."

"Lots of people were invited to that party. And I don't think he wanted to fire you."

"I *know* he didn't want to fire me, because I'm part of this goddamn game they're playing. So are you. We were the only two invited to a private audience and given an invitation to muckrake on the *Call*'s time."

"Okay, so you lead a charmed life. Daniel likes you. Juliet is in love with you. Ivan's off your neck. And I'm the guy you send for coffee. Shit, man, you got it made."

"You're not listening!" I got up, frustrated, and started pacing behind the sofa, up and back, up and back.

"I heard enough to know I wouldn't mind being in your shoes."

"Sneakers aren't your style. Anyway, tonight French summons me to his office and hands me a confidential report from the office of the Assistant U.S. Attorney. We've got a scoop. But instead of telling me to write a story based on the report, he says he wants to talk about it with me next week. *Next* week, f'Chrissake.

"If you were the managing editor of a newspaper in the country's fourth largest city and you had a story like that, would you wait a week to talk about it with the reporter? Would you give the report to that person *before* you read it yourself?"

"I don't know. What's the big deal?"

"The big deal, my friend, is the bedrock of competitive journalism: Print it first. Make the competition play catch-up."

"Well . . ."

"Am I right? Christ, video news crews will run you down with their fuckin' vans and minicams to get a picture on the air five seconds before the competition. I don't think any of it's important enough to break the speed limit, let alone put people at risk, but tell that to an AP reporter or a legman from the *Inquirer*, and he'll ask you what you're doing in the business."

"Maybe Daniel has to check it out with the lawyers."

"He'd still have me writing it while they sat on their collective fat ass and pondered the consequences. Anyway, they'd want to see the finished article before they made any legal pronouncements."

"You're right."

"But if he was handed the report and told to give it to me, to see how I'd react, or to read as background material . . . Leon, Daniel didn't get that god-damn report from the U.S. Attorney or from anyone on his staff. He got it from Juliet."

"How do you know that?"

"When I sat down in French's office I could smell her perfume on the chair. She'd been in that chair sometime within the hour. He hadn't had time to read it. She used her connections to get it as sure as I'm sitting here with you."

"Which means what? I don't see the point."

"Juliet Franklin-Rossini is running this operation, which would be fine—but her brother, as I understand it, controls the paper. She even said to me, 'I don't really have much to do with the day-to-day operation of the paper.' She was embarrassed.

"Which leaves me thinking that she's won French's loyalty with promises of who knows what and we're cannon fodder in a coup-to-be, not to be confused with a coup d'état, or, I hope, a coup de grâce."

"What's all that shit mean? I never could understand Latin."

"Not to worry, Señor Ipso Facto. What it means is she's after power. She's looking for a way to dethrone her brother and take over the *Call*."

"*What!?* I swear, Hawkins, you have got a twisted mind."

"Wanna bet?"

He laughed. "Thirty to one, right? Fuck you."

"Leon, think about what I'm telling you."

"You want to know what I think? I think you've got yourself one hellava sweet deal. All you have to do is go along with her and you'll probably end up as Ivan's boss." The idea gave birth to a huge grin. "Think about that, turkey. You could have Ivan for breakfast."

"I'd have to get up too early for such a small pleasure. And I have no ambition or desire to be a fucking newspaper editor in Philadelphia. Or anywhere else."

"Write your own ticket. If you help her get what she wants, the way she feels about you, you can have anything. Hell, she'd probably support you while you write books. What's her place like? Could you be comfortable in a mansion with a butler and maybe a hot little French maid to bring you your espresso? Whew! Beats the hell out of Sammy as a servant."

"You haven't seen the butler. They chipped him off the big rock at Stone-henge. You want more ice?"

"No, thanks."

I sat down again, and each of us fell into his own thoughts. I was reasonably certain that I'd brought Ferris around to my point of view, but the so-called bottom line still didn't add up to much. So I was 'right.' So what?

"The thing I can't figure out," I sighed, "is what they plan to do with any of this. French can publish anything for one edition, maybe two, but then what? He can't win a war with his publisher, and Juliet doesn't have the power to back him."

"They're looking for a break somewhere."

"Yeah, but what kinda break? Eventually, everyone in the Delaware River Valley will have an opportunity to read that a lot of Reichmann's boys in blue have been misbehaving. Publishing that a day or a week before all the others get it doesn't do anything for French or Ms. Franklin-Rossini unless she's trying to show her brother that she's capable of more involvement in the *Call*'s news operations."

"Hey, maybe that's all she wants," Ferris declared.

"You gotta be kidding. Alexis may fantasize about being a real live Brenda Starr, but Juliet?"

"Ask her."

"Ask her what?"

"Ask her what the fuck she wants. Why not?"

"I already did, more than once."

"What did she say?"

"Nothing . . . it was all bullshit."

Ferris laughed and poured himself a short vodka. "She's got you on a string." He was delighted with himself. "She's got the hook set and she's just reeling you in, little by little." He went on laughing, shaking his head back and forth. "It's all clear as these fine-looking crystal glasses she left here."

Well, fuck me! He was right, and I was ridiculous for not seeing it. "Shit!"

"You know I'm right." He laughed. "God, I love it."

The phone rang and I left him sitting there laughing.

"Hello."

"Hi, grump. It's midnight. Am I still on your list of hot prospects for this evening?"

"Sorry, I forgot. Why don't you come over? You got your car?"

"Sure. Be there in thirty minutes. 'Bye. Oh, you were a hit with Uncle Angelo. See you later."

Great. Her mother sends me cookies and her uncle thinks I'm an okay guy. I can't wait until we start looking at china patterns. I rolled a joint, took a hit, and walked back into the living room. "You want a hit off this?"

"One. Maybe two. I gotta get out of here. That Sheila?"

"Yeah. You remember the guy at the bar when you came in, the one I was talking to?" He nodded, holding the smoke in his lungs. "You know him?"

"No." The word came out on a cloud of marijuana smoke. "Why?"

"That's Sheila's uncle."

"I know that. I've seen him in there, and we've said hello once or twice, but I never really talked to him."

"He's a 'sector commander' in the police intelligence division, whatever the hell that is."

The joint stopped in mid-flight, halfway to his lips. "He told you that?"

"No, I just made it up. Give me that." I took the joint, inhaled, and handed it back.

"*He* told you he's with the Philly PD's intelligence division?" His surprise surprised me. "Those guys don't tell their families what they do most of the time."

"Well, Sheila hasn't proposed yet, so I'm not family."

"You should be real nice to him. And her. Or leave town."

"What the fuck's with you?"

"Ask him to show you your file."

"What file? What the hell are you talking about?"

"They keep files on every reporter in the area."

"Are you serious?" He sucked in a lungful of smoke and nodded as he handed the joint back to me. "You saw the files? Or your file?" I asked.

"Damn right. Everything. Where I work, where I live, credit record, military record . . ."

"I didn't know you were in the service."

"Reserves. How much I make, my parents, where they live, how much my dad makes, their credit record, clips with my byline, and how much insurance I carry. Car, license number, even how many tickets I've picked up. And most of it was right on the money."

"No shit." 'Since you don't have a car, I hope to hear from you before then.' I could hear his voice.

"What time is Sheila due?"

"Half-hour or so." I opened a bottle of beer. "You want anything?"

"Nope."

"Tell me how I've been hooked before you leave. Let's see how close we are to a common vision."

He started laughing again. "She finds you in a Mexican federal slam, so right away she knows you're a little different. And she's physically attracted to you. You tell her you're a reporter, right?"

"Yeah."

"Busted for possession, maybe looking at a long stay behind the iron doors. She gets you out, so now you're obligated. You owe her. And you show up to pay the debt. That says you've got some sense of honor, plus you acknowledge that there's something between you.

"She gets you a job, which is easy enough.

"She starts a fight because she wants to see how fuckin' hard-nosed you really are. If you cave in to her, then she knows to handle you one way. If you don't, then she has to deal with you in a different way. Right?"

I shrugged.

"You know I'm right. She loses the fight, which doesn't make any difference. It's like sending out a patrol, to see who's out there and how strong they are.

"But she has to do something to put it back together so she gets you out of the motel, takes you home to her mansion, and you fuck half the night.

"Then she disappears. You're confused. You know sooner or later she'll show up again. Hell, it's her paper, or half of it, and her car . . . and you're her knight, tarnished armor and all.

"Meanwhile, you can't get yourself fired. And you've moved in here, a nice ready-made place to hang out and see what happens next.

"She shows up Christmas Day like a goddamn present, gift-wrapped in a sable." He started laughing again.

"You're sure as hell enjoying this, aren't you?"

"Bet your ass I am."

"You should. If I were on the other side I'd be laughing, too. I wish I knew what the hell she and French have planned."

"Nothing."

"Whatta you mean, 'nothing'?"

"I don't think they've really got a plan." He stood up. "It's time for me to get rolling." He pulled on his overcoat, smiling. "I still say you've got a sweet deal. Just don't forget your friends when you're sitting in that corner office."

"Right. Leave your name with the secretary and I'll get back to you." I walked him to the door. "I've got to think about this shit. See you tomorrow."

A few minutes after Ferris left, Sheila came in with my "big present," as she put it. She'd bought me an Adolfo bomber jacket with more pockets and zippers than I'd ever seen, made of some of the finest leather I'd ever felt. Four hundred dollars if it cost a dime. And a perfect fit.

"I don't know what to say . . . it's perfect. Thank you."

"As soon as I saw it I knew you were meant to have it, but I thought it might be too much, y'know? That you might take it the wrong way. My mom talked me into it."

Cookies and compliments and a very expensive leather jacket. Mom was sure as hell doing her part. Ah well, what the hell. I pulled her to me and kissed her, wishing she wasn't in love with me, but as long as she was, I decided, I'd play out the hand and see what happened.

"Can we go up to bed and fuck?" she asked as she slipped her hand between my legs. "I'm so horny I had an orgasm driving over here, just thinking about you."

"You're full of it." I laughed and slid my hand under her skirt. She wasn't lying. Her pussy was wet. My finger slid in and she wrapped her arms around my neck and lifted herself onto me, circling my waist with her strong legs. Moaning, grinding her pelvis against me, she stuck her tongue in my ear. And then she yelped: "Ahh, ahh, ahh, goddamn, do it, do it, *fuck me-e-e-e!*"

— — — —

At five A.M. I came awake with a rush, riding a geyser of adrenaline to the surface, eyes wide with anxiety, my heart pounding. I was clammy with sweat and chilled from lying exposed to the cool air. My half of the quilt covered Sheila. Her half was on the floor.

A dream woke me. Or I woke myself from the dream. I closed my eyes and drifted, waiting for the images to follow me to the surface.

The first was a Chinese hexagram from the *I Ching*. Then Mama-san. Square gold coins. A temple. The snake!

The snake brought it all together. In the dream it was a time of deep twilight. I was standing at the bottom of the frame, looking into the picture. At frame right and set back was a small Oriental temple, an open structure with a gold Buddha seated on a pedestal, the perfect being in repose. He was surrounded by flickering candles. At frame left and closer to the foreground was a carved wooden table, the top covered in small ceramic tiles, and on the table was a hexagram from the *I Ching* fashioned from gold, almost like a trivet. Number Fifty-six. Lu/The Exile.

The hexagram, Mama-san said in the dream, represented a degree of danger, a time when travelers are alone and without friends. Big trouble, every-where, she said. Success would be small at first, but great success was possible.

"Great caution only way to make safe journey."

Coiled to one side of the gold hexagram was an iridescent green snake, maybe three feet long.

The message from Mama-san, in the dream, had been very much like the message she had given me at lunch. And as I thought about it I remembered that it had been five P.M., give or take a few minutes. I rolled on my side and picked up my watch, squinting at the dial. It was five after five.

My pulse had settled down and the perspiration had dried. I listened to Sheila breathing, to the clock ticking, to my conscience nagging me about a lot of shit I couldn't or wouldn't change. Fuck it, what's done is done. Looking back is too much like looking at a bad movie on TV for the second or third or tenth time. The story's gone, if a story ever existed. The plot is even thinner, the characters even less comprehensible. All I see are the mistakes. Could have, would have, should have. And then you die.

"I have a confession to make," Juliet announced as she whipped the Mercedes around a lumbering eighteen-wheeler and slid back into the north-bound lane of Highway 611.

"You always wanted to race in the Monte Carlo Grand Prix."

"I *asked* if you wanted to drive."

"I know, I know . . ."

"I've never known a man who would admit that the woman behind the wheel could drive as well as he could."

"Hell, you may be a better driver than I am, but seventy miles an hour on a frozen road in the snow is a little excessive from my point of view."

"Sixty. You want me to slow down?"

"No, just don't kill me in this piece of overrated, underpowered German junk."

"Don't make me self-conscious and I'll get us there in one piece."

"I can't wait." I lit my third Camel of the hour and opened the window enough to let the smoke out. "You mentioned a confession . . ."

"I'm in love with you."

"You're in love with me," I said after a few seconds of quiet desperation. She nodded. I put my hand on her shoulder. "Say three 'Hail Marys,' then go and sin no more." She didn't smile, or say anything. "You do know your 'Hail Mary' don't you?"

"Why do you make fun of everything that makes me feel good?"

"Do I?"

"Almost everything. Why are you so afraid of me? Or your feelings for me? I know you care about me."

"True. But do I love you? Or, more to the point, am I *in love* with you?"

"Doesn't matter. You wouldn't admit it if you were."

I tilted the passenger seat back a little and closed my eyes. *Doesn't matter. You wouldn't admit it if you were.* Maybe she's right.

"You've retreated into your shell, and it's another thirty minutes to Upper Black Eddy. It seems a shame to waste our time together because you're afraid of someone loving you."

"If I'm afraid it's not a fear of being loved. It's fear of love encumbered with expectations that I can't meet."

"Let's talk about something else. You pick a topic."

"How about my love for you?"

She snapped her head around and took a quick look. I was staring straight ahead, smiling. "Don't fuck with me, Hawkins."

Cracked me up. The tone and the content were as unlike her as poetry was to me. I would've kissed her but she was still doing close to seventy. "That was priceless," I finally managed to say. "Nothing ambiguous, nothing hidden in the silken folds of tactful word selection and careful sentence structure."

She concentrated on the road, which—thank the gods that be—was almost deserted.

"And now who's in retreat?" I asked after several minutes.

"I haven't retreated! I'm thinking about what you said."

"Oh well, that explains it. The distinction's difficult to see, but that's probably because it's so dark in here. Hell, I have trouble seeing fine lines in broad daylight."

"Oh, shut up," she laughed. "You surprised me."

"Yeah, well, *you* surprised *me.* Anyway, someone else thinks they're in love with me. I can't handle two at a time."

"You can't handle one at a time, except on the physical level."

"You're right," I said, "so why tell me that you're in love with me? Why would you even allow yourself to feel that way? Unless you have expectations that I'll change, that I'll 'learn' to be the person you require to make it sensible to be in love with me. Otherwise it doesn't make sense."

She drove in silence for ten miles or so, then turned off on a narrow gravel road that undoubtedly fell under the county's carefully planned program of benign neglect. She cut her speed to twenty.

"Is this a shortcut?"

"This is the only way to get there. I told you it's remote."

"Ivory towers and throne rooms are remote. This is the dark side of the moon. How far from here?"

"Fifteen minutes, if the bridge is standing."

"*If* the bridge is standing . . ."

"Otherwise, we hike. That'll take an extra fifteen minutes."

A nice brisk stroll on a cold New Year's Eve. One of my favorite pastimes.

The bridge, a fifteen-foot wooden span, had held its own. The Mercedes shifted into a crawl and we crossed an angry creek that was threatening to spill its shallow banks. The windshield wipers were moving faster than the pistons.

Once past the bridge it was a short drive to the A-frame perched on a low granite ridge overlooking the Delaware River. We were about sixty miles north of Philadelphia, she said, although we'd driven another twenty or so because there wasn't a straight-line route. With the traffic coming out of the city, and the slow speed once we were off the highway, the trip had taken almost two hours.

Inside the house, I looked through the huge front window into absolute blackness. No stars or lights from other houses were visible. "This window ever blow out?" I asked.

"No, knock on wood." She rapped the bar top with her knuckles.

From where I was standing the room stretched back about thirty-five feet to a wall that separated the living area from the kitchen, a downstairs bath, and a small bedroom for the maid. An ample loft bedroom, a master bath, a sauna, and a sun room took up what there was of the second floor, which covered a little more than half the first floor. The cathedral ceiling was thirty-five or forty feet high at its highest point. There were a lot of exposed beams. It reminded me of a tobacco barn converted into a condo.

"You like it?" Juliet asked, looking up from the champagne bottle with which she was wrestling. As she did, the cork surrendered with a gas-propelled *pop*, ricocheted off a beam to my left and landed at my feet. "Jamie, are you okay?" she yelled as the champagne spilled out the neck and over her hands. "Oh God, look at me," she moaned with some embarrassment, and then she got the giggles.

"Fine." I picked up the cork and sniffed it. "*Les Feet* 'fifty-one, I believe."

"You turkey, you're not helping, you know . . ." She'd grabbed a small towel from inside the bar and stopped most of the dripping. "This stuff cost seventy-five bucks a bottle and I'm spilling it all over the floor."

"I might be more sympathetic if you could control your giggling. Try to look a little despondent." I pulled a stack of cassettes out of my bag and put on *Exit*, by Tangerine Dream. I am, at times, a heartless sonofabitch.

"I feel silly. You think it's the grass we smoked?"

"Naw, probably the decrease in pollutants and your proximity to escaping vapors from that bottle. I bet you're a raucous wench when the bubbles go up your nose."

"I'm *never* raucous," she contended with absolute certainty.

"I didn't think so."

"Well, okay. As long as you understand I'm a . . . what did you call me? 'A right and proper lady of good posture, good standing, and killer bazongas.' " She was laughing so hard she spilled another five bucks' worth of the bubbly.

"Did you have any plans for us to drink that stuff, or is this some peculiar ritual by which I'm being seduced?"

She inhaled with studied concentration, and managed to subdue her giddiness. Then, clutching two champagne glasses and the bottle of Dom Perignon, she made it across the room. "You pour, okay?" I poured, put the bottle aside, and took one of the glasses from her hand. She was transfixed. "What's that music? It's so . . . strange."

"It's music for acid lovers and mushroom eaters."

"I felt myself being carried right out of the room."

"I circled Jupiter one night listening to this. Shall we toast the New Year before you lift off?"

"My God, I just remembered, I have to cook! I've never tried to cook while I was stoned."

"Can you cook when you're straight?"

"I'm an excellent cook, thank you."

"Well, put it on automatic and see what happens."

"Put what on automatic?"

"Your drug-addled and somewhat altered consciousness. Just go about your business like you know what you're doing. That's how you control this stuff. If you want to control it."

"Right." She clinked her glass to mine. "Happy New Year, Hawkins. If nothing else, it should be interesting."

We drank a little and she moved in, pressing herself against me. "Gimme a kiss," she said in a surprisingly gravelly tone.

I kissed her, grinning, wanting to laugh. "You are *fried*," I said when we parted. "You know that?"

"I know. It's fun." She drank about half of the champagne left in her glass. "Do you really love me?"

The automatic response—Love many, trust few, and always cut the cards— came to my lips, but I didn't say it. Instead, I nodded. "Yes, I love you."

"I never thought you'd say that to me."

"Neither did I, but what the fuck do I know? I'm a cynic. Remember?"

"You are hard work."

"You're not what I'd call a piece of cake, my sweet."

"I think I'd rather be a tart," she giggled.

"You've got too much money to ever be a real tart, but I'll do what I can to help you."

"Can we start tonight?" she asked as she moved closer.

"At the stroke of midnight," I promised as I slipped the mouth of the glass under her right nipple. I tipped the glass and a perfect circle of champagne-soaked cloth closed around the nipple, which was rigid and probably quivering. "This is the high-society version of the wet T-shirt contest," I said.

"Well, you missed one," she answered, turning slightly to give me a better angle of approach.

— — — —

"You've never seen the Mummers' Parade?" Juliet called from the kitchen, as if it was beyond ordinary comprehension that any being could have survived thirty-odd years on the planet without the experience of string bands and bizarre costumes.

I was stretched out on a sofa with my eyes more closed than open, nursing my second cup of coffee and staring at more odd-looking people than I'd seen in one place since the last time I was on Hollywood Boulevard. "Never saw them, never heard of 'em." And neither had anyone else I knew outside Philadelphia.

I nursed a little of the coffee past the lump that had replaced my solar plexus. "They're actually pretty good," I yelled, which made my head throb. "Better than the Pasadena bullshit."

"The *Call* sponsors one of the bands," she said as she came into the room. She looked great, smiling, humming like Scarlett on the morning after. "They're world-famous!"

"Does that mean we have to applaud when they go by?"

"No, but stay awake. This really is a Philadelphia event." She knelt beside me and brushed my hair away from my face.

"Frankly, my dear, I don't give a fat rat's rear end. I need a drink to settle my stomach." As for staying awake, I didn't have much of a choice. What I did have was a very expensive champagne hangover. I was in no condition to sleep. Christ, give me tequila any day. No matter how much I drink at least I wake up with a clear head. A lot healthier than drinking glorified grape juice with bubbles. What I needed was fresh air and a reason to go find it.

"Listen," I pleaded, "if you want to see this parade why don't we tape it and go for a walk. If I don't move around I'll be a basket case until this evening. If I get up and do something I'll feel better by six or seven, at the latest."

"Too much bubbly for Mr. Grump? How about breakfast?"

"How about the death sentence. Eggs up at sunrise."

"It's seventeen degrees . . ."

"Seventeen? God, it's no wonder all those Colonials looked like lemon-sucking refugees from Fun City. It's too damn cold to smile."

"Wait until summer hits Philadelphia. Hot, humid, and dirty air."

"Would you give me a grown-up sized shot of something with a proof rating at least twice my age?"

"Sure." She rummaged in the liquor cabinet and came back with a bottle of Wild Turkey.

I held out my cup. "Just pour it in here, with the coffee."

"We could go riding. Both the horses need exercise. And you would certainly get plenty of fresh air. There's always a wind off the river at this time of the year."

"I haven't been on a horse since I was about sixteen years old."

"You can have the mare," she whispered in my ear with a sexy murmur. "She's easy."

"Another tart?"

She bounced up, rigged the VCR to record, pushed a couple of buttons, and grabbed a short, heavy jacket from the closet. "Let's ride."

"Christ, you're full of energy and ambition. It'll take me ten minutes to get my sneakers on."

"I'll get Frank to saddle the horses and walk them around front for you. Take your time."

She left me struggling into a sitting position, hoping Frank, her caretaker, wasn't as fucked-up as I was. Lacing up my sneakers, I could hear the leathery voice of the old man who'd taught me what little I knew about riding. "Check the cinches and always keep your heels down." I wished I had a pair of boots.

I was leaning over, tightening the lace on the second sneaker, when the vapid female TV commentator loudly gushed, "Here he is! One of the great favorites in the annual New Year's Day Mummers' Parade . . . listen to the applause!"

I looked up, expecting to see Ben-Hur, at the least.

"Commissioner Reichmann, of the Philadelphia police, and the ever-popular Bullet!" the male half of the TV duo fairly shouted.

Bullet? Old Commissioner Dumdum rides a fuckin' horse named Bullet? I cackled. The camera tracked the horse and rider. The horse was an easy fifteen hands high, a black beauty with one white stocking and a satin sheen. Reichmann, in full-dress blues, pearl-handled .44 on his hip, rode with arrogant confidence. The man who would be Caesar, I thought.

"Bullet, of course, is a great favorite with the kids," the woman commentator said in her high-pitched voice. "A beautiful, powerful animal, admirably ridden by our commissioner of police, don't you think?"

"Yes, indeed, Tiffany. My son, Randy, who's only six, says he wants to be a mounted policeman when he grows up so he can be like the commissioner and have a horse like Bullet."

"Can you believe this shit?" I shouted at the empty room. "The guy's probably a child molester. Tiffany Bimbo is a week out of Altoona and needs a voice coach." I reached for my coffee, and when I looked back the camera was pushing in on Reichmann's right stirrup. "And the camera operator is either an epileptic or the director's got a foot fetish."

"There we see the commissioner's new boots . . ." Numb-Nuts announced, the camera tight on the glistening black leather.

One boot, asshole.

"A New Year's tradition with Commissioner Reichmann," Tiffany gushed. "Every year, the commissioner orders a new pair of handmade riding boots from an elderly Mexican craftsman in Albuquerque, just for this great parade."

Out of nowhere appeared a picture of a striking, silver-haired old Mexican man hunched over a boot last. The old man was stitching the sole to the welt.

"Señor Juan Cortez," Tiffany continued, "is reported to be eighty years old."

"What a handsome old gentleman," the guy added as the picture changed to one where Juan was standing chest to face with Reichmann, beaming as Reichmann examined a pair of boots. Juan was about five three, in his boots. Reichmann towered over him.

"Recently married for the fourth time," Tiffany giggled, "to a young bride of twenty-two. John, maybe you should get this guy's address." Chortle, chortle.

"He's quite the fellow," John said. He didn't care for her sense of humor and I wondered how she would have handled an equally sexist piece of suggestive 'journalism.' Poor John must be having a problem with, gasp, *dysfunction*, and Tiffany isn't getting as much as she wants.

The director switched to a wide shot on another camera and Reichmann was once again riding toward the viewer. John and Tiffany babbled on about Juan Cortez and Reichmann, how they had come to meet, Reichmann's admiration for the old Mexican gentleman. Ad nauseam. Real 'put it in perspective' reporting, better known as filling dead air.

As they struggled to make something of nothing, the camera pushed in, again, until the frame was filled with the stirrup and boot.

"Oh my God, oh my God," Tiffany screamed into her mike milliseconds after the sound of a rifle shot, followed by the screaming of a wounded horse.

The picture switched to a high-angle wide shot, and the camera zoomed in tight on Reichmann and Bullet, both of them down on the street, blood pouring from a wound in the horse's neck, Reichmann with pistol in hand. The commissioner crouched behind Bullet, a useless effort to shield himself since he was looking up and anyone shooting down would have had a clean target.

"A sniper," John cried. The commissioner is down, and, my God! He's been badly wounded! Look at the blood! And Bullet's trying to protect his master. He's moving around . . ." His voice trailed off and I hoped it was because the director was screaming at him to shut the fuck up.

In fact, as the picture shifted from one camera to another, it was clear to all but the brain-dead that it was Bullet who'd been wounded, and was in his gasping death throes, his mouth a sea of bloody froth, while Reichmann shifted on his haunches, his eyes darting from one camera to another. In the distance, unseen, the string bands continued playing, blissfully unaware of what had happened.

And then the sounds of pure pandemonium rose from the street to the platform where Tiffany and John were strangely silent. From the high-angle camera a wide shot revealed several thousand people running in all directions, stumbling, staggering, shoving each other from their paths.

The director cut to another screen, tight on Reichmann as he rose from his crouch. He'd lost his hat, and his jacket was soaked with blood. The barrel of the .44 moved slightly as Reichmann lined the sights on Bullet's head and squeezed off a single round.

"It's a coup de grâce!" John screamed over the echoing report of the Magnum. "It's a coup de grâce."

"Jamie!" Juliet shouted from outside. "What's going on?"

"El Supremo just sent old Bullet to Happy Pastures."

The door flew open and she stared at the TV, her forehead creased. "What are you talking about?" she groused as she closed the door.

"Reichmann sacrificed 'the ever-popular Bullet' to a larger cause."

"My God!" she gasped. "Is Reichmann hurt? What happened?"

"You want the official version, or do you want my version?"

She looked from the TV to me and back to the TV. "What on earth are you talking about?"

"There are two ways of looking at what a couple of million people think they just saw. I may be the only outsider who has a second view, but I think Reichmann's running a very weird scam."

"Commissioner Reichmann," Tiffany interjected, "apparently was *not* injured by the sniper. The blood you see apparently is from the wound to Bullet, we're told."

"Apparently," I said, "little Tiffany Tea Time has successfully mastered the definitive conditional parts of her job, we're told. To whom are these things apparent? And who told her? Stay tuned for film at six and eleven."

"Jamie, will you please tell me what happened? Officially."

"A sniper, not his real name, fired a round apparently meant to kill or cause grievous injury to Philadelphia Police Commissioner Rudolph Reichmann, but as luck would have it, the bullet hit Bullet, that has been confirmed, and the sniper didn't hang around for a second shot. The horse went down, Reichmann soaked up a little blood from the dying horse, and then El Supremo put a round through the horse's head. And all that, mind you, while five hundred lunatics in very strange costumes continued to do the old soft-shoe up Broad Street in time to 'Satin Doll.' "

" 'Satin Doll'?"

"I may have just made that up. But it needed a light touch at the end, don't you think?"

The director cut to a two-shot of John and Tiffany, apparently grim and almost certainly shaken by the events just witnessed. John, looking directly at the camera, said, "Tiffany, we've just heard that members of the Special Weapons and Tactics team may have the alleged sniper cornered in the nearby Academy of Music. According to one of our field reporters . . . ah, stand by, please, now there's another report that a man with a rifle has been seen on the roof of the academy. We don't want to make a wrongful assumption that anyone seen with a rifle is a sniper, but . . . okay, I think we're about to go live to correspondent Art Quisenberry. . . . Are you there, Art? Can you hear me?"

I was rolling on the sofa, laughing. "Christ on a bike, who are these people? John and Tiffany? I can't fuckin' believe it."

"What is so funny? A sniper running loose on a rooftop with a powerful rifle isn't my idea of comedy." Her tone was stern.

"Juliet, there wasn't any attempt on Reichmann's life. If that wasn't un-adulterated bullshit I'll plead guilty to fucking goats and you can hang me as a pervert."

"I don't understand . . ."

"When the bullshit settles down, I'll rewind the tape and show you some-thing"—I grinned—"odd, if Reichmann's the horseman he seems to think he is."

"He's an excellent horseman, as a matter of fact. I despise him, personally, but he rides extremely well and handles horses with ease. What did you see?"

"You need to see it in the context of what happened, but just before the rifle shot Reichmann was getting ready to bail out. The camera was on a tight shot of the stirrup while Tiffany and John-boy were chattering about Reichmann's new boots and some poor bootmaker. Reichmann didn't have any way of knowing that his boot was on close-up, but he knew when to expect the shot, and he was getting ready to get off his horse in a hurry. Otherwise, Bullet might have fallen on him and broken his leg, or Christ knows what."

"Are you sure?"

"Do I look like someone who'd fuck a goat?"

"Jamie, that's disgusting. Can't you put it differently?"

"Well, *excuse me*! The leader of Philadelphia's law enforcement just put God knows how many lives in jeopardy and you're offended by my language? Not by the information, but by the manner in which I phrased it?"

"That isn't the point."

I couldn't stop myself from laughing, which annoyed Juliet, which was understandable since she didn't know why I was laughing. I mean, there we were, arguing about my poor choice of words as if it had some importance while an obviously lunatic commissioner of police hoaxed—how many people? Three or four million, maybe? Not only do we want to kill the messengers with the bad news, we're considering long, cold showers for any who refer to having carnal knowledge of a goat.

"Are you finished?" she inquired when I settled down.

"Foot in the stirrup, heels down." I said. "First time I ever sat on a horse, the old man who let me ride told me that. 'Boy, *always* check yer cinches, feet all the way in them stirrups, and keep them heels down.' "

She was chewing her bottom lip, looking from me to the TV and back. Her hands held riding gloves which she twisted as though she meant to wring out water.

"Let's go play with your horses." I found my jacket, pulled it on, and dropped my arm around her shoulders.

"Aren't you interested in this? It's certainly big news."

"It's bullshit, Juliet. Let the tape run and we'll look at it when we get back. C'mon."

"In a minute."

I went into the kitchen and rummaged in the cabinets until I found a box of sugar cubes. I slipped a few in my pocket and went back into the living room. "You ready?" I tugged on her arm and she let me lead her to the door, casting a quick glance over her shoulder as she stepped onto the porch. The horses were tied to a post. "Do I still get the mare, *madame?*"

"Yes. She's the sorrel with the Western saddle."

"What's her name?"

"Gemini. She has a twin sister."

I walked quietly up to Gemini and whispered in her ear, "Don't make me look bad, okay? It's been a long time." As I talked I fed her a couple of sugar cubes. A little bribery seemed a reasonable investment, for whatever it might be worth. She snorted, whether in disdain or delight with the sugar I couldn't say.

"Let's go, cowboy," Juliet called.

I checked the cinches, which were snug and seemed properly secured, then mounted Gemini and turned her toward Juliet. "You lead. Ms. Gemini and I'll tag along."

Juliet's horse broke into a trot as soon as she touched his ribs, and Gemini, sensing my keen desire to be with the one I loved, bolted after them. I grabbed the saddle horn with my right hand and pulled back on the reins with my left. "Whoa, girl. Jesus, gimme a break, I'm not ready to race for the roses, okay?"

From somewhere behind me and to my left, near the barn, I heard soft male laughter. "Lifestyles of the Rich and Ridiculous," a new comedy special for New Year's Day.

— — — —

"Okay," I said, pushing the slo-mo button on the VCR remote control in French's office. "Watch his heel . . ." Frame by frame the picture developed, a cheap time-lapse visual blossoming. Reichmann worked his boot backward, ever so slowly, until the ball of his foot rested on the stirrup.

I froze the frame. "Now listen," I instructed French, and I released the tape to normal speed. The sound of the rifle report came. I hit the freeze-frame again. "Video is thirty frames per second, I was told. From the point where his foot is over halfway out of the stirrup until that rifle shot is forty-eight frames. A little over a second and a half. He fuckin' *knew* what was coming."

"Run it again, please."

I went through the drill again and we watched it for the second time.

"Where did you get this tape?"

"Channel Five. It's called a window dub, and the numbers in that little window at the bottom are a time code. The last two numbers in the sequence are frames. It counts the frames, thirty per second. Kinda interesting, huh?" Actually, Juliet had arranged for it through the station manager, someone she knew socially. She could get it a lot faster than I could, and with fewer explanations as to why she wanted it.

"Interesting, yes. Conclusive, no. You can turn it off."

I rewound the tape, ejected the cassette, and turned off the VCR and TV.

"They were supposed to be new boots, right?" Ferris asked. "What if his feet were hurting him and he was just wiggling around to find some relief?"

"I think Jamie's right," French said, "but it isn't anything we can use at the moment." He shifted his weight, and then shifted again, as though he was sitting on a stone. Something was making him uncomfortable, and it wasn't a busted spring in his chair. If there was a busted spring it was in the grand plan. If he had one. Which I doubted.

"Leon, would you be kind enough to send one of the copyboys down to the coffee shop? Get an espresso for Mr. Hawkins, a coffee regular for me, whatever you'd like, and tell them to put it on the *Call*'s account."

"Sure."

"Double for me," I said. Ferris left looking a little confused and I settled back in the chair. "Something about this business with Reichmann's stunt is bothering you. Or seems to be."

He picked up a pen and began sketching. "I'm tired. Sally and I drove to Gettysburg to celebrate New Year's with family. We didn't arrive home until well after midnight, and the phone started ringing at seven this morning."

"That isn't the problem." His head snapped up and his eyes bored into me. He actually looked a little angry, or severely annoyed, which was an interesting change. "That's not the problem, Daniel. I've seen the 'fuck me, what do I do now' look on too many faces not to recognize it. Why send Ferris out to tell a copyboy something you could have told him on the phone?"

"I wanted to talk to you, in private, about the report from the U.S. Attorney's office. And I thought you might like a cup of espresso. You're our candidate for the Coffee Olympics if anyone ever organizes a contest."

"I'd probably lose to a ten-year-old kid from Istanbul. Turkey's got some serious coffee drinkers." I dug out my cigarettes. "I know you don't smoke. Do you mind if I do?"

"Feel free. Tell me, what was your reaction to the report?"

"It's a little strange, actually. I know, in the abstract, that every city has problems with its police force. Hell, they're ordinary humans, so a percentage of them are gonna be corrupt and/or brutal.

"But it was a little unsettling to read the specifics. And there's too many for the size of the force. That shit feeds on itself, if it isn't stopped. Being a cop in a big city must be a lot like being in 'Nam. You're never sure who the enemy is, or where the next round is likely to come from. But if you lose it emotionally, you end up hurting a lot of people who you were meant to protect."

"That might make an interesting sidebar to the Reichmann interview. We'll get you in a patrol car for the cops' version of nightside and you can write your story as an allegory of Vietnam."

"Who's interviewing Reichmann?"

"You are."

"*I'm* interviewing Reichmann? Jamie Hawkins, the defender of Charlie Patton, the same Jamie Hawkins who came within a gnat's ass of being busted for his participation in the rescue of Charlie Patton . . . ? That's the lamb you want to toss to the wolf?"

"You're the perfect choice."

I got up to flip my ash in the ashtray French had put on his desk and started pacing. I was having difficulty seeing myself sitting with Reichmann, asking questions that he would either resent or refuse to answer because they were too personal. I didn't even like the idea that Reichmann knew I existed, and now French wanted to send me into hand-to-hand combat with Dumdum?

"I don't know . . ." I stopped pacing and leaned on the back of the wing chair. "When is this supposed to happen?"

"I haven't made the arrangements as yet. It only occurred to me as I was riding into work today."

"Has it occurred to you that there might be some objections to anything I write about El Supremo? It sure as hell isn't likely to be a favorable review." I was pacing again.

"As long as it's fair."

"And what about the U.S. Attorney's report? Am I going to be allowed to refer to that and ask specific questions regarding the charges?"

"No. You can ask about corruption or brutality or anything else, but you can't refer to specific charges. As far as I know, Commissioner Reichmann hasn't even seen that report. He may before the interview, but it will be a courtesy copy, not public information."

"Who's going to do that story when the report is released?"

"I'm not sure, but I want these two articles written before anything is released to the media."

I stopped pacing and leaned on his desk. I wanted him to look into my eyes when I spoke. "You're playing a dangerous game, Daniel."

"How so?" he asked innocently, but his facial muscles tightened and something flashed in his eyes. If the stakes were high enough, I thought, I could take him at five-card stud.

Sammy rapped on the door, pushed it open, and came in with our coffee. "I guess I know who gets the double espresso," he said as he handed me the cup. "I added the half-and-half and one sugar."

"Thanks." I reclaimed my seat. "What happened to Leon?"

"He's on the phone." He put another cup on French's desk and grinned at me. "I sure hope you guys are talking about something that involves me as a legman bringing back information instead of coffee."

"Actually, Mr. French was arguing for your promotion to the copy desk and I said I thought you'd prefer death at dawn."

"Well, nice talking to you, but I've got a lot of wire copy to clear off the machines."

"Nice young man," French said as he pried the lid off his cup after Sammy closed the door.

"He'd do better selling real estate. He's a hustler."

French began adding a few lines to his sketch, talking as he worked. "Do you have any interest in being famous?"

"No."

"Would a Pulitzer Prize interest you?"

"I don't know. Have you got one to offer?"

"Perhaps," he said with a smile. He sipped his coffee, waiting.

"When you do, give me a call. No pun intended."

"I'll give you a call when I've arranged the interview with Reichmann and your night out with the boys. I think the interview should follow the patrol, don't you?"

"Personally, I think I'd feel a lot better about this if I knew a little more about your goals. Protecting Philadelphia from the consequences of Reichmann as mayor isn't my idea of a worthy cause."

"Is earning a paycheck a worthy enough cause for you?"

"Depends on what kind of day I'm having. Anyway, I'd better get back to my desk or there won't be an obit page in the *Call* tomorrow." I picked up the videocassette. "You know, if the *Call*'s computer experts wired the funeral homes to our mainframe and gave them the basic obit form, the morticians could fill in the blanks and send it directly to the make-up editor."

"I'll give that some thought," French said with a smile. He was in control again.

— — — —

The National Front for Radical Action blew up Reichmann's personal police cruiser early Friday afternoon. Sixty-six thousand dollars' worth of high-performance engine and armor plating, with bulletproof windows, wiped out by fifty dollars' worth of plastic explosives. Reichmann's driver was in the Roundhouse at the time and the explosive was shaped to implode, collapsing the car on itself. No one was hurt and very little damage was done to other vehicles.

Reichmann's Second Brush With Death (headline writers should negotiate for a profit percentage based on how many papers they sell with their sensationalism) occurred a few minutes after one o'clock, and ten minutes later I answered my phone to hear Ivan bellow that I was to report to Daniel French within the next fifteen minutes. I said okay, and hung up.

The receiver was barely in the cradle when Ferris called. "The Bombers got Reichmann's car."

"I heard, from Ivan."

"Is this weird, or what? You think he had someone do his car? Or you think maybe the sniper was for real?"

"All I know is what Ivan told me, which was next to nothing. He only called to tell me French wants me in the office in fifteen minutes, minus whatever time I spend on the phone with you. So, how's the wife and kids? And how about those Eagles?"

"You know, Reichmann would have been in the car at that time ordinarily. He always has lunch at the Alliance Club on Friday. The lunch starts at one-thirty and he's always there."

"So what happened today?"

"He was touring the Roundhouse with a group of kids from a dozen local high school newspapers. All the school papers are running antidrug campaigns and some PR guy from the teacher's associaton put this together."

"That's got to impress high school kids. 'Gee, I used to smoke dope and sniff glue but after my high school editor printed that hard-hitting interview with Commissioner Reichmann, I realized I was on a dead end street. No more drugs for me. I've switched to Miller Lite.' " I lit a Camel and put my feet up on my desk. "Anyway, what happened? The tour run into o.t.?"

"So the story out of the Roundhouse goes. He was late to the meeting with the kids, the tour was slow, and he didn't want to cut it short since they offer another way to reach schoolkids. He was almost finished with them when it blew."

"Well, it's a hellava story for them. And it's great PR for Reichmann. No one was hurt, he escaped for the second time in less than a week, and we all sell more papers with his picture and thoughtful comments. Has Radio Reichmann put out anything?"

"Just bulletins. You best be hustling your buns if Daniel's waiting."

"See you later."

■■ ■■ ■■ ■■

As it turned out, what French had really told Ivan was to have one of the desk assistants call and ask me to stop in at my earliest convenience. Ivan invented the fifteen-minute deadline. And all French wanted was to talk about the ride in the patrol car and the interview with Reichmann. He'd scheduled the night ride for Thursday, and the interview for Friday, a week away.

I spent the remainder of the afternoon doing my usual assortment of fillers, rewrites, and obits. At five-thirty I logged out for dinner and ate alone at Mamasan's. Ferris was out on a story. And Sheila still wasn't talking to me. I wasn't surprised.

New Year's night, returning to the city, Juliet had asked me if I'd stay the night at her house, and I declined. She'd driven on into Center City, quiet until we stopped for a light about a block from my apartment. "Have I upset you?" she asked. "Is something wrong?"

"No, why?"

"You've been very quiet since we started back, and I can't help thinking you're anxious to get away from me."

"I've got a lot on my mind and I don't feel like talking to anyone." I massaged the back of her neck.

"You can hide in the library if you want to be alone."

"Thanks, but all I want to do is stretch out on my sofa and read until I fall asleep. It isn't anything to do with you. It's me." In truth, I couldn't stop thinking about Reichmann. And Sheila. From the bizarre to the berserk was my guess.

Our last conversation, two days before I'd left for my New Year's Eve tryst, had quickly turned into a screaming match, which Sheila won. I couldn't rise to her level of anger. I was, she'd shrieked, too goddamn egotistical to see that I was being used by a woman too old and probably too fucked-up to find a man her own age. She was a spoiled rich bitch who would dump me when she got tired of playing fuck-the-writer.

"You may be right," I'd said and hung up.

As Juliet pulled to the curb in front of my apartment on New Year's night I was looking at her. She was smiling, but she wasn't smiling at me. "I think you may have company," she said as I turned to see what had attracted her attention.

"Oh, shit," I sighed as I caught sight of Sheila sitting on the steps, staring into the street, her chin resting on her hands.

"So much for the good book," Juliet said with a grin. "But lying on your sofa may do the trick, if it's a good lie. Or should that be 'lay'?" She drove away laughing, which Sheila noted with an icy stare. It looked like a long night.

"You didn't even call to wish me a happy New Year," she said by way of greeting. "Or a happy birthday." Her face was tear-streaked and she looked like a refugee, wrapped in an old heavy coat, her hair ratted from sitting in the wind.

"Happy birthday? I don't remember you ever telling me the date of your birthday."

"John and Peter, the manager, gave me a surprise party after we closed New Year's Eve. I know John invited you, so you had to know. I was a New Year's Day baby."

"You're gonna be a New Year's Day pneumonia case if you don't get off those steps. C'mon inside, please." I hadn't seen John in almost a week, but that wouldn't help my case.

"She was laughing at me," Sheila complained as she followed me down the hall. "She thought it was funny driving up in her rich bitch Mercedes and finding me on the steps like an orphan, waiting for you to come home." I opened the apartment door and steered her inside. "If I had a key at least I could've waited inside."

I took her coat, draped it over the back of the sofa, and went into the kitchen. She followed me, watching as I took down a large can of clam chowder.

"Don't you have anything to say to me?"

"Happy birthday. I'm hungry. You want some soup? Did you eat today?"

She stomped out of the kitchen as I put the soup in a pot, added some hot sauce, butter, pepper, half-and-half, and lemon juice. When I looked up she was standing in the doorway with a loaf of bread.

"I baked this today. It's a family tradition. Always eat fresh-baked bread with someone you love on New Year's Day."

I poured soup into two bowls, put a spoon in hers, then tore off the end of the loaf. "Do you toast these people with whom you're eating the bread, or do we just eat it."

"Just eat."

We ate the bread and soup, and I made coffee while she washed the bowls and pot. She was making a supreme effort to keep her emotions in check, which she achieved by separating herself from her anguish and from me. That suited me better than rage and tears. We talked until well past midnight, about her family and my lack of a family, about her ambition to be a writer with a husband and kids, living in a house at the Jersey shore, and my desire to live alone in a stone house on the Sea of Cortez. We talked about music, writing, being a reporter, and Reichmann. I didn't mention what I thought I saw on the tape. We probably touched on no fewer than fifty different topics, but neither of us mentioned Juliet. Sheila cried a couple of times, softly, wiping the tears with the back of her hand. Her face was chapped from sitting in the wind while she had waited for me.

When we quit for the night she was so completely spent that she went to sleep in minutes, clutching my arm. No sex, no goodnight. She simply closed her eyes, sniffed once or twice, and she was out.

I'd expected the worst, and she'd remained fairly calm. Fucking amazing. Predicting women is like playing with sharp knives. It pays to know what you're doing, which I don't most of the time. They are amazing creatures without whom life would be unbearable. But they defy logic.

That thought went by a dozen times between the soup and sleep. And it was the first thought I had when I woke up and realized she'd left without waking me. My next thought was that I might well never see her again. I was too weird, and we had very few common goals. Passion and play weren't enough. What she needed was my willing surrender of choice, my agreement to ask her permission to live my life differently. If I could make decisions, whether to fuck Juliet or fly away to Baja, without her approval, or guilt, then I couldn't possibly offer anything worthwhile. Like 'commitment'. She was looking for the requisite male partner needed to start the traditional nuclear family and I was struggling to avoid an emotional meltdown. There was no way I could endure marriage to anyone, not for love or money.

— — — —

Mama-san came out of the kitchen to sit with me at the counter where I was sampling dim sum and drinking beer. She asked about Ferris and shrugged when I told her he was working on a story.

"How you like it here?"

"Philadelphia?" She nodded, and I shrugged. "I've lived places I liked better. Too cold and too old."

"You have girlfriend?"

"Yeah, I guess." Something about referring to Juliet as my 'girlfriend' seemed ridiculous. She didn't fit the term, but I couldn't imagine explaining that to Mama-san.

"You not sure?" she laughed.

"Some days, Mama-san, I'm not sure what planet I'm on. I live in a world of my own more often than not."

"Ahhh." She emptied the little beer that remained into my glass. "Make life hard. You need woman."

"I need more beer."

"You think about message from *I Ching*?" she asked as she poured icy Chinese beer into a fresh glass.

"Yeah, but what can I do? We live in a dangerous world." She watched me without comment as I ate a small dish of shrimp that had been marinated in a spicy combination of things I couldn't identify, then glazed with honey and deep fried. "Anyway, the *I Ching* referred to a journey. I'm not going anywhere for a while."

"Life is journey. You are Lu, the Exile. I make study of *I Ching* for many years. Not many times I see Lu. Always man. Always danger."

"So what do I do, Mama-san?"

"Study signs. Make wise choice when you come to fork in road." She picked up the check left by the counterman and put it in her apron pocket. "You friend of Lee-on, you no pay." She walked toward the kitchen, and stopped at the opening. "Remember to study signs."

Another fuckin' fork in the road. Weird shit. The feeling that she knew something more than she was saying made a nice lump in my stomach. Sidewalk fortunetellers and Rent-a-Psychics may be full of shit for all I know, but the ability to see beyond the veil of ordinary human perception is, for my money, a fact of life. I'd been surprised to hear Juliet say she consulted a psychic, but his ability to 'see' me, to sense my needs, and know that she and I were destined to meet didn't leave me one-tenth as disbelieving as Ronnie Ray-gun's election or Rudolph Reichmann's demented passion to be the mayor of Philadelphia.

— — — —

Walking back to the *Call*, I wondered where I could buy a gun, and then I wondered if I was losing my precarious hold on reality. Guns are part of the problem a lot more often than they're a part of the solution. Get a goddamn grip on yourself, Hawkins. This ain't fuckin' 'Nam. Weird, yes. But not even Reichmann can match free-fire zones and body counts.

Absorbed in my thoughts, I made it back to my desk and was staring at a press release issued by the Delaware River Port Authority, trying to make sense out of nonsense about total tonnage and ship traffic in and out of the river's many ports, when Allen Dark stopped by my desk to remind me that we were due at the Philadelphia Art Museum in less than an hour to cover the Catacombs by Night tour. I'd completely forgotten my promise to Juliet that I'd do my best to make the tour sound like the most exciting discovery of art since the opening of King Tut's tomb. Exactly how I would manage that was a mystery only slightly smaller than the 'total tonnage' numbers from which Ivan was expecting me to fashion a five-paragraph filler in the next five minutes.

— — — —

"Of course," the guide said as he led us down the winding stone steps toward the 'catacombs', "many of the works you'll see tonight are every bit as valuable as those displayed in the public areas."

"Of course," I muttered just loud enough to be heard by Allen Dark. "And right after we finish this tour I'm taking bids from any of you who'd like to own the Ben Franklin Bridge."

"In addition to providing storage, the catacombs are where our experts restore paintings, pottery, sculpture . . . and the occasional staff member who has run amok and injured himself."

"It's gonna be a long night," Dark whispered to me. "I've done these tours a few times, and most of the guides are as prissy as an old lady in a public loo. We had to get one who thinks he's Robin Williams."

We were trailing the group of thirty or forty mostly middle-aged, middle-class 'art lovers' who, I'd guess, wouldn't know a Goya from a Gauguin if the frame didn't come with a little brass plaque. The majority of them appeared to be couples of overdressed women wrapped in middle-priced furs and stressed-out men wearing the corporate pallor.

"Culture vultures subscribing to the belief that once you've made a little more than you can spend you should put some of the excess into art," Dark grumbled. "And I've got to take pictures. I can't wait to see what you write about this. Pulaski Day may be a forgotten story by Monday."

"Please," the guide continued as he walked backward down the hall, "do stay with the group, and don't be alarmed by the occasional rattle of chains and cries for help. They are treated well despite their pathetic appearance."

"This may be the worst assignment I've ever had. What in the name of Christ *am* I going to write?"

"Don't panic. I hate it when reporters panic. It screws up my exposures."

"Well, if you'd consider a more personal 'exposure' I'd have a story. 'When *Call* photographer Allen Dark snapped, it wasn't what you'd call a pretty picture. Paramedics who rushed to Dark's rescue said they'd never seen a whang covered with so many tiny black warts.' Can you do airbrush?"

"Fuck you, Hawkins."

" 'Potential new members of the club of small-time donors touring the Philadelphia Art Museum suffered numerous cracked ribs and coughing fits brought on by the uproarious laughter Dark prompted when he flashed for the would-be patrons of the arts.' "

"Did your mother have any children that lived?"

"None that haven't been put away for safekeeping."

We were all trooping along in a shuffling herd when I remembered that I had a joint in my shirt pocket, a sample from Sammy who, it turned out, was the nightside connection. I lit it and took a couple of quick hits, then handed it to Dark. "It's medicinal."

"Are you nuts? You'll get us both in deep shit." But he took it, and after he'd glanced over his shoulder he inhaled until his face flushed with effort.

"Christ, you can't get stoned on one hit of this stuff, I don't care how much you suck in. Jesus! Gimme that."

About five seconds later the smoke erupted from his lungs in a fit of coughing and everyone in the crowd of culture vultures looked back, wondering no doubt who these two weird people could be. The smell of marijuana was strong and the smoke was hanging in the air.

"What an asshole," I laughed. "Why don't you just scream for the dope smokers to form a line in the rear."

"They're mostly boozers, with a couple of coke-snorting yuppies, is my guess. Shit, I'm wasted."

I took another toke and snuffed the roach on the floor. A few moments later we were herded into a large room filled with work stations, artisans' tools, glazes, and God knows what else. It was a factory for repairing damaged pottery.

Our guide immmediately broke into his recitation. "One of the most common artifacts from ancient cultures is pottery. Fragile as it is, pottery can withstand the elements and it doesn't decay. In some cultures the pigments and glazes were so superior that some of their pottery has barely faded . . ."

Five minutes later I backed out of the room, and lit what was left of the joint. I was mildly stoned and more than mildly panicked. Or more than mildly stoned and totally paranoid. Christ, Sammy boy. You should put warning labels on this shit.

The hall was empty. I wandered away from the group, wondering how the hell I was going to make it through another hour or so of the tour listening to this drivel. And what the hell could I possibly write about this that anyone would find interesting? I needed an angle. Or a damn good excuse to offer Juliet. She was expecting something that would hold the reader's attention and possibly entice a few people to sign up. I didn't want to disappoint her, but this bullshit *was* boring, at least to me. I snubbed the joint and told myself to fuckin' get serious and focus on the job.

At the next opening, on the opposite side of the hall, I looked in. This room was smaller, and decidedly untidy. The two workbenches were cluttered with work in progress. I found several statues, none more than six inches high, arranged on one of the tables. They looked as though they had been freshly enameled. I moved closer, squinting through my sunglasses, trying to decide if I saw what I thought I saw. I did. All the statues depicted pairs of males in very sensual-looking wrestling holds. Or homosexual foreplay.

I spun around at the sound of a shoe scraping on the floor and came eye to eye with a plump, pretty, young girl wearing a name tag that read "Ellen." She had fair skin, hazel eyes, and reddish-gold hair cut short.

"I apologize for startling you," she said, "but tour participants aren't permitted to leave the group unescorted."

"I should've known better," I grinned. "Ellen . . . ?"

"Yes."

"I'm Jamie Hawkins, a reporter for the *Call*. I'm doing a story for Ms. Franklin-Rossini. I was trying to find something different to focus the story on . . ." I glanced at the statues. "I don't think these will work, though. Are these supposed to be wrestlers or what?"

She blushed. "I'm sorry, Mr. Hawkins, I'm not familiar with those pieces. Actually, I work in public relations."

"How'd you find me anyway? I thought I was very discreet."

"I followed the aroma."

"Of the Camel?"

"Yeah, right," she said.

"You want a hit off a joint? Wicked stuff."

"I wish I could, but I think we'd better return to the group. If you want some ideas for writing about this from a different angle, come in on Monday and we'll talk. The Museum has a nice café, and we'd be happy to treat the press."

"Ah, love, by Monday I may be history, and sure as hell this story will be." She served up one of those brave little smiles that's supposed to hide disappointment. They always look like they're made of fiberglass. "But I've never visited the museum. Maybe I could call you for a tour?"

"Sure, anytime." Her eyes brightened up noticeably and the charming smile that spread across her hungry mouth was a lot more convincing. "We have to go back to the group now . . . please."

I leaned over and touched my lips to her cheek, lightly and briefly. "You lead, I'll follow." She blushed again and turned, leading the way. Nice choice, Jamie m'boy. You may be ripped to the tits but you know a good-lookin' tush and fluid hips when you see them.

"Where the hell have you been?" Dark growled when I stopped alongside. "You got something going with her?"

"Gimme a break, f'Chrissake. I was looking for an angle to this bullshit that will allow me to write something that won't get me strung up by outraged art lovers or the patrons of this fine museum. Not to mention my boss."

"You've been smoking more of that shit you tricked me with, and putting the moves on Miss Chubby Cheeks. She's kinda cute, actually. What's her name?"

"Ellen. She's in the PR department and our encounter was strictly semi-professional, what with me being stoned."

"Except for the time you were dealing with that lunatic at the Tourist Center, *semi*professional would be above par. You should hear the shit people say about you."

"Send me a memo." Inside I was laughing. Who gives a fuck what any of them think?

The group was now on the move, the guide chattering as he led us to another chamber within the catacombs. "I can't listen to this shit for another hour."

"Take a hike."

Three magic words. Take a hike. Get lost. Play a child's game of let's pretend. Pretend you're lost in the catacombs of the museum, a lost soul seeking an exit . . . maybe I run into the ghost of Goya. Now, *that* would be a hellava tour, led around by a genius gone mad, listening to him comment on what we saw. I could work in the guide's humor about staff members run amok.

"Hey, Jamie . . . you still with me? Christ, you must be off the planet."

"No, no. Listen, you gave me a great idea. I'm gonna take a hike. Cover for me. Tell Ellen that I . . ." I laughed. "Tell her I was called away on a matter of some urgency. Get her home phone number, tell her I've got to write this piece tomorrow for the Sunday paper and I may need to check with her, since she's in PR, about something. Who knows what. Okay?"

"Where you going?"

"To get lost. I'll catch up with you later, down here or on the front steps."

"Okay, but this smells like a dope smoker's daydream."

I walked for a good fifteen minutes, pausing here and there to look at whatever caught my attention. The more I walked the more confidence I lost in my Big Idea. After fifteen minutes I was inclined to agree with Dark: A dope smoker's daydream. I pictured myself walking with Goya. Then Gauguin. Two fuckin' egomaniacs and a boy from Georgia who hadn't seen an original painting by either of them until he was almost thirty years old. Hell, maybe that's it: A woefully uneducated pilgrim in the company of giants who talk about art, trashing their colleagues, gossiping about who was diddling who . . . Shit, Jamie, this is a "family newspaper." Selective reality, remember? No talk of sex allowed.

Whatever would or wouldn't happen with the story, I suddenly realized I *was* daydreaming. I'd gotten so involved in my fantasy that I didn't have a clue to where I was. At the next intersection I turned a full circle but it all looked the same. And then I heard someone cough, off to my left. I followed the passage for thirty feet or so, until it intersected with a corridor to the right. And there sat a Philadelphia cop. He was sitting in a ladder-back chair, balanced on the two rear legs, his shoulders against the wall, the plastic brim of his hat pulled low over his eyes, a burning cigarette in his hand. He coughed again, his fifty-year-old lungs protesting the abuse.

I was on the verge of speaking when his right hand came into view and he tipped a flask to his lips. He swallowed three times before the flask disappeared again behind his leg.

What now? I didn't want to startle him. He might fall out of the chair. But I wasn't going to go away without asking why in the name of Christ a Philadelphia cop was sitting in the catacombs of the art museum. This might turn out to be some kind of story, I thought. Sure as hell should be funny.

I inhaled deeply and reminded myself not to give away the fact that I was blitzed on grass. Even a cop drinking on duty could find some reason to object.

"Excuse me," I said as I stepped forward with a cigarette in my hand. "Can I get a light from you?"

The front legs of the chair crashed to the floor and he almost fell on his face. He was more drunk than sober, and it took him a minute to stand up and gain his balance. He stared at me as though I'd dropped in from his worst nightmare.

"I think your line is 'Halt, who goes there.' "

"Aye, an' will ya be givin' me an answer I can live with?"

"Name's Jamie. I'm a deserter from the Friday-night culture tour. It is still Friday night, isn't it?" I squinted until the name on his ID tag came into soft focus: O'Riley.

"Aye."

"What in God's glorious name is a good Irish cop doing down here at this time of the night?"

"Keepin' the watch and 'avin' a bit of grog."

He held out the flask and I took a slug of Irish whiskey, which ranks right up there between prune juice and peach fuzz on my list of things I'd rather never again put in my mouth. "You moonlighting for the art museum?" I asked as I handed the flask back to him.

"Oh, laddie, if only I was."

"Damn sure you can't be on duty here."

"Can't I now? An' why not, pray tell?"

"Truth to tell, there's no reason at all. One bureaucracy is as ridiculous as another, and if I can be sent down here on patrol, so could you." I gestured with my cigarette. "Can I get a light?"

He handed me a Bic. "An' would you be wantin' to tell me who you work for?"

"The head of the antiquities acquisition department. She claimed I screwed up some paperwork she needed for customs, and we lost a piece of ancient Chinese pottery as a result. This is my punishment."

"An' the Baby Jesus makes three. Me with my thirty-two years on the force, an' them sendin' me down here to watch over a goddamn motor pool." He tipped the flask to his lips and downed another healthy shot, then offered it to me.

"You have to be more lost than I am," I said and faked a swallow. "The closest motor pool I know is at the armory."

"Lost, 'e says. Lost, me arse. It's right in there." He jabbed his finger at a set of steel doors in the opposite wall.

I laughed. What the hell was he talking about, a motor pool? "Must be for an army of leprechauns with tiny vehicles."

"What would a young pup like you know about leprechauns or motorized rocket launchers?" He hit the flask again.

"Officer O'Riley, you're a man of discriminating taste in refreshments, but a little more of that fine Irish whiskey and next you'll be telling me that the SWAT teams have decided to turn Philadelphia into a banana republic."

"Nothin' to do with that bunch of arrogant bastards. No sir. This stuff belongs to the ARTs."

"What the hell are ARTs?"

"Antiterrorist Reaction Team. Special detachments, they are."

"C'mon, O'Riley. Jesus, give me another slug of that stuff so I can get on the same wavelength."

"Would you be tellin' me I don't know me own job?" He pushed the flask toward me.

I faked another drink and handed it back with the cap off. He snatched it out of my hand and downed an ounce or so.

"Maybe I just can't imagine the ART motor pool in the basement of an art museum. It's too much like one of Vonnegut's stories."

"You wouldn't be wantin' to make a tiny wager, now would you?"

"How's a bottle of Bushmill's strike you?"

"Done. Come along."

O'Riley lurched across the corridor, fumbled out a key ring, and on his third try opened one of the two steel doors on which had been stenciled ART AUTHORIZED PERSONNEL ONLY. He stepped through and waved me in.

The room wasn't much more than an alcove, its only furniture a desk and chair. A telephone rested on the desk, and on the wall, next to another, smaller door, was a six-inch-square black box with a key pad like a telephone's.

"In there, lad," O'Riley snorted, "is ART's transport motor pool and my quart of Bushmill's." He punched a code into the key pad and the door slid open. "After you."

'There is much danger.' I could hear Mama-san's voice and for an instant I wished I hadn't started this bantering bullshit with O'Riley. But I had, and the only way to go was forward. I stepped through, into a vast chamber barely lit with red emergency lights.

"Holy shit!" Once my eyes adjusted to the dimness I did a quick count. Four tanks, four mobile rocket launchers, sixteen armored personnel carriers, two armored staff cars, a couple of half-tracks, and at least two dozen jeeps. The tanks were covered with tarps, but they're hard to miss with that cannon barrel sticking out from the turret. The rocket launchers were covered, but O'Riley pointed them out, chattering like a shill who'd snared a pigeon. At least a dozen of the jeeps carried swivel-mounted M-30 or M-60 machine guns anchored to the rear floorboard. Against the walls, covered in tarps, were a lot of crates, maybe fifty, maybe five hundred. All I could see were the ends of various stacks, and without getting closer I couldn't say for sure—but they looked like crated small arms, rations, and possibly clothing. Except for the unlikely colors chosen to 'camouflage' the vehicles, what I was looking at could qualify as a small military weapons depot. The baby-blue and white color combination ensured that no one would mistake these for anything other than Philadelphia police vehicles.

I was wondering if I could nonchalantly check the closest vehicle to see if ART had been stenciled on it when something spooked me, and a sudden feeling that I'd do well to get my ass out of there began to hammer at me like a racing pulse.

"You win, old-timer." I moved slowly but deliberately toward the door. "My apologies, *and* a quart of Bushmill's next week. Where would you like it delivered?"

"I'll be stopping by yer office in the antiquities acquisition department to see yer smilin' face later in the week."

He closed up the entrance while I stood in the corridor, smoking. The drunken old fart remembered what I'd said about where I worked. That should make things interesting if his memory stretched into the dawn's early light. Shit!

When we shook hands his grip was firm and he wasn't wobbling anymore. Christ, he could probably drink most of us under the table and go home to a hot toddy. I had the unhappy feeling he'd remember the bet, the name, and the place to collect.

It took me ten minutes to get out of the catacombs, with directions from O'Riley. He didn't seem to think it odd that an employee would be lost in the bowels of the building. Hell, I was a paper shuffler, as far as he knew, and paper shufflers, like all bureaucrats, were dimwitted, and doomed for lack of meaningful direction. Walking away from him, I could hear his laughter. Har, har, har. He'd had a surprisingly good night, all things considered, and best of all it had come at someone else's expense.

— — — —

"**Y**ou sure as hell aren't giving me much to go on," Dark complained as the elevator carried us toward the eleventh floor. "I'd like to know what you're planning so I'll have a better idea of which pictures to print."

"Just process the film and give me contact sheets. I'll pick out anything that works for me and you can select from those, okay?"

"Okay." He handed me a business card. Ellen O'Hara. "Her home phone number's written on the back. She said you could call 'anytime' and she put a little extra lilt in the word."

"Stop grinning like that. It's not what you'd try to make it if you were the glamorous, good-looking, witty writer and I was just another purveyor of overexposed happy snaps."

We parted at my desk and I parked my butt in the chair with a sigh that could be heard across the room. No one noticed.

What the fuck happens now? Never in my checkered career had I felt less adequate or more like an amateur. Did what I had seen mean what I thought it did, or was I merely overreacting to my own amazement? Heavy armor and rat-patrol jeeps might be as ordinary to big-city police departments as pin-ups in the squad room. Not common knowledge, but part of the common denominator.

And who did I want to tell about it? French and Ferris? That could be like throwing bloody chunks of beef to a pair of sharks. I wasn't real happy about the idea of them thrashing around in this while I had my ass on the line.

And O'Riley. What happens if he comes looking for his jug of Irish whiskey? He was a serious drinker, and a bet was a bet.

Christ, what've I gotten into now? Whose Big Idea was this, anyway?

I wandered toward the back of the city room where Ferris usually hung out. As I stepped around a column on which someone had fastened a basketball rim minus the net, a hard rubber black ball whizzed by my head.

"Out!" someone bellowed. I looked around and saw the Judge sitting on a stepladder, refereeing a peculiar version of a handball game and reading his Bible.

Tony Abbot, a decidedly plump copy editor, and Tiny Thomas, a huge nightside reporter and obit writer, were passing the time between editions.

"Out, my ass," Abbot complained.

"Watch your language," the Judge said calmly as he turned another page in the Good Book.

"Tony's got the rag on tonight. That's why he's playing like an old lady," Thomas announced. "My game. You owe me a buck."

"Hawkins," Abbot yelled. "You saw it. Whatta you say?"

"Bickering in the city room is an abomination in the eyes of the Lord. Where's Ferris?"

"What?"

"Where's Ferris?"

"Over here," Ferris called as he came out of the wire room. He walked between the squabbling contestants, took the ball from Tiny and stuck it in his pocket. "Game's over. And I don't care who won."

"Listen," I said as we walked back toward my desk, "let's go into the library for a few minutes. I've got something to tell you that needs a little privacy."

— — — —

"Did you fall into the punch bowl up there?" Ferris asked as I finished my inventory. "You said you were stoned, but how many pink ladies did you drink with that bunch before you went down the rabbit hole?"

"They didn't serve anything stronger than wine, which I don't drink. O'Riley was in the bag, but I was straight enough to count without using my fingers. You ever heard of ART?"

"Not a word, ever. Couple of years ago I heard Reichmann was poor-mouthin' the Feds for money to form an antiterrorist division, but he never got it. They gave him enough to hire some so-called consultants for a 'study' of Philadelphia's needs. I saw a short version of the study. Unruh had a copy. I never read it. He said it was boring and no one was going to write the story unless Reichmann got the money. Unruh said the Feds decided against it because there wasn't any clear and present danger from terrorists in Philadelphia. New York, LA, Miami, a few other places, all got federal money, but not Della-philthia."

"What about the study Reichmann commissioned?"

"They made it sound like we were under attack as they wrote the report, but what the hell, it was written for Reichmann. What else would they say?"

"Weird shit, Leon. Very fucking weird."

"Let's call Daniel. See what he says."

"No way. Not on a telephone. And I'm not driving out to see him at this time of the night."

"You know, Reichmann may have gotten that stuff from the army. Surplus."

"I don't care where he got it. Why is it a secret? Who paid for it? And what the hell does he plan to do with it?

"That's a serious weapons cache, Leon. I can see why he'd think the jeeps and armored command cars are a necessary part of the cops' ability to respond to a wholesale riot, or in the aftermath of a natural disaster, to patrol the streets. Paranoia is socially acceptable within limits. Hell, it generates votes.

"But fuckin' tanks? They're probably not the last word in high-tech hardware, but Jesus Christ, they're still tanks. And rocket launchers? He's ready to handle anything from the meatloaf that ate Toledo to the Tet offensive."

"Well, it should make an interesting sidebar to your story about the culture vultures."

"You're out of your fuckin' tree. I wasn't sure I should tell *you* about it. Damn sure I'm not ready to tell the rest of Philadelphia. I don't like this shit, Leon. Not even a little."

"What're you gonna do about O'Riley?"

"What the hell can I do? Nothing. He can't afford to squawk too loud. He was plowed and he wouldn't want to draw attention to himself or what's in there. Right?"

"You better hope he never pulls you over for running a red light. So whatta we do?"

"Wait. We can talk to French on Monday. I'll come in." I got up, wishing I was headed to the Cock'n'Bull. Or home. "And worst of all, I've got to write a nice smiley-face bullshit story about the goddamn tour or my ass will be in a sling. It's the moment of truth, so to speak."

— — — —

PHILADELPHIA
Sunday 7 January 3 p.m.
    Another Sunday in Philadelphia. Might as well be Monday in purgatory. I have nothing to do, nowhere to go that's worth the trip out the door, and no one to see. I've done my laundry for the week, cleaned the bathroom, changed the sheets on the bed, and all the dishes are sparkling. If that doesn't get me the Good Housekeeping Seal, there's no hope.
    The life of a glamorous big-time newspaper reporter with his hand on the pulse of the city . . .

Sheila flashed through my thoughts, laughing. I remembered her saying she only went into the Cock'n'Bull so she could meet reporters who had their hands on the 'pulse' of the city. If only she'd gone on laughing, instead of falling in love. I missed her.

Friday night I went with Allen Dark to do a story on the art museum's 'catacombs' for Juliet. Another pitch for money from the small-time players. Not my idea of fun, but when Madame wants a story and thinks I'm the one to write it, what the fuck do I have to say? Yes Ma'am was what she wanted and that's what she got.

The story turned out okay, considering that I went there with absolutely no idea of what to write. She had said she wanted something different without knowing what that meant. I said okay, without thinking how improbable that was. I still think I can turn the proverbial sow's ear into a silk purse without a lot of effort. When will I learn?

Took me six fucking hours to write 1500 words. But it was sure as hell different, and funny, and had absolutely nothing to do with anything. Another fine example of my journalistic skills.

The hook I took for the story was based on the premise that I'd gotten lost in the catacombs and discovered a lot of weird stuff that I mixed with the tour guide's ef-fort at humor, some real work done by the museum staff, and the ghost of Van Gogh who was searching for his ear. It was bizarre, but it worked because I made his comments and laments humorous.

Even fucking Ivan complimented me. That must be a sure sign I'm dead meat on the Call.

If not hearing anything from Juliet was a sign, I was in real trouble. It was possible that she hadn't seen the story, but that seemed unlikely. She actually thought the *Call* was a good paper and usually read the whole damn thing. When I called her just before noon, the news I got from Stonehenge was that she was away. He'd said he expected her about two P.M.

That's when I shifted into my domestic mode. Filling time.

And I was still filling time, and pages, screwing around with my journal. But when I need to sort out some of the shit, putting it on paper is the best way for me to organize my doubts, define my perspectives, and deal with my depres-sion. More often than not I'm no less doubtful, confused or depressed, but it's a more concise confusion and a well-reasoned melancholy. It's also something to do when doing something is all that stands between me and the Pit.

The doorbell cut through my thoughts. I pushed myself up from the chair as a loud, none-too-gentle knock rattled the door. I'd have bet my last day on the planet against one night with Kathleen Turner that it was a cop.

"Who's there?" I yelled as I crossed the room.

"Angelo Finori."

I opened the hall door. "You got a pass key to the street door?"

"Nope. Some people were leaving and I walked by them. Poor security for a high-risk guy like you. Can I come in?"

"Oh, by all means. I was just sitting around thinking that I hadn't had a visit from the police in such a long time."

"It hasn't been all that long, as I understand it."

He came in and I closed the door after him. "Tea and a bit of a crumpet?"

"I hear you convert French roast into first-rate rocket fuel. How about a cup of that?"

In less than ten seconds, probably in no more than two or three, he'd checked out everything in sight, then moved across the room to where he could look into my study and up to the loft.

"Tell you what," I said as I walked toward the kitchen, "I'll give you a cup of coffee if you'll give me some idea of what the fuck you're doing here. I know I make great first impressions, but this doesn't feel like a social call."

"Damn," he said as he snapped his fingers, "I forgot the Danish."

"A snooper with a sense of humor. Times are changing." I put water on the stove and cleaned the pot.

"What's that pot called?" he asked from the doorway.

"French press. Goes with the French roast. Otherwise, the French coffee police come around and close your kitchen."

"I'll take mine black."

"Whatever you say. You want to go on looking around? I don't want to hold you up, no pun intended."

"No. It's a habit."

When I'd poured his coffee I extended the cup about half the distance between us. "The deal was a cup of rocket fuel for a good reason why you're making house calls on a Sunday."

"Agreed. Can we sit?"

"The sofa's yours. I think I'll stand."

He sat down and tipped the cup to his lips. "Whew! That's coffee."

"Lef'tenant, I know you've got to have more interesting things to do than traipse through Philly sampling coffee brewed by media mavins."

"I came here to tell you, or warn you, that you're about this far"—he spread his right thumb and index finger apart an inch or so—"from falling into a bottomless pit."

"I kind of thought that was a definition for life in Philadelphia."

"You'll be laughing with the fishes if you think humor works like a flak jacket."

"So who's after my ass?"

"Who do you think?"

"Beats me. I don't sell drugs, I don't gamble on credit, and I don't fool around with married women. No dealers, no bookies, no irate husbands." I shrugged.

"Last night, while you were supposedly reporting on a tour of the Philadelphia Art Museum's catacombs, you gained entry to a very secret room guarded by a Philadelphia police officer who, it would appear, was duped by you into opening the doors. You, to put it in the vernacular, are in deep shit."

We stared at each other for a while, drinking our coffee, playing the game. I decided to show him a few cards and see how he reacted.

"*C'est la vie*. That's French for I don't give a fuck."

"How the hell did you con O'Riley into opening the doors?"

"He's Irish and he was drunk. How tough could it be?"

"Who else knows about it? Who've you told, and what did you tell them?"

"Why do I have the feeling I'm being interrogated without benefit of my *Miranda* rights?"

"I'd like to help you, Jamie. Forget the *Miranda* bullshit."

"Angelo, I've been asked more questions by more people about what I've done and why I did it than you can imagine. I'm not saying that someone couldn't get the answers if they made it a point to break my face or feed me the right drugs, but I'm not real chatty with strangers."

"You must have had an off night then, since you didn't know O'Riley before you bumped into him."

"You and Sheila have a very similar sense of humor. The side effects of English lit, no doubt."

"Do you like her?"

"Yes. A lot more than she realizes."

"But not enough to give up Ms. Franklin-Rossini . . ."

"You and Sheila also have a common nail to drive into my coffin." And I wonder how much he knows about me and Ms. Rossini?

"Sheila really isn't part of this. And since I brought it up, I'll apologize. My wife and I don't have any kids, so I've been very close to Sheila since she was four or five years old." He finished his coffee and put the cup on the table with a thump, as though he was ready to leave, but he didn't move.

"Well, what now? Do I get arrested for trespass? Or shot at sunrise?"

"I'm not here to arrest you. And I'd feel bad if you were shot, sunrise or otherwise. But it's a distinct possibility. You were made in that room."

"How?"

"Closed-circuit cameras and an alarm system. When the door opens all the cameras switch on and everything is taped until someone resets the alarm. The entry code doesn't have any effect on the cameras. In other words, legitimate entry is beside the point.

"The image isn't sharp, but it's there and your story in this morning's *Call* was like a confession. You can't very well deny you were at the museum, can you?"

"So what? It's circumstantial as it stands. O'Riley may or may not recognize me. He was totally fried. Whatever Reichmann has in there is peculiar, to say the least. And probably illegal. Regardless of legality, it sure as hell would be embarrassing in the extreme and a *lot* of questions would need to be answered. So what's he gonna do, bust me on a bullshit charge and let me tell my story in court? Not bloody likely."

"No, not bloody likely, but the solution is very likely to be bloody. And it's your blood we're talking about."

"*C'est la vie.*"

"You may not give a fuck, as you so eloquently put it, but I do."

That stopped me for a moment. He was intense, and he sounded sincere. "Why? You don't even know me, let alone know me well enough to care if I'm sent to do my routine with the fishes."

"I know a lot more than you might imagine. You remember a kid named Angelo Cocuzza . . . ?"

"Fuckin' A right," I grinned. Crazy Dago. And in the next breath the joy brought by his memory turned to low-grade gloom. "I knew him in 'Nam. He had his ticket punched in the bush."

"You ever hear him mention Uncle Angelo?"

I grinned again. Shit! "*You're* Uncle Angelo?"

"No . . . Uncle Angelo was our godfather. He's dead."

"You're talking about major-league Mafia . . ." I couldn't believe it. "Are you fuckin' serious?"

"Yes."

"What do the Feds think about that? And Reichmann? Shit, you gotta be putting me on."

"How else would I know about Private Angelo Bruno Cocuzza? I knew him, I know his family, and I know all the connections."

"You got a shield?"

He laughed, slipped his wallet from his jacket and flipped it open. "It's real," he said with a smile. "You were part of the happy trio that brought a hundred kilos of Thai stick into the country, packed in a coffin. You're also the only survivor, as I understand it."

I think my mouth may have fallen open at that point. I looked into my empty cup and started toward the kitchen. "You want another cup of coffee?"

"No, thanks. And, since you're certainly wondering, I got it from the godfather. He laughed for a week. 'My boy,' he'd say. ' 'At's my boy.' The old man never got over the kid's death."

I cleaned the pot while I waited for the water to boil, thinking about Crazy Dago. Jesus, this was like a poker game with someone who could deal any card in the deck anytime he wanted it. Four of a kind might look fine, but looks don't beat a straight flush. Fuck me. There were weeks, sometimes months, when I didn't think about Dago's dope deals or numbers pool, or even how he'd died on the side of a hill in the middle of No Man's 'Nam. And Poe, who went to hell in a shit storm. Literally.

"I'm not trying to scare you," Finori said when I came back into the room. I sat and cradled my coffee with both hands. "It's important for you to trust me if I'm going to have any chance of getting you out of this situation."

"What has my connection to Angelo the Younger got to do with this?"

"First, he really liked you.

"Second, he said you were a stand-up guy, that even though you gave him a hard time about the Thai stick, you kept your mouth shut. He'd want to help if he was alive. I'll pay off part of the debt for him, if I can.

"Third, no matter what's happened between you and Sheila, she likes you. I think you make her crazy, and she swears she never wants to see you again, but she'd never feel the same about me if I didn't try to help you.

"And fourth, I've got my own interest in you."

"And what might that be?"

The phone rang before he could answer. I answered it at my desk. "Hawkins."

"Oh, God, are you grumpy again today?" Juliet asked with a laugh. "If you are I'm not going to say anything nice about your story because you'll just brush it off."

"Does that mean you liked it? I'm off the hook?"

"It was perfect. I don't know if we'll attract anyone who hadn't already planned to join but the story was wonderful. I laughed out loud three or four times."

"Music to my ears. Can I call you? Are you home?"

"I'm not home. Am I interrupting another sorrowful tête-à-tête?"

"No, just reminiscing with someone about old times."

"I'll call you later. If you're not busy maybe I can stop by and deliver a more personal note of appreciation."

"Okay. 'Bye."

"You were about to tell me why you have, as you put it, your own interest in me," I said as I returned to my seat.

"I want to get rid of Reichmann. You may be useful."

"Well, that's an interesting confession. The way I hear it, if you'll wait a while he'll end up as mayor and you'll be free to bid for his job."

"I'm not after his job. I'm after him. He's dangerously paranoid, he's lost touch with what his job is all about, and he's very popular with some elements in the city. That's a bad combination."

"Where's your confidence in the electorate?"

"They put Sean O'Conner in office. If you'd lived here long enough, you'd know why that fact alone justifies a significant loss of faith in the Philadelphia ballot box.

"Corruption is a way of life in this city, Jamie, and party politics is the lifeblood of corruption. It isn't even peculiar to Philadelphia, it just seems to happen here more often.

"But stories about crooked ward bosses and payoffs to the zoning board will be filler material you can stuff between bra ads in the Metro section if Reichmann drifts too much further from reality. And he may."

"You remember *The Caine Mutiny Court-martial*?" I inquired.

"Yeah, I remember it. Who've you got me pegged as?"

"None of them, all of them. Who knows? The point is, who the fuck are we to decide that Reichmann should be deposed? *I* think he's dangerous. But I'm not sure I'm the one to decide that his time on the stage is up. I've been on the other end of the hook too often. Plus the fact that I don't really care if he's mayor or police commissioner or a boardwalk barker in Atlantic City. It's nothing to me."

"If he feels threatened, he'll have you hit, and knowing you were in the ART motor pool leaves him vulnerable."

We were back to staring at each other. He was holding some compelling cards, the most compelling being his position in the grand scheme of things, lower case. For all I knew, his position in the Grand Scheme of Things, upper case, could be equally impressive. He'd sure as hell brought me face to face with what a lot of people would call my destiny. Fucked again.

"Is Reichmann an honest cop? Never mind he's come unglued and his seams have split . . . is he clean or is he dirty?"

"You got any of that tequila around? Let's have a shot and a beer, and I'll tell you a story.

Finori left a few minutes after six and I have rarely been happier to have anyone close a door behind them. I knew a lot more than I wanted to know, if he was telling the truth, or even the truth as he knew it. And if he wasn't, he wasn't. He had my vote.

I made myself another cup of coffee, took two hits from a joint, and sat down to my typewriter.

6:30 p.m.
So much for my quiet Sunday at home reflecting on the merits of sobriety, the evils of weed, or addressing the real needs of homemakers who must choose between no fewer than fourteen different brands of dishwashing deter-gent. Personally, I favor Joy with the 'lemony' smell since joy is the last thing I would otherwise expect to find in a sink full of dirty dishes.
No, no time for domestic concerns. It seems I've been nominated for an appearance on the Philadelphia 'hit' parade, and to hear the story from one of Philly's boys in

blue I may soon join old Bullet in those heavenly pastures.

Reichmann wants me dead. Or so says Philadelphia Police Lieutenant Angelo Finori, Sector Commander of the
Police Intelligence Division.

Finori has proposed an alliance intended to keep me
alive and put Reichmann out of office. Reichmann's already out of his mind, so out of office wouldn't seem an
unreasonable ambition. I suggested inviting him to lunch
with three headshrinkers and picking up the certificate
of megalomania along with the check. Lef'tenant Finori
nixed that idea.

What the aforementioned Finori has proposed is that
I, in exchange for information that almost certainly
would earn me a Pulitzer nomination, write and find some
way to publish the tawdry, totally sordid story of a cop
who not only went bad, but went off the deep end.

Additional information gathered by Mr. Ferris and
myself from other sources (like who, I wonder?) will be
examined for accuracy and certified or disavowed by
Lef'tenant Finori, from his own knowledge and police intelligence files.

In the interim, the Lef'tenant will do his almighty
best to dissuade Reichmann from punching my ticket. He
seems confident that he can accomplish that.

Personally, I think my best bet is a night flight to
Cabo San Lucas.

But I've been drawn into something so outrageous,
something so compelling, that I don't know if I can hie me
out of here before it's resolved. The part of me that insists on basic concerns with survival isn't real happy
with my curiosity.

Lef'tenant Finori left me with some reading material, which I haven't opened. It's a copy of the police
dossier on one Juliet Franklin-Rossini and I'm not altogether sure I want to read what they've scraped up from
whatever sources they have.

I told Daniel French, a few nights ago, that he was
playing a dangerous game. And here I am taking a chair in
the same game, with rules I can't ask to have spelled out,
playing for stakes I can't afford, and I have the very
distinct impression that I'm the Joker that's wild.

Yo, Lord . . . listen up. You sent me a cop with a degree in English lit as a guardian angel, a spearchucker

as a partner, and a blonde widow as the love interest who
may or may not be on the side of the angels. On the off
chance that You're listening and my laments have any
bearing on the outcome: This is not my idea of fun.

I poured myself a shot and raised the glass to the heavens. Here's to destiny,
vastly overrated as a plot line in this weird little comedy you guys have scribbled,
but probably effective as a way of ensuring that all the actors are on the stage
when the curtain goes up. Not that it matters, but I've never had a strong interest
in lead roles. I'm more of an observer and commentator on Life. In case that
was overlooked.

Salud!

— — — —

Of all the uncounted, dumb-ass, dimwitted activities dreamed up by man to
occupy his time and provide him with a framework in which to exhibit his
paranoid fantasies, so-called intelligence gathering by amateurs ranks among the
most ridiculous. The term itself is just another bullshit euphemism for the
dubious art of prying into the affairs of others. And ninety-nine times out of a
hundred, the perceived 'need to know' is proof of the paranoia, not part of the
solution to whatever problems exist.

What I find most amazing about the process is the remarkable degree of
dependency the snoopers develop on clipping services.

Having written for publications from which God only knows what was
clipped and filed as gospel, I know how unreliable most published reports are,
no matter what the topic, no matter how careful the reporter. Time and space
limitations alone make reporting a full and accurate account of almost anything
very nearly impossible. Never mind the prevailing attitude of the reporter, or
the mood of the editor responsible for squeezing all nine paragraphs into a six-
paragraph slot.

Reliance on clippings as a source of information for any reason, other than
a notice that an event occurred, is an invitation to blunder, or worse. That
should be obvious to anyone who can read on a fifth-grade level.

But despite the obvious, clips, annotated with all kinds of totally subjective
observations and outright fiction, make up the majority of almost all files kept.

It's funny, unless it's your file.

For those engaged in the gathering, the trick, it seems, is in reading between
the lines, which usually means reading something into nothing. That's a basic
skill most people learn early in life. The habit of judging by appearances, or
projecting significance into a look, a word, a wave of the hand, is learned while
most of us are still in the cradle. Carried far enough—to the point, say, where
most people would realize they need help from a headshrinker—it becomes a

form of neurosis that can lead to great success in 'processing raw data', as the snoopers often call it.

A private citizen without any deep-seated suspicions, for example, probably wouldn't see any real significance in the mention of both Juliet Franklin-Rossini and Juan Valdez Madrid in the article reporting their attendance at an international newspaper executives' convention held in Miami. They were two among the many who had conned someone into paying for a four-day binge. Booze, food, and fucking, in that order, were the priority items on most individual agendas. Guaranteed.

And yet, right there in Juliet's dossier was a three-year-old clipping from *Editor and Publisher*, detailing the convention, listing names and papers, speakers, and recipients of awards. She was noted as co-author of a report, with Juan Valdez Madrid given second billing, on the use of summer interns from ghettos as a tactic in the war on drugs.

The idea, summarized in thirty-seven words, which I counted, was that if 'disadvantaged' kids were given summer jobs on a newspaper or in a TV newsroom, those kids would go back to the slums and spread the word about the negative consequences of drug use. Specific details of the miraculous process that would bring about their awakening were missing from the article in *E&P*.

And the full report delivered by her and Señor Madrid was missing from her file.

The theme of the convention had been the media's responsibility to help combat drug production, importation, and consumption. One boring seminar after another, led by lard-assed editors applauding each other for doing their part to win the war on drug abuse by running in-depth articles, hard-hitting interviews, and meaningful series of horror stories on *drugs*. They were undeterred by the fact that ninety-nine percent of their group couldn't roll a decent joint. Who among them could understand the appeal of heroin? Who among them could even say they knew a junkie, or had wrestled the demon and lost?

My jaundiced view, however tactfully couched, would never appear in print. No one was willing to even consider the very real possibility that none of them knew enough about drugs to intelligently inform a troop of Brownies about the 'dangers' in caffeine. In a war, everyone is expected to fight, however inept they might be with firearms.

The article in *E&P* was useless as intelligence, meaningless to anyone except an amateur "intelligence" operative who had the ability to discern something worthwhile in a worthless clip. Maybe the person in charge of Juliet's file was doing piecework, being paid by the number of times he found her name in print.

I counted the names listed in the article and came up with seventeen. Why had Juliet's name been circled, along with Señor Madrid's, and why were those names linked? Who the fuck was Juan Valdez Madrid? He was listed as an editor of a paper in Vera Cruz, Mexico. But other than his partnership in preparing the report, what connection did he have with Juliet? I flipped through the file, but I couldn't find any other mention of him, not even in the sheets marked Personal Summaries, where the gossip got better as reliability decreased.

I made another cup of coffee and continued reading. There was a thirty-one-paragraph article from the *Call* travel section, written by someone I didn't know, which reported on a trip Juliet had taken to Nicaragua almost two years earlier. Red circles had been drawn around several quotes from Juliet, most of which said something favorable about the country, the climate, or the people. I scanned the entire piece, looking for something that would have caused me to flag this article for her file. Exactly what did the reader see in the quotes that made it worth saving?

She had enjoyed her visit, to judge by the article, but she hadn't said anything about the country's leadership, or Marxist philosophy, or social reforms. I couldn't find one iota of political comment, positive or negative, in the entire thirty-one fucking paragraphs.

Remember the secret, I reminded myself: Read between the lines.

Looking at the *Call* article, I flashed back to a military briefing in 'Nam to which I'd been dragged by a friend, during which a full bird colonel, after ingesting the best available intelligence, declared with godlike certainty that the absence of the NVA unit he so desperately wanted to find proved—*proved!*—they were there. And he thumped the map in the area where he believed them to be. No one rejected his conclusion, and no one objected to his plan. He ordered a full-scale sweep and everyone went to war as directed.

His approach to locating the enemy seems to apply to a lot of jobs in intelligence.

Looked at from that perspective, the significance of the Nicaraguan travelogue suddenly became clear. The fact that Juliet hadn't said anything complimentary about the Sandinistas, their government, or their attempts to make life a little better than it had been under the previous, American-sponsored dictatorship, was proof positive that she sympathized with the sons of bitches who had replaced our designated crooks and cretins with their own.

And that, without a doubt, was information vital to the Philadelphia police.

— — — —

I was reading her TRW credit report when she called. I invited her over, and asked her to give me an hour to finish some reading I was doing. Then I went back to the file.

She had sixteen credit cards, ranging from American Express to Neiman-Marcus. She also had a couple of blemishes on her TRW. One from the Book-of-the-Month Club, one from a disputed charge she'd made, or someone claimed she'd made, at Hertz. Tsk-tsk-tsk. Even the rich have problems with credit-reporting companies. That's nice to know.

The 'personal summaries' were the most absorbing. They also contained the most unsubstantiated information. Gossip, secondhand, thirdhand, even fourthhand observations—and hearsay, speculation, conjecture, and pure fiction.

My first surprise came with her DOB. She was forty-two years old. I'd guessed her age at maybe thirty-eight.

Apart from the Jag, which I'd given back to her with a great sense of relief, and the Mercedes, she was listed as the owner of a '79 Jeep and a '77 Porsche 911, another piece of German junk. She sure seemed to like ugly cars.

She owned a California house, which she'd never mentioned, in Newport Beach, and an apartment building at 222 South Twenty-first Street, managed by Theodore Rondazzi Realty Management Company. Well, fuck me.

She was said to be a Quaker, a member of the American Civil Liberties Union, Americans for Democratic Action, AA, and the AAA. She sure seemed to have a fondness for organizations that began with the first letter of the alphabet.

A reformed alcoholic who still drinks socially, contrary to the guidelines of AA. Makes substantial annual
contributions to AA's operating funds, usually $5000 on
the anniversary of her membership.

In the margin someone had scribbled in pencil, "Seen drunk at Alliance Club. 8/5/82." I wondered if that was true? She'd never mentioned having a problem with alcohol, and she rarely drank anything other than wine. And why would that concern the Philadelphia police?

No known drug habits. Prescription medications in-
clude Valium, codeine, Seconal.

I'd never seen her take so much as an aspirin.

The so-called summaries went on and on for several pages, little bits and pieces of information from which a "profile" would be drawn.

She was deemed to have "leftist" political sympathies, and was known to have had intimate relationships with three Latin American males with proven Socialist or Communist Party memberships. No names were listed, but I suspected old Juan Valdez Madrid was one of them. If any of this shit was true.

And then came the big news, the last page of the personal data summary, an updated entry made one week before Christmas.

Present personal involvements:
    James F. Hawkins, news reporter, *Philadelphia Call*,
for whom subject arranged release from Mexican Federal
Prison in Mérida, Mexico, where Hawkins was awaiting
trial for conspiracy to transport 100 kilos of marijuana
from the Republic of Mexico to the U.S. (DEA/FBI)

Chester R. Denton, U.S. Attorney, Philadelphia, Pa.
Subject known to have traveled to numerous out-of-state
locations with Denton where they shared hotel room, in-
cluding verified sightings in San Francisco, CA, New
York, NY, Los Angeles, CA, and Aspen, CO. (SFPD/NYPD/
LAPD/Informant)
    See additional files: DENTON, Chester R./HAWKINS,
James F./ROSSINI, Antonio/FRANKLIN, James T./FRENCH,
Daniel E.

So Hawkins, James F., had a dossier in the files of the Philadelphia police, and Juliet Franklin-Rossini was making it with Denton, Chester R.

If the entire file was as accurate as their summary of my legal problems in Mexico and the estimate of my proposed export, all of this could be material for stand-up comedy.

I lay back on the sofa with the file in my lap, running through a mental Rolodex of questions, the most persistent being: Why did Angelo give this to me? Was it meant to turn me against Juliet, and thus back to Sheila? Was it to warn me about the kind of person I'm dealing with in hopes that I'd be less loyal? Was it to see how naive I am? To shock me? To scare me into leaving Philadelphia? I was still rolling the questions around and around when I dozed off.

— — — —

The door buzzer woke me twenty minutes later and I tucked the file in a desk drawer before I let Juliet into the apartment. As she was walking toward me I wondered if she had a key. If it *was* her building then she sure as hell could get a key without a problem.

I almost said, "You know, you look pretty good for a forty-two-year-old landlady. How about taking the rent in trade?" I even formed the first sound, which was lost in my soft laughter. It was too fuckin' funny, my image of her expression, my laughter at her puzzled questions. It wasn't the time to be smug.

As it was, my unexpected laughter rattled her for a moment. "Is something wrong?" She glanced down nervously, expecting to see something embarrassing, a food stain or a rip in her blouse.

"Naw, nothing's wrong. I was sleeping and I'm a little punchy. C'mon in."

She had brought a bottle of Fumé Blanc, which she asked me to open so she could have a glass of wine. 'Reformed alcoholic who still drinks socially . . .' As I struggled with the cork I realized that I had to tell her, sooner or later, or forever put almost everything she said and did into a modified context, one she wouldn't know existed.

It occurred to me that knowing things about someone, things they quite probably wouldn't want you to know—or even worse, wouldn't want you to discovery by reading a tacky police file—is a hell of a burden. In an intimate or close relationship, it gives you a distasteful advantage and it destroys whatever parity existed. I suspected it would also destroy any trust that had accrued. I hadn't trusted her completely before I saw the dossier. But I had trusted her enough to leave myself somewhat vulnerable, and now I find out that she's involved with Chester R. Denton, U.S. Attorney, the engine driving the investigation of Reichmann. Was it true? Ongoing or past tense? Physical or emotional? Manipulative or mutually supportive?

Was it time to get the hell out of Dodge City?

"Did Daniel call you today?" she asked as I handed her the glass of wine.

"No. Did he say he was going to?"

"He said he wanted to talk to you." She shrugged. "Do you plan to sit down?"

"Let me get a beer." I spent the time it took to get myself a beer debating what, if anything, I wanted to say, and decided I wouldn't bring up the dossier until I'd had more time to decide if I was even going to stay in Philadelphia. It might be the right time to back away.

When I walked back into the living room she was stretched out on the sofa, her skirt immodestly hiked to mid-thigh, her hair down and fanned out around her head, her eyes filled with impish light.

Ah, what the hell, we may as well enjoy ourselves while we can. Who knows when it's all going to blow up in our faces? Or my face. . . .

——— ——— ——— ———

TORTURE AS A TOOL OF INTELLIGENCE GATHERING

Now *that's* a headline. I was standing over my desk, nursing my first cup of coffee, and looking at the cover of CPA. After five hours of sleep my eyes had opened wide and I'd eased out of bed to avoid waking Juliet.

CPA, the magazine for "Latter-Day Christian Paladins," had been given to me by Atlee a few days before, along with a press release announcing the third annual convention of the Christian Paladins Association in Cherry Hill, New Jersey.

"Here's something you can have some fun with," he'd said as he dropped the materials on my desk at the *Call*. "I was thinking you can do a preconvention piece. Make a couple of calls, use excerpts from the magazine, whatever. Maybe find a local member of the group.

"Then you can cover the convention. You should have a great time with that. You might even come up with a couple of sidebars or a column."

"Let me look at it before I make any promises," I'd said, hoping he'd go away, which he did.

I'd never heard of the CPA. And I couldn't remember what, exactly, a paladin was. The only Paladin I'd ever heard of was a character played by Richard Boone in an old TV series.

God bless dictionaries. Originally, a paladin was one of the legendary twelve knight-champions King Charlemagne kept on the payroll to do his dirty work. That isn't the commonly accepted romantic view, but it's closer to reality.

So what the hell was a Latter-Day Christian Paladin? A merc for Jesus?

I'd scanned the press release, mentally shrugged, and went on with whatever I was doing when Atlee interrupted.

I should have read it then, instead of bringing it home. CPA was not the best way to start a day. "Doonesbury" is more my speed at seven-thirty A.M.

After a quick glance at the table of contents, flipping a few pages was about as much as I planned to do with it for the moment. It was an obvious knock-off of *Soldier of Fortune* magazine. I read two paragraphs of the editor's column, which addressed the need for committed Christian warriors to rededicate themselves to the war against heathen Communists, drugs, and gun control.

There was an article on fund-raising for the Contras, and a companion piece on the adventures of a Christian Paladin in the jungles of Nicaragua. A feature headlined FIELD TEST reported on the Uzi in cold weather. It was datelined Tsjokkarassa, Norway. Right.

Atlee, Atlee, I sighed. You don't really want to give these cretins publicity, do you? We can't put 'em out of business by holding them up to ridicule. And who knows who might read whatever I wrote and decide it sounded great? We've got a lot of brain-dead people out there who think *The Dogs of War* should have received a special Oscar for inspirational patriotism.

I went into the kitchen for a coffee refill, wondering what to do about Juliet, what to say to Daniel about the ART motor pool, what to say to Finori about the dossier, and how to respond to his offer of a deal. And then it hit me: I was, supposedly, on Reichmann's hit list. Jesus H. Christ! If that was for real, I might be dead before the day was done. A sobering thought, as they say. For a few seconds I felt physically sick. Adrenaline overload.

Shit, I may as well *have* a shot before I *get* shot, or run over or whatever. I poured tequila into a glass and downed it.

"Jamie?!" Juliet's voice went through me like a Magnum round and I almost dropped the shot glass on the counter. "Are you drinking already? It's not even eight o'clock."

"Don't you ever knock before you come into the kitchen?" I yelled. "It's only common courtesy."

"Knock before I come into the kitchen . . . ? Jamie, are you drunk?! What's wrong? Why're you up so early, and drinking straight shots of tequila?"

"Were you ever an alcoholic?"

"What?!"

"Were you ever an alcoholic? A bottle baby? A lush?"

"I had a problem, once. I wasn't an alcoholic because I was never really addicted. Why? Do you need help, Jamie? I know some people who could help you, if you do . . ."

"What did you do, to straighten out?"

She crossed her arms under her breasts, sort of hugging herself. Was she cold, or was she unconsciously shielding herself against an expected attack? "Is there a cup of coffee left for me?"

"Sure. I'll make it. Did I wake you?"

"No. Jamie, when my husband was killed I went into a long period of feeling guilty, of being even more angry than I had been, of feeling useless and bored, ugly and unloved. I started drinking, to blur the edges a little. To soften a reality that I couldn't handle. That lasted about a year. Some days I didn't drink at all. I never felt that I *had* to have a drink or I'd come unglued.

"After a year of that I started seeing a psychiatrist, who recommended that I also attend a few AA meetings. He said he wanted me to see how tragic life can become if the need for alcohol ever truly takes over.

"I went, and I learned a lot about people, how they struggle to stay alive, how—excuse me—totally fucked up a person can become, how painful life can be for others. I'd never thought that other people had problems as large as, or larger than my own.

"I went back from time to time, and I even managed to help a couple of them. I got them jobs, which they desperately needed.

"And I still belong to AA. I donate money and sometimes I take someone in for a few weeks, help them get on their feet."

I poured coffee into her cup and mine, thinking that on one hand the dossier was right—she had gone to AA with a drinking problem, and she did still contribute money to them—but on the other hand, the information was dead wrong. I believed her when she said she was never addicted to alcohol. Self-pity, maybe, but that's another trip.

"Jamie . . ." She slipped her arms around my waist from behind me. "There's no shame in it. We all need help at times, and dependency on alcohol isn't any different than overeating or compulsive spending, or a dozen other types of neurotic behavior. I love you, and I can get you help, if you want it. I know a good clinic, in Maryland. I know two excellent psychologists who specialize in therapy for alcoholics. I . . . I just want to help you."

I turned around to give her the cup and she was crying. I felt like a schmuck. "Juliet, the help I need isn't going to come from a clinic, or a therapist. I'm not an alcoholic. I go for days without a drink, or I drink one beer with dinner. Other times I drink in excess, for days at a time, but it's because I want to drink, not because my body's screaming for alcohol."

"You *want* to drink tequila at eight in the morning?"

"I took a shot to stop the shakes. I've been told I'm on Reichmann's hit list, and all of a sudden it struck me that I might be dead before sundown. Or lunch, for that matter."

"*What?*"

"Dead. Cease to be, for the moment anyway."

"Who told you that? Reichmann? You're on Reichmann's hit list?"

"Reichmann didn't tell me, f'Chrissake. Let's sit down. I need to ask you some questions, and I need some straight answers. Otherwise, I'm history."

She settled herself on the sofa and brushed the hair out of her eyes. She was wearing my oversized Baja T-shirt again. "What do you want to know?"

"Have you ever heard of ART?"

"Jamie, I'm on the board of the museum." Her expression was straight from a comedy that no one believes, but everyone loves. Either she thought I was the dumbest dork on the block, or she should have been Teri Garr's sidekick. "Art is one of my great loves," she said when I didn't respond.

"A-R-T. Antiterrorist Reaction Team. Philadelphia's first line of defense against Khomeini, Quaddafi, and assorted other raghead lunatics who might want to take over this city."

"What are you talking about? Is this a police group? Is Reichmann involved in this ART thing?"

"Reichmann, and a lot of other people." I told her what I'd discovered while I was looking for an angle to the catacombs story.

"How could that happen?" She was shaking her head: no, no, no way. "It's unbelievable!"

"Only if you haven't seen the evidence in the murky light of night," I snorted. "That's not all of it. Supposedly, I was 'made' by the cops. They know someone was in there, and since I wrote the story about being lost, they know it was me."

"My God! You've got to leave Philadelphia. Pick a place and I'll see that you get there, incognito. I've got friends who can arrange it."

"If I leave, no one will know where I'm going. Not even you."

"You don't trust me, do you?"

"I told you the first day I was in Philadelphia: Love many, trust few, and always cut the cards. Leaving without telling anyone where I'm going falls into the latter category."

"What else?" She sighed. "Who told you the police know it was you in the basement?"

"A cop. He says he can keep me alive, if I make a deal with him."

"What kind of deal?"

"To get rid of Reichmann."

"You're supposed to *kill* Reichmann? Jamie . . ."

"Not kill him. Jesus Christ, Juliet, I'm not an assassin. He wants Reichmann out, so far out he couldn't get elected chief plumbing inspector. I should put him together with Daniel and let them work it out."

"Do you trust this person?"

"Not entirely, but he's made the best offer I've received."

"Better than mine to get you out of town, out of the country if you like?"

"This is a hell of a story. Hard to walk away."

"Wouldn't it be better to walk away than maybe never walk again?"

"I haven't decided. Tell me something: What's your relationship with Chester Denton?"

Her mouth fell open an inch or so. She drank some of the coffee, staring at me. "I owe him a lot."

"That's not a relationship, that's a debt."

"Are you asking me if he and I are lovers?" She laughed.

"Are you?"

"Are you jealous? You with your Polish pub wench?"

"I'm not jealous. And I know that might be difficult for you to accept. But he's the power behind the investigation of Reichmann and the police department, and you have a preliminary report from him, which I don't think he handed out as a press release.

"You also were reported to have made several trips with him and quote shared the same hotel room, end quote."

"I did make trips with him. I do like him. He did help me, enormously. He's married." She was watching me closely as she spoke. "And he's gay."

"Gay . . . ?" It took me a full five seconds to react. "Not cheerful-and-full-of-fun gay, right? Gay as in he makes it with guys."

"One guy. They've been lovers for several years. It's a sorrowful and very painful secret they keep. His wife and his employers are willing to tolerate discreet affairs with women, but no one's willing to condone a sexual relationship with another man.

"Whenever he and I have traveled together, Robert, his lover, would be wherever we went, registered in the same hotel under an assumed name. I would sleep in Robert's room."

"Why would you do that?"

"It's a long story."

"It probably won't take as long to tell me the story as it would take me to recover from being killed. Tell me."

She finished her coffee, put the cup on the table, and sat back with an air of resignation. Maybe she'd known all along that one day she'd have to tell me a lot of this shit, if only because her feelings for me were too intense to keep it all on a casual basis. I could hear Sheila screaming that Juliet would dump me as soon as she got tired of 'playing fuck-the-writer.'

Life's a bitch, and love's a sonofabitch.

"My husband was from a Mafia family. You probably wonder how I ended up marrying him. It's an even longer story, but let's say I was swept away and let it go at that.

"He was educated at Choate and Princeton, earned an MBA, and was put out front by the head of the family in South Jersey. He was good-looking, well-spoken, educated, and thoroughly charming when he wanted to be. He was also vicious, foul-mouthed, and a bully when he wanted to be. Jekyll and Hyde. I'm not sure he knew who he was, which may have led to some of his erratic behavior.

"He fucked up. He screwed the wrong people and tried to get by with it on arrogance. He was killed.

"And some people thought I had it done, or had a hand in it. That either I took out the contract, or I set him up for the people who had it done. For a little while the police here had me under surveillance, and I heard that both the Philadelphia DA and a federal prosecutor were considering charging me as an accomplice.

"I had met Chester socially, and I went to him. I don't know what he did or to whom he spoke, but after that it all died down and I was left to face myself. Which is how I started drinking."

Christ, what lives we live. What secrets we keep. For the first time in a long time, I'd found someone for whom the pain of living must equal or exceed my own. Or it had. But somehow she found a way around it. She'd arrived at a point where she could help others. About the best I'd managed was keeping them at bay.

"Is this helping you?" she asked.

"It clears up some questions, but there's another one which I've asked you before. Why did you bail me out of Club Fed?"

"I've answered that question, more than once."

"Maybe it has more than one answer. You sure as hell had something in mind."

"What I told you about the psychic was true. What I said about being attracted to you was true. And you remind me of my husband in some ways, both positive and negative. I don't believe you're a bully, or the sonofabitch he was when he went off the deep end.

"But you have a way about you, an either/or attitude that makes it difficult for the rest of us to cope."

"I could give you what I consider very good reasons for that, but it wouldn't make it any easier for you, and I don't like explaining myself. Anyway, that doesn't answer the question, does it?"

"In a way, it's part of the answer. Daniel and I both want to change the *Call* . . ."

"Which means you'd have to change the ownership. The *Call* is what your brother wants it to be, so you have to unseat him."

"Or bring him around by putting him in a position where he has no other choice.

"But to have any success with that approach we needed a new face, a person who wasn't afraid of battling with the editors, someone who could find the kinds of stories we want to print.

"Someone who, in your words, doesn't give a flying fuck what anyone thinks. We could protect that person to some extent, and give them help and direction . . ."

"And hope for the best." I got up and stood over her, somewhat pissed. "If nothing happened, no big deal. And if I hit the motherlode, who knows what would happen, or where it would lead?" I walked away, then turned back. "You're gambling with my life."

Her smile was rueful, to say the least. "Who would ever have imagined this kind of development?

"And if I have any understanding of people, which I think I do, you're not what I'd call a stranger to confrontation. You may not like trouble, but you need it. Trouble and sex may be the only two things that relieve your boredom. And I wouldn't let you get hurt."

"You don't have enough money to buy off Reichmann."

"Money isn't the only medium of exchange available."

"It's the one that counts. Money and power. Everything else is chopped liver."

She came over to me and slipped her arms around my neck. We were face to face. "What about love?"

"Great stuff, but flak jackets offer more protection." I kissed her. "You know, for a landlady, you sure smell good."

"And for a tenant who doesn't pay his rent on time, you are a real pain in the ass. What else have you found out?"

"I've got all your credit-card numbers. You've got a couple of black marks on your TRW. And you own a Porsche 911."

"Ruined by BOMC and Hertz." She kissed me. "The Porsche was my husband's. . . . If you want to leave, I'll have it arranged by six this evening. Just tell me where you want to go. I know a place in St. Tropez you could have for a few months."

"I don't like the French, and I don't think I'd like the Riviera in January. If you want the truth, I don't know what to do. It's an amazing story, if I can break it open without getting lit up like Wanamaker's Christmas tree."

"I have some business to take care of this morning." She checked her watch. "In fact, I'm already running behind schedule. I should be free by eleven-thirty or so. Let's have lunch and talk some more."

"If I'm a marked target, you should stay away from me."

"Actually, the place I've got in mind is as safe as either of us can be. I want you to have lunch with me at the Alliance Club, today. A lot of interesting people will be there, and I'd like for them to see us together."

"Isn't that where all the power brokers go to refuel?"

"Most of them, yes. Will you go?"

"Shit, why not? At this point, I never know when the last supper is the one I'm eating. Is the food there any good?"

"Better than Burger King."

"What time?"

"I'll pick you up at noon, out front."

— — — —

I stood in the door, watching her walk down the hall to the street. The phone rang just as she looked back and waved. It rang again as she disappeared down the stairs and I closed the apartment door. It rang a third time as I reached for the receiver.

"Hello!" I barked.

"This is Uncle Angelo . . ."

The concussion from an explosion rattled the windows and the sound boomed through the room. "Christ!" was all I managed to say into the phone. I was out the door and down the steps two at a time, standing on the sidewalk as the last pieces of twisted metal and shards of glass fell to the street maybe twenty yards away. Small flames danced across the dash and black smoke rolled up from what was left of Juliet's Mercedes.

"Hellava mess," a feminine voice commented from behind me.

I spun around, relieved and disbelieving at the same time. She was holding a sticky bun from the deli. "Jeee-zus!"

"Well, you never have anything to eat in your place, so I went the other way, to the deli . . ."

A screaming patrol car slid to a halt several yards behind the smoldering hulk and one of the cops leaped out with a small fire extinguisher while the other appeared to be jabbering into his transmitter. In the distance I could hear other sirens, and air horns. "Fire truck, an ambulance, and probably another cop car or two. Whatta we tell 'em?"

"You go inside and let me handle it. I'll tell them I was driving through the area, inspecting my property, and I left my car to go into the deli. It blew up. Then I'll get one of them to give me a ride home where I'll throw up."

I put my arm around her and pulled her closer. She was shivering. "You're okay?"

"I feel surprisingly calm. Go inside, please, so I can talk to the cops and get this over with. As far as they know you're just another resident on the block who came out when you heard the explosion. I'll call you later."

She handed me the sticky bun, minus the bite she'd taken out of it as she was leaving the deli, and I sat on the stairs watching. She stepped around a couple of frightened but curious people who had gathered to watch the mysterious excitement. Further down the block, several more people had congregated. And across the street, three older women were leaning out their windows, looking down on the scene.

— — — —

"Uncle Angelo," I said, "the shit's hit the fan."

"I heard." A truck went by and the sound drowned out anything else he may have said. "Where you calling from?"

"Pay phone, about a block from my apartment. What the fuck is going on? That wasn't my car and I wasn't anywhere near it."

"Could be a couple of things. You okay?"

"Yeah."

"She okay?"

"She who?"

"Ms. Franklin-Rossini. The ID was made from the tags by the officer on the scene." I didn't say anything. "You there?"

"I'm here."

"Whoever it was, they weren't trying to kill anyone."

"I feel so much better hearing that. Listen, you can tell Reichmann, or someone who'll get the message to Reichmann, that I've written the story about the fuckin' motor pool, it's on file, and if I end up dead the story goes to press in the next edition. As long as I'm alive the story stays in safekeeping."

"I'll see what I can do."

"And that story isn't all I've got tucked away. Unless he plans to fry a lot of people, and I mean a lot, he'd do well to back off."

"Don't make threats you can't back up. And be *real* careful. I can't just walk into his office and tell him you know he's been playing with C-4 and you're gonna tell on him if he doesn't stop."

"Someone better tell him. 'Bye."

"Wait! Let's get together later."

"Maybe. Can you find out if my phone's tapped?"

"Probably."

"If it hasn't been, call me. If it has, get rid of the tap and then call me." I hung up before he could say anything else.

How would he know what kind of explosive was used? The question was like a yapping lapdog that just won't be shushed. Not only didn't I have an answer to that question, I didn't know why I thought it would matter. Or if it mattered.

I reached Ferris at home and told him what had happened.

"I can pick you up, give you a place to lie low for a while," he offered.

"You know what? I don't think they mean to kill me, at least not yet. I think Uncle Angelo was right. It was meant to scare me, or us. Remote-control detonation, nothing in the megaton range. Fucked up the car but no other real damage."

"Like Reichmann's car."

"Yep. Like Reichmann's car. Fuck him. I'm going to lunch."

— — — —

"If the Exile dallies with petty matters, he will draw disaster upon himself . . ."
It was the *I Ching*'s first words of wisdom from the individual lines of the
hexagram for Lu, the Exile.

I read it three times, then dropped the book on my desk and picked up my
coffee. Who cares if it was C-4 or B-12? It doesn't matter, and it doesn't matter
how Angelo knew, if he did.

The copy of CPA caught my eye as I put my cup down. How the hell did
we go from flower power to firepower in such a short time? Something is so
fucked up it defies comprehension. I opened the magazine, turning pages,
reading headlines and ads.

In the back of the book were several pages of classifieds and small display
ads. On the second page, under JOB OPPORTUNITIES, was this ad:

WANTED: EX-GREEN BERETS
Or others with background in counterinsurgency. Unique opportunity
to work with police in large eastern U.S. city.

Reply with letter outlining experience, present status, salary requirements. Adviser positions available, with short or long-term contracts.

Replies to *CPA* magazine, Box 1776, Kansas City.

And what might this be? Were they looking for training cadres or squad
leaders? I flipped the page. More bullshit.

Out of nowhere, a huge yawn that seemed to rise from my knees was
followed by a tremendous sense of fatigue. It wasn't even ten-thirty and I was
as tired as if I'd been working for the last twelve hours. This, I thought, is not
the time to be tired, or feel overwhelmed, or hedge your bets. It's time, amigo,
to get your ass in gear, or get on a plane. You can't go halfway and then turn
back. Halfway is half-assed, and that won't do it.

Pulitzer or Puerto Vallarta? Put out, or get out.

— — — —

"Hello . . ."

"Ms. Franklin-Rossini?" I asked in a not-real-great British accent.

"Yes . . . ?"

"William Witherspoon here. Witherspoon Toyota. The report of your misfortune has reached us, and I was curious, Ms. Rossini, if you might be in the

market for a new car? We at Witherspoon Toyota, Mrs. Witherspoon and myself, as it were, would be delighted to send around one of our more luxurious models for your consideration. And, this being a special offer to a very special customer, we would be willing to throw in, so to speak, a lunch at the Alliance Club for you and a guest."

"I did promise you lunch, didn't I?"

"You okay?"

"A little shaky, but I can handle lunch. How about you?"

"Hungry. Thirsty. And behind on my rent. You wanna pick me up?"

"Okay. I'll make the reservations, and pick you up at twelve-thirty."

"See you out front."

— — — —

The Alliance Club is Philadelphia's best-known Republican landmark, a massive, three-story Federal fantasy constructed of stone blocks thick enough to withstand cannon fire, its lower third faced with greenish-black marble that reputedly was taken from the palace of some minor Turkish emir in the 1800s. At the top of the immense stone steps, two totally pissed-off granite eagles guard the entrance, where a brass plaque declares in elegant, snobbish simplicity:

ALLIANCE CLUB
1881
MEMBERS ONLY

Full membership requires the right bloodlines, the right political connections, and serious money. Associate memberships are held, Juliet said, by a select few with the right connections and a proper history of suitable donations to the right political candidates. For lunch you only need the right escort.

"How's your sense of humor?" Juliet asked as the maître d' hurried away to greet some new arrivals.

"It's about the only sense I have. Why?"

"This place is a little, ah, stuffy, wouldn't you say? A sense of humor might save me some embarrassment and make the experience a little easier for you."

"Juliet, 'stuffy' is what you get in the city room when the thermostat locks in at ninety and the windows are frozen shut because it's ten degrees outside."

"This is pompous, in the extreme. Squared. It looks like a cross between a wax museum and a private mint. But I'll behave."

"Thank you."

The waiter, a thin gentleman with perfect posture and wearing a tux, bowed slightly at Juliet's side, handing her a menu as he apologized for the delay in his arrival. "Would the lady care for a glass of wine before lunch? We have an excellent dry white."

"Perrier with a slice of lemon, thank you, Harold." She looked at me with a hint of warning in her eyes.

"Absolut, on ice, please."

"Very good," Harold said.

"Vodka?"

"You said I should behave. Hell, these people don't drink tequila, and I'm not big on designer water with lemon slices." I grinned at her. "I didn't say I could do this with a straight face, but I can be polite."

"You even dressed for the occasion. You look quite nice in that jacket." She reached over and touched the sleeve. "Silk . . . my, my!"

"Not to mention gabardine slacks, Egyptian cotton shirt, and a right and proper by-God tie."

"That was the first thing I noticed as you came down the steps. I've never seen you wear a tie. I didn't know you owned one."

"You've never seen me wear a jockstrap, either, but I own one of those, too."

"Jamie!"

"It's okay, even these guys know about jockstraps." I looked past her at a clump of suits cluttering the dining room entrance. "Who's in that flock of turkeys standing in the door?"

"It's impolite to stare, Jamie."

"Be rude. I see Reichmann in the back of the crowd, and if he's standing in the back they've got to be megavolt scum."

She cast a quick glance at the crew and turned back. "The tallest one is Edmund Tyler, a banker. The one with the horn-rim glasses next to him is Mitchell Pierson, deputy mayor. The short one with the flushed face and silver hair is Sean O'Conner, our esteemed mayor. The tall, good-looking one in the charcoal-gray suit is Edison Cabot, an assistant U.S. Attorney who works for Chester. The one standing next to Reichmann is Gentry. I don't remember his first name. He's new here, maybe a year or so on Reichmann's staff. He turned up one day at Reichmann's side and no one seems to know where he came from."

"He's a merc."

"I'm not sure I understand the word."

"Hired gun." I watched the group trail along behind the maître d'. "He's running ART."

Juliet turned for another look, and as she did her eyes and Reichmann's met. He left the group, heading our way. When she turned back her upper lip was beaded with perspiration. "I shouldn't have been so obvious."

"C'mon, Magoo. Remember your sense of humor."

Reichmann came to a halt opposite me, but he only had eyes for Juliet. "Miss Franklin, nice to see you."

"Thanks. How are you?"

"Well enough, thank you. I heard about your car. I wanted you to know that I've got men working on it, although it was obviously an NFRA job." He made an effort to smile, an act so unnatural to him that he didn't seem to remember quite how it was done. He looked as though he had a nervous twitch. "Now we've both lost valuable property to a bunch of psychos."

"Thank goodness no one was hurt. By the way, I'd like you to meet Jamie Hawkins. He works for us at the *Call*."

"Mr. Hawkins and I met Christmas Eve, in Quaker Plaza." He turned slightly, conceding my presence. "And I've become quite a fan. I read all of your stories."

"It's nice to know I've got an audience. And I believe you and I are scheduled for an interview this Friday. I'm looking forward to it."

"So am I, Mr. Hawkins." He tried his smile again, with the same results. "Well, I'd better get rolling here, or I'll be late for lunch. Nice to see you again."

I watched him cross the floor, striding on a straight line to the private room where the others had disappeared. Someone inside, out of sight, closed the door after his entrance.

"You're interviewing him?" she asked disbelievingly.

"So Daniel says. He arranged it."

"I hope you won't go in there with that smart-ass smile on your face. He doesn't like you."

"He may not like anyone, for all I know. But he really *dis*likes me." I opened my menu. "Which is understandable."

"Does Daniel know about the 'motor pool'?" she whispered, leaning so close I could smell the perfume, something faintly erotic.

"I didn't tell him. I haven't seen him since last Tuesday or Wednesday. Right after I showed him the videotape." I inhaled and smiled. "What's that perfume called?"

"Joie de Vie."

"It should be called Joy of Sex."

She blushed and I stifled a laugh. I couldn't believe she'd be embarrassed after the experiences we'd had in bed. On the sofa. In the woods overlooking the Delaware. Christ, that was the coldest I've ever been. "You like it?"

"I could live with it." I thought about what I'd said, and quickly added, "In a manner of speaking."

"In a manner of speaking," she said, mocking me. She opened her menu, gave it a quick once-over, and said, "May I recommend the spineless chicken, marinaded with lemon in white wine?"

"Not nice!" I said with a grin. "And laughing at your own bons mots is too gauche to mention."

"God, I love it when you talk dirty to me. You *are* a chicken with women."

"You're right. They scare the hell out of me. Especially you. But I don't want chicken for lunch. So recommend something else."

"They serve an excellent lobster salad, huge, with truly glorious dressing. I've never tasted better. Honest."

"Sounds good. If I'm gonna sleep with the fishes I may as well go for a first strike. Boil the sucker and serve it!"

"Shhh. You promised you'd behave." She flagged our waiter down and sent him away with our orders. "Tell me something. Why did you say Gentry's a . . . merc?"

"He's got the look, the posture. Hard eyes. He wants something to happen so he can show everyone how fuckin' essential he is to whatever they've got going. Where'd they all go, anyway? Is that a private dining room?"

"A Club Room. There are eight, as I recall. That particular one is leased to your employer and my brother, James Franklin."

"No shit! Which one was he?"

"He wasn't in the crowd at the door. He's probably been in the room since eleven-thirty or so, drinking. That would be after he'd had two or three at the bar, which opens at eleven. *He's* an alcoholic."

"Did you and he ever get along? Like when you were kids?"

"James was nine years old when I was born, and he hated me on sight." She broke off the end of a bread stick, smeared it with butter and took a bite.

"He was an only child until you arrived, right?"

"Yes."

"That's not uncommon. The older kid supposedly feels jealous and threatened."

"That wasn't the problem. Years later, my mother's sister told me that after James found out my mother was pregnant he became obsessed with the idea that he should have a brother, and evidently my mother had promised him one. I guess she was like a lot of desperate parents—promise them anything to shut them up.

"According to my aunt, while my mother was pregnant James became very attached to her, which he hadn't been, and talked constantly about all the things he and his brother would do, inventing adventures for them to share, telling everyone how they'd conquer the world. He was convinced that I'd be a boy.

"Then I showed up, and my mother died giving birth to me."

"That was a long time ago."

"Some wounds don't heal with time. We got into an argument about something relating to the *Call* a few months ago and he screamed at me, 'You goddamn slut, you killed our mother and you stole the place that was meant for my brother. Rot in hell.' And then he stormed out of the room."

"What did you say?"

"Nothing. But I went out and found you three weeks later. I may still have the last word."

Right. Jamie Hawkins, boy paladin. Not a Christian Paladin, mind you, favoring Buddhism as I do. But a paladin nonetheless. Wonderful. But what the fuck am I dealing with here?

For a lot of reasons, the script was beginning to read like a late-twentieth-century version of Cain and Abel, updated to reflect the status conceded to the

'80s woman. After years of sacrifice to the sisterhood, she now gets to play the role of Abel.

The more information I got the less I wanted to know about any of it.

The waiter served, and we ate, and it was the best lobster salad I'd ever eaten. The dressing was the thing that tipped the scale.

"Champagne vinegar," Juliet said when I asked her what the chef had done to the dressing that made it so different. "Have I outdone all the other editors and publishers who've wined and dined you to win you over?"

"I don't remember anyone in the business ever trying to win me over. Once, a few years ago, the city editor of a little rag in Tennessee took me to a dingy neighborhood bar and bought me a couple of draft beers while he tried to talk me into working for fifty bucks a week less than what I asked for, which was at least fifty less than the clerks in classified ads were making."

"Did you get the salary you wanted?"

"I got heartburn from eating the pickled eggs they kept on the bar. I was so broke I hadn't eaten a real meal in two days. The tires on my car had less tread than my sneakers, and I'd coasted into town on fumes."

A busboy cleared the table and the waiter brought Juliet coffee. I kept an eye on the closed door of the Franklin Club Room, curious about what was going down inside. It had to be a lot more interesting than anything that was happening in the main salon, where we were surrounded by people whose function in life was a riddle I had no hope of understanding. What the fuck do these people think about? How to make more money? How to spend more money? Who they can fuck, or who they can fuck over?

"So did you enjoy your lunch?" Juliet asked.

"The salad was great, but I don't think I'll apply for a membership.

"I've been to a Greek wedding, a Sicilian funeral, Chinese New Year celebrations, and a meeting of the UN Security Council, but I've never seen anything quite like this place from this vantage point. These people are from another planet. I haven't heard one person laugh since we came in here."

"They're not a happy lot," she said, evidently excluding herself.

"I'd sure like to know what the hell is going on in your brother's lunchroom meeting."

"Quite probably a heated discussion regarding the content of that report on the Philadelphia police. Reichmann and the mayor received copies about a week ago. We were the only news organization to get one, so far as I know."

"What about all the other people in there? How does the report concern that banker you mentioned? Tyler? Is that his name? And where does your brother fit into this?"

"I'm not certain, but I'd say Commissioner Reichmann felt he needed moral support from a few of the city's prominent citizens."

"Looking for 'moral' support from a bank president and a newspaper publisher is like looking for virgins in Las Vegas. I think they're circling the wagons."

"What a curious idea. Why do you say that?"

"Too many off-the-wall, totally weird things are coming too quickly."

"Like the catacombs? That kind of stuff?"

"Like the catacombs, old Bullet, your car . . . Reichmann's bootprints are all over this. What I can't find is a trail that leads to an explanation of what the hell's going on."

A hint of a smile flashed on and off. "But you think it's something more than life in the big city?"

"Reichmann, and for all I know everyone else in that room, has ambitions on Caesar's chair. I keep thinking he's already running for the mayor's job."

"The mayor of Philadelphia doesn't count for much on the national political scene."

"The governor of Georgia probably counted for less before Jimmy Carter decided he was Don Quixote. Reagan and that bunch of robber barons and petty thieves he brought with him aren't nearly the extremists that were promised to the right wing. They need a champion, too.

"Think about it. If Reichmann can go on making news by confronting 'terrorists' and chasing political 'radicals' who've loosed a reign of terror in the City of Brotherly Love, he becomes a household word. Like Ty-D-Bol and Ted Koppel."

"Jamie! That's terrible."

"Okay, New Blue Cheer and Ted Koppel. The point is, this country's in bad shape, with no prospects for improvement. Who's gonna lead us out of this shit? Mondale? Haig? Tweety Bird on the one hand, and a glorified Weekend Warrior on the other. Reichmann might be a dark horse, but I think he's in the race."

"It's impossible for me to see him as anything other than a Philadelphia cop. As long as I've known him, he's been a police officer."

"I know . . . it's like trying to picture Walter Cronkite anchoring the evening news for ABC. But you'd be surprised how quickly people would get used to that."

"Shall we go?"

"I'm ready, but we need a check."

"Not here. I'll sign on the way out. It all goes on the *Call's* account."

— — — —

As Juliet was signing the check, some guy in an eight-hundred-dollar suit, nervously touching the knot in his sixty-dollar silk tie, came up and started talking to her about the museum's responsibility to become more involved with kids in the slums, or some such bullshit. I caught her eye and nodded toward the exit, then walked outside to stand on the Alliance Club's ample veranda and look down on Locust Street's pedestrian traffic.

Juliet strolled onto the veranda, frowning, followed closely by Edison Cabot, who was in an obvious rage. The Assistant U.S. Attorney's lunch hadn't gone well, if his flushed face and irate manner were a fair indication of what had happened in the Franklin Club Room. I also noticed that part of his left arm was missing. In the crowd at the door earlier I hadn't seen the stainless-steel hook.

As Juliet came toward me, Cabot headed for the steps, seemingly in a big hurry. He brushed by her from the rear, then paused on the top step, looking around, searching for someone, or maybe he was looking for a cab.

"Let's offer him a ride," I said to Juliet, taking her arm.

"Who?"

"The one-armed crusader. What's-his-name there. Cabot."

"He probably has an official car."

"Offer anyway, and introduce me. C'mon, before he rides off into the sunset."

"Edison," she called as we headed toward him. He looked over, his face still filled with anger, but he smiled when he saw it was Juliet. "Can we offer you a ride?"

"No, thanks. I've got one, I hope." He glanced at me.

"Edison, this is Jamie Hawkins, a reporter for the *Call.*"

He hooked the handle of the attaché case and held out his hand, frowning with an effort to recall where or how he'd heard my name. "Oh, right. You wrote that story on Charlie Patton, didn't you? The Christmas Eve fiasco in Quaker Plaza?"

"I did. I'm doing some research and interviews so I can write a follow-up in the next couple of weeks. Would you be available to talk to me?"

"I'd need approval from my boss, but that shouldn't be a big problem. Sure. When?"

"How about tomorrow? Any time after ten o'clock."

"Let me check my calendar and speak to Mr. Denton." He glanced quickly at Juliet as he spoke Denton's name, then smiled at me. "Call me later today, around five. If I can't answer the phone for some reason, tell my secretary who you are and she'll let you know where it stands. Okay?"

"Fine. Thanks."

A car horn beeped a couple of times and Cabot waved. "That's my ride. Nice meeting you, Mr. Hawkins. Juliet, nice to see you."

"What was that all about?" she asked as we ambled down the steps and headed toward her tomato-red Porsche 911, delivered to the curb by the valet with a foot-wide grin.

"What's any of this about? He came out of that meeting in a rage. Maybe he tried to make a deal and they told him to fuck off. Maybe they tried to buy him. Maybe he had to pay for his lunch? Who knows?

"But something happened in there, and if you can talk your friend Chester into giving Cabot permission to tell me what went down, I may be a little closer to untangling this shit."

"Jamie, I don't know . . . I'd feel a lot better if you went away until things settle down." She climbed into the car from the passenger side.

"I thought you bailed me out of Club Fed so I could dethrone your brother and leave you in charge of the *Call*," I argued as I got into the driver's seat. "Yes? No? Maybe?"

"Maybe I changed my mind."

"Once you start dancing with the bear, you can't stop just because he steps on your toes. You know that, don't you?" I'd gunned the car away from the Alliance Club and realized suddenly that I was doing forty miles an hour in second gear. It might be German junk, as I usually described cars from the Fatherland, but it was the fastest junk on the street at the moment.

"I don't remember there being a 'bear' on my dance card."

"Look again, gorgeous, there's more than one." I shifted into third and let the car slow itself. "I can't believe you drive this sucker. It must have about the same stall speed as a Cessna.

"It's fast. Zero to sixty in less than six seconds."

"Fierce fuckin' turbo. What year is it?"

"A '77, I think. It only has thirty thousand miles on it."

"This was your husband's car?"

"One of his cars. I sold the others and bought the 450 SL." She looked sad for an instant. "I really liked that car."

"You could trade this thing for a couple of those, I should think." I headed toward the *Call*. "I told Ferris I'd come in today so we could talk to Daniel about my adventures in the catacombs. You can drop me there, then call Chester. Ask him if Cabot was wired."

"Wired?"

"If I went into that room with those people, I'd have a wire, on me or in the attaché case. If he was wired, I'd really like to hear what was said."

"I'll try." She sighed. "But that's asking a lot."

"I'll make it worth your time." I squeezed her thigh. "If you haven't fallen asleep before I finish work."

"You're off today."

"I'm *off* most days. This is business."

— — — —

Leaving Cabot's office the next day at noon, I wondered if the mustard-colored Mustang that had followed me from home to the federal building would be waiting. Knowing I was being watched by people who probably didn't have my best interests at heart brought forth some peculiar ideas. I tried to picture myself in disguise, but I couldn't come up with an image I thought would work. Anything wild enough to do the trick would attract more attention than I wanted. In Manhattan, for example, a bearded Arab wearing dark sunglasses, flowing robes, and a burnoose could pass as easily through the streets as some guy in a Wall Street suit. In Philadelphia, he'd probably be mugged, or busted by the vice squad as a fag in drag.

I recalled bits and pieces of a dozen episodes of *The Rockford Files*, trying to remember what James Garner did to give the slip to tails. And then I remembered that the show was set in California, where no one walks further than the curb, so all his slick tricks probably would have happened while he was driving.

And what if the tail in the car, which was fairly obvious the third time it passed me, was meant to be seen, and another one, on foot or in a less obvious car, was waiting to take over. Using two and three people to follow someone was another trick I'd seen in movies. That would piss me off.

But why put a tail on me? If Reichmann wanted me dead, I could be killed as easily as Charlie Patton. Deleting someone from the active file in life is easier than finding a parking place in most cities. The passenger in the Mustang could have popped me with a silenced pistol, and probably have been back in the Roundhouse before the blood dried on the sidewalk.

And what if these guys weren't Reichmann's? They could be two of Uncle Angelo's hired hands. Maybe they were bodyguards.

Or maybe Lef'tenant Finori was leading me into the Valley of the Dearly Departed. I wasn't crazy about the idea, but I had to consider it. Blind faith in others was never my style.

I couldn't find the Mustang. I glanced around a few times as I walked toward the *Call*, and twice I abruptly veered into a building and stood inside for a minute or so, watching. *Nada*.

Fuck it, I finally decided. Either I die, or I don't, and whatever happens I probably won't be happy with the outcome.

— — — —

"How did it go with Edison?" French asked as I settled into a chair. "He's got a reputation for being closemouthed with the media."

"He didn't have all that much to say, actually. We spent some time talking about 'Nam. And then he played a tape for me, the one he made yesterday during his meeting at the Alliance Club."

"He *taped* that meeting!?"

"And played the tape for me, yes."

"My God. I'd love to have been there for that."

"Well . . ." I pulled an audiocassette from my pocket. "This is your lucky day, *if* you've got a cassette player available."

"Gentlemen . . ."

"Our beloved publisher," I said, reading from notes I'd made in Cabot's office.

". . . Now that you've eaten the profits from half a dozen display ads, perhaps we can turn our attention to Mr. Edison Cabot and the reason for this meeting."

"Gentlemen . . . since you aren't going to like what I've got to say, I'll keep it brief.

"My staff has uncovered and verified fifty-seven complaints of unnecessary or excessive force used by the Philadelphia Police Department within the last twelve months. And by excessive, I mean instances where moderate to severe physical harm resulted from actions by the police, witnessed by no fewer than three observers in each instance. The Commissioner himself was implicated in nine events, all of them verified."

"Fourteen of the fifty-seven incidents resulted in permanent injury to the suspects. Another eleven individuals were killed."

"Riffraff! Bolshevik terrorists. Scum armed to the teeth, and when they get their heads cracked they cry foul."

"That was Reichmann," I said deadpan. "In case you didn't recognize the voice."

"Who else was in the room?"

"A few people, including the mayor and the DA. Listen." I switched the cassette player on again.

"August seventeenth," Cabot continued. "Mrs. Juanita Rodriguez, age twenty-seven, initially involved in a dispute with an unarmed female traffic-control officer regarding a parking ticket issued to Mrs. Rodriguez in the 4000 block of Walnut Street, West Philadelphia. She claimed she was legally parked. The meter maid ignored her and attempted to drive away. Mrs. Rodriguez blocked the path of the officer's vehicle. The argument grew heated, and an anonymous caller phoned the local precinct. Three cars responded, with a total of six officers.

"Mrs. Rodriguez, who weighs approximately one hundred and seven pounds, and was at that time six months pregnant, sustained a broken jaw, a dislocated shoulder, three cracked ribs, and suffered a miscarriage—"

"Goddamn troublemaker, one of those neighborhood black radicals that causes problems and then tries to hide behind their color."

"Mrs. Rodriguez, a native of San Juan, Puerto Rico, was at that time employed by United Pennsylvania Bank and Trust, and had never been active in community protests. She was 'subdued' by four of the six officers on the scene after, they claimed, she attacked them with a beer bottle."

"Yes! Now I remember that case," Reichmann shouted.

"However," Cabot said, "fourteen witnesses, including the parish priest and two city employees from the Building Codes Department, gave sworn statements to the contrary. They said her 'resistance' consisted of telling one of the officers to, quote, Go fuck yourself, end quote."

"Lies! Lies!" Reichmann bellowed.

"Then why, may I ask, did the City Attorney attempt to settle Mrs. Rodriguez's lawsuit out of court, to the tune of three hundred thousand dollars?"

"Edison, surely you can't condemn Commissioner Reichmann and the entire Philadelphia police force for one unfortunate incident."

"That's the honorable mayor of Philadelphia, Sean O'Conner."

"I recognize the voice," French said. He'd winced at the details of Mrs. Rodriguez's injuries, and smiled at Cabot's polite reference to her birthplace after Reichmann called her a black radical, but otherwise his face had been impassive.

"Mr. Mayor," Cabot responded, "let me assure you that I do not condemn the entire Philadelphia police force. These incidents exemplify the attitudes of a tiny minority. But there is, without doubt or legitimate defense, a tendency to use unnecessary, often excessive force when none is required.

"And keep in mind, the eleven people who died were not the only people killed by the police in the last twelve months. They were eleven people who did not represent a clear and present danger to the officers involved. None of them were armed with a deadly weapon. Five of them, in five separate events, were kids who had been surprised in probable attempts to steal a car.

"Shooting an unarmed, 'suspected' car thief who does not obey a command to halt is not acceptable in the United States of America. We're not a Central American state ruled by the military. Not yet, anyway."

"You're not out there," Reichmann screamed, "day after day, night after night, in that goddamn jungle of drug pushers, addicts, whores, thieves, and lunatics who throw bricks from the rooftops and set ambushes in alleys and hallways. It isn't your life on the line, Cabot. What do you know about it? When did you ever—"

▬ ▬ ▬ ▬

I stopped the tape, grinning at French. "Cabot told me that while Reichmann was pissing and moaning he, Cabot, reached over and picked up a cannoli with that pincer he's got where his left hand used to be. I'd give a week's pay for a picture of that."

"How much more of this is there?"

"Not too much. Listen to the next one." I started the tape running.

▬ ▬ ▬ ▬

"March seventeenth," Cabot said. "St. Paddy's Day. Peter White, age twelve, observed by police, quote, 'tampering,' end quote, with the door of a new Mercedes sedan on Rittenhouse Square.

"According to witnesses, two officers arrived at the scene with sirens screaming, and one of them leaped from the patrol car with his service revolver drawn.

The boy ran. The officer fired a warning shot into the air, but the boy continued running. Both officers pursued, one on foot, the other by car. The driver left the car at one point to continue on foot, and eventually fired five shots, three of which hit the boy. He was dead at the scene.

"Subsequent investigation revealed that the Mercedes belonged to the father of the boy, who had sent him to retrieve something from the car. The keys were found in the boy's hand."

"He had a gun! I remember the case. Several witnesses said he had a gun. And the father was a known criminal, a bookie, with strong underworld connections, and a suspected dope dealer."

"He was a twelve-year-old kid with a goddamn water pistol! A plastic toy, which he never displayed. It was in his pocket. It popped out when he tripped and fell just before being shot by the officer. He did reach for it, but he was nine—*nine!*—feet from the pistol when he was shot.

"His father, indeed, does appear to be a bookie, and possibly a drug dealer, but the officers didn't shoot the father. They shot a twelve-year-old kid.

"And that incident, gentlemen, occurred at three-fifteen on a sunny afternoon, not in an alley, not in a dark hallway, not on a rooftop at night."

"That's all very interesting, Edison, and more than enough to ruin an otherwise excellent meal. What, exactly, is your point here?"

"Who's that?" French asked.

"Tyler, the banker."

"My point," Cabot said, "is that the man responsible for providing leadership to the city's police force, the man you have seemingly selected to run for mayor of Philadelphia after His Honor here finishes his term, has by deed and tacit approval encouraged the use of force and violence far in excess of what was needed, and has himself been involved in nine incidents where complaints of brutality were directed against him.

"Violation of basic civil rights by Commissioner Reichmann and dozens of his officers can be proven beyond any reasonable doubt.

"I have recommended that the federal government file suit against Reichmann and thirty-four of his officers, probably before the end of June.

"In addition, there will be a full-scale audit of funds administered by the police department, to determine if, and to what extent, some of those funds have been funneled into areas not appropriate to police activities."

Daniel waved his hand and I shut off the player. "What was that last business about?"

"All I could get from Cabot was that he, or someone working for him, thinks Reichmann's been spending federal antidrug money on the acquisition of unauthorized armaments."

"And you think you know where those 'armaments' can be found?"

"Unless someone moved them."

"Go ahead."

"That's about it. But catch this last bit by El Supremo."

"You and your kind," Reichmann said in a voice as flat and cold as a frozen lake, "will be the first to come running to us for protection when the fucking Bolsheviks and terrorists take over this city, this country. Who's gonna protect your civil rights then, Mr. Prosecutor?"

"I came here as a courtesy, on the instructions of my boss. I've said what I came to say, and I'll spare you any further unpleasantness. Thanks for the lunch."

— — — —

French sat with his elbows on his desk, his head resting on his hands, staring straight ahead while the tape rewound. The soft click of the mechanism turning itself off was like a crash of thunder. He looked at me and I thought I saw anger or disgust flash in his eyes.

Oh, Christ! Same old shit. I'm the messenger, he doesn't like the news.

"How did you talk Edison into giving you that tape?" he asked in a tone that fell somewhere between accusation and despair.

"Why? What does it matter?"

"It matters if you've compromised the *Call*, or yourself, if you've made promises that can't be kept, or misrepresented your situation in any way."

"Daniel, I've got enough shit to deal with. I don't need any more from you."

"You might want to keep in mind that I am ultimately responsible for your behavior. If you've taken liberties with the truth, or made commitments in the name of the *Call* which I can't sanction . . ."

"Skip the bullshit, okay? What's wrong? Too many high rollers and heavy hitters? Tyler. Reichmann. The mayor. The district attorney. Not to mention the real owner of the *Call*."

"Not at all . . ."

"This tape was given to me in confidence. I can't use it as a basis for a story, and I sure as hell can't print a transcript. So what are you worried about?"

"Your health."

"My 'health' isn't your responsibility. You and Juliet went out looking for a champion, someone to fight your battles. All I wanted was a bail ticket out of Club Fed and a place to park my butt while I tried to figure out what comes next."

"That's a rather self-serving analysis of your situation."

"Whatever you say, but remember that you and Juliet turned me in the direction *you* wanted me to go, and now I'm up to my ass in God only knows what. We're looking at the motherlode here. And you want me to do what? Quit?"

"No, no, Jamie, it's nothing like that. Nothing at all like that. But this *is* a delicate situation."

"Then you tell me something. Where the hell do you see me publishing whatever I dig out of this pit? If James Franklin can sit in that room, listening to Edison Cabot's laundry list of sins committed by the Reichmann regime, and not do anything or say anything about it, why do you imagine he'd allow you to publish an exposé? He's got to be in bed with Reichmann, Tyler, O'Conner, and a few others, right?"

"Your choice of metaphors . . ."

"I belong to the Metaphor-of-the-Month Club. Daniel, stop fucking around with semantics and let's come to some clearly defined, mutually agreed-upon estimation of what's going on here. Am I on this story, or not? And if I am, what do you plan to do with it?"

His phone rang while he was looking for some way to cover his ass and still keep me in the house. If I walked out he'd have to answer to Juliet. If I stayed, and the story broke, he'd have to answer to brother James. I didn't envy him his situation.

"Just a moment, please." He covered the mouthpiece and looked pleadingly at me. "Let's continue this later. I'd like to give all of it some thought, and I need to take care of this call. Okay?"

"Fine," I grumbled as I stood up. "I'll be out there writing obits and calling travel agents about flights to the Far East."

— — — —

"**W**ell shit, man, look at it from his point of view," Ferris said in French's defense. "He's well into his fifties, he's still payin' a mortgage, he needs his job, and you've left him looking at what's-his-name's choice."

"Hobson's?"

"Sounds like the guy."

"Maybe you're right. But those bozos in the Mustang aren't gonna stop following me around just because Daniel French says he doesn't want to play anymore."

"Do you have to pace up and down like that?"

I stopped at the far end of the room and leaned on a table. "It's either pace or smoke, take your choice."

"So pace, f'Chrissake."

I sat down, probably ten feet from where he stood leaning against a bookcase, and lit a Camel. "He was ready enough when he put us onto this goddamn story. Dig, he said. It's a time-honored tradition.

"And he had to know that his esteemed publisher was ass-deep in whatever's going on, right? Now, all of a sudden, he wants to 'think' about it. Why?"

"You went from saying all you wanted was a ticket out of Philly to being pissed off because Daniel doesn't want to open fire on City Hall. Why?"

"Because I'm stupid."

He gave me a long look and a half-smile.

"Fuck you," I said, laughing.

"What? I didn't say anything."

"Well, say something. You were the one who said we'd work together. You'd dig it out and I'd spread it around. What the hell have you been doing?"

"Fishing."

"You catch anything?"

"A big-mouth eunuch. Maybe. We need more bait than I've got, and to get the bait we have to talk nice to Daniel."

"How much?"

"Ten, maybe fifteen thou."

"Sheee-it! Fifteen hundred would be tough enough. Fifteen *thousand?* And what the hell is a eunuch? I mean, I know what a eunuch is in other parts of the world, but I don't think you're suggesting we buy a castrated slave . . . are you?"

"Eunuch is what the cops call the civilian clerks who work for the department, because they aren't authorized to carry weapons. I got a line on one in the Roundhouse, from a bookie I know."

"He owes the bookie a bundle, so we pop up with a lot of cash and buy what?"

"He doesn't owe the bookie anything. He wins a little, he loses a little, but he's not compulsive about it."

"Yeah . . . so what's his compulsion?"

"Hookers. Expensive hookers, which he can't afford most of the time. And one real expensive hooker, in particular. The guy's nuts about her, so I hear. But she's a thou a night, plus she expects to be wined and dined."

"A *thousand* a night?"

"Cash. In advance. She works two nights a week, Friday and Saturday."

"A thousand a night? For what?"

"Hey, whatta I know? The point is, he's already popped her a couple of times, and he's hot for her."

"You got this shit from a bookie?"

"He's righteous. I used to run numbers for him when I was a kid, and we've stayed in touch.

"Last night I ran into him, in a bar we both go to. We started talking about this and that. Shop talk. And he tells me about the eunuch. He says, 'Maybe one day you need an inside guy, this one's for sale.' That's all."

"So when do we talk nice to Daniel?"

"As soon as you straighten out your attitude."

"Okay. Let's try for the turn of the century."

"Let's try harder and make it an hour from now. I already made the appointment."

"And what do we say? Give us ten grand to go fishing? Or, We need fifteen thou for a hooker. . . . ?"

"I tell him what I told you, about the eunuch, the bookie, and the hooker . . ." His voice trailed off and he ended his thought with a long sigh.

"The bookie, the hooker, and the eunuch," I said. "Not what I'd call classic lit, but it has a certain charm, if you like lowlife."

"You're the fast-talkin' bullshit expert. *You* come up with a story."

"Ferris, even I have limitations. You've got a fish, maybe. What does this guy do? Is he in personnel or payroll or . . . Shit! Does he have access to their computers?"

"He's a personnel clerk!" Ferris's grin was a foot wide. "All those records are on computer."

I was pacing again. What the hell? He just might have access to the payroll files.

Ferris was frowning again. "What exactly are we looking to buy?"

"ART."

"Right."

"I'm serious. I think there's more to Reichmann's Antiterrorist Reaction Teams than any of us have considered. A lot more."

"Like what?"

"Like a separate, totally secret little army to operate all that shit they've tucked away in the catacombs. Maybe a hundred, hundred and fifty secret, elite cops, paid for with tax dollars, who spend their time playing out Reichmann's doomsday scenarios."

"That's a lotta guys who have to get paid, right? If they get paid, someone has to keep records."

"And the records are locked up in the mainframe computer somewhere . . ."

"Damn!" He started toward the door. "Let's go talk to Daniel right now."

"No! Whoa, wait a goddamn minute. Listen to me. Before we go in there asking for a ton of money, let's find out if the guy's for real. Can you get him to a meeting?"

"I don't know. Hell, all I've got's his name, and that he's a personnel clerk who works in the Roundhouse."

"You know the name of the hooker he's so crazy about?"

"No, but that's easy."

"What's the eunuch's name?"

"Kofax."

"Okay, we need bait, the right hook, a good story line, and a little bit of luck."

"Piece of cake," Ferris grinned.

"Yeah, well, I've got a bulletin that might make that piece of cake a little tougher to chew. How does Daniel French persuade the *Call*'s accountants to give us even ten thousand without the approval of James Franklin? That's a lot more money than this rag ever spent on checkbook journalism. Guaranteed."

"Damn!"

I lit another cigarette. "We need to think about this before we tell Daniel anything else. He's already had his first attack of second thoughts. If we sound like we haven't worked this out well enough to at least present a good story, he's gonna say no way.

"And I'll tell you something else, amigo: Until I know where he plans to publish whatever we come up with, I'm not gonna make myself a larger target for Reichmann and friends."

"Man, this might be the biggest story you and I will *ever* do. If we can't sell it to Daniel then we can sure as hell sell it to someone else. *Penthouse, Esquire, Mother* fuckin' *Jones* . . ." He was close to shouting, pacing up and back, his eyes lit with the feverish possibilities of success, recognition, and reward. All the traps in the trade.

"*Mother Jones* probably pays about ten cents a word, and no one reads the fuckin' book. *Penthouse* might do it, but we'd have a hard time getting their editors to come up with ten grand in bribe money based on what we could tell them right now. And this isn't *Esquire's* kind of story.

"You're wound too tight. Cool it, okay? We don't want to do anything totally stupid. Life's cheap, and if we aren't real careful we could be real dead for a real long time."

"Okay, okay. You're right. Whatta we do?"

"Cancel the meeting with French for now. He doesn't want to see us, anyway. Let's think about the best way to approach him with the business about the money. We need a sizeable piece of change, especially for a bribe."

"You want me to work on Kofax?"

"Yeah. Let's see what we can come up with that will get him interested.

"And keep this in mind: If we do this story and sell it somewhere else without Daniel's blessing, we're both gonna be out on our ass. I don't really care, but you might."

"Hey," he said, grinning, "I'm with you."

━━ ━━ ━━ ━━

Backlit and framed by navy blue drapes the color of his uniform, Reichmann greeted me from behind his massive oak desk. "Good morning, Mr. Hawkins. Please be seated."

He dismissed the female sergeant who had shown me into his office, but remained standing. "I've set aside thirty minutes for this interview," he said. "And before we start, I want to make it clear that my private life is not open for questions. Is that understood?"

"I understand what you said, but I'm not clear on what you consider your private life. You're a public figure. In many ways you have no private life."

"I don't want to get off to a disagreeable start here . . ."

"Good. Let's leave it at this: I'll ask whatever questions I think are relevant, and you decline to answer any question you consider too personal." I put a small tape recorder on his desk, in plain view, and opened a notebook.

"You take shorthand?"

"Speed-scribble. It's indecipherable to the ordinary eye, and I can do it quickly. Let's start with your image . . ."

"I'm as unconcerned with my image as you are with yours."

"Nice to see you have a sense of humor."

"That wasn't meant to be funny. If you worked for me I'd have you demoted for wearing sneakers and jeans to interview a public official. Doesn't the *Call* have requirements regarding appropriate dress?"

"They claim they do, but I go my own way most of the time. Anyway, dress is part of the image, and this is my image.

"Now, let's go back to *your* image. You claim you're unconcerned about it, but everything from your manner of speaking to the pearl handles on your pistols says image is uppermost in your mind. Isn't that something of a contradiction?"

"The handles are ivory. I am a leader, and leadership is created of many elements. Image, however, is something created to fool people, which I dislike. I lead by example. I don't hide behind an image, merely pretending I can do my job. I *am* what the public sees, at home, at a budget meeting, on the street, having dinner with friends. This isn't image. This is real."

"In other words, you're a man of substance . . . meat and potatoes . . . Whereas, a man 'hiding' behind his image is more like quiche and white wine."

"Well put," he said with grudging appreciation of one of my more mindless metaphors. He even sat down behind his desk, for which I was grateful. I was tired of looking up at him.

"Do you see yourself as Philadelphia's first line of defense against the elements of society that would bring us down to a level of anarchy?"

"Absolutely!"

"A general in a neverending war . . . That's a tough job."

"It will end, Mr. Hawkins. Mark my words, one day we will win because one day we will be given the manpower and firepower we need and the liberal court rulings that have us hamstrung will be reversed."

"Open season on lawbreakers."

"Even if I felt 'open season' was the right choice of words, I wouldn't want to be quoted saying that."

"Are you an admirer of General George Patton?"

"Very much an admirer. If he had been allowed to keep fighting after he beat the Germans, we wouldn't have half the problems we have with the world. Take the Russians out of the picture and what've you got? The world would've been our oyster."

"What about the problems in the Middle East?"

"Without Russian support for the militants, the British and French would still be in control."

"Do you feel they, the radical Middle Eastern countries, are a danger to us? Do you take the threats to bring terrorism to the U.S. seriously?"

"A lot more seriously than many others who hold public office or work for federal agencies responsible for enabling us to maintain a proper defense."

"Specifically, to whom are you referring?"

"I'd rather not name names. We disagree, and I believe one day soon they'll come around to my point of view. It's nothing personal."

"The sporadic bombings in the Philadelphia area—how long have they been occurring?"

"Two years."

"They've been attributed to something called the National Front for Radical Action. Who or what is the NFRA?"

"Radicals."

"What sort of 'radicals'? Are they Americans or foreigners who've infiltrated the U.S.? And why come to Philadelphia when New York, LA, and Washington, DC, offer so many more inviting targets?"

"We've had almost no luck identifying their origin. My gut feeling is that they're misled, misdirected Americans financed by money from the Middle East, and possibly Japan.

"As to why Philadelphia is a target, think about it. This is the cradle of American democracy, the home of the American Revolution, and a city of shrines to the American way of life.

"We also are the least capable of defending ourselves. We asked for special funding for antiterrorist reaction teams and we were turned down without any public hearings. Without, in fact, any real consideration. We've had more random bombings in the last two years than all other major U.S. cities combined, and still we're not considered an A-list target."

"Who's on the A list?"

"That's confidential information."

Is it now? I dug out my Camels. "Do you mind if I smoke?"

"Not at all. There's an ashtray on that table there . . ." He pointed to a table several feet away.

"How many have you arrested?" I asked as I retrieved the ashtray.

"None, other than that black bastard— Scratch that."

"None?"

"One. He hanged himself before we could get a confession."

"Charlie Patton, you mean."

"They don't have names, as far as I'm concerned. In the old days, before the liberal courts decided that it's okay to call a policeman a pig, but beating the piss out of lowlifes is a violation of constitutional rights, I'd have had a confession from the sonofabitch before he ever saw a mattress, let alone had time to hang himself."

"What if he wasn't a terrorist? What if he was just another dumb-ass looking for a quick fix to his problems?"

"He was a goddamn terrorist!" Reichmann slammed his fist onto the desktop hard enough to rattle a coffee cup nested in a saucer. "Make no mistake, Mr. Hawkins. From the time we got him into the Roundhouse until the time he left for the morgue, he smirked and smart-assed his way through the entire interrogation, saying his buddies would have him on the street before Santa made his rounds."

His buddies, I wanted to say, weren't members of the NFRA. His big-time buddies were two dimwitted newspaper reporters, one of whom quite probably was lucky he was still alive.

"As commissioner of the Philadelphia police," I said, "are you, like the ship's captain, responsible for the safety of all the citizens of this city?"

He hesitated for a moment, probably wondering if the question was loaded, or just stupid. "I'm responsible for the enforcement of law and order, and for the men I send out to do that job. If I've failed my responsibilities by neglecting to take appropriate action, or by neglecting to give the men under my command the right kind of leadership, then I'd expect to answer to the voters of Philadelphia."

"Your job's appointed, isn't it? What would the voters have to say about it?"

"They vote for the people who appointed me."

"From what I've heard, you're hoping that one day they'll vote you into the mayor's office."

"That's not police business. I will not respond to rumors about my alleged political ambitions. I don't have any."

"Okay, let's talk about leadership, what you call the 'right kind' of leadership. Are you satisfied with the way your men have responded to the job of enforcing law and order in what might be described as a lawless city?"

"Absolutely! We've got one of the finest group of men in blue anywhere." He relaxed, satisfied that he was back on safe ground. "I think the record speaks for itself."

"The record, as I understand it, often speaks of violence, corruption, and cover-up."

"You've been misinformed, Mr. Hawkins, or maybe you've just misunderstood the record. Since I took control of the force we've had very few complaints, and no serious charges filed against the department, or anyone in the department. No serious charges, no trials." He looked at his watch. "We're running out of time . . ."

"Just a few more questions," I said.

"Five minutes, and then I've got to keep an appointment."

"I rode with two of your guys last night, on a swing-shift patrol. That's a jungle out there. I kept thinking how much it reminded me of Vietnam."

"I'd heard you were in Vietnam. Won a couple of medals, didn't you?"

"Two more than I probably deserved. But the thing that got to me last night was the feeling that I was back in a goddamn combat zone, where the

enemy doesn't wear a uniform, doesn't have any regard for the rules of engage-
ment, and probably half the crime is committed by kids, street gangs that roam
around the city with impunity, not to mention automatic weapons." He was
nodding: Yes, yes, at last here's a reporter who's had at least a small taste of
what it's like.

"With all of that going on, tell me how you feel about due process, and
the principle of law which holds that everyone, even a known criminal appre-
hended in the act of committing a crime, is entitled to his or her day in court?"

"Due process is sacred in our system."

"So is human life, if you go by the book, but your officers, a few of them
anyway, seem more than willing to short-circuit the rights of those suspected of
committing a crime. And they don't seem to have a lot of regard for human
life."

"They have the highest regard for *human* life, Mr. Hawkins. But the dregs
of humanity, the anarchists and terrorists and dope dealers that stalk our streets,
are not, repeat *not*, human. They have little or no regard for human life, and
their lives have little value to me or my men. The only due process they deserve
is a long fall from a short rope."

He jumped to his feet, and I thought he was about to end the interview,
or maybe even throw me out physically. Instead, he stomped across the room
to a large map of Philadelphia and rapped half a dozen points circled in red or
yellow ink, using his blunt forefinger like a pointer. All together, the map
displayed maybe fifteen yellow and four red circles, most of which showed little
plastic flaglike markers fixed to pushpins.

"Here! Here! Here! Each of the markers indicates a bomb incident within
the last eighteen months. Millions of dollars in damage, four dead. How would
you like to tell their families about the value of life and the right of terrorists to
a day in court?"

"What's the problem with finding the people responsible? Are you under-
manned, outgunned, overwhelmed?"

"I don't have enough money or manpower. This kind of work takes specialists."

"How about the Feds? Or federal money to hire specialists?"

"None of the damage was done to federal property, so the FBI has shown
very little interest. Ane the amount of federal money we receive has been de-
creasing in recent years."

"Maybe it's a sign of the times, the decision of the people reflected in the
actions of their leaders."

"Leaders? What leaders?" His blood pressure must have jumped twenty
points. "A bunch of goddamn liberal turkeys cheerleading for the anarchists,
supported by spineless cranberry conservatives, voting billions of dollars to prop
up dictators in Africa or Asia, who won't spend a few million at home to keep
the streets safe for Americans." He walked back to his desk and stood, facing
me, leaning on his arms.

"A lot of people remember this country when it was a God-fearing, law-abiding land of hardworking individuals who lived by the Ten Commandments and the Golden Rule," he said. "Those days are gone.

"And today, Mr. Hawkins, right now, the barbarians are at the gates. We're under siege. The courts free the criminals, and turn loose the terrorists, leaving the decent citizens of this city and this country as prisoners in their own homes."

"What's the answer?"

Reichmann went from a raging crescendo to a dead stop. Maybe it was the tone of voice in which I'd asked him if he had the answer. Or maybe the whole thing was Rudolph Reichmann playing George C. Scott playing General George Patton. With conviction, with passion, without a doubt. "Internal security," he said.

"Secret police?"

"A national police force dedicated to the preservation of the American way of life. It's the only way to save this country from itself. We need internal security. The Bolsheviks have got to be rooted out, the terrorists tracked down and disposed of, the madmen put in chains. And time's running out, for all of us."

"Well, I've overstayed my time." I stood up as though to leave. "One last question, Commissioner. Where did it all go wrong?"

"I'll tell you exactly where it went wrong: permissive sex, illicit drugs, and loud music!"

"Amen."

— — — —

Sex, drugs, and rock'n'roll. It was stuck in my head, like one of those goddamn tag lines in a TV commercial. All it needed was music and we could put this country on the road to salvation. A new "Battle Hymn of the Republic," done by a rap band.

> Hey, yo, don't you know?
> The problem is sex,
> drugs,
> and rock'n'roll.
>
> Pushers, hookers, pimps,
> and guitars,
> drummers, humpers, hangin'
> out in bars.
>
> Terror in the streets.
> Terror between the sheets.
> Sex, drugs,
> and rock'n'roll

Bring 'em down,
Bring 'em down,
Decibels, Jezebels, and
dope-smokin' clowns.

By the time I reached the *Call* I had it all on tape. I decided to call it "The Reichmann Rap."

— — — —

". . . *Cranberry conservative!* What in God's name is a 'cranberry conservative'?" French fairly shouted. He looked up from the page with a pained expression. "Did he really describe someone as a cranberry conservative?"

"Actually, he was making a colorful reference to the ideology of those congressional wimps who've refused to cast an affirmative vote for Ronnie Raygun's right to initiate first strikes against Peru and Colombia, and/or suspend civil liberties and declare martial law in the war on drugs. Rather than, say, looking at George Bush through rose-colored glasses. If you know what I mean."

"I'm not sure that I do."

"Probably just as well. Why don't you go on reading? I'll just sit here and drink my eleventh cup of coffee, open my third pack of cigarettes, and hope to hell you don't insist on a lot of rewrite because I'm wasted."

"Go home," he said without looking up.

"Go home? Before you render your solemn judgment?"

"If it has minor problems, I'll see they're fixed, and you can read it in Sunday's paper. If there's a real problem you can fix it next week."

"Next week? I'm not working tomorrow?" He was reading again and shook his head, no, without looking up. "Since when do I get Saturday off?"

"It's not entirely a day off. Evidently Juliet has some plans that involve you."

"That's news to me."

He went back to reading, then looked up again. "By the way, you did a fine job on that 'night patrol' piece. That, and this interview, will play well together."

"That's what they said about Rosencrantz and Guildenstern. And we all know what happened to those guys. Killed by a copy editor in drag."

"Jamie," French sighed, "go home." He dropped his pencil on the desk and looked up, his eyes filled with sadness. "Or better still, go sit at the bar in a neighborhood saloon, one that caters to blue-collar laborers who drink shots and chase the demons with a beer. And while you're there, drinking and listening to the stories of not-so-quiet desperation, reflect on how unlikely it is that someone with your attitude and your destructive nature should be blessed with the talent you have.

"And then ponder the imponderable nature of random choice that selected

you and bestowed upon you a gift that you neither appreciate nor understand."
He held my gaze for a long moment, then picked up his pencil and resumed
reading.

"Daniel, if I wanted a day off I'd ask you. If I wanted a lesson in philosophy,
I'd ask God. The truth is, I didn't ask for either."

He grunted by way of response and continued reading. I closed the door
quietly behind me.

— — — —

The Cock'n'Bull was packed. Every seat at the bar was taken, most of them by
counter girls from Wanamaker's cosmetics department and secretaries from law
offices, and every space between the stools was filled with lechers and lushes
and lonely members of the male gender. Weekend warriors in the battle of the
sexes.

I looked around for Sheila, thinking, Big fuckin' mistake, Jamie-boy. You
should leave well enough alone. Go find a bar on Arch Street and listen to the
stories of the hookers and dime-bag dealers. Or go home and contemplate the
staggering magnitude of *indifference* inherent in all 'random choice.'

I'd been tempted to ask French, "What if random choice is from the same
school of thought that brought us the incontrovertible truth about the flat earth
and the sound barrier? What if, one day, right after we exceed the speed of light,
we discover that random choice exists only for mechanical functions, like flipping
a coin to determine who buys the next drink?" Instead, I'd walked away feeling
abused.

"Ah, what perverse destiny has brought us together on this cold winter's
night . . ." I whirled around to find Alexis, slightly ripped and somewhat unsteady on her feet, with the back of her right hand pressed to her forehead in a
poor imitation of Theda Bara. "Alone, alas—unloved, left to fend for herself.
Poor damsel in distress."

"Not to mention being half in the bag," I said with a grin. "You shouldn't
sneak up on a white knight like that."

"Just passing by when I caught sight of that unmistakable Hawkins pose. I
bet you stand like that in the goddamn shower."

"Is this my night to take a ration of shit from everyone I know?"

"Hello, creep," Sheila said as she passed on my right. She didn't smile or
slow her pace.

"Could be," Alexis said. "So you gonna offer to buy me a drink, or do I
have to go back to that fuckin' insurance salesman from Kankakee, Illinois?"

"Ivan changed jobs?"

"Ivan went home to collect the wifey for their big night at the Cherry Hill
synagogue. He's being inducted into the B'nai B'rith Blue Pencil Hall of Shame."
She put her hand on my arm and squeezed slightly. "So . . ."

"I'd be delighted to buy you a drink, but I probably should be getting home to my own wife."

"Yeah, right. How long has it been since you went home to anyone, let alone a wife?"

"Couple of years, I guess. She may be starting to worry by now. Whatta you think?"

"I think I'm probably better in bed, and you're sure as hell more interesting than Steve from Kankakee. The EPA should ban regional sales meetings. All that bullshit pollutes the air."

"Sounds like nonstop fun to me. How can you go wrong with a guy from Kankakee?"

"He's got one wife, two children, a three-bedroom 'rancher,' and five Visa cards. I hate the name Steve and I hate salesmen who promise me a great deal on my car insurance while they're looking down my blouse."

"Maybe he was just checking your hooters."

She moved closer, steeping out of the path two drunks had picked to cross from their table to the bar. "How come you've never tried to fuck me?"

"I'm shy."

"Bullshit."

"And you always gave me the impression that on your list of unpleasant possibilities I fell somewhere between a typhoid shot and an uninterrupted hour of listening to an amplified Albanian dial tone."

"Buy me a drink and I'll tell you exactly where you are on my list of possibilities."

As I glanced at the bar, two of the standees started collecting their change and wrestling with their coats. "C'mon, there's a couple of slots at the trough." We maneuvered our way to the bar and I waved at John.

"Be right with you," he called.

"I shouldn't be drinking in the mood I'm in," I said as I stacked cigarettes and money on the bar.

"So what're you doin' in here?"

"Beats me. I was told to find a saloon and contemplate the nature of random choice. Here I am."

"Was the 'random' aspect of your choice influenced at all by the fact that you'd like to bang the barmaid with the big tits? The one who called you a creep?"

"Possibly," I laughed. "Listen, I've been meaning to ask, are you related to Edison Cabot, the Assistant U.S. Attorney?"

"No. He's one of the rich Cabots. Cashmere and caviar. I'm one of the Columus, Ohio, Cabots. Polyester and meat loaf."

John extended his hand as he came toward us. "Long time, *hombre*. How've you been?"

"Okay. And you?"

"Busy, busy, busy. What'll you have? The usual?"

"Might as well. I can't dance and I'm too old for rum and coke. You know Alexis?"

"Hi, Alexis. I'm John, Mr. Hawkins's personal bartender. I've seen you in here a few times, but we were never introduced. What can I get for you?"

"Whatever he's drinking."

John looked from Alexis to me with that classic bartender expression that asks at a glance if I approved. I shrugged and he went in search of the Conmemorativo.

"That was cute," Alexis said. "What're we drinking, Malayan monkey sweat?"

"Tequila, with a beer chaser."

That cracked her up. "You are such an asshole," she finally managed to say. "What else would you drink? Shooters and what?"

John put the tequila on the bar with shot glasses, beer glasses, and two bottles of Corona. He poured the tequila. "Lime and salt?"

"As long as you're up." I smiled at Alexis. "You can still order a glass of some amusing, lighthearted white wine with a sensitive bouquet."

"Doesn't go with the black leather and chains." She picked up the shot glasses and handed one to me. "To hot flesh and a long life."

"Whew . . ." I touched her glass with mine and downed the shot just as John put a saucer of lime wedges on the bar with a salt shaker.

"Couldn't wait, huh?"

"Trying to save you a trip. Since you're here, fill 'em up, and pour one for yourself."

"Maybe later," he said as he refilled our glasses. "After the amateurs go home with their lucky Friday-night dates."

Alexis poured the beer while I lit a Camel. A lot of guys would envy me at the moment, I thought, but I'm not all that eager to get in bed with Alexis. I don't want to hurt her feelings, I don't want to fuck her, and I don't think she's gonna buy any of my bullshit excuses.

"Are you fantasizing or just trying to figure out what to do next?" she asked after a long silence with no eye contact.

"I was wondering how to tell you, without it sounding like rejection, that this isn't the right time for me to yield to my lustful instincts. And I decided that probably isn't possible, no matter how sincerely it's intended.

"The problem for me is I've got a lot of unrequited passion for the 'barmaid with the big tits,' I think you called her. We had a fling, and then we broke up. I'm not really over that."

"She didn't seem real happy to see you," Alexis said with a frown. "And I think you're lying through your teeth, but you're so goddamn weird it's hard to tell."

"Listen, don't dwell on it too much because I'm just passing through."

" 'The Dealer' . . . you know that's what they call you?"

"I heard."

The crowd at the bar was thinning out and we had more room. If a few more left and I could get something to eat, this could turn out okay.

"And some of them think you're gay," she announced after I'd sort of disengaged myself from her and the subject of who thought what about me.

"Rumors run amok: Is Jamie Hawkins light in the loafers, or merely light-hearted? Geraldo wants to know! Answers tomorrow on 'Live at Five,' on Ten."

"You don't give a damn, do you?" Alexis asked with a trace of annoyance. "It doesn't matter who thinks you're weird, or arrogant, or unapproachable . . . who thinks you're a fag or who thinks you're a real fuck?"

"I'm just a poor-ass little country boy, Alexis, lost in the big city. If it wasn't for a few fast women who took advantage of me, I'd probably still be a virgin."

"That may be . . . I heard you were fucking half the owners of the *Call*, and *Mr.* Franklin isn't your type, so you probably aren't a fag."

"Well, now that you're satisfied . . ."

"You wanna know what I think?"

"That wasn't the deal. The deal was, I buy you a drink and you tell me where I fit on your list of possibilities. I've bought two already, so it's your turn to curtsey." I caught John's eye and made a motion to refill the shot glasses. He grinned and started down the bar.

"I think you'd be hard to handle, impossible to control . . ." She frowned at John, but he filled both glasses anyway.

"I'm not all that difficult."

". . . and a great fuck."

"Naw . . . See? You've got it backwards. I'm really easy to get along with, but only so-so in the sack. No one ever called me a great fuck. Really." I drew in a lungful of smoke and exhaled in her direction. "Actually, one woman did, but she was older and she'd been in prison for three years, so she probably doesn't count."

Her hand trembled a little as she reached for the tequila. She stopped just before her fingers closed around the glass. "No way. I'll be on my face."

I slipped my arm around her shoulder and leaned in until we were face to face, separated by inches. "How you holding up?"

"I was fried when you got here . . ." She inhaled and gripped the edge of the bar with both hands. "But I'll be damned if I'll let you get out of it by getting me drunk." She managed a lopsided grin and I leaned back, smiling. She had balls, even if they weren't any larger than her little teacup hooters.

"You know what else I think? I think you and Ferris are onto something . . . a story. A *big* story. The stuff that gets you a raise, and maybe a write-up in *E&P*."

I pushed the shot glass a little closer to her hand. "Drink this and maybe I'll be in line for a Pulitzer nomination."

"The other night, a couple of guys I know on the force were in a bar we all go to, and they asked me about you."

"Cops?"

"Undercover narcs. Real undercover. Like they've never actually admitted that that's what they do, but I know from another friend . . ."

"So . . .?"

"So they were telling me that they'd been assigned to give protection to a reporter from the *Call*, all hush-hush stuff. And I asked who, and they said, 'The jerk-off that wrote about the Quaker Plaza shoot-out on Christmas Eve.' "

"Maybe they were talking about Ferris. His name was on the story, too."

"Hawkins, gimme a break. They were talking about you. I said 'Hawkins or Ferris?' and they said, 'Jamie Hawkins.' Okay?"

"That's the first I've heard about it."

"They said they'd gotten a hot tip that the NFRA is after your ass."

"Alexis, f'Chrissake . . . don't you think the cops would tell me if they put a tail on me?"

"Maybe, unless they're using you for bait. Reichmann doesn't like you much."

"I interviewed Reichmann today."

"How'd that go?"

"Well enough, after we worked out the ground rules."

She drank some beer, peering at me from behind the glass. "What are you guys up to?"

"Nothing. Who were the cops? Tell me their names."

"I only know 'em as Hansel and Gretel."

"Hansel and Gretel . . . Two narcs from a fairy tale." I downed the shot of tequila and bit into a slice of lime. "That sounds about right."

"I might be helpful, you know. I might have contacts that you and Ferris wouldn't even think of."

"Get real, Alexis."

"Listen, you can write the goddamn story, okay?" She leaned in close, almost whispering in my ear. "I already know something that might be useful."

"Useful to whom? There's no story, there's no Hansel and Gretel, there's no more tequila in my fuckin' glass." I rapped the bar with the shot glass a couple of times and John rolled his eyes, but he came down the bar with the bottle.

I couldn't decide if she was fishing with live bait that she'd picked up from God only knew where, or if she was just firing shots in the dark, based on Christ only knew what.

"It's a very small world around here, Jamie."

"No shit. You said you know something that might be useful. Tell me what it is and I'll tell you something about Hansel and Gretel."

"You first," she said.

I just looked at her for a few seconds, unsure how far to pursue it. I hate playing poker with women.

"C'mon," she said, laughing softly. "I'll show you mine if you show me yours."

"Hansel and Gretel aren't narcs."

"How do you know that?" she asked without protest.

"I know, and that's all you need to know. But think about this: Philly PD narcs wouldn't be assigned as bodyguards unless there were drugs involved. They aren't directly involved in trying to bust someone from the NFRA, and I don't deal drugs. It isn't their job and it doesn't make sense."

"If they aren't narcs, who are they? Feds?"

"Possibly."

She sipped her beer. "My friend swore those turkeys were undercover narcs." She was talking more to herself than me. "I can't believe she'd lie to me about that . . ."

"Don't make something out of nothing, Alexis. Those guys could be reading meters for the water department. Forget it. You want a fresh beer?"

"No," she sighed. "I'm already drunk."

"So, it's time for you to 'show me yours,' as you put it."

She turned to me and peered into my face. "That could be a lot of fun if you'd take me home."

"And then what? I take you home, we fuck each other into submission, we fall asleep, and tomorrow we wake up, look at each other, and then what?"

"We go pick out china patterns." I'd finally hit the right button, and for a moment she was pissed. Then she grinned. "You aren't worried about tomorrow. You're worried about the barmaid seeing us leave together."

"You're probably right." She wasn't altogether wrong, if I was going to be altogether honest.

"Do you like the ocean in the winter? I know a great little bed and breakfast place on the Jersey shore, in Sea Isle City."

"I need commitment, Alexis. A one-night stand and Sunday brunch in a trendy café that sells badly scrambled eggs at six dollars a pair isn't my style. Even worse, we work together, and you're involved with Ivan. Think about it . . . there I'd be, at my desk, up to my buns in obits . . . watching Ivan watch you watch me watching Ivan. It's a short road to a broken heart."

"We don't even work the same shift, you asshole." She spun around on the bar stool, stepped down, and grabbed the bar. "Whoa . . ."

"The floor tilts after Friday night's happy hour. You want John to call a cab for you?"

"I want you to take me home. I'm not gonna tell you what I know unless you make sure I get home okay."

"You've got to be kidding."

"C'mon, Hawkins, walk me home. It's only a couple of blocks."

"You'll be lucky if you're on your feet when you reach the front door." Shit! I waved for John while Alexis got into her coat.

"I'll be right back," she announced. "Got to make a stop in the powder room before I hit the street."

"You shouldn't have given her that last shot," John said as I finished my beer. "She may be unconscious before you get her in bed."

"All I've planned is to see her home safely. I've got enough problems without getting involved with her and I don't need a grudge fuck from some lost soul. Tomorrow she'd either dislike me even more than she already does, or she'd wake up and decide that she could tame me, whatever the hell that meant to her." I shrugged. "I've been there before."

"Did you really save her life at that shoot-out on Christmas Eve?"

"Fuck no! Who told you that?"

"The Polish Princess. She's still in love with you," he added with a shake of his head. "But she's stubborn."

"Listen, have a drink with me, okay? I'm buying."

He glanced down the bar; it was half empty and the second bartender had everything under control. He poured two shots of tequila. "Good to see you," he said as he raised his glass.

"Better fuckin' days," I said, and we drank. "Now give me a check so I can get the hell out of here. I've had all I need to drink, and more than my share of abuse. It's time to go home."

"What a fun guy. It's ten after eleven on a Friday night and you're calling it quits? Jamie, Jamie . . . what's happened to you?"

"I'm up to my ass in weirdness, and I'm tired."

He went to the cash register, totaled my bill, and handed it to me, along with a business card. "Almost forgot. Lieutenant Finori left that for you."

I put two twenties on the bar and looked at the card. It looked exactly like the last one he'd given me. I turned it over, looking for a message. On the back he'd printed:

FINORI'S TAXI
"Clean, safe transportation 6 P.M.–12 A.M."

What the fuck does he want? Is this a warning, or his cute way of saying he wants to talk? "When was he in here?"

"Last night," he said as he put my change on the bar.

"Keep it." I pushed the money toward him. Shit. I hadn't heard from him since our brief conversation after Juliet's Mercedes was turned into scrap metal. And I hadn't called him. "Can you let me make a call on the house phone?"

"Sure." He reached under the bar and pulled out a telephone. "Just like Sardi's."

"Never having been there, I wouldn't know, but somehow I don't think the Cock'n'Bull will ever be mistaken for Sardi's."

He moved down the bar while I dialed. Finori answered on the second ring. "Taxis are hard to find at this time of the night," I said.

"Where are you?"

"The Cock'n'Bull, but I'm leaving in a few minutes to escort a colleague home, then I'm going home."

"Walking or driving?"

"Walkin' for a couple of blocks, then I'll be lookin' for a cab."

"What address?"

"Beats me. I've never been there." From the corner of my eye I caught sight of Alexis coming toward the bar. "I've got to go."

"I need an address," he said.

"Alexis, what's your address?"

"Society Hill Place, Building Five. Who wants to know?"

"My mom, in case I don't come home. She wants to know where to send the cops."

"I got that," Finori said and hung up.

"Let's go," I said to Alexis.

She hooked her arm in mine and we headed for the door, with her weaving slightly. A few of the people at the bar turned to watch us, most of them undoubtedly thinking unkind thoughts about me because I'd gotten her drunk so I could take advantage of her. Right.

Alexis stumbled and almost pulled both of us to the floor. Once I had her upright, I put my arm around her and prayed that Sheila was in one of the back rooms. And then I prayed that a taxi would be sitting out front, a bored driver with no better place to park.

At the door I stood aside, holding it open, while Alexis made a careful exit. As I stepped through after her I glanced back and there was Sheila, clutching a tray of dirty beer glasses and empty bottles, staring at me.

And outside there wasn't a cab in sight. It was freezing cold, with an icy wind off the river. "Left or right?" I asked as I pulled the collar of my jacket up around my neck, wondering why I still bothered looking for help from the heavens. I was on the shit list, obviously.

"This way," she said and we lurched to the right.

The Mustang's engine came to life from somewhere behind us as we headed south. I didn't turn or look back. I didn't need to. The Japanese may own the world's car markets but all of their four-cylinder rice grinders sound alike. The rumble of the Mustang's exhaust was as distinct as the sound of its engine revving.

The distance to Alexis's apartment was closer to four blocks than two, and she was showing faint signs of sobering up by the time we arrived. Her gait was steadier, and she was complaining about the cold. I barely listened, wondering what to do after I delivered her to the door. If I went in, I'd only complicate the situation. If I hung around outside I could end up with frostbite by the time Finori's "taxi" arrived. If it arrived. And the Mustang was still behind us.

"You owe me," I said to Alexis as we approached the terraced grounds of the high-rise she called home. "You haven't told me what you know that, quote, might be useful, end quote."

"Ivan has a meeting next week with Teflon Tom . . ."

"Who!?"

"Thomas Teitlebaum, our executive editor. Did you ever meet him?"

"No. If I hadn't read his name on the masthead I wouldn't have known we have an executive editor. Where does he hide?"

"On the twenty-first floor. He's more like a corporate chief of operations than an executive editor.

"And he lives under a sun lamp, which is why we call him Teflon Tom. His skin's like a piece of old luggage."

"So what's the big deal about Ivan and Teflon Tom getting together?" I asked at the lobby door. I'd stopped in my tracks, staring at Alexis, waiting for an answer. I still wasn't convinced she actually knew something worthwhile, but I wasn't ready to walk away, either. The Mustang's engine shut down.

"C'mon Alexis, what the hell's the game?"

She put the key in the door and pushed it open. "Politics. Daniel and Teitlebaum have never gotten along well. He's been looking for a way to get rid of Daniel for years, and probably would have already if it wasn't for Juliet Franklin-Rossini. And since Ivan wants Daniel's job, helping Teflon Tom is a smart move on his part.

"But that's not the part you'll find interesting. For that," she purred, "you have to come inside . . ."

Three unkind responses came immediately to mind, but I put my self-interest ahead of my strong desire to grab her by the throat and stepped through the door. What the fuck, at least I could enjoy the game and leave those clowns in the Mustang to freeze their balls for awhile.

━━ ━━ ━━ ━━

"Ivan went in to confront Daniel about whatever's going on with you and Ferris," she said as she stripped off her coat and dropped it over the scalloped back of the sofa. "He knows something's up, and he wants to put one of his reporters on the story, too. More politics."

"That reporter being the same one to whom he tried to give the Quaker Plaza story, I should imagine."

"Of course."

"Why does 'vested interest' always smell funny? You think it's the fabric?"

"What fabric? What are you talking about?"

"Vested interest is usually cut from the whole cloth of bullshit, y'know."

"Daniel," she said, ignoring my comment, "told Ivan that the two of you are working on a major story requiring total secrecy, and only if you guys asked for help would he consider someone from dayside. He wouldn't tell Ivan anything else."

"Did it ever occur to you that French is mind-fucking Ivan?"

"Not his style."

"And since French's answer didn't satisfy Ivan, you, or the two of you, decided you should get me into bed? Then what? I have an orgasm and spill the beans, so to speak?" I wanted to laugh. I also wanted to stick her head through the window, without bothering to open it.

"No, you arrogant jerk! I've wanted to fuck your brains out since you strolled into the city room like you owned the goddamn place. I'm a sucker for hard cases. Okay? It's like some guys go bananas for bimbos, or chicks with long legs, and some chicks would die for a guy in a uniform. I love power, and you've got your own kind."

"You're a real piece of work, Alexis."

"And probably the best piece of ass you've never had. Get real, Hawkins. You think because I write all that fluffy ducky bullshit I'm an airhead?"

When I didn't answer she walked over to where I stood at the window looking down at the street. From the fifteenth floor it was hard to spot the top of a particular car, and I wasn't sure if the Mustang was still there.

"I asked you a question," she snapped.

"You also called me an asshole a couple of times, a jerk at least once, and you haven't told me what the fuck you think is so 'useful.' " I raised my glasses and parked them on top of my head. "Or if you have, you really are an airhead."

She was trembling slightly, and when she lightly touched her tongue to her bottom lip I wondered if we were even on the same planet, let alone the same wavelength.

"Okay," I said, "Let's try again. I don't know what the fuck Ivan thinks Ferris and I are doing, or why French told him it's a big goddamn secret. This all sounds like unmitigated bullshit to me. Power, politics, and somebody's fantasy trip, all in one."

"But let's say Ivan tells Teitlebaum that Daniel's got two nightside reporters working on a secret investigation. So what? Ivan says it's not fair? Who cares?"

"Ivan will claim that the full resources of the *Call* aren't being put to use. And it's *Call* policy, not to mention good protocol, to involve the day city editor in any and all stories of 'significant consequence.' Teitlebaum will agree. And Daniel will either have to deny that there's a story, which would sure as hell cramp your style . . . or he'll have to admit that you and Ferris are onto something really big, and after that it's all over the city room in fifteen minutes, tops. An hour later, it's all over the city. The mayor, the DA, Reichmann, you name the place and the people in that office will know your name, your face, and whose ass you're after."

"There's nothing I can do about any of it."

"Tell Daniel what Ivan plans to do so you guys can head him off. Give Ivan a cover story that'll keep him pacified." She smiled and I could see the light go on behind her eyes.

"Get Daniel to tell Ivan, and Tom if necessary, that you and Ferris are working on a series for *Miz* Rossini about a swindle in the art world. Possibility of major fraud. The art museum bilked. She's on the board at the museum, and she's got all the right connections, so that would sound plausible, and boring enough for Ivan to believe it. The investigation is secret because some very rich people may have been conned. Hell, the museum may have forgeries on display.

"Ivan will go very quickly and very quietly back to his desk, and that'll be the end of his curiosity for weeks."

"That's a hell of a piece of fiction to come off the top of your head," I said with real admiration. If Ivan was about to muck up our half-assed investigation, and bullshit was the only way to keep him quiet, the story was perfect. The only disagreeable thing about it was the probable necessity of bringing in Alexis.

"Why is Ivan beating the bushes? What the hell gave him the idea that we're working on anything?"

"Ivan *knows*." She shook her head as though I'd asked her to explain the mysteries of animal migration, or how Lassie always found her way home. "And he's sharp when it comes to putting little bits and pieces together. Gossip, an offhand comment made by someone, a change in routine—nothing gets by him unnoticed."

"As you said earlier, we don't even work the same shift."

"But your shifts overlap. And the other day he was talking to Atlee, and Atlee said something about you and Ferris making your own hours. Someone else commented on your visits to Daniel's office. A couple of the guys made cracks about how much time you and Ferris spend together in the library."

"And that's Ivan's basis for confronting French? Shit."

"Look me in the eye and tell me it's all Ivan's paranoid fantasy. No crapping around, no games."

"What Ferris and I are working on isn't all that interesting or worthy of secrecy," I said. It was time to tell the truth, which didn't seem the best choice, or to redesign the lie to suit the listener. "Hell, we aren't even sure we've got a story . . ."

"I'd like to believe you," she said with a smile, "but if that's true, why did that car follow us from the bar?"

"What car?"

"The Mustang. It followed us from the Cock'n'Bull."

"Who knows? You think that was Hansel and Gretel, right?"

"Let's put it this way: That was not a Center City jitney." She reached out and gripped my jacket, pulling herself up on her toes. Even in her boots she was a good three inches shorter than me, but she reached up, put her arm around my neck, and pulled my head down until our lips touched. "Kiss me," she whispered.

She had a wicked mouth, and the thought of spending the night with her in a warm bed was a lot more appealing than the idea of walking out into the frozen wilderness of Society Hill. I put my arms around her and cupped her ass with my hands. She pressed herself as close as she could get and I was the one who broke for air.

"You want a drink?" she asked as she moved away.

"I'll take a beer. And you can answer the sixty-four dollar question."

"What's that?" she asked as she took two bottles of Japanese beer from the refrigerator.

"What do you get out of this?"

"You guys fill me in and let me work on it with you."

"There isn't anything for you to work on," I said with some exasperation. "Honest."

"You're full of shit," she said, and handed me a beer. "Listen to this scenario . . . One day in October you show up and walk into a job that didn't exist until you arrived. I'd know if Ivan planned to hire a reporter. No interviews, no references, no testing, no clips, no nothing.

"You defy Ivan and survive. You write that Pulaski Day story and survive. You tell Ivan to go fuck himself when he wants you to give me the Charlie Patton story, and you survive.

"You dress as you please, you come and go as you please, and you're fucking the publisher's sister, who happens to own a piece of the paper.

"Now, realistically, if you saw all that happening, wouldn't you think the guy had something going?"

"Probably," I answered and upended the beer bottle.

"You weren't brought in here to write obits and stories about museum tours. You aren't a hatchet for management. So you've got to be a hired gun. A lot of us figured that out a while ago. We just haven't been able to identify the target." She drained about half of the beer from her bottle and burped lightly.

"Nice . . ."

"Listen, you can write the story, okay? Just give me a piece of the by-line. I want out of here, Hawkins. Off the *Call*, and out of Philadelphia. I need a big-ticket story I can ride to New York or LA."

"I'm not the only one involved in this, so I can't really say yes."

"Whatever you decide, the others will agree. We both know that."

"Maybe, maybe not." I went back to the window, drinking beer, stalling. When I looked down there was a bright yellow light on top of a dirty yellow cab.

"Listen," I said, "I've got some business that has to be handled now." I put the beer bottle on the window ledge.

"You sonofabitch." She grabbed my arm as I stepped around her. "How can you leave me?"

"Got to, for now. My friends are waiting and it's cold out there." I moved away, toward the door. "See ya . . ."

"Hawkins . . ."

I stopped. "Yeah?"

"Call me over the weekend and let me know you're okay. If I can't get laid, at least don't make me worry about you."

"What do you think's gonna happen?"

"I don't know. If those guys in the Mustang aren't your bodyguards, they may be out to get your ass. I'd feel bad if they got it and I couldn't."

"I'll be okay. I'll call you tomorrow or Sunday."

"I make a great meat loaf and mashed potatoes if you ever want to come for dinner."

"I hate meat loaf, but thanks for the thought. Good night."

━━ ━━ ━━ ━━

The Mustang was nowhere in sight as I came out of the building. I climbed into the taxi and grinned at Lef'tenant Finori. "I love curb service," I said. "Did you bring a flask? I could use a drink."

"I rarely drink on duty, but maybe after we're off the street. What'll it be? Your place or mine?"

"Mine, if it's all the same to you."

He gave the driver my address and sat back. Once, at a red light, I turned to ask him if he'd found any taps on my phone, but he warned me off with a look and a shake of his head. We finished the ten-minute ride in silence.

And thirty minutes later he was out the door, leaving me to ponder how unlikely it was that Ferris and I would ever publish anything other than our resignations. Or our obits.

A few minutes after he left I sat down at my desk with a cup of coffee and phoned Alexis. Her answering machine picked up the call on the first ring. "I'm safe at home," I said after the beep. "The guys in the Mustang were friendlies. I'll let you know how the vote goes on your petition to join the boy's club."

I hung up and lit a joint, inhaling as deeply as I could and holding the smoke until my lungs ached. Then I did it again. I wanted to be so stoned I could barely find my butt with both hands. I hoped I wouldn't need to.

By the fifth toke I was off the planet, which was a problem because I was also starving and Neptune isn't known for its fast food. Christ on a bike, I sighed. I need a good woman, a gorgeous genie in a bottle who'd take care of me and go read a book when I need to be left alone. How much longer can I live on caffeine, nicotine, and tequila?

My hunger generated four-color images of food that popped up in front of my mind's eye like flash cards, and for a moment I wondered if Mama-san might still be open. But that didn't make sense, because I wasn't going out the front door for love or money, let alone something to eat. If it wasn't in the kitchen, it wasn't on the menu of possibilities.

I was still thinking about sea bass and Mama-san when I picked up the *I Ching*, which I'd marked at the hexagram for the Exile. I started reading interpretations for the individual lines.

If the Exile dallies with petty matters he will draw disaster on himself.
Narrow-mindedness will cause misfortune. One lacks ability in his job.

No shit. I'd been a poor excuse for a soldier, and I knew even less about being an investigative reporter.

But narrow-minded? Pray tell, about what?

Alexis flashed before my eyes, sandwiched between pictures of me as a grunt, and a slab of meat loaf on a plate half covered in mashed potatoes. The image of the meat loaf convinced me that I might have taken one toke too many.

I went to rummage in the kitchen. A can of chili, a can of tuna, two cans of soup, a can of creamed corn. I was ready to quit in despair when I found a box of Frosted Flakes under the sink with the Windex and cleanser, probably left there from the last time I was stoned.

The Exile arrives at the inn. He carries valuables. He wins the loyalty of a young servant.

The Cock'n'Bull? I wondered as I crunched my way through the bowl of cereal. Starring Sheila as the young servant? If she was part of destiny's cast of characters in this strange story I'd certainly managed to fuck up that chapter.

One of my problems with the tea-leaf approach to life's mysteries is the symbolic nature of the answers. The larger problem is that I don't like hot tea.

The inn where the exile stays, burns down. He loses the loyalty of his young servant. To continue is dangerous.

I read it, and then I read it again. Weird shit. I'd sure as hell lost Sheila's loyalty. And most of what Finori had told me was less than reassuring. I was still walking point in a strange land.

The Exile finds sanctuary. He regains his valuables. He is not happy in his heart.

The phone rang, and I almost dropped the bowl I was holding. "Hello."

"Did I wake you?" Juliet asked.

"Do I sound like I'm sleeping? Scared the bejesus out of me."

"But not the grumpiness, it seems."

"I'm not happy in my heart, according to the *I Ching*. And I'm sure not happy with you."

"Why?"

"For putting Tweedledee and Tweedledum on my tail, and even more because you didn't tell me. Where'd you find those guys? Main Line Rent-a-Cop?"

"I'm not going to say I'm sorry because I'm not. I don't want anything to happen to you."

"Well, save your money. I'm off Reichmann's shit list, at least for the moment. Evidently Gentry was the eager son of a bitch who wanted to waste me, and Reichmann put a muzzle on him."

"Where did you hear that? Jamie, who're you dealing with that knows so much about me?"

"Confidential sources. That's the reporter's equivalent of 'No comment.' I'm also not happy with you arranging my days off. Daniel didn't seem real pleased, either. In fact, in the war for hearts and minds, I haven't done well with anyone lately."

"You've won my heart, and I wanted to take you away for a weekend. In Barbados."

"You'd improve your odds if you asked me before you made the plans and put them in motion."

"I'm sorry . . . I . . . ." The silence stretched out until it was as tight as a piano wire. "Are you really angry?" she finally asked. "Like, you-don't-want-to-talk-to-me angry."

"Naw, I'm too stoned to get completely bent out of shape." I got a sudden flash of a white sandy beach. "Barbados? For a weekend?"

"Wouldn't that be fun? I have tickets for a flight tomorrow morning, returning late Monday. You'd be back in time for work Tuesday."

"Thanks, but no thanks."

"Well, I'd like to see you tonight."

"I'm not going anywhere anytime soon."

"I could be there in thirty minutes."

"I may be asleep in thirty minutes."

"I'll take my chances. And," she added in a husky voice, "I'm prepared to give you a nominal discount on next month's rent if you're still awake when I arrive."

"I'll see you in thirty minutes," I said, smiling. I was about to hang up when my stomach growled. "And if you show up with a couple of sandwiches you can choose the first position."

"That's *vulgar*. I'll be there with a Care package before you fall asleep."

She may not be a genie in a bottle, but she's close. Probably too close.

Expect great success, the I Ching advised. *Those employed will have responsibility and prestige.*

I closed the book and put it aside. Considering the wisdom of the first comment I'd read, that "one lacks ability in his job," the "great success" struck me as wishful thinking. I hadn't been dealt all the cards, but the ones I had seen I would have folded weeks ago in a different game.

God, please don't let this crap signal the onset of another meaningful learning experience, the kind that leaves the putz with the short straw forever changed. Those are always painful, and I've learned as much as I want to know for a while.

I heard my prayer hit the ceiling and bounce back. That sucker wasn't going anywhere. And neither, it seemed, was I.

— — — —

"I need twelve hundred dollars," I said to Juliet the next morning. She was raking scrambled eggs onto our plates while I waited in the kitchen door.

"Do you want jelly on your toast?"

"A little. What can I do to help?"

"Wait until I've had my breakfast before you tell me why you want twelve hundred dollars. My guess is I'm going to need my strength."

I ate my eggs and a piece of toast quickly, using the time to think through what I wanted to say to Juliet. I hate making conversational outlines. And I'm not crazy about breakfast at nine A.M.

"You know, we're really not compatible," I finally said. "You're a morning person. I'm not real fond of anything that starts before noon."

"I lie awake nights thinking about that," she said as though I'd just pointed out that we had different religious convictions. "It may prove to be the fatal flaw in our relationship." She finished her food and put a little half-and-half in her coffee.

"Why do you need twelve hundred dollars?"

"For a hooker I want to meet."

"You want *me* to give *you* twelve hundred dollars so you can spend the night with a hooker?" The coffee cup was poised an inch or so from her mouth and she looked at me through a thin cloud of steam.

"Well, that's not exactly the way I would put it, but . . ."

"I probably could find you a first-class call girl for *two* hundred. Twelve seems a little excessive unless there's more to this than meets between the thighs."

"There's more."

"Like what?"

"Bribery. Blackmail. Probably a little deceit. The usual sleazy elements of good investigative journalism."

"Do I want to know about this?" she asked herself aloud. "Or would I feel better if I just wrote a check and went away to Barbados for a week or two alone?"

"Let me know what you decide. In the meantime, tell me something: Are there any conditions, or clauses, in your father's will that would affect the ownership of the *Call* if either you or your brother were convicted of a felony?"

"Either you have one hellava source of information," she said after a moment of stunned silence, "or you are amazingly intuitive."

"You're right. And I was right, right?"

She chewed on her bottom lip for a few seconds, then smiled. "You took a guess, didn't you?"

"Not really. Last night, after you fell asleep, it finally flew up and hit me in the face. Daniel says he wants to see Reichmann deposed because he's a threat to the city and the citizens of Philadelphia.

"That might satisfy Daniel, maybe even win him a Pulitzer, but you wouldn't gain anything from that.

"So the question then becomes, What do you want? You did admit that you want to defrock the other J. Franklin, but only so you and Daniel can turn the *Call* into whatever you see as an ideal newspaper.

"I can't buy that. You aren't a crusader, and you're damn sure not a journalist."

"Well, what am I, then?" she said with some anger. "Immoral? Vindictive? Deceitful?"

"Defensive, at the moment." I left her to think about it while I made myself another cup of coffee. I didn't need an argument so early in the morning. It tends to make for a long day. As I waited for the water to boil I caught the sound of the shower from the bathroom. When in doubt, hide in the bathroom.

— — — —

I was sitting at my desk when she walked in, wrapped in a bath sheet, her head covered in a turban fashioned from a smaller towel.

"Sorry I was rude to you," she said as she settled into the only other chair in the room. "And you're right. I am defensive. So what now?"

"It's time for you to make some decisions. You have to decide how serious you are about this business. So does French. I'm not exactly enchanted with this job, and doing it without knowing whose battle I'm fighting, or even where the story will be published, if—*if*—there's a story that can be published, is bullshit. I don't feel any commitment to this from either of you."

"That's fair."

"You also have to decide if you want to spend the money that I'll need. If Ferris and I can work this out, which is another big goddamn 'if,' my guess is something between twenty-five and fifty thousand dollars."

"For bribes?" she asked.

"Baksheesh."

"Bribes."

"Sometimes it's a bribe, sometimes it's more of a service charge. I don't plan to bribe the hooker, but I do want to find out about a guy she's balled a couple of times, and the only way I'll get her to spend time talking to me is if I cover her fee."

I finished my coffee while I tried to read between the lines that had formed between her eyes. She didn't look happy.

"I can afford the money," she finally decided, "but I'm not sure it's an investment I want to make. There'd be a lot of repercussions, and I'd still have James to contend with."

"You want the *Call*, and I can't guarantee you that. Even if Reichmann falls, your brother may not fall with him. The only way to take him down is to uncover something that will put him in the slam, and that isn't bloody likely, is it?"

"Not unless it's a federal crime, and even then he'd have to serve at least a year. Dad gave us that much leeway."

"Why a year?"

"He said it was possible that one of us could be locked up for contempt of court, or failing to reveal our sources to a grand jury, and if James or I wanted to be a martyr, that was our business. But if either one of us wanted to be stupid, that was his business. And to serve more than a year to protect anyone was, to him, stupid.

"I don't think he ever imagined that one of us would try to have the other put in jail for a felony." She left me thinking about that while she cleaned up the dirty dishes and made a pot of coffee.

What now? she'd asked. A damn fine, well put question: What now?

I was making a mental summary of what I knew, and what I thought I knew, and what I could defend or prove, which was almost nothing, when a piece of my late-night conversation with Lef'tenant Finori surfaced: "Check out the Franklin Memorial Art League."

"Whatta you know about something called the Franklin Memorial Art League?" I asked as she came into the room.

"It's a tax-exempt foundation, put together two years or so ago by my brother and Edmund Tyler, the banker, in honor of my father, to raise funds for the maintenance of the museum building."

"No shit. Who controls the money?"

"The foundation."

"Okay, who controls the foundation?"

"Well . . ." She sighed. "There's the head of the foundation, which is an honorary position that went to the mayor. Then there's the board. My brother's a member, as is Tyler. And I think there are three others, all male. The newer ones were added in the last year or so, and I don't remember their names. It's a very small group, and they don't give out much information. I suppose some of it's a matter of public record, but they keep a low profile."

"You're not a member?"

"No."

"What have the trustees done with the money, that you're aware of?"

She gave it some thought, then shrugged. "I can only recall one big job. Repair work on the building's foundation."

"When was that?"

"A year and a half ago. They were down there for three or four months."

"Did the museum close during that time?"

"Only for a week, during the worst of it. They did most of the work at night." She sipped her coffee, lost in thought.

"Other than working on the building foundation, have they spent any money on anything? Sandblasting? Paint? Roof work?"

"No. But they did take over the responsibility for security."

God, I love it when I fill the house with a hole card and the guy with the seven-high straight isn't even sure why I'm still in the game.

"And when, pray tell, did they volunteer for that noble commitment?"

"About the same time. We had an incident where a lunatic came into the museum and tried to destroy a couple of paintings. Just before the work started in the catacombs."

"How much time do you think your brother would do for tax fraud?" I asked with a smile.

Her eyes opened wide. "Tax fraud!? James would *never* do that. The Art League is a memorial to his father, whom he cherished. Plus, James is worth twenty or thirty million dollars. He doesn't have any reason or need to commit fraud."

"I don't care if he owns the Philadelphia mint. The fuckin' Franklin Memorial Art League is a fraud. A cover for Reichmann, and several other very irreverent people." I bounced out of my chair and did a little dance with a grin as wide as my face. She was looking at me as though I'd totally lost it.

"What kind of security did you have before the incident with the lunatic?"

"A couple of private guards on the door, and maybe half a dozen others wandering around inside. They spent as much time reading the racing forms or sleeping as they did patrolling the exhibit rooms."

"And after?"

"What are you getting at?"

"The new guys are different than the usual rent-a-cops, right? They stand straighter? The uniforms fit? There's a spark of intelligence in their eyes?"

"I suppose . . ."

"They have sidearms? Pistols?"

"Yes."

"Reichmann's SS troops."

"Are you crazy?"

"I'm not even eccentric, let alone crazy. I may be wrong, but I do believe we've found the Unholy Grail."

She didn't speak for a full five minutes, maybe longer. She sat there staring straight ahead, and for probably the hundredth time in my life I remembered the old saying, "Be cautious in what you wish for . . . you just may end up with it."

I went looking for the tequila bottle, which I'd left in the fridge for some strange reason I couldn't recall. I poured two shots and carried them back to where Juliet sat unmoving.

I waved the shot glass under her nose, back and forth. "Are you comatose, or did you drift away to observe one of Jupiter's moons?"

"I'm not sure I can do it," she said as she took the glass with a trembling hand.

"It's for medicinal purposes. It'll start your heart, the synapses will fire, and the little neurons can go about their business. Otherwise, you're courting permanent brain damage in fifteen seconds." I drank my shot and shuddered slightly.

"I meant exposing my brother."

"So far you haven't done either, and the clock's ticking. Drink." She upended the glass and gasped. Those early-morning shots can kill an amateur.

"You sure went to a lot of trouble, and expense, to get this far. Now you develop chickenheart. . . ."

"Oh, be still," she shouted berfore I could finish my sentence. She was crying a little.

Fine. Just another average Saturday morning in fuckin' Philadelphia. I finally find what I think is the missing link between James Franklin, Edmund Tyler, Rudolph Reichmann, and the mayor, a link I might be able to hammer into the righteous sword of muckraking excellence, thereby making the City of Philadelphia safe for future generations of yuppies and other assorted lowlife, and she comes unraveled.

Without Juliet, I knew French would fold faster than a wilted orchid. He might flap his arms from the pulpit for the sake of his image, but there was no way he'd put his money on the table. Or his ass on the line.

I leaned over to wipe away a tear, and she grabbed me as though I were outbound on a one-way trip to Tibet, pulling herself up from the chair, kissing me, and then, bam! Back into the bathroom.

— — — —

When she came back into the room I was looking at Saturday-morning cartoons. I couldn't remember the last time I'd turned the TV on before noon on Saturday. Old Wile E. Coyote was in deep shit, which is where I'd left him years before. Some of us never learn.

"Who do you root for?" she asked as she stood behind my chair. Her arms came around my neck, and she slipped her hands inside my shirt.

"The fuckin' coyote. The Roadrunner reminds me of all those jerks who think they've found the meaning of life in the Gold Card, a black BMW, and the white magic they pack up their nose.

"One day that little *meep-meep*ing sonofabitch is gonna hesitate for an instant and then you're looking at *pollo frito*."

"I'm sorry I made such a scene."

"I've dealt with worse. From you, actually. The first time I saw this apartment. You didn't make any sense then, and you didn't make any less sense ten minutes ago. The guy calls you a slut and says you stole his brother's place at the *Call*, and you don't want to contribute to his downfall. Are you afraid?"

"Yes." She sighed.

"Of what?"

"Of losing you."

I took her hand and pulled her around to the front of the chair so I could see her eyes. She sank to her knees, clutching my hands. And sure enough, she had the look; in mere moments she had become the abandoned female. The event hadn't actually occurred, but for her it was already a fait accompli and I was history.

"Once the game is finished," she said, struggling to control her tears and her tone, "you'll pack your stuff and go looking for more trouble, or you'll go back to Mexico and work on a book until you're bored and then you'll find trouble. I'll get a letter once in a while, and maybe even a phone call if you're somewhere in the country. But, from my point of view, you'll have left me with the spoils of war, but no pleasure in winning."

"Maybe not." Her speech was heartfelt and my shields went up. Red alert flashed through my nervous sytem. "I could end up with the fish in the Schuylkill River."

"Jamie, don't . . . Please."

I stood up and stepped over her to pour a shot of tequila. "You want one?"

"No, thanks."

I drank one and considered pouring another, then decided against it.

"What now?" she asked.

"That was my question." I went back to the chair and sat down sideways. She nestled her head in my lap. "It's your paper, sort of. And your money. It's my story, along with Ferris's, but we're a long way from having all the information we need. We don't have a publisher. And we sure as hell can't finance this with the money I've got in my Christmas Club account."

She sat up, smiling, which was a relief. "You don't have a Christmas Club account."

"And there we are, at the heart of the matter. Any right-thinking Christian with good, solid American values *should* have a Christmas Club account. And you're quite right, I don't. Now, either that makes me something of a misfit, the kind that has brought this country to the edge of ruin, or . . ."

"Or what?" she complained when I left my pronouncement unfinished.

"Or I'm destiny's child, probably illegitimate." That cracked me up for some reason. "You really know how to pick 'em, don't you?"

"Maybe I'm one of destiny's children, too."

"Wouldn't that be a piece of cosmic perversity? Two star-crossed children of the same hard-nosed deity. I wonder if that would constitute incest?"

She slapped my leg. "You have a totally perverse mind, do you know that?"

"And you're probably one of the good kids that He takes to the cosmic equivalent of PTA, while I'm stuck here, in this home for the wigged-out and the wayward. This is visiting day, which in this dimension's concept of time stretches out for months or years, but in real time is maybe five nanoseconds."

"Do you think I'll be grounded because I seduced you?" she asked.

"Probably. I know I sent off a protest after the first time you had your way with me. Retribution may be on the wing, even as we speak."

"Well, will you take me to bed once more before I'm turned into a pillar of salt?"

"A pillar of polymers. They're using a lot more plastic now. They last longer, so more people have an opportunity to see the wages of sin and repent. Amen. Now let's go fool around before retribution arrives."

— — — —

Somewhere between her third and fourth orgasms she looked up, straight into my eyes, and said with fierce intensity, "There are times when I hate you."

"Yeah, and there are times when you'd lie down and die for me," I said as I rolled over on my back, bringing her with me, yielding to her the supposedly dominant position. When she was straddling me, looking down, I saw how much anger and pain she felt.

She fucked me with fast, hard thrusts, grunting with the effort to maintain her precarious balance between carnal pleasure and emotional anguish, between her bittersweet satisfaction of control and the suffocating delight of submission.

And when she finally gave up control for those few moments of ecstasy, she erupted in a screaming orgasm. "Goddamn you, goddamn you!" she cried, slapping my arms and chest, over and over, until she collapsed, with her back to me, sobbing. A few minutes later she fell asleep.

— — — —

Sometimes I think the only possible way to ever truly understand women would be to become one. Even for a day. And I've got that on my list of things to do, right there between learning to like tofu and asking God to lunch.

On the other hand, it is possible to accept one of them, or some of them, without any genuine comprehension of their priorities or their peculiar emotional makeup. It's not a lot of fun, but it's probably no worse than menstrual cramps.

After an hour of contemplation, two shots of tequila, and a couple of tokes, I finally accepted that she was angry with me without good reason, and that I had no good reason to expect her to be rational about emotional issues. My sin was simply that I could, and eventually would, leave. That, to Juliet, meant that I needed her less than she needed me, which gave me a kind of power that couldn't be countered with money or position, with threats or tears. It meant that I was unobtainable. It would be left to me to point out that, in the long run, she was fortunate to have it so.

C'est la vie.

From time to time, I still look back at that morning and think, It could have ended there. Which is ridiculous.

And knowing how ridiculous the idea is, I think, Well, it *should* have ended there. Which is equally ridiculous.

While you were in Mexico, I say to myself, living on tequila and tacos, wrestling with your demons and trying to write another novel, Reichmann and company had already begun working on their plan to protect the city from ragheads and radicals. They didn't know and couldn't have cared less that you existed.

Before you were ever busted and sent to Club Fed, the game had escalated from Let's Pretend to high-stakes poker, and too many people had bought a seat at the table.

And by the time Juliet had bailed you out, the inevitable was already sitting on the launch pad. There was no turning back.

You had two choices: Leave, or light the fuse.

— — — —

I was asleep on the sofa when Juliet woke me to say she was hungry and offered to take me out for lunch.

"What time is it?" I asked.

"One-thirty."

I pulled her close enough to kiss her. "You go. I'm not ready to face the world."

"Are you angry with me?"

"No."

"Disappointed?"

"In you?"

"In me . . . in my reluctance to let you go any deeper into this morass. I know you can't very well pursue it without my blessing."

"Actually, it's your money and your half of the paper I need. A blessing I can get from the local priest." I rearranged myself, waking up slowly.

"What's that expression you use? 'Don't slow dance with a bullshitter'?"

"I really don't know if I'm disappointed. Maybe. Or maybe I'm relieved. Would it make any difference?"

"No." She sighed. "I don't have the courage for it. I don't want to see you or Ferris hurt. Or killed. And I don't want to lose another battle to James because if I lost he'd take away everything that's important to me. He's very powerful, and totally unforgiving."

"Okay. What are you gonna tell French?"

"The truth. He has a lot to lose too."

"I need a cigarette."

She brought my Camels and my lighter from my desk, shaking her head. "You smoke too much."

"I know, but I can't quit. At this point the tar is all that's holding my lungs together." She put the pack on the sofa, then lit the cigarette for me. "If you leave . . . when you leave, will you let me keep this?"

"My lighter?"

"Yes."

"You don't smoke." She didn't say anything, and anything I said other than yes, or no, would probably get the same response. "Okay. When I leave it's yours, at least until the next time I see you."

"Thanks." She put the lighter on top of the cigarettes, kissed me lightly, and stood up to leave. "Call me later if you get bored. I'll be home all night."

I got off the sofa and walked her outside. Standing on the stoop, I watched her walk down the steps to the sidewalk, where she stopped and looked back. "You're not going to do anything dumb or dangerous, are you?"

"What would I do that's dangerous? Stick my finger in the garbage disposal?"

"I don't know. Just be careful until everything settles down. Okay? Please?"

"Piece of cake."

"Promise?"

"Promise."

— — — —

Having made my solemn promise to avoid anything dangerous, as though I always knew beforehand when danger would rear its curious head, I decided to do something that was irrefutably dumb. I went back to the Cock'n'Bull to see Sheila. I didn't want to win her back so I could get her in bed, but I did want to win back her affection. If that was possible. I believed without question that she and I could be good friends, and I meant to do my best to give us that opportunity. But first I had to convince her that I'd be a much better candidate for friend than husband.

She wasn't real happy to see me.

"What the fuck do you want?" was her greeting, and that came from the opposite side of the bar after she'd studiously ignored me for the better part of an hour.

"I want you to stop hating me long enough to listen to what I have to say."

"I don't hate you. But I don't have anything to say to you, and I don't have any interest in anything you've got to say. So why don't you find another place to drink?"

"I like this place. Where else can I find the warmth and companionship offered here, surrounded by my colleagues, steeped in journalistic memorabilia, nurtured by the hospitable staff . . ."

She leaned over the bar until her face was only a few inches from mine. "Fuck off!" she said, and walked away.

What we've got here, I muttered in her wake, is a failure to communicate. Not to mention a little bitchiness. More than a little, actually.

"Tough lady," the guy three stools to my left commented. He shook his head, as though to say, "and I'm happy it's your problem, not mine." "Buy you a drink?"

"I'm drinking slowly since it may take me all night to get her off her high horse, but thanks. Maybe later." And please don't start talking about your problems with women. Or give me advice about how to handle this one.

I drank some of my beer, then stared at the glass as though I was lost in thought, and when I looked past him, surveying the room, he was rummaging in his sample case, one of those big rectangular leather boxes with the hard sides. Another fuckin' salesman from Kankakee. Plaid jacket, white shirt, and skinny black tie. Mr. Fun goes to Philly.

Sheila crossed the room near the front door and leaned on the bar, chattering with one of the customers, a TV reporter I recognized from his reports on Channel 11. She was smiling and laughing. Watching her made me smile. She really was a joyful spirit when she was in a good mood. I missed that.

Sheila's response to me hadn't been a big surprise, but I wasn't ready to give up, either. I'd decided before I left the apartment that I'd accept a certain amount of abuse and hope that once she'd unloaded some of her anger she'd sit down and talk. If it took all night, so be it.

John came on at six-thirty, half an hour late, shivering from the cold. The high temperature for the day had been nineteen degrees, according to the TV weather-mouth. He'd made it sound like a freak event that had caught everyone by surprise. Hell, it hadn't been above freezing all week.

"How's it going?" John asked as he poured two shots of tequila and pushed one of the glasses toward me.

"Sheila told me to fuck off, and you're thirty minutes late. On the other hand, you're buying this drink, and she didn't say fuck off forever." I raised my glass. "*Salud!*"

He downed the shot and shuddered. "That should warm things up a little. How'd it go last night with . . . Alexis, right?"

"Yeah. Alexis Cabot. I got her home, and I left her fully dressed. I told you I wasn't interested. We work together, and there aren't many people who can handle that."

"Sheila started crying two minutes after you were out the door, and went home about two minutes after that. I think she thought you'd come in here to patch things up with her, and then you left with another woman. Even I was a little surprised. She doesn't seem your type."

"C'mon, John. Alexis was too drunk to go home alone. And I did come in here to see Sheila, who didn't exactly throw her arms around me."

"She couldn't get close enough. Alexis was all over you."

"Yeah, well . . . there wasn't much I could do about that."

"Listen, Sheila's due for a break in a few minutes. If you want to fix things up, I'll see if I can talk her into sitting down with you."

"You think she'll listen?"

He shrugged. "She might, if you tell her that you love her, that you miss her, and that your life isn't the same without her."

"Jesus, why don't I just propose marriage? Then tomorrow we can go out shopping for a tux."

"Jamie, she's convinced that you were seduced by an older woman with power and position, which is rough competition, and that even if you wanted to break off the relationship you'd be afraid to put your job in jeopardy. She thinks you chose the one who could help your career rather than the one who really loves you, and she needs reassurance. She's hurting."

"She thinks that I chose Juliet over her to advance myself at the *Call?* She told you that?"

"That, and everything else that's happened to the two of you. I've heard it all, and I mean all, from the first time you went home with her. Until you came along, I'd never seen her emotional about a guy. She's had a dozen different boyfriends, but she spent a lot of time alone."

"Christ on a cross . . ." How the hell am I suppose to talk her into accepting me as a friend when she's convinced that I was led astray by an older woman and selfishly chose my career before wife, kids, and a house on the Jersey shore? "John, I don't know how to deal with that. I'm probably the most non-career-oriented person in this bar, on this block, possibly in this city if you don't count the street people. What can I say?"

"Tell 'er what she wants to hear."

"I'm not gonna bullshit her."

"You do care about her. I've seen that. You have to miss her or you wouldn't be here. And your life can't be the same without her. That's only logical. So where's the bullshit?"

"See what you can do," I sighed. "And give me another beer, *por favor.*"

"Two beers," the salesman chimed in, "and another shot for Mr. Lucky, who seems to have three women fighting over him."

John looked at me and I shrugged. "If he wants to spend his money on a philanderer, I'll drink to that." For a moment I was annoyed, but then I reminded myself that I had spent a lot of hours in bars, on buses, in coffeehouses, listening to other people's conversations and complaints, lamenting life. When you're lonely and bored with your own existence, listening to someone else's misadventures can be entertaining, and occasionally give one a breath of hope.

I watched John walk down the bar, to the far end near the door, where Sheila stood leaning against the back of a bar stool, still talking with Mr. TV News. She excused herself, and went into the corner with John. Two or three times I saw her shake her head. Once she glanced at me for an instant, a look of surprise on her face. I wondered what the hell he'd just told her.

The conversation lasted two or three minutes, and then John came back to my end with three icy bottles of beer and a grin. "You're on, for five minutes," he said. "I got her to promise that much. After that, you're on your own." He popped the caps off the beer, placed one in front of Captain Kankakee, one in front of me, and one where he expected Sheila to sit. Then he poured two shots of tequila.

"Take it out of this," the salesman said and dropped a twenty on the bar, "and hold the change until I get back from the head." He gave me a wink and headed for the bathroom.

"Is he stone strange, or what?" John asked.

"Too many nights alone in too many strange cities. Another tragic victim of Ramada-itis. But if the twenty's good, cash it. These drinks may be my meager portion of Upjohn's profit-sharing plan."

"Is he a drug rep?"

"I don't know, but he's selling something. His sample case is on the floor."

As he went to ring up the tab, Sheila strolled down the bar and around the corner to stand beside me. "Hi . . ."

"Hi. You want to sit down for my five minutes? Some lonely salesman who's in the head at the moment bought us a drink."

She slid onto the stool. "I haven't had a shot of this stuff since the last time you and I drank one." She picked up her shot glass.

"To your change of heart." We chugged the shots and she wiped tequila tears from her eyes. "Outa practice, huh?"

"Jesus!" She inhaled deeply, reminding me of what a great pair of C cups she owned.

John was standing on the opposite side of the bar, beaming. He looked altogether pleased. "Why do you think that guy asked me to hold his change?" he asked as he refilled our shot glasses. "You think he's worried about you pocketing his five dollars?"

"Who knows?"

"I'm gonna leave it here." He put the money down next to a pack of Marlboros and a Bic lighter. "Those two are on me."

"Congratulations on your interview with Reichmann," Sheila said, squeezing my arm. "That was a great piece, especially if you read the other one about being with the cops on patrol."

"Where'd you see those?"

"Sunday's paper. We always get copies in here Saturday afternoon. The guys want the sports, and the girls want to see who's having Sunday sales."

"Hell, I haven't even seen the stories since I turned them in. Did they read okay? No obvious editorial scissor work?"

"They're great. You mixed in that stuff about Vietnam, and then Reichmann is yelling about the bombings, and needing more firepower and more manpower . . . He made himself sound like a lunatic talking about the 'terrorists.' You did a terrific job."

"Listen," I said to Sheila as I stepped down from the stool, "I don't want to press my luck, but I need to empty my bladder before we talk, if you'll promise not to start the clock until I get back."

She kissed my cheek lightly and smiled. "I'll wait. But let's drink these before you go." She lifted her shot glass. "I have a toast." I raised my glass. "To a long life with a happy ending," she said, and we drank.

"I'll be back in a couple of minutes . . ."

The bathroom was freezing. The room's only window was open and a steady five-knot breeze was blowing in from the alley. Nineteen goddamn miserable degrees and some dimwit would rather freeze than inhale whatever the ventilator couldn't handle. I slammed it shut and unzipped my jeans, glancing around for some sign of the salesman. Both stall doors were open and he was nowhere in sight.

I'd zipped up my jeans and was reaching for the handle, intending to flush, when the door flew open, blasted inward by the force of an explosion. Almost simultaneously, the wall buckled and the urinal fell to the floor between my feet, splashing my legs and sneakers. At the same instant, I heard the mirror over the sinks crack, sending shards of glass crashing to the floor as a tremendous boom rattled the light fixtures in the ceiling. Some of the bulbs popped, and pieces of flying glass were everywhere. From an upright position, I'd been slammed headfirst into the wall, bounced back, and knocked on my ass. Instinctively, I covered my head with my left arm, pressing as close to the wall as I could get to protect myself from a shower of plaster that fell from the ceiling. The whole thing took two seconds, max.

It took a few more seconds for me to realize that I'd survived an explosion of some kind and consider the possibility that I'd scrambled my circuits. My head ached, and I was having a tough time processing thoughts that I could string together. I kept seeing the same images—the wall buckling and the urinal falling—over and over, always in slow motion.

Finally the howling of alarms, set off by the concussion, drew me to a reality slightly larger than what I could see from where I'd fallen. I heard screams and sobbing and someone yelling "Get an ambulance, get an ambulance." I started coughing and it dawned on me that what was left of the room was filling with smoke despite the wind coming through the blown-out window overlooking the alley.

A gas main, I thought. A fuckin' gas main exploded.

Then the wetness oozing down my neck seeped into my thoughts. The right shoulder and front of my shirt were soaked in blood. I touched my neck and looked with surprise at the red smear on my fingers. "Jesus Christ," I grunted. For some dumb reason it hadn't occurred to me that I might be wounded. The glass had cut me so quickly and with such force I hadn't felt any pain. Suddenly, raw fear threatened to sap what little control I had over my thoughts and body. I sat there staring at the blood on my fingers, my eyes filling with tears. I was straddling that fine line between resignation and panic, wondering if an artery had been sliced open. I realized that I might be living the last few minutes of my life. Never in my worst nightmare had I imagined I'd find death on the floor of a saloon bathroom, with me looking into a cracked porcelain urinal. But there I was.

The two primal reactions to fear are fight or flight. I didn't have any place to run, and I wasn't certain I could get on my feet, not even to fight my fear, so I made myself concentrate on breathing, pushing back the anxiety until I had at least some slight hold on my emotions. I touched my neck again, looking for any evidence that the blood was spurting rather than oozing. All I found was more blood.

And then I remembered Sheila and John. And the sample case the "salesman" had left at the bar while he was supposedly in the bathroom. "Merciful Father, please . . . not them."

I struggled to my feet, weaving slightly, and started toward the door, wading through the residue of glass and plaster, porcelain chips and tile fragments, all of it crunching under my sneakers. Maybe halfway to the door, which was hanging from one hinge, another spasm of coughing hit me and I lost my balance, crashing to the floor. A piece of broken glass opened the palm of my left hand and more blood poured forth.

I rolled over, cursing silently, and struggled to my knees, then to my feet. In a few moments more I made it to the door and leaned against the splintered frame, looking into absolute chaos. My head was filled with the sounds of the dying, the anguished moans and the pitiful pleas for help. Almost everything in the room was obscured by smoke. I saw maybe a dozen fingers of fire that burned despite the downpour from the sprinklers. Two bodies were sprawled on the floor within five feet of where I stood, one without a left arm. I stumbled over the missing arm a few steps beyond, closer to the bar.

I found Sheila smashed into the wall, a large section of the oak bar lying across her legs and stomach, her skirt partially burned and still smoldering. Her mouth was open and several of her teeth were missing. Her right eye was gone. A mix of soot and blood had crusted on her face.

Dear God in Heaven . . . how could you let this happen to her? I asked as I sank to the floor.

I tried to crawl past her, to push through the rubble and look for John, but I didn't have the strength to move the chunks of wood and plaster. And I didn't have the courage to touch Sheila, to put my hand on what was left of her face and say good-bye. I looked at her and wanted desperately to reach out to her, but nothing happened. No action followed the thought, no matter how many times I tried.

A fireman found me, still coughing, as I was crawling toward what had been the wall that fronted on the street. I remember hearing him yell, "Stretcher! Get a goddamn stretcher in here!" I tried to stand and got nowhere.

"Can't get up . . ." I said.

He knelt and put his arm around me. "Easy, son. Relax. You're gonna be okay. Just relax . . ."

My head dropped, and I watched the black wave sweeping in from the distant rim of my bewildered little world. And then I was out.

— — — —

I surfaced in an ambulance, bouncing along Lombard Street toward the Society Hill Medical Center. An IV needle had been stuck into my left arm, and a bandage was wrapped around my left hand. I noticed my watch was missing. So were my glasses, which I couldn't remember losing, but they undoubtedly came off during the aftermath of the explosion. My cigarettes and lighter had been on the bar.

The paramedic leaned over and checked the pupils in my eyes. "You're gonna be fine," he said. "Have you stitched up and on your way in a couple of days." Satisfied with whatever he saw, he leaned back. "How you feeling?"

"Wonderful. What's with the cut on my neck?"

"Nothing to worry about. Most of the bleeding stopped. Fifty or sixty stitches should make it right. A little different angle and you'd probably have bled to death before anyone found you." He put his hand on my arm and smiled reassuringly. "Just relax."

I drifted off, and the next thing I knew the ambulance swerved left, then made a hard right turn and bounced into the driveway that led to the emergency room. They had me on a gurney in the hall in two minutes or less.

"Thanks for the ride," I said.

"No problem."

"Easy for you to say," is what I tried to say, but I don't think it came out like that because I threw up about the time the second or third word came out. Everything that came up left the aftertaste of smoke.

From where the paramedic had parked me, I could see the nurses' station at the end of the hall. The only nurse in sight was behind the counter, pacing while she talked on the phone, answering one call after another, and occasionally marking a chart or making notes. Two clerks sat on either side of the nurse, also answering calls and making notes. The phones never stopped ringing.

Between the station and me, three other lost souls lay on gurneys that had been parked against the wall. We'd all been hooked to IV bags and left to stare at the ceiling, chilled and trembling, projecting the worst possible outcome. No candy stripers with sweet smiles passed. No one with soft cool hands came to offer kind words or ask if we needed anything. We were four seemingly forgotten casualties left in a long, cold hospital corridor. I'd decided that I was okay, more or less. I hoped the others were no worse because I had the feeling it would be a while before any of us were finished with the medical part of this bullshit and allowed to start the healing process.

Later, maybe half an hour, maybe an hour, an officious and overbearing nurse's aide came over to count my pulse and check my blood pressure. Her hair was red and ridiculous, a wiry tangle of curls that she'd lacquered with spray. She had beady blue eyes, a pug nose, and a thin-lipped mouth that probably hadn't been kissed since Christ was a carpenter. I squinted at her name tag. N. M. Steele. N. M. for 'No Mercy' was my guess.

She glanced at the paperwork left by the paramedics and started on me by checking my pulse, jabbering all the while. "Do we have medical insurance, Mr. Hawkins?"

"Yes."

"And do we have our insurance card with us?"

"No."

"We really should keep our insurance card with us at all times, Mr. Hawkins. We never know when or where that card may make the difference between life and death. And it makes our job much easier."

"What, exactly, is *our* job? Sorting out the righteous card carriers from the uninsured riffraff?"

She released my wrist and noted my pulse on the chart. "Were you drinking before the accident?" she asked as she righteously shifted from the plural "we" and stuck a thermometer in my mouth. Her voice was as unpleasant as her manner. I managed, without biting through the thermometer, to say I'd had a few, which set her off on a lecture about the dangers of drinking and driving, with a shrill emphasis on how irresponsible I was to put other people at risk with my lack of concern for the law, etc., etc., yap-yap-yap. As she lectured, she checked me out, probing here and pulling there, all of which I endured without comment until she yanked on the bandage the paramedic had applied to my neck.

"Jesus Christ, woman!" I bellowed, jabbing at her with the thermometer. "I wasn't in a car wreck. I was in that saloon that was bombed, and I'm still bleeding, so fuckin' lighten up."

"Watch your language, young man, or you'll find yourself in a good deal more trouble than you've already got." She strapped that Marquis de Sade cuff they use to measure blood pressure on my arm, and pumped with a vengeance.

I swore at her under my breath, but I was grateful for her silence. I was also exhausted. I stopped struggling, and within a few minutes I'd drifted away again.

"Your vital signs are stable," she avowed some time later, "and you don't appear to be in a great deal of discomfort. No evidence of internal injuries. Except for the alcohol and your attitude, you seem to be in stable condition."

"Wonderful. You think maybe I can get the hell out of here before sunrise?"

"That's very unlikely," she answered with some irritation. "Now turn over." She popped me in the ass with a tetanus shot and marched away with her meager victory.

Ferris found me, still in the corridor, a little before nine o'clock. I'd been sleeping, and woke with a start when he put his hand on my wrist. "Just lookin' for a pulse," he said with a grin. "How you doin'?"

"Well, a shot of tequila and a couple of aspirin would help, but all in all I'm okay. What time is it?"

"Ten to nine."

I looked past him down the hall, and saw that two of the gurneys were gone. "Listen, I forgot to take a number when I checked in. You think I'll still get to see a doctor before I'm on Medicare?"

"You won't live long enough to qualify for that, but the nurse said you'll survive this. What happened?"

"He tried to kill me."

"Who?"

"Reichmann. The guy who planted the bomb was sitting at the end of the bar, where I always sit. He bought Sheila and me a drink, then said he was going to the head. He left one of those big sample cases salesmen drag around with them on the floor, next to his stool.

"I went to the bathroom a few minutes later and he was nowhere around. The window was open. He went out that way, into the alley, never thinking I'd leave Sheila so quickly to go to the head."

"You're lucky you're alive. Are you dead certain that's what happened?"

"I'm not dead, but I'm sure. Had to be. What's Reichmann saying?"

"National Front for Radical Action, what else?" He took a deep breath and let it out slowly. "Sheila?"

"Dead." I closed my eyes and covered my face with my hand.

He gripped my arm and squeezed. "Jamie . . ."

"Goddamn it, Ferris, that scumbag sonofabitch timed this for the interview, so he could say, 'I've been warning everyone about this threat and now it's happening.' "

"We'll fix his ass. You've got to get on your feet, but we'll get him."

"You know the last thing she said to me? We had a shot of tequila, which that motherfucker bought, and she said, 'To a long life with a happy ending.' " The tears came despite my effort to preserve the little emotional control I had left. "It wouldn't have happened if I hadn't been in there. She'd still be pissed with me, but she'd be alive."

"Don't do that shit to yourself, man."

"The truth is the truth. Reichmann wanted me and he didn't care how many he fried." I moved my hand away from my eyes and took his in mine, clutching it. "I fucked up, Leon. Goddamn it, I fucked up. I shouldn't have gone in there. I shouldn't have believed Finori. He said the heat was off and I believed him."

I couldn't stop crying, and then I was coughing, which made me choke, and all of a sudden all that was left of the tequila and beer and emotions erupted and I threw up on the side of the gurney and on the floor for the second time.

"I'll be right back," Ferris said, and he came back in a few minutes with a basin of cold water and a couple of towels. He stood over me, wiping away the tears and vomit, talking softly, trying to soothe me, to reassure me that what had happened had very little, if anything, to do with my being in the Cock'n'Bull.

"It's a newspaper saloon," he said. "He went after newspeople. You're probably right about the timing. But it wasn't just you he was after. None of us have taken the bombings seriously, and he needs us. So he killed a few media people and now they'll support whatever he says he needs to fight the terrorists.

"Listen, the interview was the key, not you. He'd have hit that place even if you'd been lying on a beach in St. Thomas."

Or on a beach in Barbados . . . "Do me a favor. See if you can reach Juliet. Does Daniel know I'm in here?"

"Everyone knows. After the explosion, Ivan and Daniel both came in. They've got half the dayside staff on the story, and five or six from nightside.

"Before I got here I'd already been to four other hospitals, checking things out and looking for you. I called in before I woke you up."

"How bad was it? Anyone else we know? Has anyone done a body count?"

"I heard seven dead, sixteen injured, most of those serious to critical. Lots of burns, and hits from falling plaster and beams. The paramedics were hauling them all over the city. Apparently all the dead were toward the back of the main room, which figures from what you said about the sample case.

"A lot of people in the smaller rooms got out without a scratch. So far, Harry Weinstock, a desk assistant in sports, is the only one from the *Call* who died."

"I don't know him. Anyone from the TV stations?"

"Mike Tull, from Channel 11, and Jim Lang from Channel 4."

"I saw Tull. He'd been talking to Sheila before she came down to where I was sitting. He must have walked down there after I went in the head. Probably leaving and wanted to hit on her one last time." My eyes were stinging with tears again.

"Jamie, hang in there. And don't blame yourself. It'll make you crazy."

"Listen, go call Juliet. Tell her I'm in here and I want her to get me out as soon as possible. Then come back and stay with me."

"Okay."

"I don't want to see any cops, and I sure as hell don't want any fuckin' reporters snooping around asking a lot of questions. You can write the story if French insists on one."

"Let me see what I can do. I'll use the phone in the hall, right around the corner. If you need me, yell."

I let go of his hand and tried to smile, which didn't work out. "Thanks."

"No problem. And I'll try to light a fire under these assholes to get you into X-ray and surgery, then we'll get you out of here." He started toward the nurses' station, then stopped. "Alexis was frantic when she heard. She kept saying, 'I know he was in there. I know it.' Maybe I could give her a call . . . let her know you're okay?"

"Sure. Tell 'er I said I'll be over for meat loaf and a beer next week."

He gave me a look, and a sly smile. "Ivan assigned her to write the lead story, and a sidebar on you."

"What goes around, comes around."

━━ ━━ ━━ ━━

Juliet arrived soon after that, with Dr. Richard Mayo and a nurse in tow. Dr. Mayo was even taller and blacker than Ferris, and he looked as tired as I felt.

I winked at her and slipped my hand in hers while Dr. Mayo read my chart.

"Did you see Ferris?" I asked Juliet. "He went to call you."

"No, Daniel told me you were here. Are you okay? Have they done anything for you?"

"I got a lecture about drinking and driving, and a negative review of my attitude." She was about to blow up. "Shhh. Don't get all bent out of shape. I already did that. Let's see what the good doctor has to say." I pulled on her arm until she was leaning over me and I could whisper in her ear. "Get me the fuck out of here as soon as you can. Promise them anything, lie to them, I don't care. But I'm not spending the night in this place, and I don't want to see any cops. Okay?"

She nodded and squeezed my hand.

"Mr. Hawkins," Dr. Mayo said after he'd peeked at my neck, "everything here seems to check out. I'll have someone sew you up"—he took my left hand, moved the bandage away, and grimaced—"within the hour. You should be able to go home in a couple of days if there's no sign of infection. How're you feeling?"

"Lonely. Thirsty. I've got a headache. And I'm ready to get the hell out of here."

"Well, you've got company now. I'll let you have a little water since we're going to use a local, and you can have a couple of aspirin for your headache. Do you know your blood type?"

"A positive. But no blood, thanks anyway."

"I'll prescribe the treatment," he said as Ferris strolled up, followed by No Mercy Steele, who was telling him he absolutely could not visit a patient in the corridor. "If it's all the same to you," Dr. Mayo added.

"Where did it come from?"

"Mr. Hawkins," No Mercy said to me since she wasn't having any luck with Ferris, "this is a state-certified hospital and we maintain the—"

"Stuff it. Where did the blood come from? K-Mart blood bank? The Wino

Plasma Emporium? You can prescribe the color of the thread they use to sew me up, but I'm not leaving here with some weird disease bequeathed to me by a junkie I'll never meet."

The good doctor looked like he might blow a fuse, but Ferris said, "I'm O positive. He can have a pint of mine."

For a moment Dr. Mayo didn't say anything, then he shrugged and looked at me. "Mr. Hawkins?"

"Fine. I always wanted a permanent tan. This should do it."

Dr. Mayo and N. M. Steele left with the nurse, and I winked at Ferris. "For most of my life I've wished that I'd been born Negrito Apache. This is the next best thing. Thanks."

"My pleasure, if they ever get their act together to do it." He looked at Juliet and sighed. "I just heard that Reichmann's making the rounds of all the hospitals. If you've got any clout with these people, now would be a good time to use it."

— — — —

Three days later, Lef'tenant Finori showed up at Juliet's, where I was making everyone slightly nuts. I never learned to be a good patient.

Finori was stopped at the huge iron gate by one of the armed guards Juliet had hired. One on the gate, one moving about the grounds, around the clock. During the day, the one at the gate sat behind the stone pillar with an M-16 in his lap, while the other one was dressed like a yard man and moved from one fake job to another. I can't imagine who he fooled. Nor could I talk Juliet out of her fears.

I asked Juliet to let Finori in and leave me alone with him. I wanted to hear what he had to say, and I didn't think he'd be as chatty unless we had privacy.

He stopped just inside the entry to the library and looked around, no doubt wondering how the hell I'd ever ended up in the good graces of anyone who could afford a place so elegant.

"You have to come all the way in," I said. "Otherwise the door won't close."

"If you're as concerned about your safety as those two outside suggest, I'd stay away from the windows."

"They work for Ms. Rossini. And so do I, for that matter. If she wants to guard her estate, not much I can say. You gonna sit down? You want some coffee? A drink?"

"Not for me," he said as he lowered himself onto the sofa and put an attaché case within easy reach. "How's your neck?"

"Fifty-seven stitches, and every goddamn one of them hurt. Plus another seven in my hand. But only the scars are permanent, and they won't be much, I'm told." I wondered if the guards had searched the case. Probably not, since he was a cop. Damn sure he didn't surrender his pistol, so I had to assume he was armed.

"I'd like to talk," he said.

"So talk." I poured fresh coffee into my cup, keeping an eye on him.

"I screwed up, Jamie. I should've known what they had planned, but I didn't."

"So both of us feel like we fucked up. And we both lost someone we cared about. When are the services?"

"We buried her this morning." He held up his hand to ward off my anger. "It was family only."

I stirred sugar into my coffee and carried it to the chair where I'd been sitting for the better part of the last two days. "I loved her, Angelo. A lot. She wanted a husband and I wasn't the one, but I did love her and I went there to tell her that and to see if I could explain to her how we could be friends and care about each other without everything coming down to marriage. I never got the chance."

"Can you tell me anything about how it happened?"

"I can tell you exactly how it happened," I said and sipped my coffee. "I can even tell you who did it if you've got ID pictures of all the scum Reichmann and Gentry have on the payroll."

His eyes were wide with surprise. "How . . .?"

"I talked to the guy. He bought us our last drink." I put the cup down, got up, and walked to the French windows, chewing on my bottom lip. I'd wept more tears in the last three days than I had in the last thirty years, and they still came with no warning.

"You're positive?"

"Yeah, I'm positive."

"Describe him for me."

I turned around to face him, then turned back. I still didn't have all the control I wanted. "Why?"

"You know why, but you don't trust me, do you?"

"Not completely, but that didn't start Saturday." I went back to my chair. "I don't have any reason to trust you, if you think about it. You're still a cop, you're still mucking around in people's private lives, you're still drawing a salary to play I Spy with taxpayer money, you're still on my case. You told me Gentry was on a leash, then you come here and tell me you didn't know . . ." Shit. Of course he didn't know. He might let me be wasted, but not Sheila. Never.

"Thanks," he said without any apparent sarcasm.

"For what?"

"For waking up to the obvious. Even if I were willing to break my promise to look after you, I'd sure as hell never have let them burn her. I swore to Sheila that I'd play guardian angel for you. She didn't know much, but she knew enough to worry. Even after she backed away from you, she made me promise again that whatever I could do to help you, I'd do it. You lucked out, no thanks to me. She didn't, and I want to know who lit up the Cock'n'Bull."

"And then what? You arrest him and I testify?" I laughed without any humor. None of this was funny. "Or do you hit him?"

"We both know it wouldn't do any good to arrest him. But whoever he is, it wouldn't bother me to kill him."

"Angelo, this script is getting a little weird.

"*I'm* the one with the attitude problem and a lack of respect for the system. *I'm* the one who supposedly doesn't fit, won't conform, and commits crimes of blasphemy against God, Mother, and the American Way. I make fun of yuppies, tell editors to fuck off, write stories that my own paper won't publish . . . But I haven't thought about killing any of you.

"On the other hand, the guy who did that job was a cop, or working for them. Whoever sent him to do the job is a cop. Reichmann or Gentry. You're a cop. You guys are supposed to work on the side of law and order."

He didn't say anything.

"You're the guy with the lit degree, the bachelor of arts in the humanities, right? I'm the guy who wasted a lot of people in 'Nam and lasted four weeks in college."

"Four weeks?" He laughed, and I laughed. The first time for either of us in too many days. "Four weeks? Really?"

"Yep. Hell, I only lasted a little over seven months in the Army, and I had a contract with them. Not to mention the threat of court-martial, hard labor, and perpetual KP. College was a piece of cake."

He had a sad smile on his lips and tipped his head forward, looking down and away, rubbing the top of his head, hiding the emotion in his eyes.

"Tell me something, Lef'tenant Finori of the Philadelphia police . . . Have you ever killed anyone?"

He didn't answer and didn't look up.

"I wiped out fourteen living beings one afternoon in a place you never heard of. Fourteen, including a guy who had been my buddy. Before that I'd killed a kid maybe four or five years old, an old woman probably close to seventy, and one or two VC grunts."

"Sheila told me about that." He looked up, his eyes full of tears. "You scared her to death with that story."

"That wasn't the whole story. I was trying to show her why the approval of my peers isn't a high-priority item with me. I didn't mean to frighten her.

"But my point doesn't have anything to do with Sheila. My point is that killing people, no matter who they are or what they've done, isn't something a sane person should do unless there's no choice, and I mean *no* choice. That kid was gonna die no matter what I did. I ended her life about three seconds before it would have ended anyway, and I saved the life of a friend by doing it. But I still see her in my dreams."

He stared at me, as though I'd just taken off a disguise and the person he thought he knew wasn't there anymore. And if I wasn't the person he'd fitted into his mental pigeonhole, who the hell was I?

"All I want you to think about is the reality you'll have to face if you put the plan in motion. It can't be the heat of the moment, because the moment's gone. You've got to find him, and that takes time. You've got to set him up, and that takes more time. And you can't fuck up or you'll be the one facedown in the ditch."

"Even though I know that, I appreciate you caring enough to remind me. What I don't know is whether I could kill the sonofabitch. At this moment I think I could, and I believe I should. But if I had him in my sights and all I had to do was pull the trigger . . ." He looked at me through the eyes of despair. "I don't know if I could do it."

"Good. Remember that, because he'd kill you in a second and never look back. So would Gentry. And a lot of other people Reichmann has on his payroll. Those guys aren't cops. They're hardcore cold-blooded killers, no different from the psychopaths and lunatics and religious fanatics Reichmann supposedly is trying to protect us from. Life's a live-fire arcade to those people. You die, I die, they die. It's all the same to them."

I got up and uncapped the bottle of Conmemorativo Juliet had left on the server. I poured two shots and carried one to him. "Her last words to me were a toast: 'To a long life with a happy ending.' To Sheila and her wish for a happy ending." We clicked our glasses and drank.

"This," he said as he took a slim manila folder from his attaché case, "is all that I've got on the guy who did it. Beluga."

"Beluga? As in caviar?"

"As in the White Whale. He's huge. Two hundred and fifty pounds, at lease. Six three. On his left hand he's missing the lower joint of the pinky and ring fingers. He and a couple of his buddies are all there is to the NFRA."

"What do the guys look like?"

"Amish farmers. Both of them have black beards, dress in black suits when they work, and wear those hats that the Amish wear. Beluga looks like a member of the Hell's Angels. Tattoos, scruffy jeans, boots, headband. Wears sunglasses most of the time."

"Well, sports fans, the guy that did the Cock'n'Bull didn't look anything like that. He looked like a sales rep from St. Louis or Tulsa. Middle America. Fair skin. No taste in clothes, but what he wore was totally ordinary. Clean-shaven. Nervous fingers, but no missing parts. Five ten, five eleven. Weighed maybe one sixty. Smoked Marlboros. Used a Bic." I mentally cropped the face that I recalled. "And icy blue eyes."

Finori was puzzled. "You're absolutely certain that was the guy?"

"He had a salesman's big, boxy, leather sample case, which he was fucking with a few minutes before it happened. He left it on the floor, saying he was going to the bathroom.

"A few minutes later, less than five, I went to the head and he was gone. The window to the alley was open. The bomb went boom. It was him."

"Sonofabitch . . ." he said as he exhaled.

"What? You know the guy?"

"No." He shook his head. "I don't know him, but Saturday night Reichmann had a shoot-on-sight order put out for Beluga."

"I saw Reichmann's press conference on Sunday. And I read the story in the *Call* Monday. Reichmann claimed that you guys had some hot leads and he expected an arrest within hours. But he didn't describe anyone."

"Not to the media, but he's got his whole SWAT command on twenty-four-hour alert. They haven't been home for three days."

"So, if Beluga works for him, what's the deal?"

"The deal is Beluga and his two partners die. Reichmann looks like a hero. Beluga can't ever testify against Reichmann. The NFRA is eliminated . . ."

"Or not. Obviously, Reichmann or Gentry hired some new talent."

"Or not, as you say. Good God."

"Except Reichmann's had two or three days to do the deed."

"He can't find Beluga. The Whale got wise and went into hiding. He evidently knows that he's about to have his ticket canceled."

"Shit, he's probably in Mexico or Canada by now."

"Maybe, but he's got to assume the Feds are looking for him, too. That might make him think he's safer hiding in Philly."

"Are they?"

"Not yet. Reichmann's giving them the runaround. He wants the credit, which he won't get if the Feds make the bust."

"How large is Reichmann's special services department?"

"I honestly don't know. How did you find out about them?"

"Common sense. He's got that goddamn motor pool in the basement of the museum. Why would he have that if he didn't have a bunch of 'elite' troops to use the stuff? Not many cops I know can drive a tank or load a rocket launcher."

"I tried to get you some information on that, but it 'doesn't exist.' "

"Computer files?"

He shrugged. "That would be my guess."

"You think we could get access through Personnel?"

"I doubt it. Too many people could do the same thing, even with locked files."

"Payroll? These guys have to get paid, so there has to be a payroll file, checks, bank accounts, federal and state tax information, insurance . . .?"

"Agreed, but everything will have been laundered so many times you'd think they worked for Procter & Gamble. You'd need to know exactly where to look, and you'd need someone with access to the mainframe and codes to do the looking."

"Can you run a real discreet but very thorough check on someone for me?"

He nodded. "Guy named Kofax, a civilian clerk who works in the Roundhouse.

Occasional gambler, got the hots for a hooker. Ferris can get her name. Thousand dollars a night."

"*What?*"

I laughed. "No, I don't know what she does for that kind of money. This is hearsay, but supposedly grade-A information. He has access to PD computers, personnel files, payroll maybe."

"I'm two clerks short in my department. I'll say he was recommended to me and we'll turn him inside out, without his ever knowing it."

More Famous Last Words from our friends at White Star Line. "I need to know as much as possible."

"You want to try blackmail?" he asked in a dubious tone.

"No. I've got something else in mind."

"Which you don't want to discuss with me."

"Not yet. Listen, where do I stand with Reichmann and Gentry? Is it even reasonably safe to walk the streets, or go to sleep in my own place?"

"I'd say you're okay. His prime targets were newspeople, not you or some other specific reporter. And he seems impressed with you. Not that he likes you, but he's impressed. He probably believes he's made a convert of you, after those articles, and that now the *Call* will take an active, rather than passive, role in his battles. He already has James Franklin in his pocket."

"He's a certifiable fruitcake!"

"Who? Franklin or Reichmann?" he inquired with a joyless smile.

"Oh, Jesus . . ."

"Reichmann assumed, correctly, that once a few media people were killed, the city's entire corps of reporters and news editors and assignment editors and editorial writers would be outraged, and take him seriously when he talks about the threat and the need to counter the threat. He wants to bring out his little army."

"Why? That's nuts."

"For one thing, he wants to see if it works. For another he'd like to get rid of the financial burden of keeping it hidden. A lot of it has to be privately financed."

"Through the Franklin Memorial Art League."

"That's my guess."

"If we could get into their bank records . . ."

"Their account is with Tyler's bank."

"You got any friends at the bank?"

"None that would let me see those records." He closed his attaché case. "I have an appointment to keep."

"Not in Samarra, I trust."

He pushed himself up onto his feet, exhausted, maybe even momentarily defeated. "Palmyra, actually."

"A day in New Jersey is like a week without o.j."

"I could take you to places in Jersey that would impress you. Not all of it looks like Camden and the Admiral Wilson Boulevard."

"You're gonna check out Kofax?" I asked as we walked toward the front door.

"I'll have whatever we can dig up within a couple of days."

When he'd stepped through the front door, onto the nickel-sized porch, he held out his hand. "To a happy ending."

He started toward his car and stopped, motioning me over. When I was almost face to face with him, he nodded toward the house. "Was that a real butler or another hired gun?"

"Straight from Buckingham P., or so I was told. Why?"

"Just curious." He got into his three-year-old Corvette. "I sure hope you don't need protection. These two clowns out here would be useless if anyone was serious about coming after you. You know that, don't you?"

"I know, but she feels better thinking she's protecting me."

I watched him until he was through the gate, wondering how he would've reacted if I'd told him that in addition to the two guards Juliet had hired, Ferris had furnished an M-16, twenty fully-loaded clips, four flares, and miscellaneous combat gear.

"Strictly a loan," he'd said. "And don't ask any questions."

If it came down to defending myself and Casa Rossini, I was ready to send a few misguided souls on their way. Or, I should say I was equipped. You never really know if you're ready until the moment arrives. . . .

— — — —

Wednesday, over Juliet's tearful objections, I went back to my apartment. Except for an occasional stab of pain and limited use of my left hand, there wasn't anything wrong, and not that much I couldn't do for myself. Juliet insisted that I take one of her electric can openers, which wasn't a bad idea since I tended to eat from cans and had difficulty gripping anything with my left hand. It also allowed me the rare privilege of selecting from an assortment of appliances that rivaled Macy's gourmet kitchen department without the aggravations.

Ferris had come to pick me up and for the first couple of miles we made the ride toward Philly in silence. It felt odd to be out, among people for whom the Cock'n'Bull had been a two-day item of curiosity. The rest of the world had gone about its business in the aftermath of the explosion. The dead had been buried. The wounded were healing, some at home, some still in the hospital. The network crews and reporters from national magazines had left when the 'news' dried up. Reichmann had failed to produce the perpetrators and there was fresh blood being spilled all over the globe.

"So how you feeling?" he asked as we approached the Schuylkill Expressway.

"Strange. Do me a favor, take the East River Drive."

He gave me a look and a shrug. "Whatever you say. Any reason?"

"It's a nice ride. I like it."

A few minutes later he turned onto the drive and I settled back. The wooded, hilly terrain and stately old houses were comforting. The area was one of the few places I'd seen in Philadelphia where I thought I might find even a small degree of tranquillity.

"Have you got any idea when you'll be coming back to work?"

"Couple of days, maybe. Everyone misses me, right? 'God, won't it be great when Hawkins gets back? What a swell guy. And we're sick of doing his share of obits.' "

"I miss you. The place isn't the same without that cloud of Camel smoke and the smell of espresso. And nobody bitches the way you do. 'What the fuck is wrong with these people? Brain-dead comma police and would-be editors yellin' for copy like any of this shit matters!' It's just not the same without you."

"Fuck you very much. If I had a bigger bladder I'd probably be dead. You know that?"

He hunched his shoulders and his hands tightened on the steering wheel. "Don't say stuff like that."

"Bah! It wasn't my time." I lit a Camel and cracked the window a little. It was cold, as usual, and overcast, as ever. "Listen . . .   I never really thanked you for coming to find me, and for helping get me out of that goddamn hospital. So, before I forget again, thanks. Old No Mercy Steele is probably still mumbling to herself about what scum we all are. It's comforting to know that even if we are all divine creations, which I doubt, God's capable of a major fuck-up. She shoulda been sent back as a reject or incarnated on some planet that deals in 'seconds.' Like one of those discount shoe stores."

He was smiling, and suddenly he burst out laughing. "Did you check out all those kitchen appliances in Juliet's pantry? Hell, half of that stuff's never been out of the boxes."

"The only thing she was missing was a set of Ginzu knives and the bamboo steamer."

"She probably doesn't look at a lot of late-night TV." He glanced sideways at me. "You think you and her will get married?"

"Well, she hasn't proposed yet, but I'm hoping maybe she'll pop the question on Valentine's Day, and—dare I hope?—a June wedding?"

"I'm serious," he tried to say with a straight face.

"Right. Well, get serious. As a husband, I'm in the same league with Ginzu knives. We'd be fighting every day within a month."

"She sure as hell loves you."

"That and a road map will get you to Montana. But it won't show you the garden path to marital happiness. I tried it, and all I did was make another person very unhappy."

"Maybe she wasn't the right one for you."

"Listen, *yenta*, there isn't a right one. It's me, not them. You ever been married?"

"Nope. I've had the same girlfriend for four years, but she keeps saying she doesn't want to get married, and I don't want to screw up a good thing."

I looked out the side window at a beautiful view of the river, and for a fleeting moment I pictured myself married to Juliet, living part of the time in that huge house, part of the time in the A-frame, having all the money I'd ever need, writing, traveling, living the life of Squire Hawkins.

"You're sure quiet all of a sudden. Thinking about it? She could make your life a dream."

"Or a nightmare. Pull in over here."

"At the boat house?"

"*Por favor.*"

He wheeled into a parking area and stopped, leaving the engine running. I leaned over and twisted the key. "I know this may sound a little strange, coming from me. But after what happened, and four days in that house, even parts of Philadelphia look beautiful." I got out of the car and walked toward the river. A moment later I heard him climbing out.

"You okay?" he asked.

"I'm fine." I turned to look at him, then looked back at the river. A young kid, probably a student from one of the universities, was sculling upstream. "Remember the story you told me about Mama-san's, how close you came to having your ass fried?"

"Sure."

"Afterward, did you notice any changes in the way you looked at things? Did food taste better? Did music sound clearer?"

"All I know is it scared the hell out of me. For days I got the shakes for no reason, and it was a month before I settled down. Why? That what's happened to you?"

"I don't know. Hell, I've been cheek-to-cheek with death more than once, and mostly it just left me drained. Maybe it's more a thing of being outside, with a friend, happy to be alive for the moment, than the old 'brush with death' crap. I really don't know."

"Can I ask you something?"

"Sure."

"It's about twenty-two degrees out here, and we're standing around looking at some fool kid row a boat up-fucking-stream while you talk about food tasting better after you almost get blown away . . . do you think you're weird?"

"Do you?"

"I don't know, man. Is this the same guy who wrote the Pulaski Day story and then rubbed my nose in it? The guy who sent Ivan running to the managing editor for help?"

"Same guy," I sighed. I sat down on a log and stared after the scull. "I'm tired, Leon. This place makes me tired. These people make me tired. This whole goddamn weird-ass story makes me tired. And we haven't really even begun."

He sat down next to me. "Listen, as long as you're okay, we can sit out here until we've got blue balls and frozen noses for all I care."

"I'm okay. Really. I happen to like this little piece of Dellaphilthia. Whatta they call these guys? The Schuylkill River Navy?"

"Yeah. Real Ivy League. Something for the rich kids to do when it's too cold to play golf."

"It's nice out here, though. I hate the cold most of the time, but there's something about winter trees and vapor from breathing that's poetic."

"Don't forget frostbite and a runny nose."

I stood up. "C'mon, let's go before you start whining that you've got to make pee-pee."

"You hungry?" he asked as we climbed into his car.

"Lunch at Mama-san's. On me."

He gunned the car onto East River Drive again and headed toward Ben Franklin Parkway. As we approached the museum an image of Officer O'Riley flashed before my eyes, sitting in his chair, his back to the wall. I remembered the bogus bet I'd made with him for a bottle of Scotch, and I wondered what had happened to him after that night. Christ, he was probably walking a beat in Fishtown. I made a note to ask Finori if he could find out.

"Drive around the museum," I said as Ferris came to the back of the building. "All the way around. Then we'll go eat."

He changed lanes and circled the museum without any comment or question, which I appreciated. I couldn't have told him why I'd given him such an abrupt order. The words were out of my mouth before I had a conscious thought about saying anything. And when we'd finished the circle and were headed toward Mama-san's, I still didn't know anything more. It was going to take a few more days for the light to go on.

— — — —

A little after three o'clock I carried Juliet's electric can opener, some clothes, and about two pounds of Mama-san's spicy bass up the steps and into my apartment. I was tired from eating too much and in desperate need of a long nap.

Ferris had tried a few times to get me to keep the M-16, but I kept saying no, and he finally left with it in the trunk of his car. I dumped the clothes in a corner and walked around touching the furniture, looking in the fridge, reacquainting myself with my home. The fridge, as usual, was almost empty, so I went down to the deli for cigarettes, half-and-half, a sixpack of Pepsi, some beer, and a bag of popcorn. With the coffee and tequila already in the apartment, I had all the four basics essential to my diet: Caffeine, nicotine, tequila, and starch.

On my way back into the building I collected my mail. Several of what I suspected were get-well cards had been jammed into the box, along with an assortment of junk mail. I tossed all of it on my desk and stretched out on the sofa. Five minutes later I was asleep.

A phone call from Alexis woke me at five-thirty. "My hero," she said when I answered the phone. "How's it feel to be home?"

"Strange, but it's better than camping out." Sitting at my desk, I looked through the collection of cards and spotted one from her, which I slit open. "That was a nice piece you did on the Cock'n'Bull," I said as I pulled her card from the envelope. On the front was a pen-and-ink drawing of a well-stacked female with a pouty mouth and melon-sized boobs. The caption read, "I heard you had an accident . . ." Inside, the message continued, "Can I come over and make it all better?"

"Thanks," she said. "Listen, I'm finished for today. Can I buy you a drink?"

"I've got a card here that says you heard I had an accident and you'd like to come over and make it all better. Is that one of Ivan's cruel jokes, or what?"

"Why don't you invite me over and find out for yourself?" she said in her best imitation of a femme fatale. "I'll bring a bottle of that wicked stuff you drink if you'll tell me the name of it, and we won't have to go anywhere."

"It's called Conmemorativo. The bottle is brown. And it's hard to find."

"I'll find it. The state store where I shop has a really big selection of off-beat booze. What time?"

"How about seven-thirty?"

"I'll be there. Should I bring anything else? How about a porno movie?"

"How about your little sister?"

I heard her inhale, a sharp little gulp of air. "That's disgusting," she said, but without any disgust in her tone, and I laughed. "Don't fuck with me, Hawkins."

"Perish the thought, Alexis. A little tequila and a crumpet, that's all. I know you're saving yourself for Mr. Right."

"Seven-thirty," she said and hung up.

I put the receiver in the cradle and sat for a few minutes with my face in my hands, rubbing my forehead, pushing gently on the spot between my eyes, still searching for the reset button.

You've got to be kidding, I thought again and again. You really don't know enough to make a plan, and without a plan this is all a fuckin' bad joke. Which led me back to my first thought.

Only I wasn't kidding. Ridiculous, maybe. Half-assed, on occasion. And quite possibly headed for trouble like I hadn't seen since Club Fed, or maybe 'Nam. But while I'd been loafing in the lap of luxury for most of the last four days, I'd done a lot of thinking, and I'd decided that I owed Sheila a lot more than a sorrowful memory, and Reichmann a hell of a lot more than the few words of muck I could rake together for the *Call*. If someone didn't make it a point to break his balls he would skate away even if whatever he had planned failed. That wasn't meant to be.

And if I get really lucky, I thought, I might have an opportunity to kill the slime bag who'd packed his sample case with his plastic surprise. Unlike Finori, I had no doubt I could squeeze the trigger if I ever had him in my sights. All I needed was a clear line of fire and a weapon. Something other than Ferris's borrowed M-16. If the opportunity did present itself, it would be at close range, and for the first time in almost fifteen years I wished for something I'd left behind in 'Nam. A double-barreled .10-gauge shotgun with the barrels sawed off. Easily disguised as an umbrella, of course, so I could carry it with me night and day.

You're out of your fucking mind, my other self commented after I'd shown both of us a couple of mental snapshots that focused on the bomber being wasted. Vengeance is the Lord's, sayeth the Law.

And I'm here to do the Lord's work, I said as I picked up the other cards and slit the envelopes, one after the other, until I'd opened all of them. Two were from Juliet. I propped them on the typewriter to remind me to call her. Another was from French, one from Ferris, one from Sammy the copyboy, and one was unsigned.

I closed the unsigned one, squinting at the cover, which featured the smiling face of a Betty Boop lookalike, her head topped with a nurse's cap. The caption read "Here's seven good reasons why you should get well soon."

Inside were seven reasons, each one etched on what looked like individual rectangular wafers of some kind, which the cartoon girl had spilled from a serving tray as she tripped over some unseen obstacle. Over her head was a caption that read "Oops . . . I lost my cookies."

The cookies were numbered, but were arranged randomly, since they were supposedly flying through the air. Six of the reasons had something to do with the pleasures of life. "To eat a pizza." "To own a Porsche." "To drink champagne." "To enjoy box seats at the World Series." "To spend August on the beach at St. Tropez." "Because there's no sex after death."

The last was "Revenge."

This, I thought, has got to be the strangest get-well card I've ever seen. And no signature, not even a first initial.

I checked the envelope for a postmark. It had been mailed in Philadelphia, two days earlier. I looked at the envelope in which Alexis's card had been sent. She'd printed the address, in red ink, and she'd included a return address. The name and address on the Betty Boop card had been typed, and there was no return address.

Okay, Captain Caffeine, figure this one out. I went into the kitchen to make a cup of coffee and give my hands something to do while I puzzled over the card. Logic, I said to myself as I put the water on to boil. Logically, who could it be?

It could be Alexis, acting cute. She's sure as hell expressed her interest in spilling her "cookies" all over me.

It could be from some female I know who hopes I'll figure it out and approach her. Someone from the Cock'n'Bull or the *Call*, maybe. But who?

It could be a warning. "There's no sex after death."

But the last one was "Revenge."

As I poured the boiling water into the pot an eerie feeling settled lightly between my shoulder blades and the palms of my hands were suddenly damp.

"Finori," I said aloud as I carried my cup of coffee back to the desk. He may have thought there was some slim chance that Reichmann would have one of his people open my mail. He wouldn't want his boss to know that he had enough feeling for me to send a card. I laughed at myself for having imagined that one more hot-to-trot female was eager to spend the night in my bed.

And that might have been the end of it if I'd ever developed the habit of using coasters. Fortunately, I hadn't, and I put the cup down on the card while I went to put a cassette in the player.

With B. B. King singing "Ain't No Sunshine When She's Gone," I picked up the coffee, sipped, and was about to put it back when I looked down and saw that the ink had run slightly from the moisture on the bottom of the cup. I put the cup on the envelope and picked up the card, touching the smeared ink. It left a faint black smudge on my finger. I turned the card to the light and squinted.

"Sonofabitch . . ." The card was an original, drawn by or for whoever had sent it. My fixation on discovering the identity of a person I knew had caused me to ignore an obvious and very odd aspect of the puzzle. I turned the card over and there was, as I expected, no logo or name of a card company.

Well, now . . . what the fuck is this all about? Daniel French was the only person I knew who could draw well enough to fool the casual observer, and he'd sent me a standard-issue, garden-variety Hallmark card.

I reached for the phone, thinking I'd call him to check it out, but I picked up my coffee cup instead. French wouldn't sent a get-well card that said revenge was a good reason to get well. That wasn't his style.

Who, then? For a moment the word wouldn't go away. Who, who, who? I stopped that by reminding myself that the question of who had already caused me to overlook the obvious—that the card was a special issue. I'm not supposed to figure out *who* sent it. That's not part of the puzzle. There's a message in here, somewhere.

I read and reread the captions and the reasons to get well. *Nada.* Eat a pizza? Own a Porsche? What the fuck kinda message is that? The reference to St. Tropez held my attention for a few seconds, remembering Juliet's offer of a place to hide. But this wasn't a card from Juliet.

I was absentmindedly staring at the phone when it hit me: The seven wafers or cookies were numbered, but because little Miss Boop had spilled them they were out of sequence. They weren't listed one through seven. The numbers, if I started with the one closest to the top and read down, were 4 7 1 6 2 5 3. I wrote it out on the envelope: 471-6253.

— — — —

The number rang twice, and then I heard a series of beeps. It took a couple of seconds for me to realize that I'd dialed into someone's pager. I hung up, gave about ten seconds of thought to the possibility that I was totally whacked out, then dialed again.

When I got the beeps I punched in my own number, hit the pound sign on my phone, and hung up. The worst that could happen, it seemed after due thought, was minor embarrassment. Someone, probably a dentist, would call thinking that there was another opportunity to drill and fill some poor bastard's teeth after normal office hours, and I'd say, "Sorry, someone punched in a wrong number." And that would be that.

I was just coming out of the bathroom a few minutes later when my phone rang.

"Hello . . ." I said.

"Your name and number, please," a female with a nasal voice demanded.

"What? Who is this?"

"Your name and number, please."

I gave her my name and number, and received a dial tone in return. She'd hung up. What the fuck? I wondered.

The phone rang again in less than ten minutes.

"Yes!?"

"Jamie Hawkins?"

"Yes."

"Of the *Call?*"

"Yes. Who is this?"

"An associate of someone with information you could use. If you want the real story about the NFRA, be at the southeast corner of Eighteenth and Spruce Streets at exactly seven o'clock tonight. Dress casual. Wear a rolled bandanna or handkerchief around your head, like a sweatband. Look for a red van. You've got one shot at this. No second chance, no fuck-up, no one else with you. Got it?"

Before I could say yes, I got another disconnect.

— — — —

Walking to the corner of Spruce and Eighteenth, I checked my watch about every block. I had plenty of time, even if the other guy's watch was running fast. Plenty of time to worry, to wonder what the hell was going on, to ask myself a dozen questions for which I had no answer and no reason to expect an answer until the next act unfolded. I'd tried to reach Ferris, but he was out of the city room. Alexis was out there somewhere looking for tequila and planning our night's adventures in bed. I'd left a note telling her that I'd been summoned to a command performance and I'd call her when I got home. I had the feeling she wasn't going to be real understanding about being stood up for anything less than an audition with God.

As I walked by the restaurant on the corner I caught sight of a small thermometer on the outside window frame. It was fifteen degrees. And the wind was blowing lightly from the west. My feet were already numb and I had my hands jammed into the pockets of my coat.

I crossed Spruce at Eighteenth and looked at my watch. I was five minutes early, and freezing. My collar was up, and my head was down, which may be why I didn't immediately notice that I was standing next to a cruising gay male who presumed I was out there for the same reason. Thanks to the confusion of my thoughts since I'd received the call, I'd forgotten that Eighteenth and Spruce was a hot corner in one of Philadelphia's prime cruising areas.

And there I stood, in my jeans and sneakers and leather coat, with a goddamn red bandanna I'd made from a tea towel that Juliet had bought, wearing my sunglasses, as usual. Right.

"Hello," my would-be companion said. "I haven't seen you here before. New in the area . . . ?"

"I'm waiting on a friend I promised to meet."

"Aren't we all? Would you like to do a line or two while you're waiting? My friends have some primo Peruvian flake."

"No, thanks." I turned slightly, looking south down Eighteenth Street, praying for the sight of a red van.

"Listen, you don't have to be shy. We're all a little nervous in the beginning." He reached over and clasped my arm.

"Back off," I said, doing my own backstep. "The guy I'm waiting for will probably kick your ass if he sees you hanging around here when he shows up."

"Oh, I like the rough ones," he said and took a step toward me.

Suddenly, and seemingly out of nowhere, a Philadelphia police car screeched to a stop at the curb, its lights flashing. I backed away even more quickly, while my suitor took off running west on Spruce. The cop in the passenger seat was out of the car in a flash. He grabbed me before I could do anything more than grumble, "Wait a fuckin' minute . . ." In seconds he had me over the hood with my hands behind my back. He snapped a pair of cuffs on my wrists. My stomach churned as I listened to that peculiar grinding noise they make when they close.

"Watch your head," he said as he steered me into the back seat. They were the first words he'd spoken.

"What the hell's going on?" I yelled.

"Let's roll," he said to the driver, who'd already started the car north on Eighteenth.

"Listen, I'm a reporter for the *Philadelphia Call*, and I'd goddamn well like to know what this is about." And please tell me before I throw up in my lap.

"Where's your ID?"

"Shirt pocket, right side."

He pulled my jacket open and removed my *Call* ID, which he held up for a better view. "We got 'im," he said to the driver. "Kill the lights and let's take it nice and easy."

"What the hell does 'we got 'im' mean?"

"Relax, Hawkins. This ride shouldn't take more than half an hour." At that point he slipped a blindfold over my eyes and I resigned myself to whatever lay ahead.

Half an hour or so later, our trip ended near what I guessed was the Delaware River. I heard a ship's horn, and the air was damp and even colder than it had been in Center City.

The guy in the back seat with me helped me out of the car and took off the handcuffs. "Don't be brave. You'll only get hurt for no reason." He took my arm. "Come with me."

He steered me to a building. I heard metal scrape against metal as a door opened. He helped me inside. "Walk straight ahead ten feet and stop." The door slammed shut behind me, and I had the feeling he'd left me to return to the car. I was debating whether to remove the blindfold when I heard a booming voice from what sounded like a human foghorn.

"This way, scribbler. Left face, march!"

I turned ninety degrees and started walking, slowly.

"I ain't got all goddamn night. Just follow the sound of my voice."

I was moving, slowly, and bumped into the corner of a crate. "Goddamn it! Shit, that hurt."

"C'mon, scribbler. The road's clear. Keep walking." I took another ten or twelve steps. "That's close enough."

I stopped, and waited. He didn't speak. "This may be a lot of fun for you, but I'm kind of in the dark about what's going on."

"Take off the blindfold."

The first clear image I got of Beluga is still the strongest in my memory. I may never forget it. He was seated behind a makeshift table he'd fashioned from an old door laid across two sawhorses, a huge man close to three hundred pounds. In the intense backlight from what was easily a five-hundred-watt bulb, he was a menacing, evil-looking mass of flesh, unshaven, his eyes hidden behind the lenses of his aviator sunglasses, dressed in a red and black plaid shirt, with his own red bandanna wrapped around his head.

After a moment he reached behind him and turned off the light, leaving us in the shadows of softer lights I couldn't pin-point without an obvious visual search. I wasn't inclined to take my eyes off him. "Unless you plan to stand all night, I'd say grab one of them crates and park it."

I stacked two empty plastic milk crates close to the table and sat down. I was within a foot of the table's edge, and within easy reach of two very large pistols and no fewer than a dozen hamburgers he had at his fingertips.

"You hungry? I got a couple extras, 'case you didn't eat yet."

"I'll pass."

"Your choice." He pulled the greasy paper off a burger and consumed it in three bites. He did the same with a second burger, chewing steadily, gulping from a quart container of chocolate milk from time to time. "You gonna just sit there?" he asked as he finished the second burger. "Ain't you got no questions you wanna ask?"

"Yeah, actually. Who the fuck are you?"

"Who you think I am?" he asked as if he was irritated.

"Beats the fuck outa me. I was standing on a street corner in Center City, minding my own business, when two cops grabbed me and here I am. Wherever the hell 'here' is."

He ate another burger without comment, and I couldn't see his eyes, so I wasn't sure if he was reacting to anything I'd said.

"You sure you don't want one of these?" He pushed a burger toward me.

"I'll be damned if I'll put myself in a situation where the guy doing my obit can truthfully write, '*Call* reporter Jamie Hawkins died of a Big Mac attack last night in a deserted riverfront warehouse.' " As I finished my spiel I reached for my cigarettes, and before my hand had moved more than a few inches I was looking into the very short, very ugly barrel of a machine pistol he'd hidden in his lap.

"Those are Wendy's," he said, gesturing with the weapon. "This is a Big Mac."

"If you don't want me to smoke while you're eating, just say the word." I was looking into the bore of a Mac-10.

"Slow, scribbler. Real slow."

I took the edges of my jacket and flipped back the sides so he could see my chest. "All I've got is a pack of Camels and a Bic."

He lowered the barrel of the weapon and I lit a cigarette with a slightly trembling hand. "So what's the story here?" I asked through a cloud of smoke. "You're Beluga, right?"

"Right."

"What was the point of the get-well card? You could have called me at the paper."

"I wanted to see how smart you are. If you're smart enough to figure out what's not real obvious, maybe we can do some business."

"Whatta you got, a special on Claymore mines and kilo bricks of C-4?"

"I said smart, not smart-assed."

"Excuse me, I lost my head for a moment. What was the point of telling me to look for a red van, then scooping me up in a police car?"

"If you happen to die before you finish this interview the story'll be that

Reichmann had you hauled off by the cops." He shrugged. "All those fags'll be up in arms. A little insurance."

"Reichmann thinks I'm on his side."

"Reichmann's scum, but he ain't stupid." He put the Mac-10 back in his lap and started working on another burger, watching me smoke.

"You got anything to drink, other than the chocolate milk?"

"In the fridge over there." He jerked his head toward the wall behind him.

The sound of the chair legs scraping on the floor sent a shiver up my spine, but I kept walking, wondering if I was about to take a few rounds in the back. It seemed that I'd passed whatever silly test, or tests, he had in mind, at least for the moment. But things aren't always what they seem.

I opened the dented door of what once had been a nice little under-the-counter refrigerator. Two cans of Bud and a bottle of Miller Lite. Figured. He didn't look like the type who'd buy designer water and imported beer. I took the Miller Lite.

"You in the 'Nam?" he called out.

"Yeah, for a while."

"Me too. Shoulda stayed over there. You a writer in 'Nam? *Stars and Stripes?*"

"I was a grunt in the line company not far from Da Nang." I chugged some of the beer. "You?"

"Special Services, China Beach."

I almost choked on the beer. "Special Services? Supervising Ping-Pong tournaments and fuckin' around with the Doughnut Dollies?"

"Yeah, I know. Listen, it was a job, and they gave it to me."

"Hell, I woulda grabbed that job in a minute. It's just that you don't look the type. How long were you over there?"

"Two years. Shit, I didn't wanna leave. Fuckin' place was beautiful. Had me a girl, worked five, six hours a day, free food, all the beer I could drink, and one hellava beach. I'd still be there if the fuckin' dinks hadn't folded."

I sat down again and put my bottle of beer on the table. "Maybe I'll eat one of those if the offer's still open." He pushed one of the burgers toward me. "How the hell did you get from Special Services on China Beach to Reichmann's Irregulars in Philadelphia?"

"Classified ads." He finished his fifth or sixth burger and wiped his fingers on the legs of his pants. "Couple years ago I was doin' some time for bad checks, on a work farm up near Lewistown . . ."

"Pennsylvania?"

"Yeah. So one day I'm lookin' through a magazine, one of them kind with all the guns, y'know . . ."

"Wait a minute, wait a goddamn minute. You're in the slam and they bring in magazines about guns?"

"It was like a military summer camp. Minimum security. They had all kinds of bullshit magazines around. But in the back, there's this ad, see, with a box number and somebody's lookin' for vets with time in the 'Nam, so I sent a letter."

"Telling them what? That you'd done two years on China Beach?"

"Naw, I told 'em I was Special Forces with a demolitions specialty. I knew enough about dynamite and C-4 and stuff, y'know? I figured it was a joke. Sounded like a Catholic school for bad boys. Looks like the joke's on me." He drained whatever was left in the container of chocolate milk and belched. His burp was a lot like his voice, a booming bass that reverberated through the room.

He left the table abruptly, carrying the Mac-10 in his left hand, and lumbered over to take one of the two cans of Bud from the fridge. I watched him, wondering why he'd turn his back on me with two pistols left lying on the table. As he turned, he popped the tab on the beer, which hissed and spewed a little froth. "They ain't loaded, case you was wonderin'." He settled back on his chair and grinned with stained teeth.

"The question did cross my mind, but I'm not here to hurt you, and if I was I wouldn't make a grab for anything so obvious. Not with you holdin' the Big Mac. You like that thing?"

"It's great at ten feet if you got the advantage. Ain't worth shit otherwise." He pulled the clip and handed the weapon to me. "It's a dope dealer's piece. Ambush weapon. Me, I like an M-16."

It was surprisingly light without the load of ammo, and lacked any character. I'd grown up around guns that had a 'feel' to them. The only feeling I got from the Mac-10, or the M-16, was cheap. Not inexpensive. Just cheap. I turned it one way and another, shaking my head. "Stamped tin."

"Just about. Reminds me of them disposable razors." He took it back, inserted the clip, and put it back on his lap. "Tell me what you know, and maybe I can fill in a few of the blanks."

"I was told that you and couple of your buddies are all there is to the NFRA. Is that right?"

"Yeah."

"You a cop? Were you a cop?"

"Never!"

"Reichmann wants you dead so he can claim he's broken the Front."

"Reichmann couldn't break wind without Gentry to tell him when to grunt. Gentry's a merc, onetime Green Beret. I heard he was kicked out with a dishonorable, then went to work for the CIA."

"You said you thought the ad was for a Catholic school for bad boys. What did you mean?"

He rubbed the three-day stubble on his cheek. "The school was called the Brother James Academy for Sports and Survival Skills." He laughed. I didn't. "It's in the mountains, way the hell and gone out in Clinton County, on the Susquehanna River. Ain't nothin' around for miles and miles."

"Who hired you?"

"Gentry. Back then he wasn't wearing no cop's brass hat. He ran the school, which didn't have any students. He hired me for cadre."

"How could he hire you if you were in jail?"

"He got me paroled to the school. It was supposed to be like a community-service work-release type of thing."

"How long were you at the Brother James Academy?"

"Three, four months. I got a crash course in demolitions and I got transferred down here." He grinned again. "*Agent provocateur.*" His pronunciation was excellent, totally unlike his ordinary speech.

"How'd you get your code name? That your invention?"

"Yeah. One time in 'Nam, a buddy of mine, he was mess sergeant for one of the division generals, he brought me some caviar. As a joke. Fuckin' salty fish eggs, right? And I loved it, man. It was great. So I looked at the can it come in, and it said 'Beluga.' At that time I didn't know Beluga was a whale, too." He shrugged. "I mean, I ain't exactly a student of Jane Fonda's workout program, right?"

"You're a little on the chubby side, I suppose." You're also full of shit, I thought, but I didn't see any compelling reason to mention that. I took a pen and a small notebook from my pocket and laid them on the table. "Let's start with the school . . ."

— — — —

"What puzzles me," French said, shaking his head, "is why he doesn't run. Did you ask him?"

"Of course I asked him. He said he doesn't have a passport, for one thing. For another, he's not exactly inconspicuous, so he's not real enthusiastic about wandering around in the airport or train station. And if Reichmann starts thinking that Beluga's left the city, he'll send out a notice with his correct name, description, etc., etc., and so forth." I made a face that suggested I wasn't altogether convinced.

"And what do you think?" Daniel inquired.

"I think he's a Fed."

"Informant or agent?"

"I don't know. Probably informant." I wasn't convinced about that, either. "I don't know, Daniel. I tend to stereotype most informants as exactly what he appears to be: obnoxoius, somewhat demented, egocentric, and arrogant. They're rarely as smart as they think they are, and my guess is that most of them don't live to collect Social Security.

"Beluga *seems* to be all that and worse. But how many people, let alone what seems to be obvious lowlife, love caviar? And he pronounced *agent provocateur* with a wonderful French accent. It sounded exactly right. Then in the next ten seconds he said, 'So I looked at the can it *come* in . . .' Sounds fishy to me, no pun intended."

"I don't even want to think about it," he said.

"The pun, or the possibility that Beluga is Fed City?"

"Either of them. Or should that be neither of them . . . ?"

"Beats the hell out of me." I opened the envelope I had in my lap. "Take a look at these, and brace yourself. Viewer discretion, and all that." I handed him several pictures of Charlie Patton, deceased. He flinched at the sight of the first print in the stack. "Note, if you will, that the cell had one bunk, the bunk had one mattress, and the mattress had one cover. That cover, you should note, was on the mattress in two of those prints, even though Charlie Patton is shown hanging."

French looked quickly and immediately turned the photos face-down in his lap.

"In the three additional prints, the mattress is bare. Those three are the ones released by the coroner.

"Beluga wouldn't tell me how he got those first two, but the cell in which Patton hanged himself was not in the Roundhouse. It was a cage at a heavy-duty interrogation site that he says Gentry runs. Normally, the ones who go in there don't pass through a booking process."

"He's picking up suspects and interrogating them without formal charges, fingerprinting, and all that?"

"That's the word from the Whale. Not many, but yes, he's violating constitutional rights with abandon."

"Jamie, I don't know what to say . . ."

"That's okay. I don't know what to do."

"Do you think there's any chance that the negatives from the coroner's photos still exist?"

"I don't know, but if the coroner were served with a court order to produce all the original negatives, I'd bet the only ones you'd see would match the prints they released. My guess is that they've already destroyed the other negatives."

"Supposing we turn this over to your Assistant U.S. Attorney friend, Mr. Cabot. He could get a search warrant and have the FBI make a surprise visit."

"If he doesn't find anything, we look like schmucks. If he does, the story's all over the country in fifteen minutes and we still don't have Reichmann nailed to the cross. He won't be indicted unless the Feds do it for violation of Patton's civil rights, which isn't going to bring him a lot of grief in Philadelphia. Or anywhere else, for that matter.

"If the cops that did this were willing to implicate Reichmann, the Feds might get an indictment for murder, as an extreme violation of civil rights, but I don't believe the cops will put the finger on their commissioner. And even if they did, I don't believe a jury would convict Reichmann of murder. He's gonna say he was home celebrating Christmas with his family and didn't even know Patton had been moved from the Roundhouse."

"Well, what do you want to do now?"

"Go home. I'm tired. I didn't get out of there until midnight."

"Okay. By the way, Juliet told me that you lost a good friend in that tragedy at the Cock'n'Bull. I'd like to extend my condolences."

"Thanks. I'll see you in a couple of days." I got up to leave. "Oh, almost forgot. If I go any further with this, I'd like to bring in Alexis."

"Alexis?"

"You remember her. Ivan's protégée."

"You never cease to amaze me. May I ask why? I give you my word I'll be discreet."

"It has to do with the eunuch. I'm not sure, yet, but I'm considering something for which Alexis would be perfect. If you don't have any problem with her working on this, then I'll ask her. She already knows something is going on, and so does Ivan. That way I may get something I need, and we pacify Ivan.

"But he has to agree that she answers to me until this is over. If I want to pull her out of the city room at two P.M. or I keep her busy all night and tell her to take the day off, no bullshit from him. And we, none of us, tell him what all this is really about. In fact, I've got a cover story that you should feed him."

"Am I going to be told what you're up to?"

"Christ, yes," I lied. "If it wasn't for you, I'd probably be in Baja now, wasting away in warm weather. This is a lot better for me."

Coming out of French's office, I avoided the city room and went directly to a pay phone next to the elevator. I dialed Alexis on her direct line and let the phone ring four times, then disconnected before the call switched to the city desk.

As I hung up and turned around she was coming off the elevator. "Creep."

I grabbed her arm. "Cool it a minute."

She twisted free and started toward the city room. "You had your chance, jerk," she called over her shoulder.

"And you're blowing yours, so to speak. If you don't stop long enough to find out what I want you're gonna spend years kicking yourself in the ass."

"I *know* what you want," she said with disdain, "but I'm not that kind of woman."

My heart stopped, but so had she, so I figured I had a chance. There's no way she could know what you've been thinking, so relax. I smiled. "Come here, please." She hesitated, and I nodded toward the coffee and soda machines. "C'mon. Give me five minutes and you may get the ticket to ride that you said you want."

She came over, cautiously, but her eyes said I had her attention. "You want a coffee?"

"I wouldn't drink that stuff on a bet. Why don't you take me down to the coffee shop and buy me a cappuccino?"

"I would, but I spent everything I had except this loose change to have the window in my building repaired." I took her arm and steered her to the elevators. "Can you believe someone tied a note addressed to me to a perfectly good bottle of tequila and heaved it through the vestibule window of my apartment house?"

"Imagine that," she said as we stepped into the elevator. She pushed the lobby-level button and smiled wickedly. "You try to torment me, Hawkins, and you're gonna pay the price. I'll make you crazy."

— — — —

"You're outa your fuckin' mind!" she yelled an hour later, sitting cross-legged and naked on my mattress. And then she laughed. "You're also bad news, you know that? I mean truly goddamn dangerous."

"Yeah, yeah, yeah. That's not at issue here. You said you wanted in on this story. Hell, I haven't even told you the good parts. But I've told you enough for now. Are you interested? Can you handle what I've proposed?"

"Maybe," she said, chewing seductively on her bottom lip. "It depends on what you find out about him." She threw her leg over my body, straddling me, and leaned down with her hands on my shoulders, looking into my face. I slapped her ass and she laughed. "Don't try to bribe me until we see what he wants."

"You understand that we probably won't get what we're after the first time out, right? It may take two or three 'encounters,' and it may not work at all."

"Do I get to keep the money?" she inquired with an evil grin.

"As far as I'm concerned you can."

"Rest stop," she announced, and bounced off the bed, headed toward the steps from my loft to the bathroom below. "Does Ferris know about this?" she called as she disappeared down the steps.

"Not yet." But I can guarantee you he's not gonna nominate me for this year's Great Idea Award when he hears it.

— — — —

"What do you think she's got that's worth a thou for a night?" Alexis asked as she came back to bed. "I mean, what can she do that's so different?"

"How the hell would I know? Maybe she's really a front for the Gang of Four or maybe she's got some magical way to get a guy off five times in a night."

She slipped her hand between my legs and lightly raked her nails on the underside of my balls. "That's not real hard. To do, I mean."

"Not if you like what you're doing, but a lot of women don't."

"Would you give me a thousand for a night?" she asked as she leaned over and slipped my cock into her mouth.

"No." Her teeth tightened on the shaft and she looked with wide-eyed innocence at me. "On the other hand, I'm open to the fine art of negotiation."

She raised her head slowly until my cock was entirely free, and then licked her lips. "Let's start the bidding."

— — — —

Ferris put the bottle of Corona down on the bar and lifted his freshly filled glass. "*Mazel tov!*" he toasted, and we clicked our glasses. "You are the only person I can imagine being able to get Daniel to advance you one thousand dollars of the *Call*'s money so you can do 'research' on a hooker."

"C'mon Leon. If we're gonna find out what she's got that Kofax wants so badly, one of us has to talk to her. And she's not gonna sit down and chat for free."

"Right." He was grinning and for an instant I wanted to pour my beer over his head. "Hey, lighten up," he said, evidently sensing my irritation. "You'd be the first to make fun of me if I was in your shoes."

"You're right. And I'm wired. You're sure this is the same girl?"

"Absolutely. I called, told her I'd gotten her name and number from my bookie friend, and that a bunch of guys wanted to send a friend over, as a birthday present. She's expecting you at seven."

I shook a Camel out of my pack and Ferris took the Bic from the bar and lit it. "Now, tell me the truth. What the hell did you tell Daniel to get the money?"

"I told him we needed good-faith money for Kofax."

"That's okay, since he won't ask for a receipt. But I still don't follow this whole thing. You talk to her and maybe you find out what she does for him that makes it worth a grand a night . . . maybe you don't. But let's say you do. Then what? How does that help us?"

"Well, there's more to the plan than I've had a chance to tell you. Alexis is part of it."

"Alexis? This is our story! What the hell does she have to contribute?"

"Her body and her sordid imagination. Whatever Crystal does, Alexis will do."

"You are outa your fuckin' mind!"

"I've been hearing that a lot."

"I wonder why?"

"Listen, we've got two possible ways of getting to Kofax. Bribes or blackmail. That's it. We're not talking about someone with a sense of civic duty, or a latent hero who'd like to completely fuck up his life for Truth and Justice. Am I right?"

"What if this doesn't work?"

"I don't know. Let's drive off that bridge when we get to it."

"Why Alexis?"

"She's available, she works cheap, and she's one of those rare beings blessed with a strong libido and no discernible inhibitions. You know what she asked me? She wanted to know if she could keep the money." We both laughed. "I think she's looking forward to playing hooker. It's exciting to her."

"You've been fucking her, haven't you?"

"Once, a couple of days ago."

"Ivan would have a stroke." He sipped his beer. "And Juliet would probably turn *you* into a eunuch."

"Fortunately, neither of them will ever know."

"So what happens? I set up a meeting with Kofax and you bring Alexis?"

"You set up an interview. A story about how the civilian force working with the police, unknown to most of the public, frees the officers to keep our city safe. I may puke before I get through this. The point is, he's as vulnerable as anyone else to the idea that he might actually get some recognition for a mindless job. He'll see himself strutting around the neighborhood like Mr. Big. Promise him a picture, too, and he'll meet you in the middle of the Schuylkill River at four A.M.

"You set up the preliminary interview in a public place. Buy 'im a drink, whatever. I just happen to drop by, with Alexis. You introduce me as a reporter, I introduce her as a 'friend,' she lights his fire, and we take it from there. He's got an obsession with hookers, according to your bookie friend. I think we can pull it off if Alexis does a number on him."

"Like I said, I think you're out of your fuckin' mind. But I'll give it a shot." He looked at his watch. "An hour from now you'll be deep in, ah . . . conversation with the most expensive piece of tail either of us will ever see."

"I'll be happy to let you go in my place. I mean it. All you have to do is get the information."

"No way. What else? I know there's more."

"I met the organizer and spiritual leader of the NFRA Wednesday night. We spent about four hours chatting in a warehouse with him holding a Mac-10 and me trying not to piss in my pants."

"You've been a busy little devil, haven't you?" he asked after a long silence and a heavy sigh.

"I'm not holding out on you, Leon. God's my witness."

"God wouldn't witness your claim to employment at the *Call*, and even I know you work there. Sort of."

"Leon, tell me the truth. What the hell do you think we're doing?"

"We're going after Reichmann."

"Are we after Reichmann, or are we after the big story?"

"It *is* a big story. Jesus Christ, this is the biggest story in Philadelphia since all those white guys got together to sign the Declaration of Independence."

"And what happens when we get Reichmann, whatever the hell that means to you or me or him? James Franklin is in as deep as Reichmann. So is the mayor, and Tyler, the banker. And my guess is there are at least a few other very powerful, very rich, and very pragmatic people involved.

"French is scared half to death already and Juliet doesn't really want to go any further, although she says she'll back us. She only said that after the Cock'n'Bull blew. That same morning she'd told me no, forget it."

"You think she's involved?"

"No. And don't tell me love is blind. She's afraid, and not without reason."

"So, you tell me . . . you want to take on Philadelphia's power brokers and run the very real risk of ending up planted somewhere in the Jersey Pine Barrens?"

"Hey, I've been living with the risks since the beginning. I had to talk you into this, remember?"

"Yeah, I remember. But neither of us knew what the fuck we were getting into. Let me tell you about the Franklin Memorial Art League, the Brother James Academy for Sports and Survival Skills, and a guy named Beluga. After that you can tell me if you want to push on or piss off, as the Aussies say."

— — — —

From the moment Crystal glided into view, it took approximately ten seconds for me to realize that my idea of using Alexis as a seductive alternative made about as much sense as trying to pass off paper plates as fine china. I squandered the first nine of those seconds making a valiant effort to regain control of my ability to organize a complete, rational thought.

She was stunning, and I was stunned. I was also mesmerized by her feline grace. She walked as if she were a panther on two feet, and she did it without a trace of exaggeration or effort. She simply flowed from place to place. Everything visible was as near to perfection as I can imagine a human form achieving. A perfect nose, perfect white teeth, a perfect smile, spellbinding sea-green eyes . . . perfect honey-colored hair held in place with a thin band of plaited silk on which, I'm certain, not a drop of sweat would be found. Her skin was the color of expensive honey and had the sheen of imperial silk. She was wearing a teal-green dress that followed every curve and fondled every swell in her body, ending in a scalloped bottom that revealed heart-stopping legs.

Fortunately, she spoke first, enabling me to recapture the faculty of speech. "Hi," she said, extending a perfectly shaped hand. "I'm Crystal."

"Hi. Jamie Hawkins."

"Jamie . . . nice to meet you. May I serve you something? Espresso? A shot of tequila and a bottle of Corona?" She laughed at my obvious reaction. "I spoke to your friend, you know, and I asked for some basic information."

"A beer would be fine, although to tell you the truth, I don't believe what I had in mind is going to work out, and I don't want to waste your obviously valuable time."

"Oh, really . . . ?" She looked past me and nodded to Ramon or Raul or whatever his name was, a slender Latino houseboy/bodyguard and for all I knew, her lover. "Won't you sit down? The least you can do is tell me what you had in mind." She smiled that perfect smile, and seemed at least mildly amused by me, or possibly by the idea that anything conceived for fun in bed could be beyond her abilities. "One never knows," she said.

"Oh hell yes one does, if one's paying attention, which is difficult looking at you." I sat on one end of a large, plush sofa of modern design. She had good taste in furniture, and the money to buy the best.

A chilled glass and an icy bottle of Corona on a serving tray were presented to me by Raul. She took a rocks glass of some burgundy-colored liquid that had been poured over ice and sipped, watching me over the rim. "Well," she said at the point where polite silence was on the verge of becoming uncomfortable, "what did you have in mind?"

"What I had in mind was a scam. Nothing directly involving you, but to enhance my chances for success I felt I needed to know what you do or have that makes the gentleman in question willing to pay a thousand dollars for a night."

"How interesting. Field research."

"The plan I had in mind involved passing along to another lady the results of that 'research' so she could entice the target of this game to the table. Or the bed, in this case."

"Another lady in the business?"

"Not your business, no. But she has remarkable abilities and a healthy appetite. She also thought it would be a gas to get paid for doing something she's always fantasized about.

"Anyway, as willing and able as she is, she isn't you or anything close. You may or may not give the best blow job in Philadelphia, but it wouldn't matter. The guy would be so amazed that he was even in the same room with you, he wouldn't know good head from a horse's ass."

"You certainly have a way with words." She laughed. "So you're saying that it's the way I look that brings him back? Not my sexual skills?"

"To some extent. You may be God's gift to the oldest profession, I don't know. But I don't think what you do matters, or let's say it's probably not at the top of the list."

"Why not consider hiring me? Why buy a copy if the original can be rented?"

"You're way too expensive and even you would need some time to get what I want from him. It isn't something he already has. And it would take a lot of effort and risk for him to get it. By the time you persuaded him to do it, I'd be bankrupt." I drained the beer from my glass and stood up. "Thanks for the beer."

"You know," she said, taking my arm as we walked toward the door, "for, oh, let's say five thousand dollars, I might be willing to provide you with a videotape of our activities. Providing he isn't someone who would try to put me out of business, either permanently or by forcing me to leave the city."

"That wouldn't work. He could be fired or reprimanded if the tape was shown. Or he might be applauded, depending on his performance. But he'd take his chances before he'd run the risks involved in my plan. I meant to exploit his obsession, not blackmail him for his indiscretion. There's a very important difference between them."

"Indeed there is," she said as she opened the door for me. "Are you sure you wouldn't like to do the research anyway? The more you know about your mark the easier it is to take advantage of him."

"Thanks, but you'd probably ruin me for every other woman I know." I took her hand, kissed it lightly, and started down the stairs.

"Good luck," she said, and waved at me as I glanced back.

— — — —

"So what now?" Ferris asked as I put the tequila bottle on the table between us.

"Well, first we drink these shots of cactus juice, and then you tell me if I'm the dumbest sonofabitch in Center City for throwing away an opportunity to fuck the most fabulous-looking female in the Delaware Valley *and* charge it to the *Call*."

"Jeez," he said and dumped the tequila down his throat. "I hadn't thought about it, but you sure as hell must be in the top two or three."

"Thanks, I feel better." I downed my shot and slouched back on the sofa. "It's still a possiblity, I guess. I mean Alexis isn't exactly without her appeal."

"Jamie, we're not on the right track here. Bribes are better."

"How much? Take a guess."

"Twenty-five."

"That's his salary for what? Year, eighteen months? Why would he jeopardize himself and his job for twenty-five thousand? He probably already has ten years as a civil servant. That's ten years toward retirement." I poured us another shot. "If he was dead-ass certain that he could get away with it, he might do it for twice that amount, but not for twenty-five. If he's that dumb, he'll get caught anyway."

"Here's to inspiration." He drank the tequila. "Listen, I've been thinking about what you told me, about the Brother James Academy. I'm going up to check it out."

"No way, José. Forget it. Those guys are grief looking for a place to happen."

"Shit, I'm not gonna just walk up and say 'Hi, I hear you're running a prep school for psychos.' It's part of the story, and I think we should check it out."

"How? You gonna sign up for their course in survival skills?"

"I don't feel like I'm doing my share."

"Tell you what . . . let's put it to bed for tonight and talk about it tomorrow. In fact, let's bring in Alexis and tell Daniel we want to get together and review this whole mess. What we know, what we think we know, what we can prove. We'll brainstorm it and see what we come up with. Maybe we're overlooking the obvious. Maybe there's an easier way to go from here. Hell, I'm nobody's idea of a tactician. I have trouble planning for my next meal."

"Daniel's out of town for the weekend, but sure . . . Monday or Tuesday if he's willing." He pulled on his coat, then took a bag of grass from the pocket. "Half an ounce of wicked weed. I meant to give it to you Wednesday. It's a get-well present."

"You're a good friend. Thanks. You want to wait while I roll one and take a couple of hits before you go?"

"I rarely smoke dope and drive. I totaled a cherry '67 Mustang a few years ago, while I was ripped."

"Oh, no . . ."

"Worst part of it was, I hadn't made my insurance payment."

"Uh-huh. Did you hit anyone?"

"No. Oh, shit. I forgot to tell you. O'Riley's dead."

"The keeper of the keys at the motor pool?"

"Yeah. One-car accident. Thinking about the Mustang reminded me. It happened while you were hiding out at Juliet's, Monday night I think. He fell asleep at the wheel driving home from work."

We looked at each other without comment until he shrugged. "That could've been the way it happened. Hell, he was a lush, from what you described. The cops wouldn't say he was drinking, but they'd have to say something."

"Sleeping at the wheel," I said with a shake of the head. "Sometimes I think God and all His fuckin' elves are sleeping at the wheel. Shit."

"Okay, I'm gone. Are you coming in tomorrow?"

"No. I'm back on my regular schedule next week. Tuesday, unless we get an appointment Monday with Daniel. I'm gonna tell him that Kofax didn't show, and return the money, so you know what's going on."

"Okay. See ya."

— — — —

Alexis's response to my decision not to pursue my 'research' with Crystal was an invitation to come to her place for a night of rowdy, raunchy, nonstop sex. "No shop talk, no philosophy of life, no talk about how to get whatever the hell you're after from Kofax . . . just one long night of dope smoking, drinking, and fucking."

I accepted her offer. It was the best offer I'd had and I wasn't in the mood to sit home and think about how dimwitted I felt, or how frustrating it was to dig and dig and never know if what I was doing would produce the story I wanted or just another big hole in which to bury me.

"You know," she said the next morning as she handed me a toasted English muffin smeared with cream cheese and apple jelly, "I still don't know exactly what you want from Kofax. You never really told me."

"I thought we weren't gonna talk shop." I took a bite of the muffin, which she'd charred around the edges. Worse, she used margarine.

"How is it?"

"How is what?"

"The muffin. I burned it a little."

"That's how it is. Burned a little. With the cream cheese and jelly it's barely noticeable."

"You don't look like you're enjoying it."

"Alexis, this conversation sounds a lot like dialogue from a TV series about young married yuppies."

"Sorry . . ."

"Don't start apologizing after the first night. Your invitation was for raunchy nonstop sex, which you delivered with enthusiasm and skill unknown to most of the women who've so generously taken me into their beds. Who gives a shit if you burned the goddamn muffin? If I can teach you to buy French roast instead of this wimpy mocha java juice and to put butter where the hydrogenated palm oil was spread, we'll be in business."

"You mean we could become an item? You and me?"

"You don't want that. Ivan would have you transferred to the Trenton bureau before you managed to bring that silly grin under control. I might be great for your ego and your libido, but I'm death on careers."

"And Ms. Rossini would send you back to Mexico in a cattle car, which is really death on a career."

"I don't think so, but we can call her and ask, if you like. Of course, there's always the possibility that she'll blame you for leading me astray, and Trenton might be the high point of your career after that."

She chewed around the charred edges of her muffin, glaring at me. I smiled at her, which pissed her off even more for a few minutes. And then she asked, "Would you like to know what I find so goddamn irresistible about you?"

"My childlike innocence?"

"Your childlike insolence. You'd get up and walk out of here no matter how much you like fucking me, or what I did to blow your mind. You'd walk off and never look back. You really don't give a damn."

"You're wrong."

"Prove it."

"I don't have anything to prove to you. But I do give a damn, about a lot of things. And I've looked back more often than you'll ever know. What I don't do is linger on the view, and I don't confuse caring with need or love with surrender, which seems to give people, particularly women, the idea that I'm hard to handle."

"Whew! Sorry I hit the wrong button."

"Forget it. People use emotions like weapons and I'm not in any mood to fight. I had a good time last night and I'm going to leave here with a smile on my face."

She took the dishes to the sink, then walked behind me and put her arms around my neck, leaning over until her mouth was even with my ear. "I promise I'll try not to wander into that yuppie sitcom again," she whispered, and touched the end of her tongue to my ear. "And if I forget, you can always give me a good spanking. I need that once in a while, to remind me of who's in charge."

"I'll keep that in mind," I said, and pulled her around to sit on my lap facing me.

"Tell me what you wanted me to get from Kofax. I'm curious, and I'm supposed to be a part of the group now, right? Part of the big story team?"

"If it's a group, you're part of it. I've got my doubts that we'll get the story I wanted, but I'll fill you in, so to speak, and then you'll know as little as the rest of us."

— — — —

In the aftermath of the avalanche she let loose, I promised Alexis that if I ever wrote 'the real Philadelphia story', as she put it, that I'd give her the credit she earned, that the truth would be unvarnished, that the role she played would be reported as it happened, including the way I lured her into participating. I could, if I felt the need to sex it up a little, describe her bust as being somewhat larger than it actually was, which I haven't done, and I could omit some of the more lurid details of her sexual encounters with Kofax.

"Don't get too graphic about the whips and leather," she said. "I mean, it's okay to mention it, but don't do a page or two of description."

I didn't lure her into anything, if the truth is to be served, and she knows that, but the definition of lured is a lot like the definition of lurid: Mostly it's in the eye of the observer.

What she did was so simple and, in retrospect, so elementary that I still use it as a kind of benchmark when my ideas get too complicated. Remember the Cabot KISS, I say to myself. Keep It Simple, Stupid. She likes that. She says it's the nicest compliment I ever gave her. That's a little sad, but it's probably true.

On Monday, the day after I'd related all I knew about Reichmann, Gentry, Tyler, Franklin, Sheila, Beluga, the Cock'n'Bull bomber, and all the other assorted bit players, she waltzed into the Roundhouse, found Kofax, and vamped him into submitting to an interview about the role of civilians in police administration.

Like the story she invented for French to tell Ivan about the supposed art fraud, whatever she told Kofax came off the top of her head. She's got one hell of a spontaneous imagination, and I have no doubt that she was flashing enough flesh to make Kofax crazy. She told me that she'd gone in wearing a fitted jersey dress that was slit to the thigh on the left side, and she wasn't wearing a bra or pantyhose. I know that dress. She's worn it to the city room a few times, and it fits, from top to bottom. She's got the legs and she looks good in what I've heard other women describe as fuck-me pumps.

The 'preliminary' interview took place at Kofax's desk, in one of those mindless modular cubicles that are so popular with space planners, all of whom are one day going to be harshly judged and sent to spend eternity in a goddamn cardboard refrigerator carton somewhere very near the cosmic equivalent of the I-5 and 101 interchange. I never saw the Kofax cubicle, but I know it because they all look alike. She could steam up one of those in fifteen seconds, max.

From there she induced him to continue the interview at one of her neighborhood saloons, and from there they moved on to the fifteenth-floor bedroom of Building Five, Society Hill Place. He was dead meat, in more ways than one, before the midnight hour. By dawn he was hers.

"He hates Reichmann," Alexis said with one of her malicious self-satisfied smiles. A good Christian probably would've said she was leering.

"You're smarter than I thought, but even better, you're lucky. We need some luck." We were eating hamburgers in a dingy little café that overlooked the Delaware River, a place she'd suggested because no one from the *Call* ever ate there. "How did you get around his obsession for hookers?"

"I made him pay."

That cracked me up. "Real money, you mean? Not pay for the drinks?"

"Two hundred and fifty bucks, I told him afterward that the two-fifty was a special introductory offer."

"Okay, he says he hates Reichmann. What else? I want all the marked cards we can get into the game."

"He needs to make sex as sordid as possible. He was panting while I was talking to him at the Roundhouse. I must have looked like one of his fantasy sluts, and I worked on his head." She giggled.

"I bet you did. So?"

"When I got him to the bar, I let him cop a feel a couple of times, and he was all mine. He told me about his girlfriend who split for New York with a guy she met while she was walking her dog in Fairmount Park. That fucked him up, plus he lives with his parents, who're in their seventies."

"He'd do better to spend his money on therapy. Jesus, he's a real piece of work."

"Well, you said the same thing about me once or twice, as I recall."

"Not without good reasons. How do you feel about this?"

"I love it. He's the other half of a fantasy I've had since I was about seventeen. I've had a couple of guys willing to play it out with me, but they were always playing, and it wasn't the same. His fantasy is perfectly matched to mine, like—"

"I don't need to hear all the details."

"—tongue and groove—"

"Cool it, wench. You're gonna talk yourself into a hunger that burger can't fill."

"His tongue—"

"Gimme a goddamn break!"

"I've got something a lot better than a break to give you."

"I'm not the subservient type."

"No, no . . . Christ, Hawkins, where's your imagination?"

"Alexis, we're at lunch!"

"I'm not wearing any underwear . . ."

"How long do you think it'll take you to bring him over to our side?"

"Look under the table . . ."

"Alexis, c'mon. Please?"

"When do you want it?"

I hesitated, wondering if the bitch was setting me up. "As soon as you can arrange it. You're clear on what we're looking for, right?"

"I think so," she said, with lust lighting her eyes.

"You said you wanted to be a part of this bullshit, but you're acting like a goddamn nympho. Get a grip on yourself and let's be serious. Okay?"

"I think you should tell him yourself. That way you can't blame me if he doesn't get the right information."

"No. I don't want to take the chance that he'll see me as the manipulator or as a threat to his newfound passion. If he's willing to do this, it'll be because he wants to be used, like you said. To be ordered around, made to please. And there's a certain risk for him, so that'll probably wind him up like a banjo string. If I walk in, it may kill the thrill."

"Okay." She sighed with what seemed like disappointment.

"Whenever you think he's ready." I finished my burger and made a silent vow to never again let her pick the restaurant. Her idea of a great burger was six ounces of fatty chopped meat served *au jus*. Which is French for greasy gravy.

"Did you enjoy your lunch?" the waitress asked as she totaled the bill.

"*Très* au jus," I said, "and give the bill to my culinary guide to Greater Philadelphia. She's a working girl."

The waitress stopped chewing her gum for a startled moment and looked from Alexis to me. "Are you two restaurant critics for one of them road-map companies, like Triple A?"

"Actually," Alexis said as she dropped a twenty on the table, "we work for the *Metropolitan Restaurant Guide*."

"That's great!" she said with complete sincerity. "I bought my medical insurance from Metropolitan."

— — — —

"What's his beef with Reichmann?" I asked as she stopped for a red light on Spring Garden Street.

"I don't know. He wouldn't say. During the interview in the bar, I asked how he felt about Reichmann as the Commissioner of Police. And all he'd say was, 'I hate that sonofabitch.' And that was it, no matter how I phrased the question. I asked him again twice, in different ways, and all he'd say was 'I hate the sonofabitch.'"

"When do you see him next?"

"Tonight."

"Where's he getting all his money? The guy's a clerk."

"I don't know, but his last pleading words were 'Can I see you tonight?' That was at four o'clock this morning. I told him to show up at seven this evening, with the money."

"How much?"

"Five hundred for three hours. I've got to get *some* sleep."

"I want you to raise the price when he gets there."

"Why?" she asked as she shifted gears and signaled a lane change. "Supposing he can't afford it?"

"That would be interesting to know. Wing it, but make it humiliating no matter what he does. If he cries he doesn't have the money, give him his session anyway, but abuse him, make him feel like shit because he can't afford you. If he doesn't complain, tell 'im you're gonna raise the price again next time."

"What if we lose him?"

"We won't. If it gets too rich for his blood we may be able to use that. If it doesn't, what the hell, you'll have a nice little stash of cash to take me away from all this when it's over."

"Right. Hawkins and Cabot in Cabo." She didn't sound convinced for some reason.

— — — —

Ivan glared at us as we waltzed into the city room. Strictly speaking, she was late, but she was, strictly speaking, working for me. There wasn't anything he could say, and he didn't like that at all, which was understandable. His worst fuckin' nightmare not only was still around but it was showing signs of longevity. If I could pull Alexis and Ferris off an assignment without asking permission or justifying it, who knew what was next? The last person to whom he wanted to yield any power was A. P. Hawkins. That was Ivan's new nickname for me, since my stories on Reichmann had been put on the Associated Press wire after the Cock'n'Bull explosion. Or so I heard from Sammy.

"A. P. Hawkins?" I said. "Sounds like a Confederate general."

"I think it stands for 'attitude problem,' but I could be wrong."

"I think you must be. I don't have any problem with my attitude."

— — — —

When Ferris hadn't shown by five o'clock I went in to see French alone, to give him a sanitized report on our progress with Kofax. He was out with the flu, his secretary said.

And Ferris was out on assignment, one of Atlee's desk assistants told me, but he didn't know anything else, other than that the assignment had come from French. When I asked Atlee, he shrugged. "He called me at home yesterday and left a message with my wife saying Daniel was sending him out of town for a couple of days."

"Okay, thanks."

"Is there a problem?"

"No, not for me. I've got a lead on something I wanted him to check out," I lied, "but it can wait."

"Are you back, officially?"

"No. I came in to talk to Daniel about the story Ferris and Alexis and I are working on, but he's out sick. I've been at this all day, and I'm not feeling well myself. I think half this city has the goddamn flu. I'm gonna split as soon as I make a couple of calls."

I wasn't feeling great, although I suspected the greasy burger, rather than the flu, was the cause of my discomfort. I was also trying to hold off a low-grade anxiety attack, which unfailingly hits me in the stomach. Anxiety and undigested grease. I needed a shot of something strong enough to open a clogged drain.

Ferris being out of town on an assignment for French seemed strange. It's rare that any of us are suddenly shipped off on an out-of-town assignment to cover anything but a disaster. The editors would rather print copy from one of the wire services than spend the money and lose the reporter's warm body. And Ferris, of all people. Nightside reporters are lucky to get out for dinner.

I called French, and Sally answered. "He's sleeping. Thank God. That man is the *worst* patient. And how about you, young man? Back to work already? You should be home, too."

"I'm okay, but I still get tired before I should. You think Daniel will be in tomorrow?"

"If he leaves here tomorrow he would do well to stop and see his attorney about a divorce. I've spent the last two days and nights trying to keep his fever down and get some food in his stomach. He's really quite ill."

"Tie 'im to the bed and tell 'im it's for his own good. You can also tell him I called. If he's feeling better maybe I can get a few minutes of his time on the phone, or drive out for a short visit. I promise it'll be short."

"I'll tell him you called, but I wouldn't count on talking to him before Thursday or Friday. Now, you tell Atlee that the managing editor's wife said that you're to leave that place within the hour. I heard you lost a good deal of blood, and it's going to take a few weeks to get over that."

"I'm okay, but thanks for the concern. I'll try Daniel tomorrow or Thursday."

— — — —

I called Ferris at home and got his answering machine. I left an unkind message that I hoped would make him laugh.

I had the receiver in my hand, about to call Juliet, when Alexis passed behind me.

"Well, I'm off to give myself to the cause. See you tomorrow."

"Okay. Listen, start working on him . . . other than sexually. See if you can find out what kind of access he had to the computer system, or systems. You know what we're looking for, so just continue the interview."

"Piece of cake."

When I got Juliet on the phone her first words were, "You don't sound good. What's wrong?"

"Nothing a hug and a shot of tequila wouldn't put to rest."

"I bought a new car today. Would you like me to pick you up? Maybe we could go somewhere interesting for a romantic dinner . . . ?"

"Sure. What did you buy?"

"A black 450-SL."

"I'll look for a beautiful blonde in a black Mercedes. How long?"

"Thirty minutes?"

"Sounds promising. By the way, have you spoken to Daniel today? Or yesterday?"

"No. I spoke to Sally. Daniel has the flu and he's running a high fever."

"Okay. Thirty minutes. 'Bye."

— — — —

I was sitting quietly in the passenger seat, holding a flask of Conmemorativo and an empty shot glass, watching Juliet and thinking about Ferris's certainty that she loved me and would marry me and make my life so much easier. To him, and quite probably to most people, I would seem to be the perfect example of the brain-dead male who couldn't see a gift from the gods when it was in his lap.

I filled the glass and offered it to her.

"Not while I'm driving. How do you feel about French food?"

"Not while they're selling Exocet missiles to the enemies of America. No way. I don't even eat french fries anymore." I downed the shot and put the flask and glass in the console. "You really do take care of me. Have I told you lately that I love you?"

"It's been a while, but I've adjusted. I know I asked you before, but are you okay?"

"I've been better, but I've been a damn sight worse. I ate a greasy hamburger for lunch, and for some reason I'm worried about Ferris. The two of them are kinda gnawing at my solar plexus."

"Why are you worried?"

"He's supposed to have been sent out of town on assignment by Daniel. The same Daniel who's home in bed with a raging fever. Doesn't make sense."

"When was the last time you saw him?"

"Few days ago. I spoke to him Sunday afternoon, on the phone. He didn't say anything, and he would have. At least I think he would."

"Well, if you've done what you can to find out where he is, don't worry about it. It's hard to be romantic while you're brooding."

"You're right."

"Now, since most neutral countries don't have wonderful cuisine, can we settle on one that hasn't offended you in the last few weeks or months and get something to eat?"

"Fish. Broiled Dover sole. I'll overlook the Falkland mess for the sake of romance."

"I know just the place. It's a country inn up near New Hope. Are you sufficiently fortified for the trip?"

"Yeah. I'm fine. That shot of tequila helped. I hope to hell I'm not coming down with the goddamn flu."

"Soup, broiled sole, steamed vegetables, and a little gift I have for you . . . you'll be as good as new before the evening is done."

"You have a present for me? What's the occasion?"

"Just because I love you, and don't get all mushy and sentimental on me."

"I'll do my best."

━━ ━━ ━━ ━━

A gunshot woke me at 4:07. The knot in my stomach was the size of a golf ball and I strained to hear something, anything. Not a peep. A dream, I wondered? I couldn't recall dreaming anything. The golf ball was pulsing slightly.

I looked at the illuminated face of my new Rolex, the 'little gift' Juliet had mentioned, which she'd given to me while we were sitting at the bar waiting for a table in the restaurant she'd chosen. I hadn't really known what to say, and looking at it in the faint glow from the night light I was no less pleased with the watch, and no less disappointed that I hadn't been able to make an eloquent response, or at least say something more imaginative than "Thank you."

Looking at her, slightly curled and deep in sleep, I wished I could give her something she wanted, make a grandiose gesture, swear a glittering vow of lifelong commitment, a promise to never hurt her. And then I wished for the deed to the fifth moon of Jupiter. There was as much chance of one as there was of the other.

I closed my eyes, willing to settle for nothing more than another few hours of peaceful sleep. I tried controlled breathing combined with images of a sailboat on a beam reach, slicing through blue water, a perfect white boat on a cloudless day with a ten-knot wind . . . but the golf ball pulsed and the certainty that I'd heard a gunshot somewhere fucked up the boat's course to the dark void of sleep. What I had heard had come from somewhere else, a distant place. Most of my life, long before I'd heard of Vietnam, I'd heard voices calling me by name, an occasional phone ringing, and once in a while a hammering on the door. They've never been sounds connected to my 'real' world. The voices hadn't come through the bedroom door. No phone in the house had rung. No one outside was pounding to wake me.

I fell asleep thinking that rather than get the deed to the fifth moon of Jupiter, I'd like very much to have my brain sent out for an overhaul. Rewire the circuits, put in a couple of new chips, delete a lot of the memories filed on the hard disk, and install a surge protector in the circuitry. Right. The Stepford Squire.

— — — —

I woke to the aroma of French roast and the sensation of Juliet kissing me lightly on the forehead.

"Good morning," she said. She smiled and brushed the hair away from my eyes. "Did you sleep well?"

"Is that a trick question? What time is it?"

"Eight-fifteen," she answered before I remembered that I was wearing my new watch. "How's your stomach?"

"Better . . . I think." I inhaled without discomfort. "The golf ball's gone, which is a good sign." I struggled into a sitting position and picked up the coffee. "Do you ever think about marrying me?"

"God no!" Her expression was an interesting mix of disbelief and nervous confusion. "What ever made you ask a question like that?"

"Well, Christ, I'm not the hunchback of Wissahickon."

"I wasn't suggesting that you're undesirable." She sat on the edge of the bed, staring at me as though I'd sprung unexpectedly from a faint memory. I was familiar, but something wasn't as she remembered.

"I didn't mean to upset you," I said.

"I'm not upset. I *am* surprised, and a little confused. I never expected to hear you say anything about marriage, other than 'no way.' "

"I lost my head for a moment."

"Well, I won't take advantage of your momentary lapse." She stood up, as though to leave, but she didn't go anywhere.

"Last night," I said in the tone I might have used to confess my sins to the guy keeping the books, "I woke up. Four-oh-seven A. by-God M. I looked at the watch and I looked at you sleeping, and I wished I was a different person, someone who knew how to follow the rules."

"That's a very generous wish," she said, sitting again. She took my hand and offered a reassuring smile.

"I also wished for the fifth moon of Jupiter, figuring I had about the same chance of getting one wish as the other."

"Jamie, I've never known anyone like you, and I wouldn't trade what you've already given me for my choice of the three best-looking, most successful rule-following males in this or any other world. You've given me as much of yourself as you have to give to anyone."

"I don't feel like I've given you anything at all. Hell, I haven't even been able to help you put your brother in the slam, where he belongs no matter whose brother he is."

"You've given me the pleasure of knowing you. You've stood up to me when I was wrong, which few people have done. You've rescued me from believing that I had only meager and boring options. You've renewed feelings, both sexual and emotional, that hadn't been kindled in years. You've made me laugh—at myself, at the absurdity of my life, at the world's foolishness."

"Sounds like therapy," I grumbled.

"In a way," she said with a grin. She squeezed my hand and stood up again, relieved. "I have some appointments this morning, but I'm free for lunch and some early-afternoon shopping. I'd like to replace a couple of the other items you lost in the explosion." I was shaking my head. "It's the *Call*'s money," she added. "But it's easier for me to submit an expense report for a few hundred dollars."

"What in Christ's name do you think I need that costs a few hundred dollars?" I asked as the phone rang downstairs.

"A warm coat, for one thing. Another lighter, so you can keep your promise to leave it with me when you ride off into the sunset. And a dark suit, so you can be my escort at the opening of my Mayan collection next Friday night."

"You've got to be kidding," I said, laughing. "Me in the middle of all those Main Line art lovers?"

"Well, if you can't handle it, it's okay. I thought you might like to see what I acquired while I wasn't busy trying to bail you out of jail."

We both heard Stonehenge climbing the steps, and we both stopped talking. The golf ball returned and a stab of pain shot through my stomach. My God, I wonder if I've got an ulcer.

"Miss Rossini," he called, lightly rapping on the open bedroom door. "Mr. French is on the telephone. The gentleman insists that he must speak to you."

"Thank you, Edward. I'll take it up here."

She connected the phone as I finished my coffee and headed for the shower, grateful for the distraction. I needed time to think about what I'd asked her, and why, as well as her response.

You woke up at four A.M, I reminded myself as I worked the shampoo through my hair, filled with anxiety, fearing failure, and probably feeling a little guilty.

And what you really wanted from her was reassurance that you're not a total fuck-up, at least from her point of view. You don't know how to pull together all the elements of this goddamn civic rip-off and hang their asses out in the wind.

But if she'd answered honestly, which I could believe or not, I had unknowingly been granted the good fortune to have found acceptance in the heart of a woman who didn't want to ruin a perfectly good relationship by getting married.

It occurred to me, as I stood under the stream of hot water, that I felt good. Even when Sheila flashed before me I didn't lose the sense of having accomplished something worth more to me than any prize the newspaper business had to offer. I hadn't moved quickly enough, or found the right words to win Sheila's acceptance, but even though my effort was too little, too late, I knew that at the very least she'd died believing I cared enough to try.

As I turned off the shower I realized that I was smiling. It was the last smile I'd be able to manage for a while.

— — — —

Coming out of the bathroom, wrapped in one of Juliet's huge towels, I found her on the window seat that overlooked a garden in the rear of the house. She was looking out, her cheek supported on her right hand, cloaked in an aura of sadness.

"Juliet . . . ?"

"It's Leon," she said softly.

The knot in my solar plexus instantly swelled to the size of a tennis ball. I sat on the edge of the bed. "Is he dead?"

"No. But he's been seriously hurt. He's in a hospital in Williamsport."

"What happened? Did he wreck his car?"

"He was beaten, and shot once."

"What!?"

"Allen Dark, the photographer, is dead."

"Where the hell is Williamsport? And what the fuck were they doing there? Does French know? Who called him?"

She turned to face me, her hands clasped between her legs, her upper body slumped forward. Tears were streaming from her eyes. "They aren't sure that Leon will pull through. He has internal injuries, he's lost a lot of blood, he may have brain damage, and he hasn't regained consciousness."

"Where is Williamsport?"

"Northwest of here, two hundred miles, I guess. Maybe a little less. I've never been there. It's off Interstate 80, kind of in the middle of nowhere."

"On the Susquehanna River?"

"I think so."

"Since you're dressed, will you go downstairs and get the atlas? Or even better, a Pennsylvania road map? And get old Stonehenge to make me another cup of coffee and some scrambled eggs and toast?" She didn't move, and I wasn't sure she even heard what I said. "Juliet . . ." She came back from her distant thoughts. "I need to see a map, and I should eat something. It's gonna be a long day."

"I'm sorry, I drifted away. My God, how can this happen?"

"It happens all the time. Don't you read your own paper? This country is the murder capital of the world." I leaned over to tie my shoes. "Are you gonna get off your ass or do I have to beg the butler for something to eat?"

"Yes, of course." She left me staring at the laces of my shoes, picturing Ferris on a gurney, hooked to a respirator, heart monitor, and other associated hospital hardware. And Allen Dark on a morgue slab, KIA. Two more victims of the Brother James Academy cadre. Two more victims of Reichmann's delusions of grandeur. Two more victims of my own half-assed dumb-fuck fantasies about bringing law and order to the office of the Philadelphia Police Commissioner.

And damn Leon Ferris for going off on his own fantasy trip.

— — — —

"I *told* him not to fuck with those people," I shouted at French a couple of hours later. "Jesus jumpin' Christ, how can he have grown up in a city as corrupt as this fuckin' place and not known better?"

"Jamie . . ." Juliet said pleadingly.

"Do you want me to try to answer that?" French asked.

"No. I'm sorry. I'm yelling at you because I can't yell at him." I looked away from French and caught Sally glaring at me. "And I apologize to you, too," I said. "I feel like it's my fault, and I hate that."

"How is it your fault?" French asked.

"I saw his eyes light up when I told him what Beluga had told me about the school. He wanted us to go check it out and I said forget it. Leave it alone. He said he didn't feel as though he was making a contribution to our investigation and I didn't take the time to convince him that he was."

"You can't be responsible for another person's ambitions or mistakes," Sally asserted. "He wanted to show you that he can do his part."

"You're right," I said, pacing the room. "You're right, you're right." She wasn't even close, as far as I was concerned, but I couldn't see any point in arguing with her. It wouldn't change anything if she agreed with me. "So what's the deal with the med-evac? They're gonna fly him back to Philadelphia this afternoon?"

"As long as he remains stable, yes," French said. "The doctors at Williamsport Hospital have stabilized him.

"Ferris's X rays were flown to Hahnemann Hospital this morning and the neurosurgeons there say they don't see any signs that he suffered brain damage. No clots, thank God. A bad concussion, possibly a hairline fracture of the skull, but they don't think so."

"The bullet wound is the most serious," Sally added. "It lodged near his heart, but it's not life-threatening if the surgeons are precise. The Williamsport Hospital surgeons think the best move is to transfer him to Hahnemann. He should arrive by helicopter about two o'clock, if all goes well."

And if all doesn't go well he'll come home in a pine box.

Sally left us to answer the phone and Juliet went to the kitchen to make some coffee. French looked at me with the pain and despair of someone watching his world split at the seams, incapable of doing anything to stop the action.

"I presume we're doing a story on this."

"I think we have to," he said. "It's certainly going to make the wires, and we'd look peculiar, to say the least, if we ignored it."

"I'll do it. We've got to sanitize the whole damn thing."

"It's yours. I'll tell Ivan." His breathing was labored and his face was covered in a thin film of sweat.

"I'll tell him. You stay in bed and get well."

"I wish I could go into the office, but I'm fortunate to make it to the bathroom and back without Sally's help. She wants to put me in the hospital." He wiped his face with his hand. "I'll be damned if I'm going to give in to that."

I felt bad for him, sick as he was, with no real hope of feeling better for at least another two or three days. Freezing one minute, afire with fever the next. Too damn sick to eat solid food, and sick to death of broth and dry toast. At his age, I suspected, it seemed even worse and probably took longer to recover.

Juliet came in with two cups of coffee, followed by Sally with a mug of bouillon. I took the coffee and went on staring out the window. It was snowing again. The flakes were large, wet, and already sooty by the time they drifted past the leafless trees.

You *could* be somewhere else, I thought. You could be on a warm beach with a bottle of cold beer, wondering if the chubby blonde with the big hooters floating on the air mattress would remember to retie her top before she turned over to broil her nose and kneecaps, wondering if you'll ever write the next ten pages of your 'work in progress,' wondering if you'll ever find a purpose and a point to breathing in and breathing out.

But you're here, and here there is a purpose and a point to your life, at least for the moment. A few hours ago you were filled with inadequacy for the lack of some grand gesture you could make to Juliet. If only you knew how to live by the rules, you lamented. If only you had the courage to 'do the right thing' by her. You're full of shit. And now Leon is fucked up, Allen is dead, Sheila's been buried, and the lunatics are still running loose. Wake up and smell reality, Jamie-boy. There's something rotten in the Roundhouse.

Forget the rules. It's time to go to work.

███ ███ ███ ███

"I've been fucking off, playing a game with people who own the deck," I said to Juliet as she drove us toward Center City. "They not only own the deck, they own the casino. They've made the rules and put their people in the right places to ensure that they never take a big loss. I think it's time to put a joker in the game."

"This morning," she said calmly, "you told me that you felt a need to do something for me, to show me that you care, to repay me for taking care of you." She paused. "Do you still feel like that?"

"Sure."

"What I want won't be easy for you to do, Jamie. And it's something that may even prove to have been as pointless as what happened to your friend at the Cock'n'Bull, and Leon, and Allen."

"I'll do my best to help you any way I can. Tell me what you want."

"I want you to leave Philadelphia." I couldn't have been any more surprised if she'd asked me to jump off the Ben Franklin Bridge.

"You said you wanted to give me something. Give me a reason to believe you'll be alive in a week, a month," she continued in a perfectly modulated tone. No pleading, no slow dancing. "Give me a reason to believe that you'll come to my next birthday party, that you'll invite me to spend Christmas with you in Cabo San Lucas."

"Juliet . . ."

"Yes or no. Don't give me rationalizations or a lyrical rejection."

"No."

After a moment she turned to say something, and I expected her to ask why. Before she could ask, I said, "Don't ask why. Either I do or I don't, either I will or I won't. In this case, I won't."

"Actually, I was going to ask if you've ever had a thought about us spending Christmas together in Cabo."

"That's the third time today I've expected you to say one thing and something completely different came out. Maybe I didn't get enough sleep."

"Are we still going to eat lunch together?"

"Sure, but someplace easy to deal with." I lit a Camel and coughed for a few seconds.

"I don't know why I worry about your life when you're so determined to kill yourself with cigarettes."

She drove in silence, leaving me to think about my decision. If I would let her, she'd take good care of me. I could walk away and not worry about losing her respect, simply because she's more afraid of this crap than I am.

"Listen," I said as she left the expressway, "do you know the difference between sex and a ham sandwich?"

"I don't think so," she said, shaking her head.

"Great, let's hit the deli on my block, then go have a picnic at my place."

"You want to take me to bed now . . . ?"

"No, I want to fuck you on the kitchen counter. Rossini on rye, with a little spicy dressing."

"In that case, let's see if this turbo works as well as they claimed when they sold me the car." She pushed the accelerator to the floor and we passed four cars in about half that number of seconds.

— — — —

"I've got to go in early," I called from the kitchen. "And it's already almost one o'clock."

"I'll be dressed in a few minutes," she answered, still buttoning her blouse as she came down the steps from the loft. "What's the rush?"

"I've got to get the Williamsport police to tell me what they claim to know and write the story before first edition. Ivan already has someone working on it. He's gonna be pissed when I tell him I'm doing it."

"Do you still have problems with him?"

"Is it still winter in Philadelphia? We don't butt heads as often as we did in the beginning, but only because I don't have to deal with him most of the time."

"We're going to make one stop on the way to the *Call*, five minutes for you to try on a jacket I saw in the window of a leather shop last week. It's on Chestnut."

"I don't need—"

"You *do* need a warm coat, I *don't* need an argument. Please?"

"Okay, okay. One-stop shopping. Jesus!"

"I wish I could buy you a bulletproof vest. Come on, your car is waiting."

— — — —

She reached over and took my hand as she steered the Mercedes to the curb in front of the *Call*. "Tell me what you need."

"I need money. I need a car. And I need a lot of luck."

"You can use the Porsche. How much money do you want?"

"Twenty-five thousand, in hundred-dollar bills. Nonsequential numbers. Don't take it all from the same bank if you can avoid that. I don't want anyone to take note of a large withdrawal.

"And forget the Porsche. It's too flashy. I need an older car with a strong engine." And please, God, don't let her have a friend with an '81 Buick. Or a five-year-old Chrysler that accelerates like the QEII and steers like a Conestoga wagon.

"I'll think about it. I must know someone."

I leaned over and kissed her. "Thanks again for the jacket and the watch. If I had five functioning brain cells I'd let you take me to some warm beach and forget all this happened. I can't, and I wish I could, for you."

"Call me later? I'm going to stop by Hahnemann and check on Leon. I'll arrange for the money, and see about a car."

"Oh, see if you can get your friend Chester to agree to a meeting. I don't know when. An open date on short notice."

"That shouldn't be a big problem as long as he's in town."

"Okay. Call me later."

It took me an hour to write the story about Ferris and Dark. That was after I'd spent ten minutes arguing with Ivan. He'd already assigned the story to Alexis, which didn't surprise me, but she walked up during the argument and handed me all her neatly typed notes, which did.

"I spoke to Daniel a few minutes ago," she lied, "and he told me that he wanted Jamie to do the story. That's okay with me."

Ivan looked from her to me and back to her. "Daniel called and didn't ask to speak to me?"

"Actually, he did, but I told him you were arguing with Jamie about who was going to write the story, so he said to tell you that it's Jamie's, and he hung up."

Ivan's blood pressure went up twenty points, at least. I thought he might actually sputter when he finally managed to speak, but he just muttered, "Fifteen hundred words, and I want it for first edition."

If I'd been in a better mood I would've laughed out loud. Alexis was a world-class bullshitter.

My phone was ringing as I sat down at my desk. "Hello."

"Nice watch you're wearing," Alexis said. "A gift from an admirer?"

I looked across the room but she wasn't at her desk. "Yeah. So?"

"I've got something for you, too. Or I should have by late this evening. Kofax said he's bringing me something special tonight. A 'nice surprise,' he claims."

"You just surprised the hell out of me, giving up the story like that, and lying to Ivan on top of it."

"It should be your story," she said. "You're the best friend he has on the *Call*. I can't believe that could happen to him and Allen. What the hell is going on?"

"Combat maneuvers."

"Can you come by my place tonight, around eleven?"

"Sure, but what if Kofax's surprise is a leather harness instead of information?"

"We'll find some way to use it."

"How about a coffee when I finish this fairy tale?"

"I'm out of here in ten minutes. See you tonight."

Working from the notes Alexis had given me, and what I could get from a few calls to Williamsport, I put together the official *Call* version of what had happened to Ferris and Dark.

According to the Williamsport police, two hunters walking to a favorite location on the edge of a state forest found Ferris and Dark. Dark was dead from a single round through the chest that had pierced his heart.

Ferris had also been shot in the chest, but the slug had passed through a secretarial notebook clamped on a fiberglass clipboard he had tucked inside his shirt. The 5 × 9 notebook, about an inch thick, and the clipboard were enough to slow the bullet. I'd ragged him about his Toys 'Я' Us clipboard a dozen times, but I'd never really paid any attention to what it was made of.

The investigating officer had reported that Ferris quite probably had been left for dead, that the assailants possibly had been scared off by the sound of the hunters, and that Ferris owed his life to the notebook, the clipboard, and probably a faulty load in the shell. The officer who read all of this to me from the report said that if, for example, the round normally would have a two-hundred-grain load, it might actually have had only half that amount. "Or less," he added.

"Like a 'short round' in artillery fire?"

"Exactly."

Both Ferris and Dark showed signs of having been beaten, the officer said. Their wallets were missing, along with Dark's cameras. The cops had found Ferris's *Call* ID in a shirt pocket.

I reached one of the hunters, who couldn't tell me anything useful. They'd been out hunting, found the bodies, loaded them into their truck, and driven them to the hospital.

And that was that. One or more unknown assailants ambushed two newsmen, beat them up, shot them, stole their wallets, and disappeared. The snow and the hunters had screwed up any possiblity of finding tracks. The bullet that had killed Dark had passed completely through him and wasn't recovered. The one in Ferris's chest was so fucked up it probably wouldn't be worth looking at from a ballistics point of view. No shells were found. No clues. No witnesses. No nothing. The only positive aspect of all of it was that Ferris was alive. For the moment.

━ ━ ━ ━

I told Atlee I had an appointment to keep, left the *Call* a few minutes after five, and called Finori's Taxi from a pay phone in the coffee shop. When he answered, I asked, "Is this a secure line?"

"Absolutely."

"Can you meet me at my place, around seven o'clock?"

"Yes."

"Bring me a detective's badge, if you can." I hung up. He might be certain that the line was secure but I wasn't.

I called Juliet to see if she'd made any progress.

"My mechanic loaned me a car, a '75 Firebird he bought to restore. He says all the mechanical work has been finished, but the body's a little rough."

"That's great. I don't want anything that looks new or attracts attention. When can I pick it up?"

"It's parked two doors up from the deli on Twenty-second Street. The keys are in one of those magnetic boxes, stuck under the left rear fender. Registration is in the glove compartment."

"What did you find out about Leon? Anything changed?"

"I spoke to the head of the surgical team. He said he's done this same operation five times, and all of his patients recovered. His principal assistant on this one was with him for three of those operations.

"There's no brain damage, no fracture in the skull, and the internal injuries are relatively minor. Bruised kidneys, four cracked ribs, loss of blood. Minor frostbite on one ear. The cold slowed the blood flow from the wound and probably helped save his life. He was conscious for a while, but not during the time I was at the hospital. No visitors except immediate family."

"Any cops up there?"

"I didn't see any."

"Thanks for finding me a car. I gotta go."

"Jamie, the money's in the trunk."

"In the trunk?"

"It's safe. Don't worry about it."

"Whatever you say . . . I'll call you tomorrow."

"Be careful, please."

— — — —

I decided to walk home. I think better while I'm walking and being on the streets was my only alternative to pacing up and down my living room. But long before I actually arrived at my apartment, most of my thoughts were on how goddamn cold it was and how ridiculous it is to live in big cities. The evening rush hour made idle thought a dangerous game. Every corner was a killing zone. Forty minutes in the cold night air and all I'd managed to do was stretch my legs.

I made it home a little before six o'clock, opened a beer, and poured a shot just as the mannequins were taking their places on the Channel 7 news set and the booth announcer was roaring through the headlines. The same old shit, night after night. The only thing different about this night was Ferris and Dark, who weren't mentioned.

I switched to Channel 4. They had a copy story, with still photos of Ferris and Dark from the *Call*'s files. The news anchor spent more time talking about the death of their reporter Jim Lang in the Cock'n'Bull explosion than he did about Ferris and Dark.

Channel 11's anchor, Edward Portero, the distinguished, gray-haired elder statesman of Philadelphia's TV news corps, was reading the lead-in to their report in a dirgelike tone as I switched channels, lamenting the death of one more Philadelphia newsman, and the critical wounding of *Call* photographer Allen Dark.

Jesus Christ! I downed the shot and closed my eyes. How can they fuck up like that and stay on the air?

He introduced some poor blonde bimbo freezing her ass outside Hahnemann Hospital. I looked up as the director switched to the minicam picture, catching her frantically checking her notes, obviously panicked, wondering how to correct the inaccurate lead without making Mr. Ed look like the horse's ass he was.

Her hundred-dollar haircut was flying in four different directions, and she had almost nothing to report. Even worse, she had to shout to be heard above the sound of Vine Street traffic. She excused herself, and tried to justify the confusion, by explaining that the Flash News Team had learned of "this terrible tragedy" only one hour earlier.

Mr. Ed picked up on that when the shot switched back to the studio, claiming that Flash News was the first on the scene with a 'live' minicam, and apologizing for the error in declaring the wrong reporter dead. He didn't mention the lack of content, or explain how the hospital had become the 'scene' when the shooting had taken place two hundred miles away, but he did promise a more complete report on the eleven o'clock news.

He also looked like he was in the fast lane to Outrage City. I could see a screaming fit brewing like a squall on the horizon.

And Ms. Minicam undoubtedly wished she was doing a 'dead' report on the soup of the day from the station cafeteria.

— — — —

Finori showed at ten after eight. I was rereading the interpretations of the individual lines in the I Ching when he leaned on the buzzer.

Sixth in the fifth place: He shoots a pheasant, losing one arrow. In the end he gains honor and position.

No shit. I wondered if I could substitute peasant for pheasant and blow away Reichmann?

Finori looked like he hadn't slept for a week. "Don't say it," he said, reading my thoughts. "I could pass as the last survivor of a three-day drinking binge."

"What the hell have you been doing? Black beauties?"

"I'm a worrier. I don't sleep much when I worry, and I don't rest when I do sleep. Here . . ." He pulled what looked like an official Atlantic City police badge from his overcoat pocket, along with a picture ID. The picture was the same as my *Call* ID. "Detective second grade. Narcotics division. Be careful where you flash it, and if you're challenged you damn well better have a good story to tell."

"I'll just tell 'em you gave it to me as a going-away gift. How the hell did you get this picture?"

"What else do you want?" he asked, ignoring my question.

"Can you put someone on Ferris?"

"You think it's necessary?"

"You do know what happened, don't you?"

"He and his photographer went to the Brother James Academy is my guess."

"A little supplementary health insurance doesn't seem an unreasonable precaution, considering what's happened. Hell, your section's responsible for the media. Since someone tried to kill him, wouldn't that be reasonable?"

"Not to Gentry or Reichmann, but I'll see what I can do."

He'd flopped on the sofa and was looking around the room. "You got anything to drink?"

"Tequila, vodka, and beer."

"Vodka on ice. How's your neck?"

"It's fine. I pulled the stitches myself." He winced. "Fuck those hospital yahoos. A pair of tweezers and a little peroxide. Saved them and me a lot of time and aggravation." I went into the kitchen to make him a drink and pour myself another shot.

"How did they get onto the Brother James Academy?" he asked as I handed him the vodka.

"I had a long conversation with Beluga. That was one of many topics we discussed. I told Ferris about it, and he hopped on his white horse to check it out."

"You had a face-to-face meeting with Beluga? Christ, Gentry and his boys have been looking everywhere for him."

"Yeah, well, Beluga was looking for me. That made it a lot easier. Interesting story he told me."

"I know the story." He rattled the ice in his glass and took another sip. "What did the Whale want with you?"

"He wants me to get Reichmann and Gentry off his ass, but neither of us came up with any big ideas about how to accomplish that. How the fuck can you work for these people? Whatever you are, you aren't like them."

"Who'd be here to look after you if I had quit?"

"My fairy godmother." I left him staring into his drink while I went to get my cigarettes.

"Jamie," he said when I came back, "there isn't a great deal I can say about why I'm still where I am. I don't approve of Reichmann or Gentry. But I work for the people of this city, not the people who run it. Someone has to do my job, and better me than one of Gentry's boys."

"That's okay with me, but I'll tell you what I think. I think you and Beluga are tied real tight to some U.S. government agency. FBI, Secret Service, the fuckin' CIA for all I know."

"Don't get paranoid. That's the first step to another boring media conspiracy theory about the subversion of local political rule by the federal government. Can you see Reagan as a dictator?"

"He'd be the last one to find out it happened." I drank my tequila. "I'm not conspiracy-oriented, Angelo, though conspiracies do occur. Nor am I suggesting that there's a conspiracy to overthrow the legitimate government of Philadelphia, or Pennsylvania, or the United States.

"What I'm talking about is counterterrorist groups in the government. They exist as sure as I'm sitting here with an empty shot glass in my hand. For all I know, there may even be a need for them, but the lack of a need wouldn't prevent any one of half a dozen U.S. government agencies or departments from forming one. Right?"

"Jamie . . ." He closed his eyes and sighed.

"C'mon, Lef'tenant. The FBI? Without a doubt. The Secret Service? I'd bet money on that one. The CIA? I'd bet just as much. The Defense Department? Absolutely. They'd say that if we're attacked by terrorists it's a prelude to an attack by radical group X, Y, or Z, and they need to protect all our military installations.

"And then there's a supergroup of some kind, to which all these others are supposed to report. Probably a Joint Chiefs type of thing.

"Then we have the locals. That's where Gentry comes in. Every major city in this country probably has or wants to form a counterterrorist division within the police department. I'd bet my butt against a stringless bass fiddle."

"You got any more of this vodka?" he asked, extending his glass.

"As much as you want." I filled it halfway and dropped a couple of ice cubes into it.

"Let's say you're right, just for the hell of it." He took the glass. "So what?"

"So every one of the federal groups, especially the FBI and the Secret Service, would like to have at least one of their own people in every local operation, to keep an eye on things. And I think that's where you come in. For better or worse, no one trusts anyone anymore. And they're all trying to score the big one so they look good when it's time to hand out money. It's all politics.

"And these are all civil servants, right? Answerable to the public that pays their salaries. Only the public doesn't know they exist. They don't really answer to anyone unless they fuck up, which the Feds would like to prevent. Else, the media starts mucking around, the story gets out, the liberals get righteous, the ACLU gets on everyone's case, the House and Senate hold hearings . . . and all of a sudden, the American public knows as much as the ragheads and radicals who'd like nothing better than to give back some of the shit we've handed out for the last forty years."

"Let me ask you something," he said, sitting up straight. "How do you feel about terrorism?"

"The same way I feel about using nuclear weapons and writing parking tickets. It's just one more way of fucking over the people who work hard and pay the bills for this deficit-ridden bullshit excuse for a government, on every level from the goddamn school board to the fuckin' White House.

"The 'horror' of terrorism, we claim, is its disregard for the value of life among civilians. It's 'dirty pool' and no right-thinking person anywhere can condone the use of terrorism to achieve political ends. We certainly would never do anything like that.

"You want fuckin' terror? Ask the survivors of Dresden and Hiroshima and Nagasaki about terror. And don't tell me that was war and this isn't. This *is* war. And most of the people killed in those bombings I mentioned, plus a lot of others I didn't mention, were goddamned civilians.

"People keep talking about World War Three as though it's only a frightening possiblity. It's a frightening reality, Lef'tenant. The world was at war when I was born and it'll be at war when I'm gone."

"Have you ever made anything easy for anyone?"

"Couple of times . . . big mistake." I poured another shot and sat down with it. "I really don't expect you to tell me who you report to, but I know there has to be someone. Otherwise, you'd have quit the department and gone to work in some place like Cape May.

"And I think Beluga is on someone's payroll, but not in an official capacity.

"Gentry's got to be Reichmann's chief of operations for counterterrorism. It was probably his idea to put together this private army, and God only knows who he's imported. That was his boy that put the case full of explosives in the Cock'n'Bull."

"What do you plan to do?"

"I'm going to open a window on a world most of Philadelphia doesn't know exists."

"How?"

"I haven't figured that out yet, but it'll come to me. By the way, what did you find out about Kofax? You never gave me a report on him."

"There isn't anything worth mentioning, except that he had a brother on the force, an older brother. He retired a little over two years ago, after he got caught dabbling in the drug business. He and a buddy freelanced some drug busts on their days off, took the stash and sold it to the dealers they'd met on some other occasions."

"And he was 'retired'? No trial? No time in the slam?"

"Nope."

"Doesn't that seem stone goddamn strange, especially considering Reichmann's raving about the evils of drugs?"

"I'd give you odds that Patrolman Kofax took a cushioned fall, shall we say, for someone else. One of the brass, probably. He retired on a medical."

"Jesus Christ." Beluga had alluded to Reichmann sanctioning drug deals by selected cops to help support his little army. He wouldn't be specific, and I'd shrugged it off as Whaleshit.

But Reichmann had one hell of an arsenal in the museum, and hungry mouths to feed. Maybe he needed drug money to supplement the funds raised by the Art League. God Almighty. I had as much chance of unearthing all that as I did of stealing NASA's moon rocks.

"You know they'll kill you, don't you?" Finori asked, pulling me back to a less speculative reality.

"Only if I fuck up."

"That wouldn't be a novel experience, now would it?"

"No. More like a short story. 'A tale told by an idiot, full of sound and fury, signifying nothing.' And so it goes."

"I wish I knew you better, Jamie," he said with a smile. "I don't deal with a lot of people who quote either Shakespeare or Vonnegut. And none who can quote both in the same thought."

"Lucky for you, I'd say. Unless you like old Shake-a-spear. I don't. On the other hand, I still have difficulty speaking the language, so I probably shouldn't be too unkind."

Finori had been gone almost an hour when I discovered the pistol he'd left. I'd gone down to the deli to pick up some food, took the keys from under the Firebird's fender, made a sandwich, and called Juliet to find out if she had any more news about Ferris.

"He's out of danger," she said cheerfully, "and the chief surgeon said he should be fine. No major problems."

"Thank the gods that be. Finori said he'd try to put a guard on him."

We talked for a few minutes, and then I hung up, poured a shot, and raised the glass in toast to a surgeon I'd never met. "Nice work. Send the bill to Reichmann."

It was too early to call Alexis, so I stretched out on the sofa, thinking I'd take a nap, and immediately sat up, grumbling. I couldn't imagine what the hell was making such a hard lump where Finori had sat for an hour without complaining. I found out soon enough. He'd slipped a .44 Magnum revolver behind a cushion, the first pistol I'd ever seen packaged in a Ziploc freezer bag. I pulled it out and checked the cylinder. Five rounds. The chamber under the hammer was empty. Another twenty rounds of loose ammunition in a smaller sandwich bag had been put inside the Ziploc with the pistol.

And what the hell am I supposed to make out of this little surprise, Lef'tenant? Mincemeat? I'd be lucky to hit a bull in the ass with a pistol of any kind. Firing this fucker's like lighting off a cannon. Course, if I hit anything, that's it. Except in the movies, nobody gets hit with a .44 and keeps moving. Most of them don't even go on breathing for a long time. Especially a hollow-point .44, I thought as I looked at the loose bullets.

I emptied the cylinder, closed it, cocked it, and pulled the trigger. The sound of the hammer hitting home was enough to scare the hell out of me. For that matter, the sound of the hammer being pulled back would discourage a lot of people.

Now what? Does he think I should carry this thing around, like a fuckin' urban cowboy? Should I put it in the car? Leave it next to my bed? Throw it in the river and go about my business? Shit!

I got up to take the pistol to my desk, and leaned over to straighten out the cushion. That's when I found the holster and harness. I slipped into it, put the pistol in the holster, and pulled on my new leather bomber jacket. Perfect. I checked myself in the mirror. No one could possibly tell I was carrying a pistol, as long as they didn't hug me. Now, I thought, all I need is a license to make it legal . . . What the fuck am I talking about? I'm officially an Atlantic City police detective. And if anyone asks what I'm doing in Philly, I'll tell 'em I'm here moonlighting as a copy editor for the *Call*. I've got about the same aptitude for both jobs.

Jamie Hawkins, detective second grade, Atlantic City police, narcotics division. Right.

— — — —

The sound of the Firebird's engine, like the sound of a woman's sultry voice or the unintentional flash of thigh, was enough to make the standard-issue American male heart beat a little faster. The engine's exhaust was a rich baritone, forced through glass packs or some other illegal replacement for the usual GM exhaust system. I figured every cop in the Delaware Valley reached for his ticket book as soon as I switched on the ignition.

It was a powerful, probably fast car that, as Juliet had relayed to me, needed some body work. Not to mention new seats, rugs, headliner, and door panels. Rust spots the size of saucers were scattered from hood to trunk lid, but there were no real dents. The tires looked new, for which I thanked any and all to whom thanks were due.

I drove to my meeting with Alexis, and as long as I didn't downshift, the exhaust didn't invite undue attention. Except for the exhaust, there was nothing to attract attention, and nothing to encourage anyone to steal the car or break into it. All in all, a perfect vehicle for me.

— — — —

Alexis took one look at the badge and ID and collapsed on her ass, laughing. "James Hawkins, Atlantic City detective?" she howled. "I'd hoped to be around when you came out of whatever closet you were in, but I never expected to see you as a cop."

"Yeah, yeah, yeah. So what happened with Kofax? What was the big surprise?"

"He brought me a 'floppy disk full of artwork.' His description."

"*Artwork!?* Shit! That's it? What is it, pirated copies of Vatican porno painted by Leonardo?"

She came toward me wearing her vamp's grin, her eyes filled with lust. "We didn't spend the time looking at computer files," she said as she pressed her body against me and slipped her hand inside my jacket. "What the hell?" she yelped as she abruptly stepped back.

"It goes with the badge."

"Let me see . . ." She pulled the zipper down and flipped back the side of my jacket, uncovering the .44. "Holy shit." She put a lot of emphasis on 'holy.' "Where'd you get that?"

"That's interesting . . . most people would ask why I'm wearing it. You want to know where I got it."

"Where *did* you get it? And the badge?"

"Casper, the friendly spook. He's on Reichmann's payroll, but he's on the side of the angels. That's us."

"Can I hold it?"

"No, you can't hold it. It's a goddamn loaded gun. I'm not even sure why I brought it. But all of a sudden I've got one and I feel like I should carry it."

"Hey, somebody killed Allen and put Ferris in the hospital. And someone thinks you should have this. I'd carry it if I were you. You want a beer?"

"Okay." I walked over to look out the window. She had a hell of a view if you like city skylines. "So when do we see what kind of art your friend brought?"

"Now, if you'd rather work than have fun. He left some notes for me, what to do with the keyboard to look at the files." I heard her open two bottles. "Any news on Ferris?" she asked.

"He's okay, at least for the moment. They got the bullet out. No big-time complications."

"Thank God." She came out of the kitchen with the beer and a handful of 5¼-inch floppy disks. "C'mon, let's take a look."

She led the way into a small room she'd set up as an office, a room I hadn't seen before. It was filled with a large desk, a lot of books and magazines, a sofa, and a desktop computer with a modem and printer. "You really got that stuff from a cop?" she asked as she switched on the computer and took a dust cover off the monitor.

"Yes. And don't ask anything else about it, okay?" She shrugged. "This is a serious-looking arrangement. You work at home?"

"Sometimes. Ivan had this set up for me. I can send anything I write directly to the *Call*'s mainframe with this modem." She put one of the floppies in the disk drive while I was looking at her collection of books and magazines. She had, among other things, about fifty back issues of *Penthouse*. Uh-huh . . . and which pages have the most fingerprints on them, little girl?

"Jamie . . . ?"

"Yeah?"

"Take a look at this." There was a note of disappointment in her voice and when I turned to the screen I could understand why. Kofax had managed to come up with copies of the blueprints used to do the 'repair' work on the museum basement. It took a few minutes to figure it out, but that's what it was. At first glance it looked like nothing of importance.

She checked the notes she had and punched a couple of keys. The picture changed to a three-dimensional drawing of a room I hadn't seen during my brief visit.

"What the hell *is* this, the bridge of the USS *Enterprise?* It looks like something from *Star Trek*."

"That, my enterprising accomplice to crime and other fun, is Rudolph Reichmann's combat command center or I'm out to lunch on another planet."

"For real?"

"It may be nothing more than a fantasy, but I'd say yes, it's for real. In the basement of the Philadelphia Museum."

"Are you serious?" She looked at me as though I had just returned from lunch on another planet. "Jamie, are you holding out on me?"

"Nope. I told you I found that motor pool. That was all I saw with my own eyes, but I know a lot of work was done in the catacombs a couple of years ago. Which is where that particular room is, or will be one day. I think it's already there."

"Is this what you wanted?"

"It wasn't on my shopping list because it never occurred to me that it might exist. Which goes to show you how dimwitted I am. But of course he'd have something like this. He needs it."

"You're saying Reichmann needs this? Why?"

"Because it's the keystone to their whole wigged-out trip. Reichmann, Gentry, the mayor, our publisher, what's-his-name the banker . . ."

"Tyler!?"

"The same. Make that thing do something and let's see if we can get a different perspective. That's a rendering done by an artist and one point of view wouldn't satisfy Reichmann."

"I don't know what to do."

"Figure it out from the notes. C'mon, Alexis, we're hip-deep in shit here. I want to see just how grandiose El Supremo's vision is."

Reichmann's combat command center, at least as the artist envisioned it, was what I'd call baroque-tech. Or maybe high-tech/no taste. It was straight out of a Saturday-morning cartoon. *Sentinels of the Universe.* Or *Galactic Space Police.* Huge wall screens displaying electronic street maps. High-tech consoles with enough control buttons to pilot a NASA shuttle. TV monitors, computer screens, electronic tracking displays. The chairs, with their high backs, wrapped arms, and posture-fitting curves, symbolized someone's idea of power.

"Can't you see Reichmann and his asshole buddies in there playing with all those Darth Vader toys?" I said as the images changed from wide shots to close-ups. "This is like a scale model of NORAD. The most sacred chapel of the Philadelphia Order of the Defenders of the Faith."

— — — —

Alexis and I had our first real fight since our Christmas Eve disagreement in Quaker Plaza when I tried to leave with the disks and notes Kofax had given her. She argued that I didn't have a computer so I couldn't possibly use them unless I involved someone else, and she didn't intend to be replaced.

"You've got something in mind and I'm going to be a part of it. *I'm* the one who came up with these disks. Remember?"

"But that isn't the issue, is it? You think I'm going to steal the story. Right?"

"It's also safer for me to have them," she said, ignoring my question, "since no one knows I'm involved in this."

"But if they get onto Kofax for some reason, they may make a connection to you, and then they'll show up here, looking for the disks."

"How could they do that?"

"It wouldn't be difficult. Listen, let's act like we're grown up, okay? First, let's make dupes of the disks and I'll take a set with me, as well as a copy of Kofax's notes."

She chewed on her lip for a few seconds while I lit a Camel, then finally said, "That makes sense. And this is still your story more than mine."

— — — —

Much to her professed disappointment, I left within the hour and drove back to my apartment. I'd made two copies of all the disks, one for safekeeping and one for everyday use. I also had hard copies of several images, made on Alexis's printer.

This, I thought, is the closest I've come to an unguarded view of Reichmann's psyche.

It's also as close as I'm likely to come to tangible evidence that he's a fanatic, which isn't a crime unless you wear a turban and ride a camel.

Even if these drawings were published in conjunction with a story about the motor pool, who would care? Who'd make a serious move to have him defrocked? Most of what I know I can't prove, and the little I can prove ain't shit to a swan. It would be the hot item in this week's news, but next week it would be 'follow-up' material. Maybe.

And then there would be another massive explosion and a lot of people would die and he'd scream that his ability to react to terrorism had been crippled by the media. He'd still end up with everything he wanted and come out of it looking like a hero. I'd come out of it looking like a tomato strainer.

I arranged a meeting for the following night with Beluga. He didn't sound surprised to hear from me and I got the feeling that he'd been expecting my call.

— — — —

"That's a lotta money for a scribbler," Beluga said as he stacked the hundred-dollar bills on the table in front of him.

It didn't look like much to me, even though the last time I'd seen that much cash in a pile I was AWOL in Las Vegas and I couldn't imagine what I'd spend it on.

The five stacks of fifty hundred-dollar bills that Beluga was fondling were fairly crisp and neatly bandaged. Barely enough to make a small-time drug deal, I thought. Or buy a new car. It had all been tucked into an old nylon shaving kit and left in the trunk of the Firebird.

"Where'd you get it?"

"Where I got it isn't the point. Is it enough to get the job done?"

"Where you got it can be the difference in whether I do this or not. Scribblers don't have twenty-five Gs in loose change to spend on anything. I wanna know who's bankrollin' this."

"The person who gave it to me doesn't know what I've got planned. And if they did, they'd have a fuckin' fit."

"Sit down," he said after studying my face for a moment. "You want a beer?"

"Depends on what kind you've got," I answered as I stacked my empty plastic crates. "I don't like most American beer."

"There's a bottle of Jap brew in here, I think." He yanked open the door on the beat-up fridge. "Yeah, here's one. You want it?"

"Okay."

"So?' he growled as he plopped the bottle down in front of me and drank from his Rolling Rock.

"So you want the job or not?"

"Talk to me, scribbler, convince me it'll work, and convince me I should do it."

"I haven't even convinced myself that it'll work." I drank some of the beer and lit a cigarette. He waited, watching me. "Okay . . . let's take the two people we'd both like to speed on their way to the next life.

"Reichmann's an egomaniac and a fuckin' lunatic. Gentry's a stone killer. They've got some real hardcore cadres working for them. Agreed?"

"Go on."

"Reichmann and Gentry believe that if they create enough paranoia they can justify bringing their little army out in public.

"The problem's been that the media haven't paid a lot of attention to the National Front for Radical Action. If this whole silly game were a political campaign, instead of a half-assed attempt to scare everyone into supporting him, they'd have used a media strategist. Someone who knows how to manipulate the press and get the best coverage. They didn't."

"Reichmann was scared of overdoin' it. He's scared of the Feds. Gentry was the one who picked the Cock'n'Bull, months ago. Reichmann said no. They talked to me, and I said I'd have to think about it. I wasn't about to blow that place."

"Which put you on the shit list."

"Maybe. They didn't come back for a while, and that job was never talked about after that."

"So they did the Cock'n'Bull without consulting you. Maybe Gentry did it without telling Reichmann. What does Gentry get?"

"Reichmann's job after the commissioner becomes the mayor. Until then, he'll settle for being head of the counterterrorist division—if he could get it out in the open."

"Then what?"

"Shit, I don't know. Maybe he'd use the organization like a labor pool for mercs and run his own employment service. You need fifty guys in Angola? Call Gentry."

"But to get the whole thing sanctioned, they have to win public support. To do that they need a major event, something so big that when it happens and Reichmann shows up with all his hardware and elite troops, everyone is so happy to see the cavalry no one asks why it exists. Or where it came from. The TV reporters will do their usual glamour shots and superficial reports on numbers and costs."

"So?"

"So, there's a national convention of mayors from around the country convening here in March. A three-day 'window of opportunity.' " I drank some more beer, watching him. "I saw a press release yesterday. And you want to take a guess as to who organized it? And the theme?"

"Oh, God . . ."

"Organized by the office of the mayor of Philadelphia. The theme is 'America's Cities under Siege: Drugs and Terrorism in the '80s.' "

"He's gonna run a live-fire exercise . . ."

"But we can't prove it. I can't prove anything, other than the existence of his motor pool."

"So you wanna smoke him out before the convention."

"Yes. You said you'd have a computer here tonight."

"It's here."

"Let's take a look at some artwork and you tell me if you can do the job."

"With the right tools and enough time," he said, standing up, "I can do any job. But that art show thing you mentioned is next Friday." He walked away from the table and I followed. "That ain't a lot of time."

"It's all we've got."

— — — —

Ferris dragged out a puny smile as I approached his bed in the ICU. It looked like the last of the lot, but I couldn't have been happier. He was awake and the nurse had said he wasn't in any great danger.

"Listen, we gotta stop meeting like this. I hate hospitals."

"I wondered how long it would take you to talk your way in here."

"Piece of cake. I'd give you a hug but I doubt if I could get through all that tubing. How do you feel?"

"Like shit."

"That happens a lot when people try to kill you. The lady in white says they'll probably move you to a private room in a day or so. They must think you're gonna survive."

"Whatta they know?"

"Not much, but they did manage to dig all that shit out of your chest. Just don't get an infection and you can be out of here in a few days."

"I sure fucked up in a major way, didn't I?"

"Ah! You got your cherry busted, that's all." I pulled a small gift-wrapped package from my pocket. "I brought something to commemorate your initiation into the Loyal Order of DBA Survivors."

"The *what?*" he asked as he labored to tear off the paper which Juliet had so gracefully wrapped. Evidently he was even weaker than he looked.

"The Loyal Order of Dumb-But-Alive Survivors. A lot of us belong. No membership fees, and your dues are paid for life. So you won't need to pull this kinda stunt again."

He pulled the lid from the box, and for a moment he looked as though he wasn't sure whether to laugh or cry. "A Purple Heart?"

"I had a couple left, from 'Nam. Here . . ." I took the medal and pinned it to his hospital gown. "We who are about to go out and get laid salute you who haven't got a prayer in hell." I gave him a half-assed salute.

"It hurts too much to laugh," he said, trying to keep a straight face.

"No more fun."

"I don't know what to say. I feel like I fucked up and you give me one of your medals. I ain't nobody's hero."

"Ah, bullshit." I took his hand in mine. "You know, after I was back a couple of years, one night I was watching TV with the former First Runner-up to Miss Chatham County, to whom I was rumored to be married, and they were airing one of their mindless, overrated PBS specials that has about the same social significance as a car commercial. Drivel cleverly disguised as a documentary, and I heard this full bird colonel say, 'There's a very fine line between the Medal of Honor and a general court-martial.' " I could still hear the voice of the guy being interviewed, and I smiled.

"I loved that fucker, whoever he was, for saying the only honest thing about war I'd heard since the night a buddy of mine and I were sitting in a hole half full of water and he said, 'Man, this shit sucks.' "

He grunted and put his free hand over the wound. "Dammit, don't make me laugh."

"Listen, I *said* 'No more fun.' Okay? Just relax, don't laugh, and when you're trying to piss in that bedpan remember the Buddhist concept of small pleasures. This kind of stuff renews our appreciation for things like hot showers, leaning on a bar with a drink telling outrageous lies to unsuspecting young girls, and urinating from a standing position."

He tried to smile, but he didn't have anything left. "I'm beat." He sighed.

"And I've already overstayed my limit. I'll come by in a couple of days, after they move you into a private room, and you can tell me what happened. In the meantime, just relax, do what these yahoos tell you to do, and don't worry about anything. Finori's got a guy in the hall out there, so that's covered. You get well and we'll get even."

"Say hello to everyone for me."

"Okay. They'll all be here soon enough. Juliet told me to give you a kiss for her, but I said no fuckin' way, so you'll have to wait on that."

He was sleeping before I finished the last sentence.

— — — —

After three long nights with Beluga I felt as though I could walk blindfolded through the catacombs, or any of the adjacent passageways. And that, I kept reminding myself, is not only stupid, it's dangerous.

I'd memorized everything Kofax had put on the computer disks, plus I'd gotten copies of some old drawings of the original waterworks on top of which the museum had been built, and copies of the original construction plans for the museum's foundation and basement. I love the concept of public record.

"Get bored and die," Beluga would bellow from time to time, usually to be sure I was still paying attention. "Bein' bored is dangerous. Bein' cocky is dangerous. Listen up, troop. Might save your ass."

"This whole goddamn plan is dangerous," I finally yelled in exasperation. "And probably stupid."

"It's *your* plan, scribbler." He must have said it ten times if he said it once. "It's your plan. You wanna call it off?"

"Not unless you've got a better one," I said over and over, and we'd go back to studying the drawings, mapping the road to Christ only knew what strange end.

I noticed on the third night that he was limping a good deal, favoring his right knee. I had thought he was limping the second night, but I wasn't sure. It was only after I was certain he was hurting that I remembered he usually moved around the room while I was busy with something. He could fake it for a short distance, but anything further than the fridge and he had a serious problem.

"You took a round in the knee," I said while his back was to me. "That must have hurt like a mother."

"Claymore. It's the goddamn screws that hurt, 'specially in the cold."

"Theirs or ours?"

"It was ours first." He limped to the chair in which he'd been sitting the first time I saw him, flopped down, and propped his foot on the makeshift table, rubbing the knee. "It was theirs when I walked in front of it." He was wearing baggy combat fatigue pants, and pulled up the right pants leg to expose a knee brace and a network of scars that looked a little like a freeway interchange. "Ain't much actual knee left."

"I can't imagine why. What were you doing before China Beach?"

"Don't ask questions you don't need answers to, scribbler. We all got some sorry history behind us."

"And a sorry fuckin' future in front of us." I got out two bottles of Corona. "Enough of this shit for tonight," I said. "Couple of shots to warm us up, and I'm going home to bed."

I put the beer in front of him, poured the tequila, and drank. "I see a little problem I hadn't anticipated."

"Better now than Friday night. What's the problem?"

"How much total weight in explosives do we have to take in there?"

"I've got maybe three hundred pounds here. May as well place half of it."

"We need another mule. You'd be lucky to carry fifty pounds across this room. What did we figure from the entry to the command center? Quarter-mile?"

"I been thinkin' about that, and you're right. I was tryin' to talk myself into a couple of shopping carts, but they're too goddamn noisy." He poured another shot for himself, then one for me. "You got any friends who like to live dangerously? Other than the one in the hospital?"

"Nope. How about those two guys who grabbed me the first night?"

"They got other work to do."

We drank in silence for a few minutes, and I kept trying to think of a way to move the explosives mechanically. Nothing worked. KISS, I reminded myself. Keep It Simple, Stupid.

I was almost finished with my beer when Sammy came to mind. This is a copyboy's wet dream. He'd love it.

"Actually," I said to Beluga, "I do know a strong young kid who needs material for his war stories. He's always telling me how he never gets out of the city room . . ."

"Can he do it and keep his mouth shut until it doesn't matter?"

"Yes."

"Okay. Tomorrow night we do a little recon."

— — — —

Five hours after we went into the tunnel behind the museum, armed with his Mac-10, flashlights, and five different colors of packing tape, we came out, unharmed and seemingly unnoticed. He was limping badly, and twice we stopped so he could sit until the pain subsided. Not only did he have a totally fucked-up knee, he was easily a hundred pounds overweight.

Sammy was shivering. It was cold, and he looked a little scared.

I don't know how I looked, but I knew how he felt. I was happy to be outside. Even the frigid five A.M. darkness was better than the dank, frightening interior of the tunnels.

"It's gonna work," I said with a sudden surge of confidence. I was grinning.

"Let's get in the car and get the hell out of here before you start celebrating," Beluga grumbled. "And I hope you've got a bottle of something in there, because I need a drink."

— — — —

At five-fifteen A.M. I dropped Beluga at his van, which we'd left parked just off Rittenhouse Square, and took Sammy home with me. He looked exhausted and was talking a mile a minute about nothing of consequence.

Inside the apartment, I poured two fingers of tequila into a water glass and handed it to him. "Drink, and shut the fuck up for a few minutes."

"Hey, Jamie . . ."

"Drink!" I thundered.

He drank about half of it before his eyes filled up with tears and he gasped for breath. "Holy mother . . ." he gasped.

I upended the bottle and drank an ounce or so. "Kinda takes your breath away, doesn't it?"

"You drink this stuff all the time?"

"Practice. Sit down over there." I pointed to the sofa, and he sat. "You want something to eat? I've probably got some eggs and cheese, maybe some bread, but I wouldn't count on it. A bowl of Frosted Flakes?"

"No, no . . . thanks." He hiccupped.

"Well, I'm hungry. You drink the rest of that Mexican monkey sweat and calm down while I fix my hearty breakfast and make a pot of coffee. You do drink real coffee, don't you?"

"Yeah, sure. With two sugars and lots of milk. If you got it, I mean. I can—"

"Stifle it, Edith. Sip the rest of that and I'll be right back."

I practically inhaled the cereal while the coffee brewed, and when I went back into the living room Sammy was much more relaxed, and very close to being drunk. He looked up from the latest issue of *Penthouse* as I handed him a cup of coffee, a silly grin on his face, his head filled with fantasies. I should fix him up with Alexis, I thought.

"Can you *imagine* a night with Miss February? My God!"

"I can imagine it. I'm not sure it would be what I imagined but what the hell? I could always go home early."

"Aw, c'mon, Hawkins. Look at this!"

"I did, about an hour after I bought the magazine. Sammy, a lot of those girls are so fucked up you wouldn't want to spend five minutes with them. You think she's a perfect sex machine, and she may be. Or she may be in scream therapy. Or maybe she only enjoys fucking guys over fifty. Or maybe she's gay."

He closed the magazine and put it on the coffee table. I'd ruined his fantasy, which is what I intended.

"Listen, Sammy . . . Friday night is for real. No comic-book fantasy, no fuckin' around. It's a job. You do it, and get the hell out of there, and you keep your mouth shut. You said you could handle that . . ."

"I can!"

"Yeah, well, I'm giving you a chance to change your mind. No one will ever know you did because no one but the Whale and me knows where you were tonight."

"I'm no chicken, Hawk." He giggled.

"I'm not a chicken, either, but I'm sure as hell scared of all the things that can go wrong."

"You?"

"Sammy, I'm not immodest, immortal, or particularly immoral, nor am I stupid. One mistake, one fuck-up, one thing that I didn't or couldn't anticipate, and I'm gonna be history. I can't afford to fuck up, or have anyone else fuck up.

"You wanted in, and I need help. I didn't choose lightly when I asked. But if you're in, you're in. You can't let me down."

"I'll be there." And for the first time all night he spoke with conviction. "You're my fuckin' hero."

Oh, Christ. "Listen, you want a hero, I'll give you the names of a couple of guys. You can find them on that goddamn black wall down in Washington. In the meantime, think of me as a role model, the personification of the proper attitude to assume when you're dealing with those who abuse authority. And learn to write a good lead. You've got talent, but you don't work hard enough on the craft."

His eyes were wide. "You really think I have talent?"

"Would I ask a guy with no talent to get involved in this shit? You may be the only survivor, and someone's got to write it."

"Jeez, thanks, Jamie."

"You want to sleep here, or you want to go home? You can have the bed and I'll camp out on the sofa."

"I gotta get home. My mom's probably still up, waiting on me."

"Okay. Thursday night we place the poppers. Friday we'll go through the drill again on what you do when the party starts Friday night. Now go home so I can sleep."

— — — —

Sleep wasn't in the cards I was holding at the moment. Maybe if I smoked a joint someone would deal me a new hand. Or give me a new head.

Maybe, maybe, maybe. What if and suppose and possibly and if I don't stop thinking about how many ways all of this can go wrong, I'll never do it. If I don't, somewhere down the line, probably at the convention of mayors in March, a lot of people are going to die. Even if I could expose Reichmann and Gentry and reveal the existence of the motor pool, I can't prove he has an elite and illegal counterterrorist army. They would become a 'dedicated, highly trained group of police specialists' paid for by 'citizen donations' before the ink dried on the first edition. Dubious financing, maybe, but so what? By the time the two-hundred-dollar-an-hour lawyers finished making deals, the whole thing would fade to black and they'd be free to start all over again.

But if I fuck up, a lot of people may well die anyway.

I rolled a joint, took two hits, and laid out the chart I'd made in the tunnels. The location for each charge was color-coded, marked on the chart and on the wall or floor of the interior.

Beluga had designated red for the heaviest charges, blue for lighter charges, yellow for "stuff that'll scare the hell outa people but probably won't do any real damage," black for satchel charges, and green for the route. All the charges could be detonated electronically, and I'd have control with a couple of small transmitters the size of pocket calculators.

"I sure as hell hope you're as good as you say you are," I'd whispered at one point, deep inside the bowels of the building, "because this is definitely not my strong suit." We were sitting so we could rest his knee.

"You ever see pictures of those tall buildings they bring down with explosives, right in a city? Make them fall in on top of themselves?"

"Yeah . . ."

"The guy who taught me most of what I know could do that shit in his sleep. When I'm finished you'll get what you said you wanted. Just don't fuck up and pop the wrong one. I'll give you the sequence and the transmitters. Rest of it's up to you."

"Ohh-kay."

"And remember, I don't give refunds."

The more I looked at the chart I'd made, comparing it to the blueprints, the more my thoughts drifted, and finally I said to hell with it. Either it works, or it doesn't, and I can't think of anything else I can do to improve the odds.

As I was drifting away to the void of sleep, the line from the I Ching drifted with me: He shoots a pheasant, losing one arrow. In the end he gains honor and position.

At some point during the five hours of sleep I got, I dreamed I was walking with Sammy through the elephant grass in 'Nam, shooting turkeys with an M-16. Despite the scarcity of feathered turkeys in 'Nam and my no-more-than-average skill with Colt's contribution to the world's thirst for high-tech instruments of death, I actually brought down four or five birds, which Beluga retrieved and stuffed into an enormous nylon shaving kit.

Juliet woke me a little before noon, hammering on the door to my apartment. Her first question, which came through the narrow opening with more than a touch of contempt, was "Jesus Christ, are you drunk?"

I closed the door, removed the chain, and opened it to let her in. "I'm not drunk," I said as she stepped inside. "I'm not hung over, and I'm damn sure not in the mood to listen to you or anyone else rant and rave. About anything."

"I haven't heard from you in two days."

"So?"

"You haven't been in the office—"

"I quit."

"Jamie?"

"Listen, to you it's eleven-thirty in the morning. To me it's five A.M. How would you like to wake up at five in the morning with someone hammering on the door, and as soon as they can look you in the eye they start yammering: Are you drunk? Where've you been? Why haven't you called? Jesus Christ, woman, do something useful and make a pot of coffee while I shower."

I left her with her mouth slightly ajar and closed the bathroom door behind me. I figured she'd either make the coffee, which I needed, or she'd leave before I came out again. Either one was okay with me.

She handed me a cup of coffee as I came out of the shower. "I was worried," she said.

"Parents do that kinda crap. Yell at their kids because they were worried. You aren't my mother." I pulled the towel around me and leaned over to kiss her on the top of her head. "On the other hand, if you're thinking about adopting me, I'll give you my lawyer's number and you can work it out with him."

"The day you have a lawyer for anything other than a criminal trial, I'll petition the state to adopt you."

She followed me up the steps to the loft, watching me dress. Then she followed me down the steps to the kitchen and stood there while I made another cup of coffee.

"Did you have anything in mind when you knocked?" I finally asked.

"Today is absolutely the last day we can select your suit for Friday night. I saw one in a custom shop on Walnut. I think you'd like it."

"I'm not going to be fitted for a suit, and I can't be your escort to the Dreams of Hunab Ku exhibition." I grabbed her as she spun on her heel and started toward the door. "Don't get bent out of shape. There's a very good reason why I can't go."

"Why don't you tell me what it is? I don't ask a lot from you, and—"

"Don't start with that, okay? You don't ask much, and I think you're wonderful, and I'm still not going."

"I could have you assigned to cover the story. Except you already quit." She suddenly looked as if she might cry. "Jamie, I deserve better than this from you."

"You want a cup of coffee?" I poured a cup for me and looked at her.

"No. Have you really quit?"

"No. I've been spending a lot of time with Beluga."

"Who?"

"The head of the National Front for Radical Action."

"Does Daniel know about this?"

"He knows as much as you do. Let's go sit down. You want a shot?"

"God, no. It isn't even noon yet."

"I'll think about that while I'm pouring." I poured a shot, downed it, and lit a Camel. "Okay, my heart's ticking again . . ."

"Why haven't you called?"

"I told you, I've been busy." I sat on the opposite end of the sofa and tried to decide what, if anything, I should tell her.

"Are you going to tell me why you aren't going?"

"I plan to tell you, and Daniel, when the time is right. Will he be at the opening?"

"Sally said he's feeling a lot better, and they both plan to attend."

"Okay, Friday afternoon, let's say three o'clock, you and Daniel meet me on Boat House Row. What does he drive?"

"I don't know. Some kind of Toyota or Datsun, I think."

"Good. Nothing that will attract attention. I'll be in that rustbucket your mechanic loaned us. Or sitting out by the edge of the river. Dress casual, and warm. We're gonna walk or sit outside, like tourists."

"Will I see you before then?"

"How about tonight?"

She smiled and I held out my hand. She slid over until she was nestled against me.

"Will Brother James be there?" I asked casually.

"Without a doubt. He's on the museum board. I think he's bringing one of his aging bimbos."

"And Herr Reichmann?"

"He had his secretary call me to say he's attending . . ." Her tone changed from lighthearted to suspicous before she finished the sentence. "Why are you so interested in the guest list?"

"Curious. The picture of Reichmann standing around making small talk with all those rich and fashionable people is comical." She *was* a good person, a loving woman who cared for me, and I wished I didn't have to deceive her. As she'd said, she deserved better, but she'd find it hard enough to handle even the part of the truth I intended to tell her and Daniel.

"Actually," she said, "he's been very generous in supporting the museum. And he mixes well. Remember, he wants to be mayor."

"Who's covering the big event for the *Call*, anyway?"

"Oh, Ivan's little tart, I imagine. Alexis."

I laughed. "I never heard you refer to any of your staff like that. What's your problem with Alexis?"

"My God, Jamie!"

That was it. "My God, Jamie!" From that three-word comment, I was expected to infer significance so obvious no other explanation was needed. And there probably wasn't a woman within the scope of the universe as we know it who wouldn't have known precisely what she meant. The rest of us would have to guess, at least with regard to specifics. If a man had been asked the same question he would have said, specifically if not accurately, "She's a slut," or "She can't write," or "She's the worst possible excuse for an objective journalist."

They can equalize opportunities for work, money, political power, and the right to give up your life to keep some shithead dictator in power, but no law ever written will enable men to truly understand women, no matter how 'equal' they become.

So I gave her a kiss on the top of her head and said, "Silly me. Too much sleep and not enough tequila."

And she gave me a look that said I wasn't nearly as amusing about some things as I might think.

But we didn't argue, which was good, because I planned to bring Alexis to the boat house meeting.

— — — —

The installation of the explosives went well. Sammy kept his anxiety to a minimum. Beluga's knee endured the strain. And I found an entry to the command center through an air vent. I didn't go in, but I did loosen the screws holding the screen in place, and I left a small satchel charge just outside. A ten-pound package of C-4 should convert the room from high-tech to Stone Age in about five nanoseconds. It wasn't my idea of a great hole card, but it beat a threat to report Reichmann and Gentry to the cops.

From the bench where Alexis and I were sitting, the hazy outline of West Philadelphia provided an interesting backdrop of urban poverty for the two Wonder Bread rowing teams sculling up and down the Schuylkill River. A bunch of Future Yuppies of America in their underwear pulling their rinky-dink boats through a freezing, filthy river in the dead of winter for no good reason. What enormous conceit.

"It's all too weird," Alexis said after staring into space for a few minutes. She'd pretty well turned the paper napkin issued with her Whopper into confetti.

"How can it be anything else, considering the cast of characters? You want out?"

"Get serious, Hawkins. Do you remember what you said to me Christmas Eve, when I wanted to go into the Tourist Center and trade places with one of the hostages?"

"I said a lot of things, most of them unkind. 'You're out of your mind' was probably one of them."

"You said I should check my caulking because my brains were seeping into my bowels. My head was up my ass, in other words."

"So to speak."

She shifted her gaze back to the river, or the bare trees, or whatever she used to focus on while she contemplated how to talk me out of what I'd told her about my plan, and her part in it.

"There must be another way." She turned toward me and swung her boots up on the bench, crossing her legs. Her skirt was short and I had a full view of her knees and a few inches of thigh.

"You've got cute dimples on your knees," I said, touching one of them.

"If we talked to the *Call* legal counsel . . ." Her voice trailed off.

"Right. The same shithead lawyers sworn to protect James Franklin. Those the guys?"

"Other laywers then, outside lawyers."

"*Nada.* That's what we'd get."

"Goddamn it, you can get killed doing this! You know that, don't you?"

"Could have happened Christmas Eve, too."

"Okay, so you and Ferris conned a dumb fuckin' asshole into surrendering to you. Great. That doesn't mean you're ready to take on Darth Vader."

"You're probably right."

"So . . ."

"Alexis, whether I die or not isn't any big deal in the grand scheme of things. Whether Reichmann is stopped or not makes a difference. All I'm planning to do is smoke him out, in a manner of speaking.

"You wanted in on this, remember? You hit on me, lured me down the garden path, seduced me, tricked me into telling you what Ferris and I were doing . . ."

"Oh, fuck off."

"And now what? You want out?"

"No, goddamn it! But you and I already know Reichmann's exactly what Philadelphia really wants. If Beluga works for the Feds, why don't they bust Reichmann?"

"Who can read the mind of the U.S. Justice Department? They make more crooked deals than a roadhouse cardsharp. If you doubt that, just read what's available on the witness relocation program. And I mean 'available,' never mind what they've managed to keep hidden."

"Okay, so they might not be the right people to ask for help. There has to be someone."

"I don't think so. No one wants this job. It's dirty and it's sure as hell thankless. At best, they'd start another bullshit investigation that would last until Thanksgiving." I pinched her knee. "In or out?"

She stared into my eyes with such intensity I thought she might suddenly hit me, or say something wonderfully profane and walk away. "In! Okay? I'm in and if this blows up in our faces you damn well better be ready to have me hound you straight to the gates of hell because I'm gonna be on your ass from now until it freezes over."

"It'll be nice to have company. You're sure you can handle your part?"

"Yes. Absolutely."

"Okay. Relax. Our employers should be here any minute."

— — — —

Juliet and Daniel arrived a few minutes after three o'clock in Daniel's bronze four-door rice grinder.

As I stood up to greet them a gust of wind blew my jacket open and hooked it on the handle of the Magnum. Daniel's eyes filled with surprise.

"Are you carrying a gun?"

"Sure looks like it." I pulled the jacket together and zipped it up a couple of inches. "And don't ask why because that isn't what we're here to talk about."

"Well, that may be, but I've never sanctioned the possession of weapons by one of my staff. Never."

"You've got one dead photographer, one dead would-be sports editor, a critically wounded reporter, and another reporter with a seven-inch scar on his neck. That last guy isn't gonna roll over for you or anyone else. I'll give this back to the person who owns it tomorrow." I winked at Juliet. "If I'm still employed."

"I hear you haven't been in the office for several days now," Daniel said. "And Juliet tells me you've been with that Beluga person. Is that what we're here to talk about?"

"It's either that or the prospects for Penn taking Yale in the annual sculling meets this spring." I inhaled as deeply as I could and for a fleeting moment I thought about how good a shot of tequila would feel, something to settle me down. "Tonight," I said, "if all goes well, we're going to wake up Philadelphia with a midwinter fireworks show that should rattle windows from here to the capital of this great nation. It probably won't, but it should."

▬ ▬ ▬ ▬

They were easier to convince than I'd thought they would be. Maybe my reminder that the *Call* staff had already suffered four casualties, two of them fatal, made a difference. That plus the fact that I didn't tell them about the explosives in the museum.

What I did tell them was that Beluga and his two friends would set off a number of small explosions around the city, triggering a massive number of fire and police alarms. That, we'd decided, would make it seem as though the city were under attack.

"You know Reichmann will probably react like a lunatic," French said.

"Christ, I hope so. If he doesn't I'm gonna look like the Mad Hatter on an acid trip. I'm counting on him and Gentry and a couple of others to run straight to the command center in the catacombs, where I'll be waiting."

"Jamie, that's crazy," Juliet said. "If they find you in there they very well may shoot you."

"Not with you and Daniel standing in the door watching. When they make their move, you move right along with them, and don't take no for an answer. In fact, don't ask. Just do it. I'll show you a diagram of the route from the main gallery."

French looked from me to Juliet to Alexis and back to Juliet, shaking his head slowly. Juliet kept looking at me.

"Reichmann's already paranoid about the NFRA being out of his control. He's afraid of Beluga running amok. When it seems that's exactly what's happening, he'll have the perfect excuse to bring out his little army, however many are available. But before he can get them assembled, the game's gonna be over."

"And what if this doesn't work out as you anticipate?"

"Then give me a Viking funeral and tell everyone that the shock of the explosion at the Cock'n'Bull pushed me right into Froot Loop City. You shouldn't have a problem convincing people of that."

"What time do the fireworks begin?" French asked.

"Nine o'clock. We've got to leave ourselves enough time to write a story for the last couple of editions. Alexis has floppy disks with a lot of interesting graphics, plus she knows almost as much about all of this as I do."

"And if we say no?" French inquired.

"You can say whatever you like, but I can't reach Beluga at this point. The cards have been dealt. All that's left is to see how everyone plays their hands."

— — — —

From 8:35 until I removed the cover over the ventilator at 8:55, I sat in the narrow crawlspace outside the command center and let my mind sort through all the pleasant images it could pull from the files. They were, for the most part, related to Juliet, Alexis, Ferris, Sheila, and the Cock'n'Bull . . . leaning on the bar, bullshitting with John, making him laugh. Eating at Mama-san's with Ferris. The first night I'd seen Sheila, while I was with Juliet. I caught an image of Marybeth and held it for a moment, wondering whether, if I died before the night was over, she would ever know. I thought about Juliet waltzing into Club Fed with fresh lobster and a carton of Camels. From the beginning she'd made my day-to-day life a little more enjoyable.

And then I thought with a sigh, Aw, what the hell, an hour from now it will all be over, one way or the other. And either way is fine with me.

As I was quietly removing the last two screws from the screen, Beluga's parting words came to mind.

He'd said, "Listen, scribbler, you and me both know your chances of gettin' out of there alive ain't much better'n my chances of playin' middle linebacker for the Eagles. What's in it for you? Gotta be somethin' more'n a goddamn story for that rag you work for."

"Vengeance."

"That's suppose to be God's game."

"I'm playing His hand," I said. "Just while He's having a beer with the serving wench from the bar."

"You better hope He's got one eye on you, 'cause if Reichmann takes the bait you probably gonna be way the fuck and gone up a creek in a leaky boat."

"I've been there before, and I know how to row."

"Maybe," he'd said with a grin, "but I ain't so sure you got both your oars in the water." Then he had reached into his jacket pocket and pulled out a scarf made of camouflage silk. "For luck."

"Thanks." I took it, curious if he'd been wearing it when he hit the tripwire on the Claymore. And then it occurred to me that he may have been, and that's why he only lost a knee, and not his head.

Reichmann's command center was everything a man with delusions of grandeur could want. Well, almost everything. He'd given away the edge with the unprotected opening through the ventilator, so obviously he needed to re-consider his security system. But who would ever have imagined, as someone later wrote, that anyone would actually find the plans, crawl through the tunnels and sneak in through an air shaft?

I doubt that any of them ever gave a moment's thought to facing the truth of the matter: They'd been outsmarted, and the wiseass grinning at the camera that tracked me around the room had the upper fucking hand. At least for the moment.

The surveillance camera, anchored in the ceiling, swiveled to track me, probably following a heat signal or the sound of my movements. I sat down at the console marked C-IN-C, which I took to mean Commander-in-Chief, throne of the Lord High Reichmann. The lens barrel rotated as the camera came in for a close-up.

"Ready phasers, Mr. Sulu . . ." I made a rude gesture with the middle finger of my right hand, then pulled the .44 from inside my jacket and lined the sights on the lens.

Squeeze the trigger . . . The voice of SFC Terry Muldoon slipped through my concern that I'd miss the whole goddamn camera. I steadied my hand and squeezed.

Christ, what a racket. The pistol kicked like a karate student. The slug missed the lens but ripped through the housing of the universal joint and left the camera dangling by a thin piece of electrical wire, barrel down, the lens looking at the floor. If any lens was left. That, I thought, should raise the pulse rate of a few people. If anyone was watching. I'd have wagered a nominal sum that someone had seen it all on a monitor, and probably they were playing back the tape even now.

"Intruder in the combat control center," a feminine voice announced in the next moment. Actually, she—it—may have made the announcement several times before I heard it. My ears were ringing despite the cotton I'd stuffed into them. A large-caliber pistol fired inside a small room makes one hell of a loud noise.

"Intruder in the combat control center . . ."

I quickly scanned the multitude of switches spread across Reichmann's throne, looking for an override of the computer's voice. I couldn't find the shut-off switch, but I did find some other potentially interesting toggles, one of them labeled LOCK-OUT and another labeled SYSTEMS OVERRIDE

'Lockout' is one word, turkey-fuckers. I just wished I knew what it did. I flipped the toggle down and heard something in the area of the door. Ahhh so . . . And for whatever reason, the computer voice stopped in mid-sentence. "Thank Christ," I muttered under my breath.

I found another set of toggles grouped under the sign EXTERNAL CAMERAS. I flipped all four switches and four tiny 3 × 5 black-and-white screens on the console flickered to life. One camera appeared to be pointed down the hall outside the door I hoped I'd just locked. There were two knobs beside each of the switches, and I twisted one. The light level was raised in the hall and I could see what looked like a key pad beside the door. The second knob controlled the direction of the camera. I set it to look straight down the hall, and settled back to wait for the Commander-in-Chief to come hammer on the door.

While I was waiting I removed the spent shell and replaced it with a new hollowpoint. I put the Magnum on top of the console within easy reach and studied the other TV screens. One of them, I noticed, looked into the motor pool. No one was moving around. The other screens showed empty room interiors, one with a small conference table. The Roundhouse, maybe. The other was just a room, nothing visible.

A clock on the console read 9:08. I checked that against my watch. They were about thirty seconds apart. Close enough. At 9:10, if Beluga was on schedule, the boat house furthest from the museum would be reduced to splinters. That should put a little speed in the aging feet of El Supremo and his band of mirthless men. It would also signal Alexis to herd the TV crews to the side of the museum where they could witness a live demonstration of plastic explosives on the sliding doors guarding the motor pool.

"These tracks shoulda been shielded," Beluga had said when he first saw the computer sketches. "Buried in cement. Cheap construction."

Alexis told me later that the explosions blew the doors completely off the tracks and left a 20 × 40–foot opening into the motor pool. Instead of one big boom, Beluga had set three charges on each side. I sent the signal at 9:15, and faintly heard the explosions, one after the other, like firecrackers on a string. I thought I'd fucked up, and I couldn't see anything in the monitor on the console. The concussion knocked out the camera.

At 9:18 I caught a glimpse of Reichmann and Gentry jogging along the hall toward the camera, followed by enough warm bodies to make a crowd. The two of them slowed as they approached the door, allowing the others to catch up. Tyler, Franklin, O'Conner, French, and a couple of guys I'd never seen were dressed in tuxedos. Juliet was last, encumbered by high heels and a formal gown.

"Penguins at twelve o'clock, Mr. Sulu. Stand by to beam them aboard." I flipped the lockout toggle up just as Gentry punched in the code; then I stood up and clutched the .44. He and Reichmann and the two unknowns poured into the room, with the others in quick pursuit. Juliet barely made it through the doors, which closed automatically.

Gentry and Reichmann were the first to notice me. Gentry's right hand automatically moved toward the lump under his left arm. I pulled back the hammer of the Magnum and smiled. He hesitated. "Do it and die."

"You miserable little cocksucker!"

I squeezed the trigger just like Sergeant Muldoon had taught me, and Gentry went backward with amazing force, smashing into Tyler, knocking the banker to the floor. "Watch your language. There's a lady present."

Juliet gasped in disbelief. Everyone else seemed stunned for the moment. Tyler's wailing broke the silence and Reichmann, maybe thinking I was distracted, made a slight move with his right hand toward his left side. He stopped as the hammer came back for the second time.

"Easy, Hawkins . . ."

"Easy enough. Just squeeze the trigger."

"What the hell are you doing in here, in my chair?" he asked. "Are you part of this bombing attack?"

"Who the hell is this?" Franklin bellowed as if he'd suddenly been given a voice and had no idea how to control its volume.

"My name's Hawkins."

"This jerk works for you, James," Reichmann snarled.

"*You're* Jamie Hawkins?"

"On my good days, yes. For the moment you can think of me as an avenging angel."

"Are you part of this plot?" Reichmann asked again.

"Not me, Commissioner. I've been here a while, waiting for you and the dead guy there to show up." I made a brief gesture toward the dangling camera. "You can ask your guys. They must have seen me come in."

"He's dead! My God, he's dead!" Tyler squealed, scrambling suddenly to his feet. Blood was splattered on the front of his crisp white shirt, and his eyes were wide with fear.

O'Conner suddenly fell to his knees and began reciting "Hail Marys," one after the other.

"You two," I said to Reichmann's aides or bodyguards or whatever the hell they were. "Outside." I checked the camera and no one was visible. I flipped the toggle to open the door. "Out!" They went without so much as a glance at Reichmann. The door closed and I depressed the lockout button. The mayor went on praying.

"Exactly what have you got in mind, Hawkins?" Reichmann asked. "You sure as hell can't believe that you'll simply walk out of here after you've killed the second-highest-ranking officer in the Philadelphia Police Department."

"I erased another of Mother Nature's unfortunate mistakes from the planet. He was a disgusting failure as a human being. He was a murderer, dishonorably discharged from Special Forces, wanted for mercenary activities and drug running by Interpol, and his name wasn't Gentry. You better shake up your personnel department, Commissioner. They don't do what I'd call a thorough background check." I stared at him for a moment, wondering how close to the truth I'd come. I figured, at worst, I was at least half right. "Unless, of course, you hired him *for* those peculiar talents."

"You're crazy!" Franklin shouted. He turned to French. "You hired this hooligan, and I'm holding you responsible for this fiasco. Now get him out of here or you'll be looking for work in Alaska."

"Jamie," French pleaded, "we've got the story. Let's go before anyone else gets . . . hurt."

"He's not going anywhere," Reichmann shouted. "And there's not going to be any goddamn story!"

"Jamie . . . ?" Juliet spoke for the first time since she'd come into the room. She looked genuinely horrified. "Please!"

"Are you people crazy?" Reichmann screamed. "He's a killer and you're all witnesses. He murdered my deputy."

"You want to go to trial with that, *mein Führer?* You want all this shit to come out in court? How you recruited Beluga to stage bombings in Philadelphia so you could get money to fund a counterterrorist group? I've got Beluga's statement. You want the Feds checking his story? And looking into the Kofax drug deals? And the national media hounding you about this private army of yours, funded by contributions to fraudulent charitable organizations? The Franklin Memorial Art League, supported by our esteemed publisher and Mr. Bigbucks Tyler? The IRS, all by themselves, can give you guys enough problems to last a lifetime."

"My God, Rudy," Tyler said, his first words since he'd realized that Gentry was no longer among the living. "We'd be ruined. All of us."

"He can't prove any of that shit!" Reichmann shouted. "He's bluffing."

"Don't make the same mistake your deputy made, El Supremo. I don't have to 'prove' it. The Feds will do it for me. What do you think they'll come up with when they look into the Brother James Academy for Sports and Survival

Skills? A place devoted to the betterment of unfortunate children, or a para-military training center for Reichmann's Irregulars?"

No one said anything and I wasn't sure what the hell I'd accomplished, other than killing Gentry, which was almost as big a surprise to me as it must have been to him. I didn't have any regrets, but it hadn't been part of my conscious plan. In a court, I'd plead self-defense, and a good lawyer undoubtedly could prove that he'd been most, if not all, the things I'd described. And if I had to answer to some pissed-off Supreme Being, I'd simply say, "Hey, he had it coming. All I did was what You should have done before I got here."

It was 9:31 according to the console clock. Time to wrap it up and see if I could get the hell out before they regained their arrogant confidence. That's when, from the corner of my eye, I caught sight of the two turkeys I'd forced out of the room, coming back down the hall, armed with what looked like Uzis. They'd shed their jackets, and they'd acquired very determined expressions for their ugly faces.

Now look at that, I thought as they stopped at the door and punched the combination to open it. Jackets off, sleeves rolled up, extra clips stuffed into their cummerbunds. Two half-dressed penguins come to save the biggest turkey of all. It finally dawned on them that something or someone had them locked out.

"What's it gonna be, gentlemen?" I asked after probably close to a minute of silence. "There's three TV crews and probably half a dozen print reporters waiting. We've all got deadlines to meet, and that includes you."

"What kind of deal are you offering?" Tyler asked, moving forward until we made eye contact. "The Commissioner is all that stands between us and the anarchists who'd turn these streets red with our blood."

"The only fuckin' anarchists I've met in Philadelphia either have blue blood or they're wearing blue coats. The deal is I walk out of here, write a story about this high-tech war room tied to the story about the NFRA, and we all go home to a night of fitful sleep.

"Gentry was shot accidentally while being subdued by those two bozos who were here earlier, after he freaked out under the pressure of the bomb attacks. A little creative work with his personnel records should produce a psychiatric report from a local shrink that talks about his painful military experiences, and how they'd troubled him since he left military service following the Vietnam war.

"What the hell, you're all well paid and highly skilled liars anyway . . . you don't need me to write your script."

"And if we don't accept the deal?" Reichmann asked with a sneer.

"There's ten pounds of C-4 in a satchel charge right outside that ventilator. Just say the word and I'll turn us all into crispy critters."

"Jamie, for God's sake!" French wailed.

"I've also got five rounds left in this .44. Your choice."

"Chief," Tyler said to Reichmann, "there's no reason for us to die down here."

Reichmann glared at Tyler, at the mayor, and finally at me. "Get away from my console and get the hell out of here," he said in a voice so low and so full of rage I could barely understand him.

"It's all yours," I said. As I stepped down from the riser Reichmann brushed by me and I spun in a half-circle, leveling the barrel and backing away.

"Don't even think about reaching for whatever you've got tucked under your jacket," I warned him, "or you'll have to share the obit page with your dearly departed deputy over there."

"Fuck you. Your ass isn't worth the price of crosstown postage."

I continued backing away, my eyes never leaving him while he made a couple of adjustments to his chair. Satisfied, he flipped the lockout toggle up and punched the door control. The door opened and his two bodyguards emptied their Uzis into the place where I'd been when they left the room. Reichmann was dead before he ever saw them.

The two assassins stood rooted in shock, thin tendrils of smoke rising from the stubby barrels. "Oh my God," one of them finally mumbled.

"And God said, 'Hey, life's a bitch and then you die.' "

The one further from me spun in my direction, raising the barrel of his Uzi.

"The breech is open, asshole. You're empty."

He made a move to swing at me but stopped at the sound of his name.

"Blanchard!" Finori yelled from behind him. "Drop the weapon. Now!"

The Uzi clattered to the floor and Blanchard's face collapsed into a puttylike paste of tears and fear. His buddy let his weapon fall without being told.

"Hawkins!"

I carefully lowered the hammer, turned the pistol around, and held it out by the barrel. "I never liked dropping a loaded weapon. They have a tendency to go off."

He holstered his own pistol and took the .44 from my hand. "I can't believe you're still alive."

"I can't believe it took you so long to get here, so we're even."

> One toke over the line, sweet Jesus,
> One toke over the line.
> Sittin' downtown in a railway station,
> One toke over the line.

Some things never change. Some things had changed. Some things looked as if they'd changed, but I wasn't convinced.

I was stoned and singing to myself as the train rolled through Wyoming, or Montana, or maybe fuckin' Idaho. I didn't know for sure, and I couldn't have cared less. I was a long way from Philadelphia, far from harm's way. I couldn't even remember how long I'd been riding behind the great iron horse in my aluminum womb. Seemed like a week, but who could say? It felt like a month since I'd seen anything other than snow-covered landscapes, cityscapes, and the inside of my rolling cell.

I was traveling under the name of Jan Sluchak, detective second grade, Philadelphia police, en route to Vancouver, British Columbia. I had a letter of introduction from Lef'tenant Finori to the chief of detectives, Vancouver police. I also had a new badge, a new ID, and a new pistol, a .38 Colt revolver.

Finori swore on his badge that the Vancouver guy in the letter of introduction actually existed, and if it was critical to my escape I could show the letter to anyone who might have a thought about arresting me and the guy would back it up if anyone called.

"Get the hell out of the country, and stay out for a while," he'd said while we were driving to Harrisburg. He wouldn't let me near Thirtieth Street Station. "And let me know where you are when you settle down for more than a month."

"I'll drop you a card, sometime around the turn of the century."

Somewhere between Chicago and whatever frozen city was next on the Amtrak itinerary, I finally realized what the problem was with Finori. We liked each other. The feeling was too strong to allow us to be casual, and there was no way we could be close. Our values were similar enough, but our priorities were very different.

I also scared him, he said. "Do you know how close you came to getting killed?" he'd asked me on that ride to Harrisburg. "For that matter, do you have any goddamn idea of how soon you'd been dead if you stayed in Philadelphia?"

"Is there a bonus if I get the correct answer to both parts of the question?"

"Yeah . . . I drive you all the way to the train, instead of dropping you at the Harrisburg interchange."

"How close did I come to being killed? About the width of a gnat's ass. How long could I expect to remain whole and healthy in Philadelphia? Two or three days, give or take a sunrise."

"You're crazy."

"I took a calculated risk, but I knew what I was doing."

He kept saying he couldn't believe I'd given control of the console back to Reichmann knowing his two goons were standing outside the door armed with Uzis.

"The whole damn gamble was dependent on the fact that they *were* out there armed with Uzis. If you're edgy, which they were, and kill-hungry, which they were, you can empty a load from an Uzi in about one second. Right?

"I knew they were convinced I'd still be in Reichmann's chair. I knew they were worried he'd rip them a new poop chute for letting me take control, not to mention that I'd wasted Gentry, all of which meant they were gonna be fast and pull hard on the trigger. No discipline. I saw it in 'Nam. There weren't ten guys out of a hundred who could, or would, fire three-round bursts with an M-16, let alone something like a fuckin' Uzi.

"It's like Beluga said, a great ambush weapon at ten feet."

"And what if they had been disciplined?"

"I guess I'd be explaining the basic nature of check and raise to the angels."

He never asked me why I'd wasted Gentry. And he never said thanks. It was payment, in kind, for some good people who'd died, especially Sheila. I didn't have any guilt about it, and if he'd asked, I'd have told him I was goddamn happy that I'd done it. Surprised, but happy.

— — — —

Juliet did ask, and she wasn't happy with my answer. It was the first time she'd ever seen anyone killed. Probably the first time she'd actually seen anyone die under any circumstances. She came totally unglued after we were out of the museum, and nothing I said was right. The value of life, and the perceived permanence of death, were so ingrained in her view of the world that she couldn't accept the fact that I had, seemingly in 'cold blood', ended another person's existence. When I said all I had really done was erase one of God's many mistakes, she screamed at me, and was still sobbing and screaming as I walked away.

I spoke to her once after that, on the phone, an awkward conversation that lasted less than five minutes. She was calmer but she couldn't reconcile or rationalize the conflicts that raged in her. I ended it by telling her that I had to go and that I'd write to her the next time I had a return address to put on the envelope.

Alexis had written the lead story and a sidebar while I was being hustled to one of Finori's safe houses, a garage apartment which belonged to a friend of his. I thought he was a little on the paranoid side of worried, but I didn't argue. And I didn't care who wrote what, or who got the by-line. Brother James, the Mayor, and Tyler would skate through the shit as surely as Charlie Patton had tripped over his own destiny and died for having the goddamn gall to seek some kind of justice.

I dumped the Colt in Puget Sound, caught a PSA flight from Seattle to LA, and checked into the Beverly Hills Hotel with Detective Sluchak's American Express card.

For two days I sat by the pool drinking overpriced frozen margaritas and listening to a half a dozen New Yorkers pretend to be impatient to leave the palms and balmy weather for the overcast, cold, and crowded canyons of Manhattan. They were all males in their 50s, hooked on gin and gin rummy. Each of them had acquired a bronzed bimbette and varying degrees of sunburn. They looked like six old scrub oaks that had mysteriously sprouted in a rain forest. They laughed at everything that was LA, and told more lies in two days than I've told in this life. I liked them.

Ferris haunted my idle time, and I kept saying to myself that I should call him, but I didn't. The possibility of a tap on his phone made it easier to postpone from one hour to the next and finally it was too late. On the evening of the second day I returned from a place called R.J.'s, a Beverly Hills saloon with a floor covered in peanut shells—if you can picture that in Beverly Hills—and found a message for Det. Sluchak from Uncle Angelo. "Di Di!" it read.

I took the message to my room and looked at it for a few minutes before it occurred to me that Finori probably meant 'Get the fuck out of there'. I had an urge to call him, too, and decided against it. It was time to move on and the less trail I left, the better.

The next morning, by the pool, I 'borrowed' one of the bimbettes from the New Yorkers and had my picture taken with her by the hotel photographer. She was blonde, bronzed, and sleek as a Ferrari.

On the back of the picture I scribbled: Jamie Hawkins meets an LA Fuckmuffin. I mailed it to Ferris and I smiled every time I thought of him showing it to Alexis. They'd know I was alive and well, and for a while they'd think I was living in LaLa Land.

After I'd checked out of the hotel I shopped on Rodeo Drive and bought a Dunhill lighter which I instructed the salesman to mail to Juliet. "Keep it until I see you again . . . in this life or the next."

Then, with a cash deposit, my Philadelphia police ID, and some line of bullshit only a brain-damaged clerk would believe, I rented a car and drove to San Diego. If Finori could trace me so quickly through American Express, which was the only way I could imagine him finding me, I didn't want him or anyone else to trace the next leg of my journey.

In San Diego I picked up a visa and headed for Baja. None of the Mexican immigration officers in Tijuana gave a fat rat's ass if I'd been *persona non grata*'ed out of the Yucatan. There's a lot of live and let live in Baja. And since it appeared that I was gonna live for awhile, I was happy to be in that kind of place.

On the Mexican side of the border, once I'd passed through the immigration process, I stood outside the building looking back. For a brief moment I felt an overwhelming sadness for what I'd lost and a huge sense of uncertainty about what lay ahead. What the hell had I done? Would I ever be able to go back? Did anyone of them truly understand?

And then I laughed, at myself, remembering the Fifth and Final Law of Hawkins: Fuck'em if they can't take a joke.